HEAVY LIES THE CROWN ...

"The Kings of Tarshish Shall Bring Gifts" by Stephen R. Donaldson—The Caliph's only heir, Prince Akhmet, had been "gifted" with dreams since childhood, but whether they would prove to be a curse or blessing for the Caliph and his kingdom remained to be seen. . . .

"Journey into the Dark" by Jane Yolen—The prince was far too young for the journey he must take, but with his family's love and magic, he would dare all the perils that barred his way. . . .

"The Kiss" by Alan Dean Foster—Sometimes even the most highborn of men may be enchanted into a frog for a very good reason. . . .

These are just a few of the twenty enchantment-filled, original tales in—

THE
BOOK OF KINGS

If you and/or a friend would like to receive the *ROC Advance*, a bimonthly newsletter featuring all the newest and hottest ROC books and authors, on a complimentary basis, please fill out this form and return it to:

ROC Books/Penguin USA
375 Hudson Street
New York, NY 10014

Your Address
Name _____
Street _____ Apt. # _____
City _____ State _____ Zip _____

Friend's Address
Name _____
Street _____ Apt. # _____
City _____ State _____ Zip _____

THE BOOK OF KINGS

EDITED BY

Richard Gilliam
and Martin H. Greenberg

A ROC BOOK

To Stephen R. Donaldson with thanks

ROC
Published by the Penguin Group
Penguin Books USA Inc., 375 Hudson Street,
New York, New York 10014, U.S.A.
Penguin Books Ltd, 27 Wrights Lane,
London W8 5TZ, England
Penguin Books Australia Ltd, Ringwood,
Victoria, Australia
Penguin Books Canada Ltd, 10 Alcorn Avenue,
Toronto, Ontario, Canada M4V 3B2
Penguin Books (N.Z.) Ltd, 182–190 Wairau Road,
Auckland 10, New Zealand

Penguin Books Ltd, Registered Offices:
Harmondsworth, Middlesex, England

First published by Roc, an imprint of Dutton Signet, a division of Penguin Books USA
Inc.

First Printing, July, 1995
10 9 8 7 6 5 4 3 2 1

 REGISTERED TRADEMARK-MARCA REGISTRADA

Printed in the United States of America

Contents

Introduction: In the Name of a King

Richard Gilliam

There is power in the name of a king. Many people, particularly those of European descent, can trace their names back to their ancestral homelands and a well-known king. Certainly that's true in my family. My given name, Richard, is the name of three kings of England, while my family name, Gilliam, is a variant of Guillaume, the eleventh-century Norman king who was a cousin and close ally of the English king Edward the Confessor. What a person does with their name is rather important. For much of his life, Guillaume was known as *le batard,* or bastard, due to the illegitimacy of his birth. History granted Guillaume a new name when in 1066 he sailed his armies across *La Manche* and defeated Edward's successor, King Harold—which is why the name by which the French king Guillaume le Batard is much more remembered today as the English king William the Conqueror.

Kings are prime material for storytellers. When "The Kings of Tarshish Shall Bring Gifts" by Stephen R. Donaldson came to the attention of Roc, they liked the story so much they commissioned this anthology to showcase it. For that, Marty Greenberg and I would like to thank Steve—for writing the sort of story that inspires others to also write and create.

History abounds with kings named Stephen and Donald. The latter is the name of three kings of Scotland, the third of whom, Donald Bane, was the younger son of Duncan I. When his father was killed in battle against the provincial chieftain Macbeth, Donald Bane fled into exile, returning when his brother, Malcolm III, captured the throne from Macbeth. Assuming the kingship upon his brother's death, Donald Bane ruled for most of the next four years, trying valiantly to solidify his Celtic–Scots rule. The events of history were not with him, however, and in 1097 he was dispossessed by an alliance of nobles who favored closer ties with England.

By coincidence, England's only King Stephen was born in 1097. The grandson of William, the Conqueror, Stephen was noted for his brave and chivalrous leadership. Alas, the latter was sometimes a questionable asset, as when Stephen generously provided safe passage for his treacherous cousin Matilda. After a long, difficult struggle, Stephen successfully thwarted Matilda from taking the crown, forcing her to flee to her estates in France. When his son and heir, Eustace, died in 1153, however, Stephen recognized Matilda's son who, upon Stephen's death the following year, ascended to the throne as Henry II.

Richard I was a popular king with his people and an even more popular king in storytelling. Never mind that he rebelled against his father (Henry II), ruinously overspent the English treasury, waged war on more civilized nations, and spent only a few months of his ten-year reign in England. Richard I had the good fortune to be succeeded by his brother John, who proved to be so bad a king that people longed for the good old days of Richard. You don't really need to say John I—England has never had another King John, a name which royal families have ever since tended to avoid bestowing on their children.

From the songs of the troubadours to the films of Hollywood, for eight hundred years Richard the Lion-Hearted has been one of the great heroes of popular fiction. Does he deserve such praise? Probably not. The Arab nations which Richard and the other Crusaders attacked were the center of the known civilized world, and by comparison the monarchs of Europe were rank barbarians. What good did come of the Crusades was the knowledge that the Crusaders took back to their homelands—the great writings of Greece and Rome, and a stronger knowledge of mathematics.

Not until the early fifteenth century and Henry V did an English king use the English language in a court document. Even so, like many of his predecessors, Henry V died in France. The process by which English kings became English was a very slow one and is still incomplete. Only in 1917 and under the pressures of World War I did the current British royal family, the House of Saxe-Coburg and Gotha, give up their German names and become the Windsors.

If Richard I gets too much undeserved good press, then Richard III (1452–1485) gets too much undeserved bad press. He was forced into battle by his enemy, Henry Tudor, but only after Henry arranged for Richard's armies to be weakened by treachery. Historical evidence indicates that Richard III died in battle, bravely fighting alongside his badly outnumbered troops. Alas, the popular image of Richard III is that of an insane hunchback who murders children. William Shakespeare needed the support of his Tudor patrons, and thus made their ancestor Henry VII look good at Richard Plantagenet's expense. For a more balanced fictional account of Richard III, try Josephine Tey's 1951 novel, *Daughter of Time*.

Stephen has also been a popular name with saints and popes. There have been either nine or ten of the latter, depending upon how you count the first Stephen II, who was elected pope in 752 but died two days later without having his papacy consecrated. The most recent pope to choose this name was Stephen IX (or X), one of the church's great reformers and whose plans for the defense of northern Italy helped convince Guillaume le Batard to seek conquests elsewhere.

Stephen I of Hungary ruled just prior to these events. His coronation on Christmas Day, 1000, marked the entry of Hungary into the family of European Christian nations.

Though born pagan, Stephen converted at an early age, and effectively utilized the church to stabilize his reign. Following a prosperous and peaceful reign, Stephen died in 1038 and was canonized in 1083. The patron saint of his country, the Feast of St. Stephen is celebrated each September 2nd.

Stefan Dusan (1308–1355) was by far the greatest king of medieval Serbia. The events of his reign bear striking similarity to the regional turmoil faced by Serbia during the twentieth century, starting with the conquest of Herczegovina—then the westernmost province of Serbia—by the neighboring Bosnians in 1326. An able military commander, in time Stefan greatly increased the borders of Serbia, including the conquests of Albania and most of Macedonia. In 1346 he had himself crowned "Emperor of the Serbs and the Greeks," and by 1348 he ruled a vast territory that reached from the Danube River to the shores of the Adriatic and the Aegean. Stefan died suddenly in 1355. His heirs were unable to hold his lands, and within fifteen years the borders of Serbia were smaller than they had been at the start of Stefan Dusan's reign.

Stephen the Great of Moldavia faced similar challenges. With the help of his friend Vlad, the Impaler, he secured his throne in 1457, only to find himself menaced by powerful neighbors. After repulsing an invasion by Hungary in 1467, in 1471 he attempted to retake Vlad's homeland, Walachia, from the Turks. This prompted a full invasion of Moldavia by the Ottomans, with Stephen winning decisive victories in 1475 and again in 1476, though it wasn't until his treaty with the Turks in 1503 that his country's independence was preserved. Despite the region's persistent strife, the reign of Stephen brought much cultural development to the area, and saw a considerable increase in the influence of the church.

These are, of course, just a few of the kings who reigned during the Middle Ages. The Vikings, alas, did not have a king named Stephen, although Viking publishing certainly has one who is very famous. One can only wonder what Penguins name their kings.

Being a real king, I think, might be not so much fun as being a fictional hero. The responsibilities are enormous and can only be escaped at the risk of civil unrest. Far too many kings died on the battlefield or were murdered back home. You have little choice of whom to marry, and are expected to provide for a great many retainers and supporters. Very few kings really excelled at being kings, which is a big part of why modern nations have other forms of government, and why current-day monarchies rarely have any real power to rule. Having the same name as a historical king counts for very little in the modern world, and almost all the kings of history lived in eras whose values were much contrary to those of the latter part of the twentieth century.

You'll find a wide variety of kings in this book. Some kings ruled well, some kings didn't, and many were somewhere in-between. The name of a king pretty much meant only what the king's life made it mean—which is quite true of what the names of the rest of us mean also.

Green Bay, Wisconsin
December, 1994

The Kings of Tarshish Shall Bring Gifts

Stephen R. Donaldson

People who dream when they sleep at night, know of a special kind of happiness which the world of the day holds not, a placid ecstasy, and ease of heart, that are like honey on the tongue. They also know that the real glory of dreams lies in their atmosphere of unlimited freedom. It is not the freedom of the dictator, who enforces his own will on the world, but the freedom of the artist, who has no will, who is free of will. The pleasure of the true dreamer does not lie in the substance of the dream, but in this: that there things happen without any interference from his side, and altogether outside his control.

[The dreamer is] the privileged person to whom everything is taken. The Kings of Tarshish shall bring gifts.

—Isak Dinesen, *Out of Africa*

I have often wondered why there are tyrants, and I have come to the conclusion that it is because some men remember their dreams. For what do we know of dreams? What is the truest thing to be said of them? Surely it is that we forget them. And therefore it is also sure that this forgetting must have a purpose. Hungers are conceived in dreams in order to be forgotten, so that the dreamer and his life may go on without them. That is why most men remember nothing—except the sensation of having dreamed.

But men who do not forget are doomed.

Such a man was Prince Akhmet, the only son of the Caliph of Arbin, His Serene Goodness Abdul dar-El Haj.

After a reign enviable in every respect except the birth of male offspring, in his declining years His Serene Goodness at last produced an heir. This, as may be imagined, was a great relief to the Caliph's wives, as well as a great joy to the Caliph himself. Thus is it easily understood that from the first young Akhmet was coddled and pampered and indulged as though he came among us directly from the gods. In later years, during the Prince's own brief reign, men looked to his childhood as an explanation for his tyrannies. After all, Arbin had no tradition of tyranny. His Serene Goodness Abdul dar-El Haj, like his father before him, and his father's father, was a man in whom strength exercised itself in the service of benevolence. Some explanation was needed to account for Prince Akhmet's failure to follow the path of his sires.

But I do not believe that a childhood of indulgence and gratification suffices to explain the Prince. For with his pampering and coddling, young Akhmet also received example. The Caliph was demonstrably benign in all his dealings. Therefore he was much beloved. And the Prince's mother was the sweetest of all the Caliph's sweet young wives. Surely Akhmet tasted no gall at her breast, felt none at his father's hand.

His Serene Goodness Abdul dar-El Haj, however, remembered none of his dreams. His son, on the other hand—

Ah, Prince Akhmet remembered everything.

This was not, of course, a salient feature of his childhood. For him, in fact, childhood was what dreams are for other men—something to be forgotten. But his ability to remember his dreams was first remarked soon after the first down appeared on his cheeks, and he began to make his first experiments among the odalisques in his father's harem.

That is always an exciting time for young men, a time of sweat at night and fever in daylight, a time when many things are desired and few of them are clearly understood. It is, however, a strangely safe time—a time when attention to the appetites of the loins consumes or blinds or transmutes all other passions. Men of that age must think about matters of the flesh, and if the flesh is not satisfied they are rarely able to think about anything else. So it was only after he had more than once awakened in the bed of a beautiful girl about whom he had believed he dreamed, thus at once deflating and familiarizing such visions, that his true dreams began their rise to his notice, like the red carp rising among the lilies to breadcrumbs on the surface of his father's ornamental pools.

"I had the most wonderful dream," he announced to the girl with whom he had slept. "The most wonderful dream."

"Tell me about it, my lord," she replied, not because she had a particular interest in dreams, but because his pleasure was her fortune. In truth, she already knew how to be enjoyed in ways which had astonished him. But she was also prepared to give him the simple satisfaction of being listened to.

He sat up in her bed, the sheets falling from the graceful beauty of his young limbs. His features were still pale with sleep, but his eyes shone, and they did not regard his companion.

"I can see it now," he murmured distantly. "I can see it all. It was of a place where there are no men."

"No men?" the girl asked with a smile. "Or no people?" Her fingertips traced his thigh to the place where her notion of manhood resided.

The Prince heard her question, but he did not appear to feel her touch. "No people," he answered. "A place where there are no people, but only things of beauty."

The girl might have said again, "No people?" with a pout, thinking herself a thing of beauty. But perhaps she knew that if she had done so he would not have heeded her. All his attention was upon his dream.

"The place was a low valley," he said, showing the angle of the slopes with his hands, "its sides covered by rich greensward on which the early dew glistened, as bright in the sunshine as a sweep of stars. Down the vale-bottom ran a stream of water so clean and crystal that it appeared as liquid light, dancing and swirling over its black rocks and white sand. Above the greensward stood fruit trees, apple and peach and cherry, all in blossom, with their flowers like music in the sun, and their trunks wrapped in sweet shade. The air was luminous and utterly deep, transformed from the unfathomable purple of night by the warmth of the sun.

"The peace of the place was complete," murmured young Akhmet, "and I would have been content with it as it was, happy to gaze upon it while the dream remained in my mind. But it was not done. For when I gazed upon the running trance of the stream, I saw that the dance of the light was full of the dance of small fish, and as my eyes fell upon the fish I saw that while they danced they became flowers, flowers more lovely than lilies, brighter than japonica, and the flowers floated in profusion away along the water.

"Then I gazed from those blooms to the flowers of the trees, and they, too, changed. Upon the trees, the flowers appeared to be music, but in moments they became birds, and the birds were music indeed, their flights like arcs of melody, their bodies formed to the shape of their song. And the shade among the treetrunks also changed. From the sweet dark emerged rare beasts, lions and jacols, nilgai deer with fawns among them, oryx, fabled mandrill. And the peace of the beasts, too, was complete, so that they brought no fear with them. Instead, they gleamed as the greensward and the stream gleamed, and when the lions shook their manes they scattered droplets of water which became chrysoprase and diamonds among the grass. The fawns of the nilgai wore a sheen of finest silver, and from their mouths the mandrill let fall rubies of enough purity to ransom a world.

"I remember it all." A sadness came over the Prince, a sadness which both touched and pleased the girl. "I would have been content if the dream had never ended. Why are there no such places in the world?"

His sadness brought him back to her. "Because we do not need them," she replied softly. "We have our own joys and contentments." Then she drew him to her. She was, after all, only a girl, ignorant of many things. She took pleasure in the new urgency with which he renewed his acquaintance with her flesh, and saw no peril in it.

But I must not judge her harshly. No one saw any peril in it. I saw none in it myself, and I see peril everywhere. When he came later into the cushion-bestrewn chamber of his father's court, interrupting the business of Arbin with a young and indulged man's heedlessness in order to describe his dream again for the benefit of the Caliph and his advisors, none of those old men took it amiss.

His Serene Goodness, of course, took nothing that his beloved son did amiss. The sun shone for his son alone, and all that his son did was good. And he was entranced by the Prince's dream, full as it was with things which he had himself experienced but could not remember. The truth was that the Caliph was not an especially imaginative ruler. Common sense and common sympathy were his province. For new ideas, unexpected solutions, unforeseen possibilities, he relied upon his advisors. Therefore he listened to young Akhmet's recitation as if in telling his dream the Prince accomplished something wondrous. And he cozied the sadness which followed the telling as if Akhmet had indeed suffered a loss.

With the Caliph's example before them, Abdul dar-El Haj's advisors could hardly have responded otherwise themselves. Each in his own way, all of us valued our suzerain. In addition, we were accustomed to the indulgence which surrounded the Prince. And lastly we enjoyed the dream itself—at least in the telling.

We listened to it reclining, as was the custom in Abdul dar-El Haj's court. His Serene Goodness was nothing if not corpulent, and liked his ease. He faced all the duties of Arbin recumbent among his cushions. And because none of his advisors could lay even a distant claim to youth, he required us all to do as he did. We were stretched at Prince Akhmet's feet like admirers while the young man spoke.

When the telling was done, and His Serene Goodness had comforted his son, the Vizier of Arbin, Moshim Mosha Va, stroked his thin gray beard and pronounced, "You are a poet, my lord Prince. Your words give life to beauty."

This was not a proposition to which the High Priest of the Mosque, the Most Holy Khartim a-Kul, would have assented on theological grounds. Beauty was, after all, a creation of the gods, not of men. As a practical matter, however, the High Priest nodded his head, shook the fringe around his cap, and rumbled, "Indeed."

For myself, I primarily wondered whether it was the recitation itself which enabled Akhmet to remember his dream so vividly. Nevertheless, I expressed my approval with the others, unwilling to launch a large debate on so small a subject.

But the Prince was not complimented. "No," he protested, at once petulant and somewhat defensive. "Words have nothing to do with it. It was the dream. The beauty was in the dream."

"Ah, but the dream was yours, my lord Prince, not ours." The Vizier was disputatious by nature, sometimes to his own cost. "We would not have been able to know of its beauty if you had not described it so well."

"No!" young Akhmet repeated. He was still close enough to his childhood to stamp his foot in vexation. "It was the dream. It has nothing to do with me."

"Of course," His Serene Goodness put in soothingly. He liked nothing which vexed his son. "But Moshim Mosha Va is quite correct. He only means to say that your words are the only way in which we can share the beauty of what you have seen. Perhaps there are two beauties here—the beauty of your dream and the beauty of your description."

For some reason, however, this eminently reasonable suggestion vexed the Prince further. His dream had made him sad. It had also made him fierce. "You do not understand!" he cried with an embarrassing crack in his young voice. "I remember it all!" Then he fled the court.

In puzzlement, the Caliph turned to his advisors after his son had gone and asked plaintively, "What is it that I have failed to understand?"

The Vizier tangled his fingers among his whiskers and pulled them to keep himself still, a rare effort of self-restraint. Perhaps he knew better than to venture the opinion that Prince Akhmet behaved like a spoiled brat.

"My lord Prince is young," commented the Most Holy Khartim a-Kul in his religious rumble. "It may be that his ideas are still too big for his ability to express them. It may be that his dream came to him from the gods, and he rightly considers it false worship to compliment the priest when praise belongs only to Heaven."

This notion "rightly" made His Serene Goodness uneasy. A son whose dreams came to him from the gods would make an uncomfortable heir to the rule of Arbin. The Caliph's eyes shifted away from his advisors, and he resumed the business of the court without much clarity of thought.

As for the Prince, when he returned to his apartments, he kicked his dog, a hopeless mongrel on which he had doted for most of his boyhood.

At the time, no one except the dog expressed any further opinions on the subject.

But of course it was inevitable that the Prince would dream again.

Not at once, naturally. In him, the carp had only begun to rise. The breadcrumbs on the surface were few, or the fish did not see them. He was in a sour humor, and his attention was fixed not on the hope of new dreams but on the failure of other people to understand the significance of the first one. For a time, he lost interest in women—at least to the extent that any young man can be said to have lost interest in women. At the same time, he experienced an increased enthusiasm for the manly arts of Arbin, especially for hunting, and most especially for the hunting of beasts of prey, creatures of disquiet, feasters on blood. Arbin is a civilized country. Nevertheless, the great forests do not lack for leopard and wild pig, with tusks which can gut a horse with one toss of the head, and packs of hungry langur often harry the flocks on the plains. By the standards accepted for a young lord of the realm and his father's son, Akhmet expended a not unreasonable amount of time upon matters of bloodshed. Until he dreamed again.

He and his companions, several young men of the court and a commensurate number of trusted retainers and hunters, had spent the night camped among the thick trunks and overarching limbs of a nearby forest. In this forest was said to live a great ape which had learned a taste for human flesh—a small matter as the affairs of the world are considered, but by no means trivial to the villagers whose huts bordered the trees—and for three days Prince Akhmet with his entourage had been hunting the beast under conditions which can best be described as gracious hardship. Apparently, fatigue enabled him to sleep especially well. On the morning of the fourth day, he sprang from his bedding like a dust devil, chasing in all directions and shouting incoherently for his horse. When his companions inquired as to the meaning of his urgency, he replied that he had had another dream. His father must know of it immediately.

Clattering like madmen in their haste—a haste which no one but the Prince himself actually comprehended—Akhmet and his entourage raced homeward.

Now when he burst among us, hot and flurried from his ride, with stubble upon his cheeks and a feverish glare in his eyes, and announced, "I have dreamed again. I remember it all," I felt a serious skepticism. To remember one dream is merely remarkable, not ultimately significant. To remember a second, however, so soon after the first—if a few weeks may be called soon—as well as after the confusion of a hard ride, and without the exercise of relating the dream to anyone else—

Well, in all honesty, I doubted young Akhmet. I

watched him closely for signs of stumbling or invention which would call the accuracy of his memory into question.

In contrast, His Serene Goodness appeared to feel no skepticism at all. Perhaps he was simply delighted to see his son after an absence of a few days. Perhaps he was delighted by the idea of dreams. Or perhaps he saw in Akhmet's eyes that the Prince would brook no opposition. Unlike his advisors, who exchanged uneasy glances as unobtrusively as possible, the Caliph only beamed pleasure at his son and said, "Another dream! Tell us at once. Was it also wonderful?"

"It was," the Prince pronounced, "wonderful beyond compare."

Steadying himself as well as his excitement allowed, he said, "I stood upon a great height, and below me lay the city of Arbin at night, unscrolled with all its lights as legible as any text, so that the movements of the least street-sweeper as well as the activities of the mightiest house were plain to be read. Indeed, the city itself was also alive, breathing its own air, flexing its own limbs, adding its own superscript to the writings of the lights. I knew that the truth and goodness and folly of all our people were written there for me to read.

"Yet as I began to read, the height on which I stood grew even greater, and the city itself expanded, and I shrank to a mote among them—a mote without loss or grief, however, but rather a part at once of the lights and of the darkness between the lights, much as a particle of blood partakes of all blood while it surges through the veins." The Prince spoke with a thrill in his voice which answered my skepticism, a blaze in his eyes which bore me with him. "Thus at the same time I rose and shrank, losing myself within a greatness that transformed and illuminated me. I rose and shrank, and the city grew, and the lights became stars and suns and glories, lifting every living heart to heights which we have never known. And the darkness between the lights was the solace in which every living heart rests from wonder.

"While I dreamed, I was among the heavens and the gods."

There he stopped. His chest rose and fell with the strength of his breathing, and the fever in his eyes abated slowly.

"This is truly a wonder," said His Serene Goodness when he had collected his thoughts, "a wonder and wonderful." Like his advisors, he had no intention of repeating the mistake of the previous occasion. "Is this not so, Vizier?"

"It is, my lord," replied Moshim Mosha Va sagely. He tugged at his beard for a moment, then ventured to add, "Perhaps it is also something more."

"More?" The Prince and his father spoke at once, but in differing tones. Abdul dar-El Haj was naturally delighted by anything which would enable him to think even better of his son. Young Akhmet, however, appeared strangely suspicious.

"To remember one dream, my lord," said the Vizier, echoing my earlier ruminations, "is pleasant and desirable. More so when the dream itself is peaceful and lovely. But to remember two—two such dreams in so short a time—is unusual. It may be that Prince Akhmet has been given a gift. It may be that he has been touched by wisdom or prophecy. In that case, his dreams may have meaning which it would be folly to ignore.

"Perhaps we would do well, my lord, to seek interpretation for his dreams."

Both the Caliph and his son were startled by this suggestion, and now their expressions were nearly identical. His Serene Goodness had too much common sense—and too little imagination—to believe that a gift of wisdom or prophecy would be a good thing in an heir. And the Prince seemed to dislike any deflection of attention from the dream itself. Nevertheless, he held his peace, and his father turned to the Most Holy Khartim a-Kul.

"Do you concur, High Priest?"

Khartim a-Kul waggled the fringe of his hat to conceal his squirming. Wisdom and prophecy were matters of religion, and did not belong to spoiled young princes. Yet he could not ignore his responsibility to His Serene Goodness, or to Arbin.

"Two dreams are only two dreams, my lord," he murmured judiciously. "It is, however, better to search for meaning where meaning is absent, than to ignore it where it is present."

Sadly, Abdul dar-El Haj was not judicious where his son was concerned, and so did not enjoy judiciousness in others. Somewhat sourly, he demanded, "Then interpret this dream for us, High Priest. Give us the insight of the gods."

The Most Holy Khartim a-Kul rumbled inchoately past the dangles of his hat. He did not enjoy being made to squirm. Neither did he like to fail either his religion or his ruler. After a moment, he said, "The language of dreams, my lord, is private, and requires study. There are interpreters who make a speciality of such matters." Seeing the Caliph's mounting vexation, however, he hastened to add, "Yet I might hazard to say, my lord, that this dream speaks of Prince Akhmet's future. At that forever-to-be-lamented day when your Serene Goodness ceases to be Caliph in Arbin, and Prince Akhmet ascends to his inheritance, he will be one in spirit as well as in body with all his people—'much as a particle of blood partakes of all blood.' He will see the good of the whole as well as the good of each individual, and will rule with the same selfless benevolence which has made Abdul dar-El Haj beloved throughout this land."

Thus the High Priest of the Mosque extricated himself from his lord's displeasure.

While I, who see peril everywhere, saw peril not in Khartim a-Kul's interpretation, but in young Akhmet's reaction.

So vehemently that spittle sprang from his lips, he snapped, "Nonsense, Priest. You rave. Dreams have no meaning. Only the memory of them has meaning."

In fury, he withdrew himself from the court.

The Caliph was shocked. "Now what have we done amiss?" he inquired plaintively.

None of his advisors answered. Apparently we had once again misunderstood Prince Akhmet's reasons for relating his dream.

Later, we learned that the Prince had gone straight to his father's harem, where he had covered one of his favorite women savagely, leaving the marks of his teeth on her breasts—marks which took weeks to heal.

So the seeds of concern were planted.

Those seeds did not sprout, however, until the Prince dreamed again, despite the fact that during the interval he tended them in a desultory fashion, giving them occasional water and fertilizer. In a time of unusual application to the study of weapons, he presumed upon his favored station to do one of his instructors an injury. He became increasingly rough in his treatment of women. His commands to his servants were sometimes farfetched—and sometimes his anger was extreme when those commands were not carried out to his satisfaction. Such signs, however, such bubbles rising from the depths of the pool, were generally ignored. We are taught to be indulgent of the behavior of princes. And he was still young. In the words of one of his grooms, he had conceived an itch which he did not know how to scratch. Therefore he was irritable. And he had not yet learned the benefits of self-restraint.

Finally, Akmet's actions passed unheeded because our fears were focused elsewhere. After many years of health, His Serene Goodness Abdul dar-El Haj began to fail. A cough which the physicians could not ease brought blood to his lips in flecks. His appetite left him, and his flesh began to sag from his bones. His wives lost the capacity to comfort him. Often he needed assistance to rise from his cushions. Because he was so much beloved, the sight of his decline filled his advisors and all his people with grief. We had little heart to spare for the vagaries of the young Prince.

So he committed small hurts without reprimand, performed small acts of unreason without restraint, caused petty vexations throughout the court and was ignored. Too little notice was taken of him until he dreamed again.

This time, his dream brought him out of sleep in the lonely hours of the night. Such was the power he remembered that he could not contain himself until morning. He must relate what he had seen. Regardless of the Caliph's weakness, Prince Akhmet hurried at once to his father's chamber, where physicians stood watch at his father's bedside, and maidens dabbed away the blood as it came to his father's lips.

"I have dreamed again," he announced peremptorily, ignoring his father's weakness, his father's uneasy sleep, "the most wonderful dream."

With difficulty, His Serene Goodness opened his eyes. Perhaps because he was still partly in sleep, or perhaps because his pain ruled him, or perhaps because he could not be blind to his son's inconsideration, he replied in a weary tone, "I, too, have had a dream. I dreamed that I had a son who loved me."

At this time, young Akhmet was still within reach of chagrin. He seemed to see his father's illness for the first time, and all his demand left him. Falling to his knees at the bedside, he cried, "Father, forgive me. You are ill, and I have been heedless, heartless. What can I do to comfort you? Why do these physicians not heal you? Why do you tolerate them, if they have no power to heal you? I will do everything I can."

This at once dispelled whatever anger the Caliph may have felt toward his son. Stroking the youth's beautiful head, he said, "You will give me ease if you tell me of your dream. Only be still while my advisors are summoned, so that they may hear you also. And permit the High Priest to bring his interpreters, so that the truth of your wonderful dream may be understood."

Prince Akhmet bit his lips, plainly distraught. Yet he acceded to his father's wishes.

And so the advisors of the court were summoned to Abdul dar-El Haj's chamber, along with interpreters roused and admonished by the Most Holy Khartim a-Kul himself.

In the corridors of the palace, upon the way to the Caliph's sickchamber, I encountered Moshim Mosha Va. The High Priest of the Mosque strode some paces ahead of us with his interpreters. We were able to speak quietly.

"This is unseemly," said the Vizier, with disgust hidden under his beard. "I am old. I need more sleep."

"You are old," I replied, "and need less sleep, not more. You have no more use for dreams."

He snorted to me. "You are glib, wizard. I know of no other reason why the Most Pompous Khartim a-Kul has not branded you a heretic. But glibness will not save you when that little shit becomes Caliph. For myself, I believe I will put an end to my life. I do not wish to spend my waning years tormented by his fancies."

I smiled at the thought that the disputatious Vizier would ever consent to death. Pleasantly, I answered, "That is because you do not understand him."

He paused to peer closely into my face. "Do you?"

"No," I admitted. "But I will." I must. Have I not said that I see peril everywhere?

Together, we followed the High Priest into the sickchamber of His Serene Goodness Abdul dar-El Haj.

The young Prince still knelt at his father's side. The Caliph's fingers stroked his son's fine hair. In that pose, the lord appeared to be passing his blessing to his heir.

"Come and hear what my son has dreamed," said His Serene Goodness when we had gathered around him. "This is the third dream, and must have meaning." It seemed that the Caliph had reconciled himself to the idea of a gods-gifted scion. Or perhaps he realized, in his unimaginative way, that Prince Akhmet must be reconciled to himself in order to become a fit lord for Arbin. "High Priest, are these men the interpreters of dreams?"

"They are, my lord," answered the Most Holy Khartim a-Kul, sounding more than ever like a subterranean mishap. "We have prayed over the young Prince and consulted the stars."

I knew for a fact that this was pious falsehood. Khartim a-Kul had had no attention to spare for Akhmet. All his hours had been spent in preparation for the rites and ceremonies of the Caliph's passing, and of the installation of a new lord. I kept this knowledge to myself, however.

"We are ready," the High Priest concluded, "to bring you our best insight."

"Very well," said His Serene Goodness as though his breath were fading. "Let my son speak his dream."

At the Caliph's bedside, Prince Akhmet rose to his feet and told us what he had dreamed.

"In my dream, I saw a mighty suzerain, a nameless Caliph in a land I have never known. He was in the time of his best youth, and though I did not know him and could not name him, his features were the features of the Caliph of Arbin, His Serene Goodness Abdul dar-El Haj, my father."

Had the Prince been more of a politician, I would have believed this beginning false. But it was impossible to mistake the ardor of his stance, or the growing hunger in his gaze.

"His head was crowned with light," said young Akhmet, "and love lived in his eyes, and his limbs were of such beauty that all hearts were drawn to him. He was the center of the storm, where peace lives untouched by pain. He was the pause between the beats of the pulse, the rest between respirations, and his gift to all who knew him was balm.

"Yet he was more than this. Indeed, when he spread out his hands, the world was shaped by his gestures, so that nature itself took on the form of his will. He stretched his fingers, and plains were made. He shrugged his shoulders, and mountains grew. Where he pointed, there were rivers. The seed of his loins gave birth to new peoples, and his caress left all women faint with pleasure."

While he spoke, I observed, as I should have observed weeks ago, that he had changed. His lips had grown pinched like a simoniac's, and his cheeks hinted at hollowness, and his form was as gaunt as his youth and beauty permitted. Regret is useless, but still I regretted that I had not turned my attention to him earlier.

"And in my dream," he continued, "the storm of pain which drives all men, but which could only run in circles of folly around the nameless Caliph, took notice of him and grew wrathful, for it is not given to men that they should be free of pain, or that they should free others, or that the world should shape itself to their will. Therefore the storm moved against him. Great was its wrath, and terrible, and whole lands and peoples were bereaved by its power. The reach of his beneficence was constricted as pain bore peace away and his place in the center of the storm shrank.

"Then there was grief everywhere, for all men were hurt, and so all men believed that the nameless Caliph could not endure against pain.

"At last the storm withdrew, thinking itself victorious.

"And yet the Caliph stood as he had stood before, with light upon his brow and beauty in his limbs. Nothing about him was changed, except his eyes. There love still shone, love for all peoples and all lands, love which healed all it saw. But with the love was also knowledge of pain, understanding for the injuries and losses which drive men to do ill, forgiveness for frailty. He had accepted pain into his being and searched it to its heart and taken no hurt.

"That was my dream," concluded the Prince. For a moment, he seemed overcome by sorrow. Then, however, he lifted his head, and in his eyes was a look which might have signified both love and the knowledge of pain. Or perhaps it was only madness. Softly, he added, "It was wonderful. It lives with me still, and will live always. I will forget nothing."

His Serene Goodness did not reply. But his eyes also shone, and there were tears upon his cheeks, and his hand clung to his son's until it trembled.

"Such dreams must be valued," murmured the Most Holy Khartim a-Kul. He may conceivably have been sincere. "To have such dreams is surely a gift from Heaven. We are blessed to be in your presence, my lord."

During the pause between one heartbeat and the next, Prince Akhmet's face lost its look of love and knowledge. At once, it became as tight and miserable as a miser's.

"Wonderful," breathed the Caliph past the blood on his lips. "Wonderful. Oh, my son.

"High Priest." A fit of coughing gripped him. When it passed, it left fresh red upon his chin. Nearly gasping, he asked, "How is this dream to be interpreted?"

Khartim a-Kul was nothing if not a politician. Graciously, he deferred to his chief interpreter, not because he doubted what to say, but because he knew the words would carry more weight if they came from a professed student of dreams.

The chief interpreter was a plump individual with more oil in his manner than most men can comfortably digest. "My lord Caliph," he began, "I pray devoutly that you will live forever. The reading of dreams is at once a mystery and a science. This is because the language of dreams is a language not of words but of images, and images do not speak. They only show themselves and leave their meaning to the insight of the observer. And yet they are a language, and all languages must be coherent. Their meaning can be learned, much as other men learn to speak foreign tongues."

This disquisition left the Prince shifting his weight from one foot to the other like a man restraining outrage. For his father's sake, however, he did not speak.

"Usually, my lord Caliph," the chief interpreter went on, "we do not presume to explain dreams until we have studied them, until we have had time to learn the language of their images." Nevertheless, even he could see that His Serene Goodness was losing patience. He hastened to say, "But the present case is exceptional. Prince Akhmet's dream is so precise that its import is unmistakable.

"My lord Caliph, your son has been given a vision of the journey of man from life to paradise. The nameless suzerain of the dream bore your face as a symbol of goodness, of the virtue and value which the gods intend for all men. If all men were ruled by goodness, the world would be remade into a place of joy. Thus the nameless suzerain has the power to shape the world. He is opposed, however, by the storm of pain, the storm of death, by the conflicting and petty intentions which assail goodness out of fear. And against this storm goodness cannot prevail because it is mortal and must die.

"But when goodness has faced death and understood it, when goodness has learned the true compassion of experience for all fear, all pain, then goodness itself becomes paradise, the perfect and healing home of the soul. Pettiness and hurt are made whole, conflicts are swept away, and joy becomes the heart's demesne."

As the chief interpreter spoke, the impatience faded from His Serene Goodness' face. The strain of his illness also seemed to fade, and peace filled his eyes. He was pleased by what he heard. Who would not have been pleased? Watching him, however, I believe that he would have been pleased by any interpretation which did not falsify the tone of the dream. For a moment, I was fascinated by the contrast between the two lords, father and son. The father thought of reasons to go to his death unafraid. The son could barely contain his fury. At the sight, I was struck by the odd notion that the true benefit of dreams comes, not to those who have them, but rather to those who hear about them.

Then the Most Holy Khartim a-Kul began to intone a prayer, and the notion was forgotten.

But Prince Akhmet had come to the end of his restraint. Despite the prayer—despite the necessity of reverence for the High Priest, or of respect for his father's pain and contentment—he left the Caliph's bedside and swept across the chamber to confront the chief interpreter. Knotting his fists in the plump man's robes, he hissed so that his father would not hear him, "You are a fool! You are all fools. You will not demean my dreams with your unc-

tuous pieties. Do you hear me? When I am Caliph, I will
have you beheaded."

The Vizier Moshim Mosha Va cast me a look which
said, I mean what I say. When this little shit becomes Caliph, I will put an end to my life.

Standing much closer to the chief interpreter than to the
bedside, Khartim a-Kul heard the prince's words. He was
shocked, of course, and outraged. But he could not stop
his prayer without drawing the Caliph's attention to the
fact that something was amiss. Grinding his teeth, he continued his unheeded appeal to the gods to its end.

By that time, young Akhmet had left the sickchamber.

He kept his word. As soon as his father's corpse began
to blacken and shrivel on the pyre, he commanded the beheading of the chief interpreter. The man was dead before
sundown.

Abdul dar-El Haj's death was still some days away,
however. His son's dream seemed to give him respite in
his illness. He rested well that night, and for a day or two
he grew stronger. And when his decline resumed, draining him steadily toward his death, he remained contented,
blessed with peace. He, too, believed the Prince's dream.

During those days, Akhmet had a number of dreams.

He remembered them all and told them to whoever
would listen. The only restraint he exercised was that he
did not trouble his father again—and did not permit his
dreams to be interpreted in his presence. Yet his look of
simony worsened. More and more, I came to think that he
was paying the price for his father's ease.

And at last His Serene Goodness Abdul dar-El Haj
died.

At once, all Arbin was plunged into a veritable apoth-
eosis of mourning. That is to say, the entire land was
seized by such a frenzy of religious prostration, ceremo-
nial grief, and ritualized emotional flagellation that it became nearly impossible for men like the Vizier and
myself to remember that the love underlying the
Mosque's extravagances was genuine. The advisors of su-
zerains became cynics of necessity, and the Most Holy

Khartim a-Kul was surely the most cynical among us. Therefore Moshim Mosha Va and I were hard-pressed to perceive the relationship between show and substance, between the public display of grief and its private truth. But we were grieved ourselves, perhaps not at our best. And, like the High Priest, we had reason to wonder what would become of us with the loss of our lord—but, unlike the High Priest, we had no outlet for our uncertainty.

We were not made less uncertain by the beheading of Khartim a-Kul's chief interpreter. For that act of tyranny, however, we had been forewarned. We had had time to accustom ourselves to the concept, if not to the actuality. As a consequence, we were more deeply disturbed by young Akhmet's other contribution to his father's funerary commemorations.

In tribute to His Serene Goodness, Khartim a-Kul revived a number of extreme liturgies and worships which had not been used for several generations—had not been used, in fact, precisely because they were so extreme. Like several of his fathers before him, Abdul dar-El Haj had become Caliph not as a youth, but as a man, and as a man, with the common sense of his forebears, he had forbidden the exercise of any liturgies or worships which he considered excessive.

Doubtless the Most Holy Khartim a-Kul deserved blame for his breach of recent custom, even though his decisions were made understandable by his fear of his new lord. But he could not have been blamed for the use young Akhmet made of his example.

Entirely to the High Priest's surprise, the new Caliph revived the old custom of suttee.

As an idea, suttee was alive among the people of Arbin. Upon the death of a Caliph, all the ruler's wives and odalisques were expected to join his corpse in cremation. And this harsh practice was not utterly unjustified. It preserved the succession of rule from the confusion which could result if one of those women bore a son after her lord's death. For several generations, however, no wife or odalisque had actually been required to commit suttee. Each new Caliph of Arbin had spared his father's women by the simple expedient of claiming them for himself, thus at once establishing his own reputation for benevolence and resolving any questions of legitimacy of his father's offspring.

The consternation among Abdul dar El Haj's harem must have been profound when young Akhmet announced that he would not follow the path of his predecessors. Specifically, he refused to claim or exempt any woman with whom he had shared carnal pleasure. He wished, he said, to begin his rule in Arbin pure. As a demonstration, he said, of his devotion to virtue and the Mosque.

The Most Holy Khartim a-Kul looked as ill as a fish as his priests led the beautiful and innocent women whom Akhmet had loved up onto Abdul dar-El Haj's pyre. The High Priest was only cynical, not heartless. Primarily to contain his own anger, the Vizier Moshim Mosha Va insisted that the High Priest deserved his distress. I found, however, that I had lost my taste for things which distressed Khartim a-Kul.

When the funerary rites and ceremonies were concluded, the new Caliph disposed of the rest of his father's wives by divorce. Doubtless he had no interest in hearing what his mother or the other older women might say about his purity or virtue.

The question in Arbin was not, What manner of Caliph will Akhmet become? It was, Who will he kill next?

The necessity of understanding him had become imperative.

"How long will it take, do you think?" asked the Vizier when we were alone. "You are a wizard. You have strange arts." His tone was bitter, although I knew he meant me no harm. "Read the signs. How long will it take before he has one of us beheaded? How long will it take before he has *me* beheaded?

"*Suttee,* by my beard! We are all disgraced. No civilized people will have dealings with us again for a hundred years."

Well, I am no prophet. I do not see the future. In the

case of young Akhmet, I could hardly see my hand before my face. Nevertheless, I had seen Arbin flourish under a line of benevolent rulers. I had watched Arbin's people grow in tolerance, as well as in religion and wealth. And I had loved His Serene Goodness as much as any man.

"Moshim Mosha Va," I said formally, so that the Vizier would heed me, "your death is already written—but it is written in the heart of the rock, where I cannot read it. Yet you are the Vizier of Arbin. Safe or doomed, you must uphold your duty."

"Oh, truly?" he snapped at me. "And must I uphold suttee? Must I uphold the murder of interpreters? Must I uphold the whims of a spoiled whelp who remembers his dreams?"

"No," I snapped back, pretending to lose patience with him simply to conceal my own fear. "You must uphold the succession in Arbin. You must uphold the integrity of the realm. Leave this new Caliph to me."

The Vizier Moshim Mosha Va studied me until I dropped my gaze. Then he breathed softly, "Yes. Wizardry and dreams. I will leave this new Caliph to you. And may the gods pity your soul."

"If you will prevent the Most Holy Khartim a-Kul from interfering with me," I replied, speaking half in jest to dispel the seriousness of the moment, "my soul will venture to fend for itself."

Moshim Mosha Va nodded without hesitation. Still studying me, he asked for the second time, "Wizard, do you understand our lord?"

"No," I answered for the second time. "But I will."

The truth was that I did not need understanding to know that Caliph Akhmet would come to me when he had dreamed again. He had already rejected the interpretation and counsel of the Mosque. And he surely had little use for the Vizier's manner of wisdom. Where else would he turn?

He did not dream again for some weeks. During the same period, he did nothing outrageously cruel. Apparently, the beheading of the chief interpreter and the burn-

ing of all his lovers had sated him in some way. The state
and luxury of his new position he enjoyed. The responsibilities he ignored, except as they gave him opportunity to
demonstrate new powers or obtain new satisfactions. For
the most part, his time was spent replenishing his harem,
and there his instinct for tyranny showed itself most
plainly, for he seemed to choose his women, not because
they were ripe for love, but because they were apt for hu-
miliation. Nevertheless, in the eyes of Arbin, women
were only women. Unthinking people began to believe
that perhaps Caliph Akhmet's rule would not prove intolerable.

I did not make that mistake. I readied my arts and
waited.

At last, in the small hours of the night, when even such
men as I am must sleep, I was summoned to the Caliph's
chambers.

I arrived to find him busy atop one of his women, and
it was clear from the sound of her moans and whimpers
that she did not relish the nature of his attentions. I would
have withdrawn, of course, but I was commanded to at-
tend and watch.

Had I been Moshim Mosha Va, I might have withdrawn
regardless and accepted the consequences. Sadly, I lack
the Vizier's pragmatic soul. Therefore I stood where I was
until the Caliph had achieved his satisfaction. Then I
risked saying, "It appears that I have misunderstood your
summons, my lord. I believed you wished to discuss the
matter of dreams. If I had known you wished me to comment on your performance, I would have prepared myself
differently."

"Wizard," Caliph Akhmet replied as if I had not spoken, "my advisors are fatuous in all things, but especially
where the wonder of my dreams is concerned. Pious
Khartim attempts to interpret what I dream. Sour Moshim
attempts to interpret the fact that I dream—and remember.
Only you have not made a fool of yourself on this subject. Why is that?"

"Two reasons, my lord," I said at once. "First, I am a

wise man. I understand that there are powers which lie beyond mortal interpretation. There the Vizier makes his mistake. He sees nothing which surpasses his own mind. Second, I am a wizard. I know that those powers will not allow themselves to be limited or controlled. There the High Priest makes his mistake. He fails to grasp that religion is not an explanation or a control for that which transcends us, but is rather an explanation or a control for how we must live in the face of powers which will not be defined or interpreted."

"Very good," said the Caliph and his eyes glittered with the confused penetration of the simoniac, at once insightful and blind. "I see that you want to live. Now you will earn your life.

"I have dreamed the most wonderful dream. I remember it all. Every detail lives in my soul, shining and immaculate, never to be lost. No man has ever remembered such things as I remember them.

"Wizard, I will tell you what I have dreamed. Then you will tell me what to do."

I bowed my acquiescence calmly, although my mouth was dry with fear, and my heart trembled. I had not come to this crisis adequately prepared. I still did not understand.

"I dreamed of wine," said the Caliph, his gaze already turning inward to regard his dream, "of strange wine and music. There were colors in the wine which I have seen in no wine before, hints of black with the most ruby incarnadine, true gold and yellow among straw, regal purple swirling to azure in my cup. There were depths to the liquid which my eyes could not pierce. Its taste was at once poppy and grape, at once fermented and fresh, and all its colors entered my body through my tongue, so that my limbs lived and burned and grew livid because of what was in my mouth. My member became engorged with such heat that no mere female flesh could cool it.

"And while my nerves sang with ruby and gold and cerulean, the music about me also sang. At first it was the music of lyre and tambour, plucked and beating. But as the colors of the wine filled my ears, the music became melody, as if strings and drum had voices full of loveliness, sweet as nectar, rich as satin. Those voices had no words for their song and needed none, for the song itself was as clean as air, as true as rock, as fertile as earth. And the music entered my body as the wine had entered it, came through my ears to live and throb in every muscle and sinew, transporting all my flesh to song. It was promise and fulfillment, carrying comfort to the core of my heart.

"Then the heat of my member grew until it became all heart, all passion, and my whole body in its turn became a part of my member, engorged with the same desire, aching with the same joy. And because of the wine and the music, that desire, that joy, were more precious to me than any release. I knew then that if my member were to spend its heat, all my flesh would experience the climax as part of my member, and the sense of ecstasy and release which would flood my being would be glorious and exquisite beyond any climax known to men—and yet that ecstasy and release, despite their greatness, would be only dross compared to the infinite value of the engorged desire, the aching joy.

"Therefore I was not compelled to seek release, as men are compelled by the lesser passions of wakefulness. Transformed by wine and music, I hung suspended in that place of color and glory and song until the dream ended and left me weeping."

The Caliph was weeping now as he remembered his dream, and his voice was husky with sadness when he again addressed me.

"Wizard, tell me what to do."

He might have been a small boy speaking to his father. Yet his need was not for me, but for a father wiser than I or all the old men of Arbin.

It is conceivable that I could have helped him then. But still I did not understand. I have lived too long in the world, away from dreams.

"My lord," I said, "you are the Caliph. You will do what you wish."

He strove to master his emotion, without success. "And what is it that I wish?"

There I failed him. As if I were wise and sure, I replied, "You wish to make your dreams live. That is why you have summoned me."

He stared at me while the tears dried in his eyes, and his mouth drew down into lines of simony, and I knew then that I had failed him. "Explain yourself, wizard," he said in the tone of a man who hurt women for pleasure.

Now, unfortunately, I could not stop or recant. "My lord," I answered as well as I could, "dreams and wizardry have much in common."

From within my robes, I produced a bouquet of rich flowers.

"Both are composed of illusion and freedom."

When I spread my hands, the flowers became butterflies and scattered themselves about the chamber.

"Yet the freedom and illusion of dreams are internal and may only be reached in sleep, without volition."

Again I spread my hands, and now music could be heard in the air, soft voices whispering melodiously of magic and love.

"The freedom and illusion of wizardry are external, matters of choice."

A third time I spread my hands, and this time flame bloomed in my palms, rising toward the ceiling as I spoke.

"You wish the power of wizardry to make the wonder and glory of your dreams accessible to your waking mind, to make wonder and glory matters of choice."

When I lifted my arms, the flame enveloped me entirely, causing me to disappear from his sight. Only a pillar of fire remained before him, burning the air, consuming nothing. From out of the flame, like the voice of the music, I said, "Wizardry is the path you must follow to pursue your dreams. You must turn away from cruelty and become my disciple. You will find no true happiness in the pain of helpless girls."

Then I stepped from the flame and let the fire go.

"My lord," I said, speaking quietly to contain my fervor, "allow me to serve you. I have knowledge which will enable you to make your dreams live."

That was my best effort, yet I had already lost him. He held a harsh bit clenched between his teeth, and his eyes were as wild as an overdriven mount's.

"So you are a fool after all, wizard," he snarled. "You do not understand. For all your knowledge, you cannot comprehend the worth of my dreams."

The truth must be told. Behind my aged composure, I was near to panic. Nevertheless, fright has its uses. It gave me the courage to say, "You are mistaken, my lord. I comprehend very well. Dreams have no worth in themselves. Their only value is the value we find in them, the value we bring to them with our waking eyes and hearts. Because they stir us or move us or teach us, they are precious. Otherwise they are nothing."

The Caliph regarded me, a twist of loathing on his lips. "Do you believe that?"

I made some effort to hold up my head. "I do, my lord."

"Then, wizard," he said grimly, "you will have the satisfaction of dying for your beliefs. They are a fool's beliefs, and they become you."

I could think of no way to appeal to him as his guards dragged me from the chamber.

For reasons which I did not grasp at the time, however, he let me keep both my head and my life. Instead of sending me to the block—or to the lion-pits, or to any other more imaginative or painful death, he had me sealed in my workrooms, with little food and water, less light, and no companionship. Indeed, the only contact I had with the court or Arbin came daily at noon, when for a brief time the Vizier Moshim Mosha Va was permitted to stand outside my door and report on the state of Caliph Akhmet's rule.

At first, of course, I believed that I was simply being held in my rooms until a suitable torture and death could be devised. By the second day, however, I began to think that young Akhmet had other intentions. When the Vizier came to my door, I asked him, "Why am I not dead? Does the Caliph imagine I fear death so extremely that I will go mad here among my arts and tools?"

In a sour tone, Moshim Mosha Va replied, "He is not done with you, wizard."

"What remains?" I inquired, daring to hope that I would be given one more chance.

"Who can say?" The Vizier's words were deferential, but his manner of speaking was savage. "Our illustrious lord surpasses us all. There are signs, however, which perhaps you will read better than I can. This morning he commanded one of his wives to be stretched upon the rack. And while her limbs strained with agony, he mounted her. His thrusts caused her to bleat like a sheep."

"Indeed," I muttered to myself. "How quaint." Then I asked, "And what pleasure did the Caliph take in this action?"

"He appeared blissful," retorted the Vizier, "if such fierceness may be called bliss, until he had spent himself. But then his joy curdled. He ordered the torturer racked until he died, as though the fault lay in the instrument of his will. I think, however, that he meant the man no harm. He was merely vexed."

Perhaps that was the point at which I began to understand Caliph Akhmet and his distress.

"Indeed," I said again. "You have become sagacious since the passing of His Serene Goodness, Vizier. You have grasped an important truth. He means harm to none of us. He is merely vexed."

Moshim Mosha Va made a noise which would have been a curse if the Caliph's guards had not stood beside him, listening. After a moment, he resumed, "Nevertheless, the hand of our good lord's vexation is heavy. Why do you not free yourself, wizard? Surely wizardry is good for that, if not for Arbin."

It may have been possible for me to do as he suggested. I could have conjured an affrit to appear before the guards and command them to unlock my prison. Perhaps they would have obeyed instead of fleeing. Freedom lay no farther away than the other side of the heavy door. Yet the distance was too great for me. I had loved Abdul dar-El Haj. I loved Arbin. And I had begun to hope again.

"Wizardry is illusion," I replied to the Vizier. "It is not power. And it is assuredly not freedom. I will await my Caliph's pleasure."

Then, whispering to reduce the hazard that the guards would overhear me, I added, "In the meantime, you must provide for the succession."

The Vizier snorted in disgust and went away.

For a number of days subsequently, he came at noon as he was permitted, bringing me the news of Arbin, which was essentially the news of Caliph Akhmet's attempts to achieve the sensation of his dreams through the exercise of power. He caused considerable pain and occasional death, striving to grasp a knowledge of mortal hurt. At unexpected intervals, he was generous, even benign, so that he could see gratitude on the faces of his subjects and compare it to the look of their distress. Well, he was young, and the young are foolish. He had had too few years in which to learn that power binds rather than releases. It was little wonder that he was vexed.

Therefore I readied myself for the time when he would summon me again.

He did not summon me again, however. Instead, covered by a bright blaze of daylight and torches, he came to see me in my workrooms. The door was flung open, allowing me sunlight for the first time during my captivity. Among guards armed with light, Caliph Akhmet strode forward to confront me.

I endeavored to hold up my head, but failed. My old eyes could not bear the brightness. As if I were weeping and ashamed, I bowed and hid my face before my lord.

"Wizard."

I was unable to see him. I could only hear the strain in his voice, the struggle against frailty and grief.

"I need you."

"My lord," I mumbled as if I had become decrepit, "I will serve you."

"Tell me what to do."

"You are the Caliph. You will do what you wish."

"I do not know what I wish."

Indeed. This I had already grasped. Softly, I said, "Tell me what troubles you, my lord."

Out of the light blurred by my tears, young Akhmet answered, "Wizard, I am only myself."

There at last I became sure that I had gleaned the truth. "The same may be said of all men, my lord," I responded gently.

"But all men do not remember their dreams!" If a tyrant can suffer anguish—if such pain can be ascribed to a man who causes so much pain in others—then the Caliph deserved pity. "They are the most wonderful dreams! And I remember them all. Every touch, every color, every joy. Nothing is lost. I have with me now the first dream as clearly as the last, and both are desirable beyond bearing.

"But when I have dreamed, I awake, and I am only myself.

"Help me, wizard."

"I will, my lord." My voice shook, and I cursed the blindness of so much light, but I did not falter. "You wish to live your dreams. You desire to be possessed by dreaming, to give yourself to that glory and freedom always. You wish to cease to be yourself. Therefore you resent anything that takes you from your dreams, any interpretation, any distraction, any release which restores you to your mortality. Waking, you strive for joy and accomplish only dross.

"My lord, I can make you dream always, waking or sleeping. I can enable you to be entirely the dreamer who remembers, beyond interpretation or distraction or release."

I felt his hands clutch at my robes, felt his fingers grip my shoulders to implore. "Then do so. Do so. Do it now."

"Very well, my lord. Give me a moment in which to prepare myself."

In order to gather my strength, as well as to draw the attention of the guards to me, I stepped back from Caliph Akhmet.

Rising to my full height, although I was still effectively blind, I said in the resonant voice of wizards, "Let all witness that what I do now, I do at my lord's express command. He has made his wishes known. I seek only to fulfill them. By my arts he will become his dreams, become dreaming incarnate."

Before the guards could ask whether it lay within their duty to permit this to happen to their lord, I spread my arms and filled the room with fires I could not see.

I did not need to see them, of course. I knew them well. Their suddenness made them seem hotter than they were, and they blazed among my tables and periapts and apparatus as if Caliph and wizard and guards were about to be consumed in conflagration. They did no hurt, however. Instead, as they leaped roaring silently toward the ceiling, they began to spew out the known stuff of young Akhmet's dreams. Mandrill leaped and snarled, spitting rubies and blood. Nilgai chased silver fear across the flames. City lights unfolded maps of tyranny across darkness implied by the cruel gaps between the fires. His Serene Goodness Abdul dar-El Haj stretched his mouth to let out a cry of love or pain. Akhmet's swollen member ached for the most glorious and rending ejaculation. To all appearances, my workroom had been filled with dreams come to madness and destruction.

Caliph Akhmet saw those fires no more than I did. They were intended for the edification and appeasement of his entourage. He saw, rather, that I reached among my vials and flasks, uncorked a dusty potion, and poured a liberal draught into a goblet ready with arrak.

"Drink this, my lord," I said as my arts distracted the spectators. "It will enable you to live your dreams even while you are awake."

Young Akhmet had not been a tyrant long enough to learn the fear which corrupts and paralyzes hurtful men.

He took the goblet and drank. I could not see the expression on his face.

Several days later, after Akhmet had died, and I had out-faced the accusation that I had killed him, and a previously forgotten relation of his His Serene Goodness Abdul dar-El Haj, discovered and prepared by the Vizier, had been installed as the new Caliph in Arbin, Moshim Mosha Va took me aside and challenged me.

"The truth, wizard," he demanded. "You killed that little shit, did you not?"

"I did not," I replied in feigned indignation. "Did not the guards declare that I gave our lamented lord no draught or potion, but only a vision of his dreams? Did not the best physicians in Arbin proclaim that our lamented lord showed no evidence of poison? This truth is plain, Vizier. Caliph Akhmet brought about his own death by refusing to eat or drink. He died of thirst, I believe, before he could have died of hunger. Can I be blamed for this?"

"Apparently not," growled the vexed Vizier. "Yet I will continue to blame you until you answer me. By what miracle have we been freed of him? What wizardry did you use? What power do you have, that you do not reveal?"

"Moshim Mosha Va," I responded piously, "I gave our lamented lord exactly what he desired. I gave him the capacity to dream his wonderful dreams while he remained awake. Sadly, his dreams so entranced him that he neglected to live."

The Vizier treated this answer with disdain. He could not obtain a better, however, and in time he grew to be content with it.

Wizardry is illusion. I put the potion which had drugged Caliph Akhmet away in my workroom and made no use of it again. I am a man, and all men dream. But I have forgotten my dreams. I have no wish to become a tyrant.

Journey into the Dark

Jane Yolen

Translation from the altar stone at the great temple at Chichén Itzá, excavated May 14, 2030

Let me tell you a story, my children.

When the young prince Ho ch'ok lay dying on his small bed, he had around him the four that he loved best.

Kneeling by his head was his lady mother, the queen, who had pulled out all the pins from her hair in mourning and likewise the pin from her lip.

His brother, the king-that-was-to-be, Qich Mam, sat by his feet, tears kept in check by the slow breathing he had been taught since a child.

His sister, who was to have been the young prince's bride, sat closer to his heart, by the left side, the tears like rivers running down her unpainted cheeks.

And standing at the bedfoot was his old nurse, weeping loudly and beating upon her bosom with a closed fist.

The young prince Ho ch'ok opened his mouth to speak and all four about him fell silent, for his voice was but a whisper. He reached out his hand and his sister took it loosely in hers.

"I am afraid," Ho ch'ok said, for though he was a prince he was, still, a small boy. "I am afraid of the journey. I am afraid of the dark."

"Then," his mother said softly, "I shall give you something to light the way." She plucked her heart from her

breast and held it out to him. And when he took it, it
shone with a light that was even and white.

"And I will give you that which can tell dark from
light," said his sister, plucking out her third eye and putting it on his forehead. "It can tell the hard places from
the soft."

"And I will give you a weapon that you shall not be
afraid," said his brother, breaking off a little finger, the
last one on the left. He placed it on his brother's chest.

"But still I am cold," said Ho ch'ok. "So cold."

At that the nurse took a great leather wallet which was
hanging from a thong on her belt. She opened it and there
was the young prince's foreskin. Since he had not yet wed
his sister, the foreskin was as soft and supple as the day
it had been cut from him. The old nurse took it from the
wallet and shook it out, and it became as great and as
wide and as warm as a cloak, and she wrapped him in it.

And the young prince smiled, closed his eyes, and rose
up out of his body for his journey, leaving but a rough-
ened hulk behind.

The first step he took went to the East where the sun
hit him full in the face, leaving a bright red scar on his
cheek. The next step he took went to the South where a
branch of the world tree slapped him across the chest, and
a sliver of wood slipped in under his nipple into the meat
of his breast. The third step took him to the West where
the wind whirled his cape up over his head and burnished
his buttocks with hot sand.

But the fourth step took him to the North and the Cavern of Night, where all those who die have to go.

The way into the cavern was dark and winding, like the
stomach of a serpent. Ho ch'ok held aloft his mother's
heart. The light it cast crept into all the pockets of the
dark and sent the shadows screaming silently from its
rays. At that Ho ch'ok smiled.

But as he went deeper into the cavern, even his mother's heart light grew dim.

"Oh, my mother," cried the young prince, "what am I
to do?" And receiving no answer, he reached into his own

breast through the opening made by the sliver of the
world tree. But his heart would not leave his body, for he
was not a woman. Still, there was just enough light from
the opening of his chest with which to see, and so he
went on.

After a while, he came to a cavern flooded with water
that seemed to be both red and black. Ho ch'ok stopped,
and bent close to the water, but he could not tell if it was
possible to cross.

He opened his sister's third eye and saw that that which
was black was, indeed, water; but that which was red was
a bridge of smooth stones. So being careful to step only
on the stones, he started to the other side.

He was halfway across when his sister's eye, being
tired, closed. And as he was a man he had no third eye of
his own.

"Oh, my sister," cried Ho ch'ok, "what am I to do?"

He would have thrown himself down and wept except
that a man does not do such a thing, except that he did
not know how to tell the wet places from the dry. But as
the first tear touched his cheek, it touched also the red
scar. And where it touched the scar, the tear turned aside.

The young prince felt the turning of the tear, and so he
bent down and, gathering up a handful of black water in
his hand, he splashed it against his face. Where it touched
the scar, the water turned roughly aside. So then Ho ch'ok
did throw himself down, but not to weep. And when his
face touched the water, the water rushed away from his
sun scar and in this way he was able to walk upon dry
land.

Soon he came to the farthest side and there he stopped,
for ahead, in the feeble light, he could see three diverging
paths. Guarding the paths was a giant vulture, the curved
knife of its beak snapping at the shadows. At its feet were
the bones of false princes who had gone before.

"Oh, my brother, Qich Mam," said the young prince,
"may I use the weapon you have given me well." He took
out the finger which had been kept in a pouch around his
neck, and held it in his right hand. There it grew and grew

until it was a great spear as strong as muscle, as sharp as bone.

When the vulture saw the spear, it laughed, a sound like death itself, and the bones at its feet rose up and assembled themselves into a cage whose door gaped wide. Then the vulture sucked in a great breath which pulled Ho ch'ok forward until he was all but in the cage.

But the young prince took his spear and flung it at the vulture. It pierced the great bird's breast, but not very deep. With a snap of its curved knife of a beak, the vulture snapped the spear in two.

"Oh, my brother," Ho ch'ok cried, "what am I to do?"

The vulture leaned down and picked up the young prince by the back of his cape and shook him from side to side. But Ho ch'ok, like his brother, knew the trick of the little finger. Still, he did not break that one off, but instead broke the second finger, the one with which a man points to his eye to show that he understands. The finger grew into a spear even greater and sharper than the one Ho ch'ok had had before. With one mighty thrust, he pierced the vulture's breast exactly where the first had gone, thus sending the piece of Qich Mam's spear straight into the monster's heart.

Then Ho ch'ok gathered up the vulture's bones and locked tight the bone cage. Next he looked at the three paths, hoping to find a sign pointing the way.

The left path was rocky and narrow and there was barely room for a man to pass. The right path was smooth and wide, and an army could walk between. But the path in the middle was as dark and hidden as a secret.

Wrapping his cloak tightly around him, and trusting to the light of his heart, the young prince Ho ch'ok chose the secret path because the unknown way always holds the deepest rewards. And it was this path that led him safely to the garden of delights where all true princes live forever.

And if you, my children, can unriddle this tale, at the end of your days you may live in the garden as well.

Keeper of Souls

Owl Goingback

Digging Owl opened his eyes but could not tell if morning had arrived. The tiny dungeon room was windowless, the stone walls as cold and hard as the hearts of his Spanish captors. A torch of resinous wood was set in a bracket high on the far wall, but its amber glow did little to push back the darkness, revealing only a few of the forty or so other occupants of the room.

Naked and enchained, they were wedged together so tightly there was barely enough room to sit, let alone lie down. Members of several different tribes from the land their captors dubbed "Florida," they had survived the journey across the big water in the belly of a Spanish ship. The same miserable journey Digging Owl had made. Most of the others had been prisoners for years. Some had been forced to labor in the mines and slave camps of the islands before being brought to Spain.

From the shadows beyond the glow of the torch came moans of pain and the sounds of someone gagging. Sickness had descended over the occupants of the room, bringing with it vomiting and diarrhea. A few feet away, a woman prayed for death to come and end her suffering.

As a medicine man, Digging Owl, though suffering from sickness himself, had done what he could to help the others. But the Spaniards had taken his medicine pouch from him, leaving him with nothing to offer but prayers.

There was the sound of metal on metal from the far end

of the room. A lock was turned and the door opened with a squeak. Light spilled across the stone floor, illuminating even more naked bodies. Digging Owl squinted against the glare as two Spanish soldiers entered the room, holding torches above their heads. They stepped to the side of the doorway, allowing an Indian woman to enter. The woman, naked except for a small piece of fabric covering her loins, carried a wooden bucket of water and a small metal cup. She moved amongst the prisoners, offering drinks to those with the strength to receive them.

Digging Owl watched with interest as the woman approached him. She was young, probably in her early twenties, her hair long and dark. Her body was oddly free of tattoos, except for a large "C" branded on her left cheek. The "C" was a Spanish brand of ownership; it stood for the island they called Cubagua. The woman had obviously once been a slave there.

The woman dipped the cup into the bucket and offered it to him. Noticing the tattoos on his chest and shoulders, her eyes went wide with surprise. Her hand trembled slightly, causing some of the water to spill from the cup. Digging Owl grabbed her hand to steady it.

"Careful, little sister," he said, taking the cup of water from her. "This is much too precious to waste."

She looked quickly behind her to see if any of the guards were watching. None were.

"You are the holy man," she said, squatting in front of him. It was more of a statement than a question.

Digging Owl nodded. "I am a holy man. But if you are sick, I can offer no cures. They have taken my medicine."

She shook her head. "I am not sick, but there are others who need your help."

He shrugged and showed her his manacled wrists.

"That does not matter. Some things do not require the use of hands. What is your tribe? Your village?"

"I am Timucuan. My village is Casti."

Recognition showed in her eyes. "The Timucuans are said to have powerful medicine. Know you of the one called Tacachale?"

Digging Owl nodded. "It is said she lives in the forest near the village of Ocali. It is she who guards the fountain of eternal life. Many have tried to possess the sacred waters, but all have failed."

"So I have heard," she said.

"But tell me, little sister, how is it you know of such things? You speak my language, yet your body is unmarked. Are you Timucuan?"

She shook her head. "I was born a slave and have served the Spaniards all my life, first in the silver mines and now here in the castle. I am named for the village of my people, a village that no longer exists. I am called Tawasa."

The destroyed village of Tawasa lay four days' travel to the south of Digging Owl's home, near the junction of two small rivers. The Tawasan warriors had tried to stop the Spaniards' encroachment upon their land, but failed. Those not killed were taken as slaves, along with their wives and children. The village was burned to the ground.

"You said you knew of my coming. How?"

"There is much talk in the castle. The king speaks of bringing one who has the gift of sight, one who can see into the future."

So that was the reason for his capture. His village had always been friendly toward the Spaniards. Knowing of their cruelty to others, the chief thought it best to pay a tribute to the Spaniards in food and labor, rather than allow them to forcibly take what they wanted. Digging Owl had helped out by accompanying one of their expeditions, accurately forewarning them of any danger along the way. It was just after such a prediction that the soldiers, under the orders of their leader, turned on him, talking away his medicine pouch and shackling him in chains.

"And if I refuse to help?" Digging Owl asked.

"Then they will kill you, and the others as well."

She took the empty cup from him. "There is a man named Antonio. A priest. He is a member of the Holy Office, in charge of what is called the Inquisition. He and the other priests torture and kill all those who do not believe in their God. Many have already died. Many more are imprisoned. I have heard that he is very angry that you have been brought here. You must be careful. He has the king's ear and is very jealous of anyone with power."

She stood up and turned away. Digging Owl watched as she offered water to the others. A few minutes later she was escorted out by the guards. The door slammed shut, casting them back into darkness.

There was no way of telling time in the dungeon cell. Digging Owl suspected that a full day must have passed before the door again opened and three guards entered the room. Carrying candles, they weaved their way between the prisoners, stepping around, or over, those lying in their path. Stopping to shine their lights on the face of each prisoner, they at last made their way to Digging Owl. Circling him, two of the guards grabbed him from behind, dragging him to his feet. They turned and headed back across the room, taking Digging Owl with them.

Digging Owl was led through the door and out into the dimly lit hallway. Still chained at the wrists and legs, he was marched through a series of passageways and up several flights of stairs to a small, circular room. Sunlight streamed into the room through a pair of narrow, rectangular windows. The windows, mere slits to shoot arrows through, were a welcome sight. It was the first time in days that he had seen the light of day or smelled fresh air.

From where he stood, Digging Owl could look out over the surrounding countryside. The land beyond the castle was barren-looking, with empty fields and stunted trees. There were no great forests where a man could be on his own to hunt and fish, like in the land of his people. Instead, houses and villages of stone dotted the plain like a repulsive rash.

No wonder the Spaniards want our land. Theirs is dried up . . . dying.

He was only allowed a moment to view the countryside. Shoved from behind, he was marched out of the circular room and down another hallway.

Unlike the previous hallways they had passed through, this one was brightly lit with both windows and candles. Colorful tapestries depicting scenes of battle decorated the walls. Digging Owl ran his finger over one of the tapestries, amazed at the softness of the material.

How can those who create beauty such as this have hatred in their hearts for others?

The hallway emptied into a large room. Digging Owl was halfway across the room before realizing they had arrived at their destination.

The room's floor was of polished stone, its ceiling trimmed in gold. Tapestries and paintings decorated three of the walls. Red curtains covered the fourth. Two massive wooden chairs sat in front of the curtained wall, midway along its length, elevated upon a raised section of floor. One of the chairs was empty. In the other sat a young man dressed in clothing of bright yellows and reds. He was a thin man with a pale complexion, dark hair, and a beard. His eyes bulged slightly, and his mouth hung open as though something was not quite right with his mind. If it wasn't for the crown he wore, Digging Owl would never have guessed that he was standing before Charles, the king of Spain—the most powerful man in the world.

Behind the king stood four armed soldiers, his personal guards, while to his left stood a man dressed in a long black robe. A priest. It was the priest, more than the king, that drew Digging Owl's attention. A short, thin man with a cruel face and eyes, he had an aura of negative energy so strong it was almost a physical blow.

Stopping a few paces in front of the king, the guards ordered Digging Owl to kneel. When he refused, they shoved him roughly to the floor.

The king leaned forward in his chair, watching Digging Owl with open curiosity.

"T-this is the great soothsayer I was p-promised?" he asked, a noticeable stutter to his voice. "I think m-my money could be b-best spent elsewhere."

"It is true, Your Majesty," one of the soldiers standing

behind the king spoke up. Digging Owl recognized him as being a member of the expedition he had accompanied. "I have seen it for myself. If not for his predictions we would have been ambushed many times."

"A sorcerer. One of Satan's own," the priest said, his voice cold with malice. "He should be burned."

The king laughed. "Have you not enough to keep you b-busy in the dungeons, Antonio?"

The king turned his attention back to Digging Owl. "Do you s-speak Spanish?"

Digging Owl nodded. "A little." Actually, he spoke Spanish fairly well. He'd learned during his time with the expedition.

"Good, then there will b-be no need of an interpreter. Very well, show us what p-powers you have. Tell me of the f-future."

Digging Owl looked around and shrugged. "I cannot. I do not have the things I need."

"He lies," said the priest. "He only stalls for time. He has no power."

The king held up his hand for silence. "Tell me what you need and m-my men will get it."

"I need the leather bag that was taken from me. It contains the things I need."

The king turned to the soldier from the expedition. "Have we such a bag?"

"Yes, Your Majesty. It was turned over to the treasury for safekeeping."

"Then go and fetch it. B-bring it here."

The soldier bowed, walked briskly across the room, and exited through the doorway.

Digging Owl's heart leaped with joy. He'd feared that his medicine pouch was lost forever. The items it contained were irreplaceable, for they were objects of power—gifts from the Great Spirit.

"Anything else?" the king asked.

Digging Owl nodded. "I will need the room to be made dark and a small fire . . . here." He pointed at the floor in front of him. "I will also need food and water."

"So be it," the king nodded. He motioned to one of his guards. "Cover the w-windows with tapestries and b-build a fire where he stands. And b-bring this man some food and water."

"The food is not for me," Digging Owl interrupted. "I want only the water. There are others, in the rooms below, who hunger."

The king cocked an eyebrow at Digging Owl, then smiled. "You drive a hard b-bargain. Is there anything else?"

"No," Digging Owl said.

He seated himself cross-legged on the floor, watching as the soldiers covered the windows to block out the sunlight and built a small fire in front of him. A short time later his medicine pouch was brought to him. A flagon of water was also brought.

Wiping his hands on his breechcloth, Digging Owl opened the leather pouch and removed a small wooden bowl. The inside surface of the bowl was painted solid black, while its outside was decorated with symbols representing different animals. Setting it in front of him, he slowly filled it with water. The blackness of the bowl caused the water to also look black. Setting the water jug back down, Digging Owl scooted the bowl closer to the fire until the glow of the flames were reflected in the water. He was ready to begin the seeing ceremony.

"What is it you wish to know?" Digging Owl asked.

King Charles leaned forward in his chair, his eyes wide with anticipation. "I w-wish to know all that you see about the country to the north of Spain. F-France. I w-want to know about F-Francis I, its leader. Is he p-planning to invade Navarre? Can we defeat him? Will we b-be able to drive F-France out of Milan once and for all?"

The questions made little sense to Digging Owl. All he knew was that Charles was worried about this place called France. Could there be another country powerful enough to oppose Spain?

"I will do what I can," Digging Owl said.

Taking a deep breath, he began to quietly pray. At the same time, he gazed at the flickering reflection in the water, allowing his mind to relax. Almost immediately, a tingling began in his toes as the energies and powers he called upon entered his body. The sensation spread upward, causing a numbness in his legs, a stirring in his loins. His breathing slowed; his shoulders slumped. As the tingling reached his chest and upper torso, his body began to contort, his arms and legs thrashing about on their own. Digging Owl, his mind still focused on the bowl of water, barely noticed the contortions. He'd become accustomed to such things.

The tingling, like an almost unbearable itching, poured over his face, causing his lips to pull back from his teeth. It entered his head, flooding his mind with a rush of energy. His eyes rolled back as he fell backward, his body convulsing on the floor. The tingling pushed onward, found an invisible doorway in the top of his head, and exited his body. It took his spirit with it.

There was the nauseating sensation of speed as Digging Owl's spirit left his body, racing to where it was being asked to go, into the future. Images of a vast countryside flashed through his mind. Villages of many buildings with fortresses of stone appeared and disappeared, giving way to mountains taller than he had ever seen before. In the fertile valleys between those mountains soldiers gathered and prepared for war. The soldiers were like the Spaniards, yet dressed differently. Since they approached from the north, Digging Owl guessed that they were the French army the king had asked about.

In what could only have been minutes but seemed like days, Digging Owl watched several battles take place. Victories went to both sides as the two opposing forces fought for control of the mountainous region. In the end it was the French who finally fell back. Satisfied that he'd seen what he had been asked to see, Digging Owl allowed his spirit to continue its journey. He thought he would return to his body, but instead found himself being pulled to the west, to a walled village beside a river. The name

Tordesillas popped into his head, but he knew not what it meant. He assumed it was the name of the village.

A darkness seemed to hang over Tordesillas. A sadness. The feeling came from the largest building in the village, a fortress of stone towers and iron bars. Before he realized what was happening, Digging Owl found himself inside that building, in one of its many rooms. He was not alone in the room. With him was a woman.

She wore a long blue dress, her dark hair tied up in a matching ribbon. Her skin was very pale, as though it had been a long time since she'd walked in the warmth of the sun. She sat on the floor, her shoulders hunched, staring blankly at the bare wall in front of her. The woman's eyes were filled with sadness, the eyes of one who'd known much suffering and pain.

In the brief instant that Digging Owl shared the room with the woman, he learned everything about her: how she was being kept a prisoner against her will, how others were saying she was crazy though her mind was quite sound. He also learned her name and who she was. She was Juana, the mother of King Charles.

Why would the king keep his own mother locked away in such misery?

The vision started to blur and fade. But before it did, Digging Owl knew the answer to his question.

Because she is the legal ruler of Spain.

Digging Owl found himself back in his body, staring up at a ceiling covered with gold. He quickly sat up and looked around.

The king and his men were staring at him, their faces grim. Obviously his body's contortions, which always accompanied his seeing, had terrified them greatly. A few moments passed before the king found his voice.

"You have s-seen something?"

Digging Owl nodded.

"Tell me."

"I have seen a great army marching from the north."

"Yes, yes. Go on," the king ordered.

"There will be many battles. Villages will trade hands. Much blood will flow."

"B-but who will win?"

"You will," Digging Owl said.

King Charles smiled, satisfied with the outcome of the future.

"Lies," hissed the priest. "He has not seen the future, Your Majesty. He tells you only what you wish to hear."

King Charles turned to the priest, then back to Digging Owl. "How can I be sure that you s-speak the truth, that what you say will come to p-pass?"

"I have seen other things . . ."

"What things?" Charles asked.

"I have seen a village many days travel from here. In this village a woman is being kept, a prisoner, shut off from those she loves. It is believed this woman is crazy, yet it is not so. What is said about her are only lies to keep her locked away. Her name is Juana. She is your mother, the one whose place you have stolen."

Charles leaped from his seat. "L-liar!" he shouted, his face twisting with rage. He strode toward Digging Owl, raising his staff as though to strike him. Digging Owl remained seated.

"I only tell what I have seen," Digging Owl said.

Charles halted, suddenly aware of the others in the room watching him. He lowered his staff.

"You know n-not what you s-see, savage." He nodded toward the guards. "Take him away. P-place him in a cell by himself, away from the others."

With that, the king of Spain turned his back on Digging Owl and walked away, leaving the throne room through a private doorway hidden behind the curtains. Digging Owl was grabbed by two of the guards and yanked to his feet. He was led out the other doorway and returned to the dungeons by the same way he'd been brought. But this time, instead of being placed with the others, he was tossed into a much smaller cell.

He only had a moment to survey his new surroundings before the door slammed shut behind him. The walls were of gray stones, wet with moisture and spotted with white patches of mold. The floor of the cell was covered with a thin layer of straw that smelled of sweat, excrement, and urine. On two of the walls, chains and shackles had been set into the stones. The conditions were made that much more unbearable by the fact that he was completely alone, with no one to talk to or share his thoughts with. Worse yet, as the door closed behind him, Digging Owl realized that the guards had not furnished him with a candle or torch. He was cast into complete darkness.

It might have been only a short time since the door closed behind him. It might have been days. Digging Owl did not know. After some thought, he decided to explore his surroundings further. Such a feat was no easy task in darkness so deep he couldn't see his own hand in front of his face. But he was determined to try anyway. Perhaps there was some way to free himself from the tiny room.

Sitting on the floor, Digging Owl pushed himself back until he touched the stone wall. Turning to his right, he lay down on his stomach, his body parallel to the wall. Moving slowly, he began to pull himself along the length of the wall using his elbows and forearms. In the darkness his eyes were useless. So he allowed his fingers to be his eyes for him. He felt along the floor and wall, searching for a loose stone or crack in the mortar—something that with a little effort he might widen to facilitate an escape. He found nothing by the time he reached the first corner.

Turning left, he crawled his way along the second wall until he reached another corner. He'd only gone about two body lengths down the third wall when a whiff of cool air caressed his face. Exploring with his fingers, he found that he'd reached the door.

Sitting up, Digging Owl traced along the edge of the door, hoping to find a crack or niche he could use to his advantage. Unfortunately the door was set flush in the wall. He doubted that he could have opened it even if he had possessed the tools to do so. Discouraged, he continued on.

On the other side of the door he discovered a bowl of water and a few pieces of stale bread. Thanking the Great Spirit for his find, he tore off a piece of bread and began chewing it slowly. Whatever their plans for him, it was obvious his captors did not want him to starve to death.

Digging Owl started to tear off another piece of bread, but his hand brushed against something else lying in the darkness. His heart raced as he ran his fingers along the leather bundle, touching the tiny shells sewn along its edges, feeling the familiar shapes of its contents.

My medicine pouch.

Why was it here? Why had he been allowed to keep it? Did the Spaniards hold his medicine in such low regard that they felt it wasn't worth keeping? Or were they planning on asking him to again see the future at a later date? Either way, he was extremely glad to have the pouch, for it might provide the means of discovering a way out.

Picking up the pouch, Digging Owl slid across the floor until his back was against the wall opposite the door. Sitting cross-legged, he set the pouch on his lap and untied the leather cord that held it closed. He knew what every item was, so even in the darkness it only took a moment to find what he was looking for.

Selecting a smooth stone that he knew without seeing was as clear as water, he resealed the pouch, setting it beside him. Holding the stone tight in his left fist, he sang a prayer. As he did, he felt it begin to pulsate, like a tiny heart, and radiate heat. It was only a mild warmth at first, but it quickly increased until it was all he could do to continue holding the stone.

The vision bowl used to predict the king's future was not the only means Digging Owl had of seeing. In fact, of all his medicine objects, it was probably the least powerful. That was exactly why he'd used it. If the Spaniards were to learn the powers of his other objects, they might take them, or force him to use them for evil purposes.

As the stone heated up, a familar tingling started in his left hand, quickly spreading up his arm. The sensation spread across his chest, down his other arm, and into his lower torso. The muscles in his legs began to twitch as mild surges of energy coursed through them. The skin around his temples pulled tight, making his scalp itch. As he had with the vision bowl, he felt the energy surge into his head and blend with his spirit. And as before, he felt the tiny invisible doorway open in the top of his head, allowing his spirit to be free of the flesh encasing it.

But unlike earlier, Digging Owl did not let his spirit race forward through time, nor did he allow it to fly. He kept a tight rein on it, making sure it remained in the here and now. Invisible to all but those of medicine, Digging Owl's spirit looked exactly like the body that encased it—minus the breechcloth. Casting a brief glance back at his body, he glided across the room and through the locked door.

Time was running out for him. What he'd said earlier to King Charles about his imprisoned mother had enraged him. Digging Owl guessed that the king was terrified that others would find out that his claim to the throne was false. It wouldn't be long before the king decided to silence Digging Owl forever.

But what evil would cause a man to lock away his own mother? Could the Spaniards be so corrupt that they would do such a thing without a second thought? Was their thirst for power so great that it could not be shared?

Moving into the corridor, Digging Owl retraced his previous journey to the upper levels of the castle. He slowed down as he passed two guards. Though he could not be seen, his presence could be felt as a slight wind or a cool draft. As he slipped past the guards, the flames of the candles on the wall behind them flickered slightly.

Reaching the upper levels, he quickly crossed the throne room, searching for the rooms that must lie beyond, one of which had to be the king's sleeping quarters. There were many rooms in the castle, and the searching took longer than he'd anticipated. Every moment he spent away from his body was dangerous. There was no telling what would happen if a guard discovered his body without its spirit. Digging Owl was about to give up his quest and return to his body when he found what he was looking for.

He located the king's chamber on the level above the throne room. It was decorated with layers of deep-red fabrics, etched vessels of crystal and numerous items of gold. In the center of the room, upon a raised dais, sat a massive bed, framed by four pedestals of ebony wood and crowned by a canopy of the finest silk. The king looked like a little boy in such a big bed, his pale face illuminated by the moonlight streaming in through an open window.

Still not knowing why he'd come, or what he could possibly do to procure his freedom, Digging Owl moved to the foot of the bed. There he stood, looking down at the most powerful monarch in all the world. Had he been in the flesh, he would have killed the king to avenge the suffering of his people. But while he was in the spirit form even his most violent attack would be but a gentle caress of wind. Instead, Digging Owl willed himself to relax, turning off the tiny voice that always spoke inside his head. With the voice gone he was able to listen to another tiny voice—that of the king's.

The king's troubled thoughts came bubbling up like water from an underground stream. They were confusing, and it took a great effort to decipher them. They were mostly thoughts of conquest and power, and of those who had ruled Spain in the past.

Picking through the thoughts, Digging Owl learned of a woman named Isabel and her husband, Fernando. They had united several squabbling provinces into the powerful empire of Spain. It was Isabel who'd ordered the torture and deaths of all those whose faith was different from her own. And it was her hand that had signed the document allowing the soldiers to enslave and murder Digging Owl's people.

Digging Owl probed further, learning of the tragedies that befell the children of Isabel and Fernando. He saw the death of her only son, Juan, barely six moons after his marriage, and the death of her oldest daughter, also named Isabel, ten moons after that. He witnessed the suffering of the one called Juana—the one he'd seen in the vision—as her husband turned against her, then her father, and finally her son, Charles.

At first Digging Owl thought that a curse must have been placed on the royal family, perhaps by one who had died because of the orders of Isabel. But he quickly dismissed the idea. Whatever plagued the family had been around long before the time of the Inquisition, long before the one called Columbus set sail for the land of Digging Owl's people.

Stepping closer, he broke the contact with the king's mind and began looking at his body instead. He squinted his eyes and cocked his head slightly, studying the face and outline of the young monarch. A blackness, like a shadow, clung to the body of the king. It was the same blackness worn by the sick and dying. But this was not a sickness of the flesh; it was one of the spirit. Looking closer, Digging Owl realized he could only see two spirits aligned within the body of Charles. One of the king's souls was missing.

Digging Owl looked again, just to be sure. There was no mistake. The king only had two spirits. Could it be that the Spaniards only had two souls? Digging Owl didn't think so. As far as he knew, everyone had three. One soul was the tiny light in the pupil of the eyes. Another was the shadow that each person makes. The third was the image one sees in clear water. Even the Spaniards he'd accompanied on the expedition had three souls.

So where was the king's other soul? Had it wandered off? Doubtful. If it had, it would have left a trail clearly visible to anyone of medicine. No, someone had taken Charles's soul. That same someone could have also taken souls from the other family members. That would explain all the suffering. But who would do such a thing, and why?

As he pondered over the whereabouts of the missing soul, the door to the king's chamber opened and someone entered the room. Digging Owl was so surprised he almost ran for a hiding place before remembering he was invisible.

It was the priest named Antonio who entered the room, the same priest who'd stood beside the king's throne. Closing the door behind him, the priest made his way quickly to the king's bedside. Digging Owl expected him to wake the king, for he moved like a man on urgent business. Instead, Antonio leaned closer to the bed, pulling something from beneath his robe.

It was a tiny glass bottle, fastened around his neck by a gold chain. The bottle was a translucent blue. In it something glowed and wiggled about as though alive. Digging Owl knew at once that the priest possessed the missing soul of King Charles. And the person who owned the king's soul also controlled the king.

Leaning forward, the priest whispered. "Time is running out. You must act now. Your mother is a danger to you as long as she lives. She must be killed, but it must be made to look like an accident. Only then can you rule Spain with a free hand. Only then—"

He stopped suddenly, turning his head to the left, looking straight at Digging Owl. Though he hadn't moved, hadn't made a sound, Digging Owl was certain the priest could see him. Worse yet, as Antonio's eyes began to glow red with a fire all their own, Digging Owl realized that the man before him was not really a priest after all. Nor was he a man.

"You!" hissed the priest, his voice becoming more animal than human. His eyes glowed brighter as his body began to change, shaking off its disguise.

Digging Owl stepped back in fear. The priest's body shimmered like smoke over a cooking fire. The black robe, no longer a necessary part of the disguise, fell to the floor. What once was a man became something far more terrifying.

A shape-shifter!

Digging Owl watched in horror as fingers lengthened and sprouted claws. Teeth became fangs. The priest's lower jaw cracked and popped, like logs on a fire, his face elongating into that of a wolf. His body hunched, shortened, and grew muscular. Hair sprouted, thick and dark, like grass after a spring rain.

The transformation complete, Digging Owl stood staring at something that could only have sprung from the loins of the evil one. It was this creature, born of darkness, that had stolen the king's soul and possibly the souls of the leaders before him, manipulating the Spanish monarchy to cause the greatest suffering to millions. Worse yet, it was about to add Digging Owl's soul to its collection.

There was no place to run. No time to flee. Though he was still in spirit form, the shape-shifter could easily kill him, for it was a creature of darkness, existing in both the physical and the spiritual worlds. Digging Owl braced himself as the creature lunged for him, but it knocked him over as easily as one bends a blade of grass.

Across the floor they rolled, Digging Owl trying desperately to keep away from the creature's deadly fangs. He grabbed its wrists, but it changed into mist and slipped between his fingers. Once free, the shape-shifter changed back into a beast and resumed the attack.

Claws ripped across Digging Owl's side, sending tiny rivers of fire through him. He screamed in pain.

The shape-shifter slashed at him again, but Digging Owl ducked and threw his shoulder against it, knocking it across the room.

The shape-shifter changed from a wolf to a cat, then to a serpent, and back again to a wolf.

"You cannot kill me, seer," it taunted, "for I am too powerful. The blood of the dark one flows through my veins. I will destroy you as I have destroyed your people."

The shape-shifter made a diving lunge, grabbing Digging Owl's left leg and tripping him. As he fell, Digging Owl brought his right leg up and stomped on the shape-shifter's face, freeing his other leg. Jumping to his feet, he ran for the doorway, but the shape-shifter cut him off.

The only exit blocked, Digging Owl took advantage of being in spirit form and dove headfirst through the floor.

He felt a slight tingling as he passed through stone, falling from the king's bedroom to the throne room. The maneuver must have thrown the shape-shifter off, for Digging Owl made it across the room without the creature coming after him. He was just about to leave through an open doorway when the shape-shifter burst into the room from the other side.

Digging Owl was knocked backward. Powerful hands wrapped around his throat, claws digging into his neck. He lashed out, striking at the shape-shifter's head and chest, trying to break free. His right hand brushed against something smooth. Cold.

The bottle.

An idea sprang into Digging Owl's head. He reached out and grabbed the tiny glass bottle hanging from the shape-shifter's neck. Yanking hard, he broke the gold chain.

Realizing what was happening, the shape-shifter released its hold on Digging Owl's neck and snatched at the bottle. It was the break Digging Owl was hoping for.

Twisting, Digging Owl tore free of the creature's grasp. He did not run to get away this time. He flew.

Tucking the bottle against his chest and sealing it in a protective layer of energy, Digging Owl flew through the doorway as fast as he could. There was a roar of rage from behind him as the shape-shifter gave pursuit.

Through hallways and down stairs, Digging Owl flew. He started to head toward the dungeons, hoping to reenter his body, but then he realized it would be a fatal mistake. If he did regain his body, there would not be time to work any medicine to defend himself. Worse yet, there was only one way in or out of the dungeon. He would be trapped. No, he had another idea.

He turned left at the next passageway he came to. A quick glance behind him showed that he was still being chased. A patch of darkness, deeper than the surrounding shadows, raced along the corridor behind him. In its passing, torches flickered out and flowers wilted. Another turn brought Digging Owl back to the throne room.

Standing in the center of the room, looking wildly about, Digging Owl searched for something he'd seen earlier.

Where is it? It has to be here. This is the right room, isn't it?

Just as he thought he'd chosen the wrong room, he spotted what he was looking for. At the same instant, the shape-shifter burst upon the scene.

As Digging Owl ran across the room, the shadow turned back into a beast again. Reaching the corner of the room, Digging Owl turned around to face it.

"Here," he yelled, holding out the bottle. "Is this what you want? Come and get it."

Howling in rage, the shape-shifter raced toward him. Digging Owl hesitated for a moment, waiting until the creature was upon him, and then threw the bottle at a large mirror on the opposite wall. The creature leaped after it.

The shape-shifter caught the bottle in midair, but could not stop itself from crashing against the mirror—crashing against it and vanishing inside of it.

There was a flash of blue lightning and a clap of thunder loud enough to shake the castle. The mirror exploded outward, its glass shattering into tiny pieces. Its gilded frame rattled and fell to the floor. As it did, a scream of agony—of a soul being shredded—rent the night. It was followed by a silence so complete, so utterly final, that it gave Digging Owl chills.

Digging Owl stared down at the pieces of glass lying on the floor. There were many doorways leading to the world where darkness lived, but only a few leading out. Though he had suspected it might be, Digging Owl had no way of knowing if the mirror was also a doorway. He'd only seen one such looking glass before—a small one, carried by one of the soldiers on the expedition he'd accompanied. Fortunately his suspicions had paid off and the mirror's surface—like the reflection on water—was indeed a portal to the home of the evil one. With any luck, it would be a long time before the shape-shifter found its way back out.

He awakened to the sound of keys jangling in a lock. A few seconds later a bolt was thrown back and his door was opened. Digging Owl sat up and rubbed his eyes, ignoring the pain that racked his body.

Two soldiers entered the room carrying torches. With them was the woman named Tawasa. As before, she carried a small pail of water. But unlike before, she was smiling, as though it was all she could do to contain her happiness.

Crossing the room, she kneeled down before him. Tawasa frowned slightly as she noticed the claw marks on his body. The ones on his legs and neck were already scabbed over, but the ones on his side still bled. Though the shape-shifter had clawed his spirit, the marks had appeared on his flesh.

"They beat you?" she asked.

"It is nothing," Digging Owl said, accepting the water she offered.

As he drank, another guard entered the room carrying a large metal ring upon which hung several keys. Digging Owl raised his eyebrows in curiosity as the guard squatted down and began removing the chains from his legs.

Tawasa could no longer contain her excitement. "Good news. The king has ordered that all the prisoners in the castle are to be freed and sent home."

"Why?" Digging Owl asked.

"I don't know," she shrugged. "It makes no sense. I have never heard of the Spaniards freeing slaves. Maybe the king has had a change of heart. But we should hurry before he can change his mind."

His legs free, the guard removed the chains from Digging Owl's wrists. Grabbing his medicine pouch, he followed Tawasa and the guards out the door and down the corridor. It felt good to walk without chains again, to be free.

As they rounded a corner, Digging Owl hung back until the others were out of sight. Reaching inside his medicine pouch, he removed the tiny blue bottle on the gold chain. Something inside the bottle shimmered and glowed, wanting to return to the body from which it had been stolen.

Digging Owl was surprised the bottle hadn't broken when the shape-shifter crashed against the mirror. He was thankful too. Even though a person had three souls, it was not easy stealing one away from the other two. But once you had possession of one of the souls you held some control over that person.

Of course, that control did have its limitations. There was no way Digging Owl could continue to manipulate Charles after returning to his own land: the distance was just too great. Besides, without all three of his souls, the king would eventually sicken and die, leaving the throne vacant for maybe an even worse monarch. Possession of the soul could also be dangerous if the shape-shifter ever returned to reclaim its stolen property.

Wanting nothing more to do with shape-shifters or kings, Digging Owl decided that, once they were safely on board the ship, he would break the bottle, releasing the soul of Charles. Until then, however, having control over the Spanish monarch was just the thing he needed to unlock the door to freedom. He smiled as he slipped the bottle back into his medicine pouch.

A change of heart? Maybe ... but I don't think so.

Seeds of Death

Larry Segriff

"**Y**es, my lord," she replied, her long red hair streaming out from behind her black leather mask. At his signal she extended her left hand and gripped the worn wooden handle. At the front of the platform, the priest made his gestures and intoned his words, while within her the anticipation built. A nod from the young king, a hush from the crowd, and she pulled the handle. Not hard, not suddenly like she used to do, but slowly, steadily, so that the victim could feel the moment approach.

There, just at the friction point, she paused, so briefly that only she and one other could tell. Smiling slightly, enjoying the moment but all the while wondering if her little ploys would ever work, she pulled the lever hard toward her. Instantly the trapdoor sprang open and, together with a combination gasp and sigh from the assembled crowd, his heavy body fell a foot and a half before snapping to a stop. He had time for two quick kicks and a sort of ungainly dance as his whole body convulsed, and then it was over, his cooling corpse swaying rhythmically at the end of his rope.

The crowd dispersed. The king looked over at her once, his eyes narrowing thoughtfully, but she avoided meeting his gaze. Instead she focused on her latest hopes, watching her most recent chance at fulfilling her dreams as it swung, pendulum-like, ticking off the moments of mortality.

Soon, but never soon enough, her helpers had deposited the body in her workroom and departed. The little outbuilding, claimed by her when she first took over the post of Royal Executioner, had the thin odor of death worked into its woodwork, but she no longer noticed. The privacy it provided was worth a little sacrifice.

Now, to see if she'd been lucky. Loosening the drawstring of the roughspun breeches, she worked her hand inside and felt downward. Almost instantly her fingers encountered that cold, sticky fluid that sent her hopes plummeting.

"Quite a feeling, isn't it?"

"What?" she nearly gasped out her response, startled by the unexpected voice. Spinning her head and unobtrusely removing her hand as she did so, she turned toward the only doorway.

He was old, the lines of his face disappearing beneath his thin white beard. His robe, hanging loosely on a skeletal frame, must have been nearly as old as he. Bare spots showed at the elbows, and the cowl was stained and frayed. His voice, though, was still strong.

"Holding a man's life in your hands, that is," he said, an odd emphasis on the word "life," making her wonder how much he'd seen and how much he'd understood. "It is quite a feeling."

"Yes," she replied simply, unwilling to make a more revealing response.

"You know, it's amazing"—His gray eyes had locked onto her green ones, the power in them boring into her like a knife—"what happens to a man who hangs to death." He glanced briefly at the body beside her and then once around the cold, stark room before returning his gaze to her. "They say," he went on, "that most of the time, a man will have a reaction at the moment of death, an involuntary, instinctive reaching toward life. Do you know what I'm talking about?"

She smiled slightly. "I've heard the stories," she said, still unwilling to commit herself to anything with this strange old man.

"They say," he continued, still holding her gaze, "that there's a rare power in a dead man's seed, a power of life and a power of death."

She felt her eyebrows lower at that, her face closing up in a dangerous expression. He was getting far too close to the truth with his vague little hints. "I've heard the stories," she repeated, adding a question of her own. "Just who are you, anyway?"

He smiled, but his hands dismissed the matter. "No one important, Lady Death. Merely a curious bystander, trying to confirm some old rumors."

She laughed, a harsh sound in that arena of death. "You want proof, old man? Come, see for yourself. Here is a dead man, a man who died only a little while ago by the very method you've mentioned. These are his britches. Why don't you pull them down and find your answers?"

Again he smiled, an amused, possibly insulting, twisting of his thin lips. "No, my lady. I think not. There is a dignity to death that I will not disturb. Far better, I believe, to ask one who knows. Tell me, Lady Death, if you will, have you seen this marvel that we've heard tell of? Can you say whether the stories are true?"

For a long moment she merely looked at him, her own hooded gaze probing at his open one. At last she nodded, saying, "I've seen this reaction, yes. As to the power in a dead man's seed, I do not know. You're talking witchcraft, and we all know that the Church has proscribed any such dealings. Such knowledge carries severe penalties, perhaps even a visit by old Garcia, the head witch-hunter himself."

At that her visitor blinked, straightening as best he could with his ancient bones. "Ah, yes," he murmured. "Well, in that case I'll press you no further. Thank you, my lady, for your time, and a good day to you."

She nodded, turning back to the cooling corpse beside her. She noticed as she did so that she had not yet closed the dead man's eyes, and now they seemed to stare at her accusingly. Chuckling softly, she reached out and pressed them shut before attending to the rest of her duties. All the while, however, as she went through her familiar routine, her thoughts kept returning to that odd little man and his dangerous questions.

He was wrong, of course, at the end. Oh, there was power in a dead man's seed, all right, a very special and very rare power. At the moment of death a man's spirit, as though in violent protest to what was happening, reached instinctively for life. That impulse, that reaching, was what the old man was referring to. The power that lay in that act, however, could only be obtained if the act itself was aborted. If the seed spilled, if the body was allowed to complete the gesture, the power was gone, and all she was left with was the useless remains, as cold and lifeless as the man himself. Why this was so she couldn't say, any more than she knew why this reaction only occurred at hangings and not at any other form of sudden death. She knew, however, what she needed: a way to keep the reaction from occurring.

Crossing over to the door, she pulled it shut again and locked it, just as she normally did when closeted with a corpse. Funny, but she was sure she'd done it this time as well. She shrugged, dismissing it, and went back to the worktable that held the body. Crouching down, she ran her hands over the smooth and solid-seeming wood that made up the base of the table. Pressing in certain spots, sliding in others, she succeeded in opening one of the several secret compartments. Out of this one she took a single black candle, a slender wooden rod, and a tanned leather cap.

Standing, she placed the cap on the corpse's head and arranged his hands around the candle so that he appeared to be holding it on his stomach. Touching the wick with her wand and speaking a word under her breath, she brought a flame into existence and then leaned down and touched the cold lips with her own. She breathed once, exhaling deeply, and whispered a name of power into the empty shell.

The dead man groaned, hands tightening around the candle's shaft as if in agony. Satisfied, she straightened, laid her rod upon those same lips briefly, and abruptly rapped him in the groin.

"Tell me," she ordered, "how I can prevent this."

Again the corpse groaned, a pitiful sound that rolled off her without effect. She rapped a second time. "Tell me."

"Noooo." The voice was faint, coming as it did from a long way off, yet she could hear the determination in it.

She smiled. "Grudolf," she said, her voice caressingly soft, "do you remember confessing to me?" Her tone held an edge, hidden like a dagger in a velvet case. "More importantly, Grudolf, do you remember how I got you to confess?" A third groan, and her smile grew broader. "I can do the same thing to you now, Grudolf, only worse, much worse, and you won't have the surcease of unconsciousness. A soul can't faint, Grudolf, but believe me, it can feel such pain as you've never even imagined." She manipulated her wand, giving him just the tiniest taste of what she meant. His groan this time was more like a shriek. "Tell me," she said, shifting the rod.

He sighed, an eerie sound that, though empty, contained all there was to know of loneliness and despair. "You've brought me back, Galicia, against my will, as you've the power to do, but not even you, Tormentress, can make me tell that which I do not know."

She frowned and wielded her wand again, briefly. "You know something, Grudolf," she said over the sounds of his distress. "I can tell. You never could lie to me."

"All right," he groaned. "It's true that I do not know what you need, but I can guess where you might find it."

He hesitated, defiant, and again she used her rod, tracing lines of agony across his burning soul. At last he spoke, his lifeless lips squeezing out a single word, a name she thought she recognized.

"Of course," she said, her smile growing even wider. "I should have seen that myself. Thank you, Grudolf, and good night. Go now, to the reward you've earned for yourself."

One last cry, louder and more horrified than before as it tapered off into the distance. She nodded, her grin one of complete satisfaction. A noise intruded where no sound should have been, and she spun, startled, toward the door.

Nothing. Imagination, she thought, or merely an echo. Still, for a moment her mind filled with the image of the old man who had interrupted her earlier. On an impulse she went over to the door and checked its locks, but found nothing. They were all in place, all secured, even those that mere mortals couldn't see.

Satisfied, she opened that door herself and summoned her assistants. She was done with Grudolf; it was their turn. Pausing only long enough to remove her mask, something that she was loathe to do, and to don a couple of other items she kept on hand for such times, she headed out to seek a woman.

The hut was actually outside the city, beyond the notice of the regular guards, and it wasn't really a hut. It was a small house, similar to those of other peasants, thatched and whitewashed and well kept. It just seemed as if it should have been a hut.

Similarly, Lady Armagan, the woman who did her business in the little cottage, was neither a lady nor a witch. The one was merely her title and the other her hope. To Galicia, who was both, she was simply amusing. On this day, however, in this instance, she might prove helpful.

"Greetings, madam, and welcome to my shop." As Galicia had hoped, she was apparently unrecognized. She so seldom went anywhere without her mask that few people would know her face. The red hair was more distinctive, but a shawl easily covered that, and a gaily colored cloak hid her black leather formfitting outfit. "Is there something I can help you to find?"

Galicia smiled, nodding. "Indeed, Lady Armagan, I certainly hope so. Tell me," she went on, surprised to find that she was a little uncomfortable with what she had to ask, "do you sell items devoted to, ah, the art of love?"

The shopkeeper, an older woman, thin of frame and tight of face, who nonetheless had the air of one who was no stranger to that art, smiled slightly, as though trying to hide her own amusement. "Yes," she said, her eloquence in her simple gestures rather than her words. "Yes, I carry such devices. What in particular do you wish?"

Again Galicia's own response surprised her, as the beginnings of a blush warmed her fair cheeks. Embarrassed more by her reaction than by the subject, or so she chose to believe, she pressed on, "I need something that will prevent a man's seed from spilling."

Now Lady Armagan did laugh, a brief but bright and tinkling sound. "Someone from the palace, eh?" she asked, her eyes still twinkling merrily. "Most of the men there are renowned for their unseemly haste. Quite a disappointment, I've heard." Galicia's cheeks flamed, but she refused to bow her head or otherwise give in to her discomfort. "Yes, milady," the proprietress went on, "I think that I can help you. Come."

Beckoning to Galicia, she led the way around the counter and into a smaller, softer room. The walls had all been draped in cloths dyed a wide range of gentle colors. Pillows littered the floor, and even the top of the little table where she had some of her wares displayed. Incense wafted lightly on the air, a delicate scent of flowers and herbs.

The Royal Executioner took one look around her and felt her own level of discomfort increase. She was not used to such surroundings. Her own quarters were spartan, by choice, not by necessity, as was her entire life. Most of her thirty-odd years had been devoted to hardness, the strength of steel and the durability of stone. This softness, this decadence, was new to her, and decidedly unwelcome. It did, however, have the effect of stiffening her spine, allowing her to forget the embarrassment of before and concentrate on her own iron will.

"Now, milady," the shopkeeper was saying, "there are several types of devices that can produce the results you desire." Stepping around the table, she reached into some covered boxes beneath it and began pulling out different items. Some she replaced without comment, but most she described for Galicia and then, depending on her customer's response, either handed them to her or placed them on the table.

"This first one is the least expensive: a scroll. You don't actually use it in the act itself—although you could, I suppose, with some possibly interesting results. Rather, it explains several techniques whereby *you*, milady, can help your gentleman remain in control for a longer period of time. There are pictures, as well, showing you where to pinch—"

Galicia cut her off with a quick shake of her head. "No. Inappropriate. Show me more."

Lady Armagan merely smiled and went on to the next item, unruffled by her client's brusqueness. "This one is very popular among the ladies of the court. It's a cream, guaranteed by Doctor M to decrease a man's pleasure for up to ten minutes, thereby improving his performance. It also has a wonderful flavor—"

Again Galicia gave her head a rather imperious toss, hard enough to loosen her shawl slightly.

"Indeed, my lady, most unsuitable for someone of your station, I'm sure. Perhaps this next item . . ." Reaching into another box, this one set slightly apart from the rest, she pulled out a small object that immediately drew Galicia's eyes. A little loop of leather, it seemed very familiar to her. Her hands were reaching for it even as Lady Armagan named it. "This is the Lover's Noose. Slip it over a man at some point prior to inviting him in, tighten it like so, and he is yours to command. Simply make sure when you put it on that this little silver bar here—see how cleverly it's cushioned by this pad?—is positioned properly on the underside of the man. Would you care to try it?"

At that, Galicia looked up sharply, her attention wrenched away from the entrancing device. "What?"

The shopkeeper smiled, but instead of replying she reached once more under the table. Galicia's eyes widened at what she expected to see, but instead Lady Armagan came up with a small silver bell, which she rang softly, twice. Before the echoes had died, a curtain in the far wall parted and a gorgeous young man stepped through, a bored look on his face and a rather large, and quite erect, member in his hand.

Needing no instructions, he came forward and positioned himself in front of Lady Armagan, angling his body slightly so as to provide Galicia with a clear view.

"Now, milady, watch. It goes over like this, quickly and easily. See, here's that small bar I showed you; see where it goes? Here, at the base, underneath. Now, I pull on this strap to tighten it, and all is ready." Her strong, practiced fingers loosened the noose and handed it to Galicia. "Now you try it, my lady."

The executioner hesitated, drawing a coaxing from the proprietress. "Really, milady, it's better to fumble here and now than in the darkness of your chambers."

Smiling at how wrong Lady Armagan's assessment was, Galicia reached out, plucked the loop from her fingers, and in one graceful motion slung it over the young man. The pressure of her fingers brought it into alignment, and a quick tug pulled it snug. For a moment she just looked at it, admiring its beauty, blind to the man who was wearing it. Then, satisfied, she removed it easily, her fingers every bit as strong and knowing as those of her hostess. When it was once more lying loose on the table, she glanced up and found the shopkeeper's eyes upon her.

"Very good, milady. I see you are no stranger to the ways of love."

Galicia merely smiled, content with her secrets. "I'll take it," she said. "How much?"

Lady Armagan named a price and seemed surprised when there was no haggling. Galicia paid her, slipping the noose into her wallet, and left, leaving gold and gossip in her wake.

Coming out of the shop, she nearly bumped into that strange little man again. For a moment only their eyes met, something like humor showing in his. That knowing smile touched his lips, and then he was gone, disappearing up toward town before she could decide how to react.

Damn! That old man was everywhere! Had he recognized her? If so, how much had he read into her actions? Surely he was too new to the city to know this place for what it was; even if he did, he couldn't possibly guess her reasons for shopping there. Could he?

Turning and heading in the same direction, she dismissed him from her thoughts. If only she could get him out of her life as easily.

Her workroom was on the way, so she stopped off there to regain her mask and to divest herself of her concealing garments. Then, appropriately accoutred, she made her way to the castle. Another execution was scheduled for the following morning, which meant she still had a lot of work to do today.

His name was Bok; his crime, treason. He was also something of a problem for Galicia. The king suspected him of being a fairly high-ranked member of a particularly difficult cabal and so, wanting to send a signal of swift and sure justice, had wanted the execution immediately. Unfortunately, he also wanted her to provide him with some very important information without giving her nearly enough time to extract that knowledge.

These and similar thoughts consumed her as, ignoring the honor guard at the entrance, she swept into the castle's anteroom and beyond, taking her normal shortcut to the cells below. Technically, when arriving for duty she was supposed to use the servants' entrance, but she never did. She was not aware of being concerned about her image, but she protected it, even unconsciously, nonetheless.

"Ah, Galicia."

Startled out of her thoughts, she looked up and saw the king himself standing before her. He had a large goblet in one hand and a rather unsteady look to him, a combination which sent shivers of dread through her. Once before, while similarly intoxicated, he had importuned her for service above and beyond the call of her normal duties. She had demurred, and when he would have insisted, used her fledgling powers to make it stick. He had been close enough to unconsciousness that it hadn't been hard, and she had done her best to make him forget the display, but still there were times when she wondered how much he might remember.

Either way, he had never bothered her in that fashion again. Still, when he got drunk, she got nervous.

"Ah, Galicia," he repeated, his reddened eyes catching hers. "On your way to see Bok, are you?" Unsteady, yes, but not yet drunk enough to start slurring his words.

"Yes, my lord," she replied, holding his gaze firmly. "There are some questions that he has not answered. Yet," she added confidently.

The king chuckled. "Ah, Galicia, it is so gratifying to see someone who enjoys her work as much as you."

She could find no answer to that, so she gave none other than a cryptic little smile. "Speaking of work, Your Majesty," she began.

"He hangs tomorrow, doesn't he?"

"Yes, my lord. As you instructed."

"Oh?" The king paused for a long swallow, draining the goblet. He looked around for the wine steward and frowned when he saw no one.

Galicia, too, sent her gaze roving around the small chamber and saw that they were quite alone. What, had the king been waiting there just to accost her? Why else would he be here in this little-used and untenanted room? Again that feeling of dread rose up within her.

"As I instructed?" he went on. "I don't recall that."

Her dread was solidifying into something darker, something that, as yet, she couldn't put a name to. "Why, yes, my lord. You were quite explicit at his sentencing. If you wish, I can find the proclamation you signed ordering his death at sunrise tomorrow."

"Ah, yes," he was nodding, his index finger beating rhythmically against his empty goblet. "His death. I do recall ordering his death. What I'm having trouble with, Galicia, is remembering a single instance where I used the word 'hanging.' "

She gave a confused little toss of her head, unsure what

he was driving at. "Why, I don't believe that you did, Your Highness. I just—"

Again he interrupted her. "Yes? You just what, Galicia?"

"I don't understand, my lord. Is there some problem? Are you dissatisfied with my results?"

His eyes locked once more with hers. "There have been a lot of hangings lately, haven't there?"

She met his gaze. "Yes, Your Majesty, there have been. They're quick; they require very little cleanup; and the people love them."

"Is that all?" He still wouldn't release her gaze.

"Why, my lord," she replied, "what else could there be?" There. Let him accuse her or make him drop it.

For a long moment he didn't respond as he searched for some sign within the windows of her soul. At last he turned away, growling, and called for more wine. She took that as a dismissal and hurried on past, wondering what all that had been about. That uneasy feeling still resting in her soul, she resolved to start using the servants' entrance in the future.

Bok was waiting for her where she'd left him: stretched naked upon the rack. In the short time she had to work with him she knew that the rack couldn't break him. It was just supposed to soften him up, to make him uncomfortable and to get him thinking about what other things she had in store for him.

"Hello, scum." Her usual greeting. He ignored her, which was also normal for this stage of the interrogation. Locking the door behind her before coming up close to him, she paused to examine him with a critical eye. She enjoyed her work, as the king had said, and she took pride in her ability to achieve her goals without making any marks. Even now, she was glad to see, when time was at a premium and she'd had to make some aesthetic sacrifices for the sake of results, even now she could find few blemishes on his heavily muscled frame.

His hair was rather long, its mass of dark curls pulled into a headpiece she'd designed herself. Painful, yes, but again, its main purpose was to serve as a constant reminder of what his future held for him. His eyes were blue, she knew, although she couldn't see them under the blindfold she used as a matter of course. Keeping the victim in the dark, she'd found, and allowing him to know only what she wanted him to know, greatly enhanced the effects of her ministrations.

She worked on him for a while, asking questions she had no interest in. Who he had worked with and what their goals had been were of far less importance to her than the fragile gift he carried between his legs. Oh, he did talk, eventually, and she did listen; after all, it cost her nothing to carry out her duties to the crown as well as to herself.

When he'd told all he knew, or at least all she felt she needed, she gave her creative impulses full rein. Quickly, perhaps too quickly, he retreated into the depths of unconsciousness. Nodding, satisfied with her results, she withdrew her Lover's Noose from her wallet, worked it over him, and cinched it tight. When everything was situated properly she released him from the rack, knowing that even if he awoke, he would be in no condition to put up a struggle. She dressed him, then, in the same prison garb he'd been wearing before she'd had her assistants strip him and place him on the rack. It was the outfit he would wear at his hanging, and it would effectively mask her little device. He might sense it, might feel the pressure where it wrapped around him, but, then again, he might not. She'd certainly left him with enough other distractions to make such a minor irritant seem invisible.

The only problem that she could see was if he had to relieve himself. Granted, she'd allowed him no water during the day, but, just to be sure, she took a moment to bind his hands behind his back. The jailers, she knew, would let him soil himself before they would stir to help him.

When she had done all that she could she left, a nervous anticipation roiling in her gut, to go and give her report to the king. Three new names and the details of an heretofore unsuspected plot should please His Majesty.

The next morning she was on the platform before dawn, feeling the effects of too little sleep. It wasn't that she'd gotten home late, or even gotten to bed much past her normal time; it was that nervousness within her, that excitement, that sense of imminent success after so many failures. Standing there by the lever, her back straight, her hands clasped behind her, she could feel the sweat starting beneath her leather.

Still, it felt good. She'd take the tension of possible victory over the ashes of certain defeat any day.

Already a crowd had gathered, causing her to recall her words to the king. Of course people liked a hanging; it was something the whole family could see. Impalements, drawing and quarterings, and even burnings at the stake— these were not spectacles suitable for children. A hanging, though, that was an event for everyone, whether they were peasants heading out to the fields or whores heading in to sleep.

She snorted then, amused by her own sense of civic duty, and turned her attention to the castle. She could feel the moment approaching, and so she was not at all surprised to see the Death March, that black-clad group of elite guardsmen, come parading out to the street. As always, they were in perfect step, their leathers shining brightly in the new day's sun, the gleam of their silver buckles and clasps tinged with the color of blood. Quite a sight for the assembled crowd, who sent up a roar of greeting and appreciation.

In the midst of the Death March, Bok stood out, his dark, tangled hair and his dirty prison clothing in sharp contrast to his escort. Even from a distance she could see that he was being dragged, lacking either the strength or the will to walk on his own. Good.

In short order the Death March presented their charge and turned him over to her. When this had been accomplished, the king joined them on the platform. The herald read the proclamation, the priest made his pronouncements, and the king nodded. Just that quickly it was over, the memory of the final pull still tingling in her palm. Bok was dead, and the crowd was trickling away.

Out of the corner of her eye, she glanced toward the king, hoping to gauge the expression on his face. He wasn't looking at her, though. Instead, his eyes were turned toward the crowd, his lips set in a thoughtful frown. As she watched, he gave a sudden nod and then turned away.

She slowly sent her eyes across the crowd, half expecting to see a familiar, ancient face among the peasants, but there was no sign of the old man.

Back in her workroom she gestured for her two assistants to lay the body on the table and then to depart. Normally she liked to do all that herself, but Bok was bigger than her usual victims. A lot bigger. Still, she smiled. His size hadn't helped him in the dungeons, and it was of no use to him now either.

Nodding her thanks to her helpers, she ushered them out and sealed the door. This was not the time for interruptions. Quickly, then, her nervousness exploding into full-fledged anxiety, she hurried over to Bok's still form. Loosening the drawstring, she worked his breeches down and felt her heart soar. The Lover's Noose was still firmly in place, and so was his seed.

Hidden beneath her mask, she allowed her face to show her satisfaction. "Well, Bok," she said in a soft, contemplative tone, "what should we do?" Working around the dead and the near dead for as long as she had, she'd fallen into a comfortable routine of talking to herself in their presence. "After all, here I have everything I need, everything I've worked so long for," she reached out and lightly cupped his testicles in her right hand, half imagining that she could feel the power they represented. "On the other hand, I'm not sure that now is the time to pursue this. That old man worries me. There's too much about him that I can't explain, and the timing bothers me. What if he's Garcia himself, or even an official of the Church?

If he walked in that door right now, Bok, I'd be safe; I've done nothing illegal. Assuming, of course, that he didn't find the compartments in the wood beneath you. Should we proceed, however, and should he come in then—well, I guess you'd have some company in whatever corner of Hell you've found for yourself." She let out another soft little sigh. "What should I do, Bok?"

The answer, however, was already in her grasp, and she knew it. She had intentionally put off examining this question until now, knowing that the whole issue would be moot if her Lover's Noose hadn't worked. Now, though, with success just a few minutes away, she knew that she couldn't wait. Once the ritual was complete, she would have the power to deal with a dozen Garcias, or an army of nosy old men.

Humming quietly to herself, she set about her task. Kneeling down, she worked her fingers in the proper fashion and opened one of the drawers in the base of the worktable. From this she removed a small silver bowl and a steel, rune-engraved, straight-bladed dagger. Sealing up this hidden compartment and opening another, non-secret one, she grabbed a couple of cleaning rags, just in case.

Standing, she placed her acquisitions on Bok's stomach and then stepped back to examine him. His hands were still tied beneath him, bowing his middle up and, not incidentally, giving her slightly easier access to his groin area. His ankles were bound also. She had no cause to fear him, dead, but she simply hadn't had any reason to loosen the ropes.

Nodding her satisfaction, she raised his knees and spread his thighs, giving her room to set the silver bowl beneath his scrotum. She fussed with it for a moment until, pleased at last with the placement, she went back to her concealed compartments for several pieces of colored chalk, three black candles, and a small, severely weathered book of spells. Using these, she drew a diagram on the ground, enclosing the worktable at the center of a pentacle, with the candles burning at strategic points around the perimeter. From all she'd learned, this was actually unnecessary. On the other hand, it couldn't hurt.

When all was ready, she stepped out of her own garments, leaving on only her mask, and stood at the corpse's side. She smiled down at him. "Consider yourself lucky, Bok. You're the first man I've been naked with, willingly, in a very long time." Still chuckling, she reached out and picked up the knife. "You know," she added, "it's too bad that you can't feel anything. You'll get no pleasure out of this. On the other hand, you'll feel no pain either. What a shame."

She could feel the leather-wrapped hilt of the dagger pressing into the palm of her right hand as, with her left, she reached out and moved his member, flopping it over to lay flaccidly upon his stomach. As she did so, the Lover's Noose caught her eye and she raised her knife. Above all, she needed to be sure that her device had worked completely. If even a single drop of his living seed had emerged, then all her preparations had been for naught. Half fearfully, half hopefully, the pulse of power still throbbing in her mind's eye, she brought the tip of the steel blade down and sliced through the leather strap.

At that point all Hell broke loose.

As the noose parted, so, too, did the ropes binding his hands and ankles. She barely noticed, however, as, beneath the fingers of her left hand, she felt his manhood stir, swelling and rising like a lance lifting for battle. Instinctively she swiveled her head to look at his face and gasped in shock. His eyes were open, his lips twisted into an horrific grin around his protruding, swollen tongue.

She tried to step back, but his hands shot out and caught her by the wrists, holding her in place. Slowly, his eyes taunting hers, he pulled himself to a sitting position, and then to his feet.

A sound came from behind her, a soft, attention-getting cough, and suddenly a lot of things made sense.

"Garcia," she said, not even trying to turn to face the old man.

"Indeed, Lady Death. My congratulations on figuring that out."

She snorted. "A little late, though, wasn't I?" He didn't bother to respond, so she pressed on. "You're a sorcerer, aren't you? That power I was feeling, the sense of magic that I thought was Bok's seed, that was a spell of yours, wasn't it? Sympathetic magic, tying the Lover's Noose to the ropes that bound him."

"Oh," he replied, "it was more than that. It was also responsible for reanimating the body. Personally, I thought that was a nice touch."

"But why?" she half cried. "Why do you, a magician in your own right, work for the Church to suppress magic?"

He chuckled. "Who better to deal with witches and warlocks than one of their own? Besides," he continued, his voice losing its mirth, "I won't always be working for the Church. There are few powerful sorcerers left in the world. Soon I will be the mightiest mage alive and proclaim myself the king of all the magicians. At that point, the Church and I will go our separate ways. After, that is, I make sure that it lacks the power to hinder me in my new career."

"Clever," she acknowledged, "but risky."

"It's worked so far," he said, to which she could find no reply.

"So," she ventured, "what now? You've got me. I admit it. The question is, what are you going to do with me? I could help you, I think, if you're looking for a partner."

He laughed, cutting her off in mid-appeal. "A partner? Or do you mean a queen?" He laughed again. "I don't think so, though if I was even a hundred years younger I might consider it. No, my dear, I think that I will do nothing with you."

"What do you mean?" she asked, the edges of doubt working into her voice for the first time. She had thought all along that he had something in mind. Now, though, she was beginning to wonder.

"Why, simple, Lady Death. I am simply going to let

you finish what you started. You wanted this man's seed. I think it's only fitting that he give it to you."

A vision of horror slowly filled her mind as Bok, motionless as a statue through this entire exchange, began to move, pressing her down onto the worktable and climbing on top of her. His strength was enormous, and he had the added invulnerability of already being dead. Her struggles didn't even slow him.

Garcia was speaking, but she drowned him out with her cry as Bok entered her. He was cold, so cold, feeling more like clay as he moved within her than like a man.

The old man's final words came to her through her haze of pain. "Seeds of power, my lady. Seeds of death."

As if on cue, Bok climaxed, filling her with the coldness of the grave. Darkness claimed her, releasing her from her ordeal, and from everything else, as the world drained away on the wings of the old man's laughter.

Le Roi S'amuse

Esther M. Friesner

It was spring, but already there were roses at Versailles. "*Pardieu*, sire, it is almost as if Mother Nature seeks to spoil you as much as our own dear *Maman* ever did," remarked King Louis's brother Philippe, le duc d'Orleans. He tossed the dark locks of his curled wig with the practiced coquetry of an aspiring royal mistress and made a great show of sniffing the pale pink blooms.

Louis XIV regarded his brother with the old familiar mixture of condescension and contempt he had felt for him since boyhood. *Monsieur de France!* he thought, in his mind naming the duke's more familiar appellation. *He looks more like mademoiselle.*

Pity never entered into his fraternal sentiments. Not that Louis held himself to be the better of the two merely on the basis of Fate's choice as to their birth order. Oh, no! He knew that by a trick of an ever-tricksy Nature he might just as easily have been born second, or third, or not at all.

But really, in his heart of hearts, he knew that no matter if there had been a hundred other healthy male siblings born ahead of him, he would never in ten thousand years have permitted Maman and the all-powerful Cardinal Mazarin to foist upon him the life they had inflicted on his brother. When Louis was born some fourteen years into the royal marriage of Louis XIII and Anne of Austria (a pretty Spanish broodmare, for all her title), it was greeted as a miracle by the people of France. More miracle than they knew—almost a virgin birth, if truth be told. Anne's royal husband seemed to have no interest in performing his marital and political duties. Rumor had it that he might have been more eager if Anne had been Antoine.

Like sire, like son, Louis thought, watching Monsieur pick his dainty way down the path between the carefully clipped roses. *Oh, Maman, how thoroughly you've done your work on this one!*

It was so: Louis did not know whether to lay the responsibility for his brother's mincing ways at the doorstep of Nature or Nurture. Papa had had such leanings, sure enough, but he cowered quite satisfactorily before the edict of Cardinal Richelieu that, like it or not, there must be an heir begotten for the kingdom's sake. *Papa always obeyed Richelieu,* Louis recalled. *I believe he actually enjoyed being dominated by that man. And so I was born. Poor Maman! It can't have been much fun for her, that enforced begetting. I wonder if she took lovers? She must have. I would be disappointed if she had not. Nay, I should be ashamed of her if she turned out to be as spunkless as Papa. Every marriage needs at least one man in it.*

"Louis! Louis, come here and see what I've found!" Monsieur's musical voice trilled from somewhere down the garden path. The king peered after the sound but could not see his brother. Reluctantly he abandoned his musings and strolled along to see what new marvel-of-the-hour Monsieur had found now.

But memories linger longer than unwelcome guests and are as bad about taking hints that it is past time for them to depart. The king's scarlet-heeled satin shoes crunched a lazy rhythm from the gravel path, his jeweled ivory walking stick setting up a pretty counterpoint, and between the two the melodies of the past played themselves out.

My poor brother. Little more than a child, with his pets and his pretty playmates and all his toys. I suppose I ought to feel sorrier for him, but how can I? He might

*have been other than he is. He could have fought against
Maman and Richelieu and, after Richelieu's death, Mazarin. Well—! Against Maman, at any rate. When Philippe
was born, there was still more rejoicing, although not
quite so long or so loud as that which greeted me. Even
the poorest peasant tries to keep a spare pot in the pantry,
just in case the first should crack. How fervently are you
supposed to celebrate the birth of the spare pot? But once
the cheers had died down—and no doubt Papa had wiped
his regal brow with an air of relief to have done his marital duty and to have his marital duty done with—the Cardinal cast his all-seeing, all-knowing eye over my brother.*

"Louis! Louis, you spiteful thing, come here, I tell
you! I don't know if it will stay. You must come now, at
once, immediately!" A staccato crunching came from
deep within the roses. Monsieur was likely stamping his
foot with impatience.

"Yes, yes, I'm coming," the king murmured. It would
not do for him to shout. That would fetch his suite of
guards and courtiers posthaste. Sometimes it amused the
Sun King to slip away from his attendant swarm of servants and sycophants. Moreover, shouting would shatter
his image, and he was jealous of the bright, perfect shell
of dignity and beauty he had constructed around himself.
"Don't be such an infant, Philippe."

*As if you had any choice, an afterthought chimed in. As
an infant, you were no threat to anyone. Once you were
safely born and seen to be healthy enough to survive,
Maman's pet cardinal Mazarin at once stopped regarding
you as the security of the succession and began to think
of you as a threat to the same. Richelieu, too, had similar
thoughts. The old fox was an excellent example to the
younger, even if both foxes wore the scarlet robe instead
of the russet brush. They knew it was not unheard of for
the younger brother to challenge the elder for his throne,
especially if the younger were of a martial turn of mind
and ambitious. Well, one way out of that problem would
be to train me up to be no easy target for a scheming sibling, too assertive a man to brook such challenges. But*

*that would make me also too strong a king to brook the
Cardinal's . . . friendly guidance.*

He didn't want that either.

*So, my innocent brother! How to keep your good
qualities—the Bourbon succession's assurance, your future worth as a pawn in the marriage market—while elim-
inating the disadvantages you might represent? Solomon
only had to cleave a baby in two to solve his problem.
The Cardinal had subtler ways.*

"*Louis!*" This time Monsieur's voice was most definitely *un*musical. In fact, he sounded a good deal like a
fishwife.

"*Coming!*" His brother's shrilling so grated on the
king's delicate nerves that he forgot himself and hollered
back. Under his breath he grumbled, "You miserable *mi-
gnon.*"

Louis hastened his steps by the merest tick of the
clock. The memories were fading. The vacancy they left
was being gradually filled by the one of Lully's spritely
airs. The king hummed as he strolled along, glancing to
left and right at the hosts of timidly opening roses, the le-
gions of plump, promising, yet-unopened buds. By all
rights his thoughts should have wandered to the sweet ladies of his court—those he had already favored and those
he had yet to honor. There was a small, shy thing in his
wife's suite. He would have to ask her name. But that
thought was blown from his head by a puff of spring air
and in its place a riddle formed:

How can you raise the perfect second-born prince?

*How easy! Any cardinal worth his red hat knows the
answer to that one: By making sure to raise that prince as
a princess.*

As Louis rounded the corner of the rosebushes he gave
the matter one final, decisive thought: *I don't care if it
was none of your fault, Brother. I would never have let
them do that to me!*

"There you are at last, Louis." Monsieur's pretty face
was screwed up into a sour expression. "I am surprised it

hasn't run away in the meantime." He gestured at the roots of one of the rosebushes.

"Or been scared away by all your clamor," the king returned with lazy good humor. "What is it you've found? A bunny rabbit?" Louis tilted his head to see, doing it carefully so as not to disturb the perfect set of his mountainous curls.

"You won't see anything like that." Monsieur was peevish. "You must kneel down." Twin smears on the knees of his hose revealed that the king's brother knew from experience of what he spoke.

"I don't think so," Louis replied, still in that sleepy tone which seemed to imply that here was one not really at home anywhere beyond the bedroom doors. "Apart from Holy Mass, I lack the practice. And I don't think you've found a Sacrament in the bushes."

Monsieur snorted just the way Anne of Austria had when she was out of patience with her royal eaglets. "Suit yourself, then," Philippe snapped. "*Don't* see it." And he dropped to his knees and crawled into the rosebushes with the huffy air of a miffed duchess sailing out of an intolerable social situation.

"Brother, be reasonable," Louis drawled. To no avail. All he got by way of reply was a fine view of Monsieur's royal backside energetically wiggling into the thicket. The king's lip curled with sardonic humor.

If anyone asks about the stains, I shall have them executed, he resolved, half in jest, and, laying aside his walking stick, he followed his brother into Monsieur's mysterious bower.

"Ah, there you are!" Monsieur crouched in a little arbor made by the fragrant blooms and the thorny stems. He grinned at Louis. "Curiosity triumphs even over you, eh?"

"I think it is better for you and for France if I am the only one privy to the fact that you are mad," Louis retorted coldly. "I feared that if I left you to your fool's tricks, you'd remain in your earth until one of the gardeners found you. I should hate to have to banish a decent gardener solely because my brother is a lunatic."

"So good of you, sire, to put the welfare of France first." (Was there a hint of Louis's own bite in his brother's reply? But that would require backbone, and Monsieur seldom had enough of that to do more than stage the occasional tantrum at court.)

"Well, as long as you've dragged me in here, where is this marvel you so ardently desired me to see?"

"Here." Monsieur gestured. It was a bit difficult to follow the motion of his fine white hand in the dappled shadows beneath the roses, but Louis had a good eye. He looked, then peered, then squinted so as to be quite sure that what he was seeing was no trick of the light.

"Bon Dieu," he breathed.

Compressed into a tiny brown shaggy ball, the infant faun moaned in its sleep, cloven hooves running in place over greenswards of dreams.

"This is not—this cannot be real," the Sun King murmured, unable to take his eyes from the small impossibility.

"I see it the same as you, sire," Monsieur reminded him. His voice was steadier, with none of that unpleasant shrilling from before. In the presence of a wonder, Philippe had regained as much self-possession as his majestic brother seemed to have lost. "One of us might doubt the evidence of his eyes, but two—?"

Louis's hand stretched out as of its own free will, the diamond rings glittering. He could see the delicately curving horns, black as ebony; he could even count their bony ridges. The creature was the color of good brown earth all over: skin and ragged, hairy flanks, and the silky curls like a cherub's that covered the horned head. It slept snuggled up on its side, like a grub, legs and arms drawn in tight. The finely modeled knobs of its backbone implored the skeptic to touch, to learn whether they were real. The king was only human. His ringed hand trembled as it reached out toward the dreaming creature, itself a thing of dreams.

Philippe's hand fell heavily on his brother's. "What are you doing?" he hissed.

For an instant, Louis forgot to be insulted at Monsieur's audacity. "I only wanted to know—"

"You'll wake it! Then it will leap up and dash away, and *then* where will we be?"

"We could seize it," Louis suggested. "Take off your coat, Philippe."

"Why?"

"To throw over it. To use as a net."

Monsieur laughed quietly at the idea. The sound of mockery was enough to awaken Louis, if not the faun, to the fact that he had somehow let slip a measure of his control. That would not do.

"If I command you to take off your coat and use it in any way I might direct you, you will do it, Brother," he said in a voice not far removed from a low, rumbling growl.

"But of course." Philippe made a small, fussy motion with his beautiful hands. "How could I have so far forgotten myself? Your pardon, sire."

Louis's thick underlip pouted out. There were times, he reflected, when it was *not* such a good idea to slip away unattended by any save his beloved brother. For one thing, it appeared that his beloved brother had a tendency to drop the mask when there was no audience present to witness his performance as the frivolous but faithful Monsieur.

A disquieting thought touched the king's mind. *How much of Philippe is mask, after all? For the court, for me . . . and for Maman and the Cardinal?*

All this, however, captured no fauns.

Philippe was just squirming out of his jacket when the creature stirred. Fists no bigger than a hen's egg stretched slender arms to their fullest length as the miracle yawned, arched its back, and revealed—a greater miracle. Small, brown, deftly pointed breasts surprised the king, their rosy tips stirring thoughts he would never have dreamed to entertain when confronted with a female who was as much livestock as lady.

Then the creature's eyes lit upon him, and she was on her feet in less time than it takes to blink. She was not even as tall as the rosebushes surrounding her. A warm breeze shook the leaves, painting her limbs with dancing shadows. Her lips parted, showing off small teeth, perfectly formed but yellow as fresh-churned butter. A fearful, shaking sound came faintly from her mouth.

"*Pardieu,*" Monsieur whispered. "She bleats."

"She bleats," Louis agreed. "But she'll bolt in a moment. See if you can't throw that jacket over her before she's away."

"I don't think it will work." Monsieur shook his head sadly. "The bushes will snare it before it can snare her. Besides, we've seen her. How many men can say their eyes have beheld so splendid a sight? A breath of legend stirs our lives; let that be enough. What would you do with her if you caught her, anyhow?"

Louis's jaw clenched. "You question *me*?" Monsieur said nothing, but the king caught the merest twinkle of a sardonic smile playing over his brother's girlish lips. "Give me that, if you're incompetent to the task." He grabbed Monsieur's jacket from him and knelt, every muscle tensed, eyes never leaving the shuddering faun.

It was a moment that held its breath so long, an artist might have captured it in the ivory curves of a cameo. But in truth, time did not suspend itself forever. The faun's tail twitched and the next instant it sprang away.

Louis was ready. He threw Monsieur's jacket and himself after it. True to his brother's words of caution, the garment did snag itself on an outstretched thorny branch. Indeed, Louis himself felt the claws of the roses as he sailed through the undergrowth. But the escapade that dared to shed the priceless royal blood had its reward: he caught her. His hands closed over the hard swellings of her breasts as his weight carried the two of them to the ground.

She fought him like a beast, hooves lashing out, the

sharp nails of her small brown hands adding their own scarlet tracks down his cheeks beside the marks of the thorns. He laughed without fully knowing why the urge rose in him so strongly. More than the compulsion to laughter rose as well. The heat of lust kindled a sweet, liquid fire that flooded every fiber of him, body and mind, washing away all the perfect shell of Louis the king, leaving only Louis the man.

"Louis!" If not for Monsieur's shrill cry, who could say where it might have gone. Philippe forced a way through the brambles and helped his brother immobilize the thrashing faun. The creature's huge, dark eyes rolled wildly in her head, showing a fear-thread of white. "All right, you have her." Monsieur looked as ready to bolt as his royal brother's prey. "Now have your look, let her go, and let's be gone ourselves."

"Why—why the haste, Brother?" Louis panted, still struggling to maintain his grip on those lithe brown limbs. The touch of her skin was silky, almost as if the hair, which had the appearance of a goat's rough coat, was in truth no more substantial than down or spiderweb.

This is either a lie or a dream, the king thought. *Or else I have blundered into a miracle.* Lie, dream, or miracle, he was not the sort to let such things escape him easily. "What are you?" he whispered in the faun's enticingly pointed ear. "What more are you than mine?"

The dappled sunlight vanished. A cool, unhallowed darkness fell over the brothers and their captive. It was not the sort of midday shadow cast by an errant cloud traversing the face of the sun. This was a removal of the light at once sudden, complete, and without hope of return. And yet the darkness was not the impenetrable black of night. Louis could see Philippe's face clearly enough in the dim shelter of the rosebushes for him to wonder whether his own face too reflected such a shameful expression of icy terror.

Louis's lips parted to speak, to ask Philippe if he had any notion what had befallen the world, the heavens, his own august self. Then he heard voices, many voices approaching. They were raised high and insistent—voices that, calling, sought another voice to answer them.

The servants, Louis thought. *Merciful God be praised, they've found us. Now we're safe.*

He pictured how his faithful retainers would react when he raised his voice to let them know, "Here I am!" They would crawl in among the tangled thorns eagerly, readily, like good hunting hounds flinging themselves on a badger's earth at a word from the Master of the Hunt. They would assist him out of this thicket—him first, then Philippe—all the time taking good care not to let the king's precious quarry escape their keeping, constantly murmuring reassurances in the royal ear that the darkness all around was nothing unnatural, that there was a reason for it, and that it would soon pass.

He cleared his throat and in a loud voice that never deliberately stooped to the vulgarity of a shout let them know where they might find him.

Coarse brown hands plunged through the rose leaves, seizing the king as if he were a street urchin caught filching from a fishmonger's stall. Voices chattered, their tone rude and jeering, their words unknown, unrecognizable, as they dragged His Majesty backward through the prickers, indifferent to how the barbs caught and cut the regal flesh.

"Let me go! Let me go! By the Mass, I'll have you whipped for this!" Louis bawled, his limbs flailing. He had lost hold of the little faun long since. His ringed hands clasped at nothing and closed on more thorns. He fumed and demanded and finally ended by simply screaming in pain like a girl.

At last they had him pulled clear of the roses. He looked down and saw the ruin of his fine clothes, looked to the side and saw his brother in similar pathetic case. The pair of them stood in the midst of a leering mob of brown-skinned beast-men as hideous as the she-faun had been delicately sweet to see. Noses broad as saucers flared cavernous nostrils, snuffling up the king's scent. Grins wide enough to split a human face showed yellow teeth that did not look as if they were strangers to meat, of whatever kind might present itself. Goat feet danced and fidgeted all around the king, cloven hooves treading heavily on his toes. Horses' tails swished away the flies. The stink of the farm was everywhere.

And then the king looked up.

Philippe's gasp was no more than the breath of a butterfly. Louis was no longer capable of uttering even that much sound. Wonderstruck, he felt his heart withering in shame within his bosom. All the courtiers' toadying flattery, the fawnings of ten times a dozen lovely women, the paintings and the carvings and the ballets he had himself commissioned to equate himself with a title he had once been fool enough to dream he deserved—the Sun King!— all fell to the ground before him, burnt to ash.

The true Sun King sat enthroned upon the verge of a golden fountain, nymphs and satyrs at his feet, and regarded Louis with an illusion-searing eye.

Louis fell to his knees, despite the efforts of his jailers to keep him standing. They could not support so large a man when he was weighed down with so tremendous a burden of awe. "Ma—majesty," he stammered.

The god gestured with a rod of gold twined thickly with the sacred myrtle. Laurel leaves crowned his radiant brow, and glittering sandals kissed his feet. Apart from these few ornaments, he was naked. He spoke, and Louis knew the anger of a god, even if he could not tell one word of the divinity's speech from another.

"He says we have offended him by laying hands on one of his followers," Monsieur whispered in his brother's ear. Louis jerked his head, startled to find Philippe at his elbow, kneeling beside him.

"How—how do you know this?"

Monsieur shrugged. "It seems I had fewer affairs of importance than you to distract me from the study of Classical Greek."

"Can you speak to him?"

"I can try."

"Then do so!" The command was quickly softened. "I

implore you, do so. Tell him we did not know. Tell him
we are deeply sorry. Tell him that the hospitality of
Versailles—of the kingdom!—is his."

Philippe spoke according to Louis's wishes, then listened gravely to the god's reply. "He says he doesn't give
a mouse turd for your Versailles or your kingdom."

Louis sensed his face reddening with rage. "Then why
did he and his ragtag suite come here?" he gritted.

Monsieur spread his hands. "*Sol lucet omnibus,* sire.
One resting place is as good as another to the rout of the
sun. It was a divine whim that brought them here, perhaps. Who knows? That's immaterial. All that need concern us now is the fact that a god has been offended." His
eyes added, *By you.*

Louis knew too much of the unpleasant turns that royal
displeasure could take to trifle with that. "In that case, tell
him that if there is some sign of our sincere repentance
that he requires, it shall be his without question."

Philippe cocked his head to one side. "Are you certain
of that, sire? Those are the words you'd choose?"

Louis frowned with all the old arrogance. "You question me? Tell him!"

"Very well. But I am trying to recall whether you were
also elsewhere when our tutors taught us not just the language but the ways of these old deities." He made a
pretty moue and set to the task of translating.

The sun god heard, and his expression lost a measure
of doom. He spoke to Philippe almost courteously, leaving Louis in a perplexing state of ill-suppressed envy. To
think that frothy, fussy Monsieur should have conversation with a god while he, the king, was left waiting at the
door like a beggar!

Therefore, when Philippe informed Louis that Apollo
did indeed have some small service in mind as an apt
penitence, Louis snapped, "Very well, then! Let him but
name it! I will do as he asks myself, freely, gladly, so
long as it be a task worthy of a king!"

"He has already named it," said Monsieur. "It is, indeed, a kingly task, and one that in the past was given to

none other than a famous ruler. If I have not yet told you
what it is, it is because I seek to give you time to find
some astute way of avoiding the god's assignment."

"What! Avoid it? Am then I a coward in your eyes?"

"No, but—"

"Tell him I'll do it."

"My dear Louis—"

"*Tell* him, I say!"

"Sire, only hearken—"

Louis gave a snort of disgust and pushed Philippe
away. Monsieur landed on his rump in the dirt while
Louis rose to his feet and sailed toward the sun god,
doing everything in his power to convey by signs and
smiles and signals that he was Apollo's man in this and
all things.

Apparently it worked, for the sun god extended his
myrtle-draped wand and graciously permitted Louis to
touch its tip.

At the touch of the wand, Louis's world blossomed into
light. The unholy dark fled, pursued by the hounds of the
sun's own splendor. Louis cast an arm across his eyes,
dazzled to the point where an icy voice within him dared
to suggest that he had made a grave mistake and that
Apollo's price of peace was Louis's sight.

But the dazzlement passed. The king blinked away the
last few drifting whorls of shadow. He saw now that the
gardens of Versailles had melted in the face of Apollo's
majesty. He and Philippe stood in the midst of a fair
meadow, starred with tiny wildflowers fairer than any
strictly brought-up rose of France. These blooms knew no
etiquette, nor where a decent flower should keep place.
They danced and rioted over gently rolling hills and
dreaming valleys as far as the royal eye could see. Here
and there they raced their tendrils up the gaily painted pillars of a local shrine or were laid in rustic baskets at the
feet of small statues of the sun god within.

One such shrine was before the king and his brother.
Apollo and his suite had disposed themselves comfortably
in the portico, beneath a frieze depicting the many ven-

geances the true Sun King had taken on his foes. Here the Python lay dead and there Niobe wept over her murdered children—their deaths the price of their mother's unwise words of pride in the teeth of Apollo's mother. Louis might not have understood his tutors' efforts to instruct him in Attic Greek, but his eyes now tutored him most effectively in the grisly fate that might be his at the god's hand. He shuddered.

The god was speaking. Monsieur stepped forward, cupping his ear beneath the elaborate court wig, the better to hear the divine decree. "Oh, dear," he said, shaking his head, when Apollo fell silent.

"What? What?" Louis seized his brother by the jacket and pulled him close, desperate for something safe to which he might cling.

"He says the contest will begin at once."

"What contest? Philippe, I never agreed to set myself against a go—" He stopped himself. Visions of Hell licked his inner eye with flame reserved for those who name gods other than the Holy Trinity. "—against Apollo," he finished.

"No, of course not!" Monsieur said. For those simple words of reassurance, Louis felt a surge of love he never before had thought to feel directed at his too feminine brother. "The gods hate all mortals fool enough to imagine themselves their peers." The quondam Sun King's heart dropped in his chest. "Not that they care what a man *calls* himself, you understand," Philippe went on, not knowing how badly he was pulling his brother's spirits hither and thither, from joy to despair and back again. "Rash words may be forgiven. It's when a mortal is bold enough to face a divinity and offer to *prove* himself slyer than Hermes or fleeter than Artemis or more belligerent than Ares that there's ado. Arachne came out of her weaving contest with Athena as a spider."

"I—I would never hold myself Apollo's equal," said the king, who had secretly and often fancied himself Apollo's better.

"Your wisdom commends you, sire. No, no fear of that.

Apollo merely wants you to stand and judge a contest for him. That is all." Philippe's words should have let Louis breathe easy at last, but there was something in his tone that left the king prey to a peculiar feeling that Monsieur had said something more, for a man with wit to hear it.

Louis did not have overmuch time to puzzle it out. He was seized by his still-bleeding hands and dragged forward by a pair of rough satyrs. They flung him down at Apollo's feet in the general area of fragrant cushions set out for his use. The king settled himself more comfortably than his escorts had done and gazed up at Apollo with a look of inquiry on his face.

The god rose, magnificent (as he could not help but be). He passed his golden rod to a staid old faun's keeping and held out his hands to the air. At once a nymph appeared, bearing a lyre, the mother and model of all sweet stringed instruments on Earth (for the gods of Greece, being gods, had their little tiffs and foibles long before there were Greeks to worship them, or Sumerians to string their own harps, or Pharoah's dancing girls to tune the seven strings of the bazinga. It was made by Hermes himself, while still an infant, and given to his elder brother Apollo to buy peace after that tricksy babe stole the cattle of the sun.

Apollo stepped from the portico of his shrine into his own full sunlight. The flowers, feeling his radiant presence, wreathed themselves around his ankles as he took a seat upon a jut of stone that had miraculously sprouted from an otherwise smooth greensward. And then he waited.

The waiting of a god is never a time of ease for lesser beings. Louis felt the nymphs and satyrs all around him twitch and fidget. He wanted to turn his head and see where Philippe had got to—his brother had unaccountably vanished—but he knew how angry he himself got when an idle-minded courtier found something else more fascinating to gaze at in a room blessed by the king's own presence. Louis also knew how he punished such inattention, and he was only mortal. He did not wish to know how Apollo might reward the same slight.

And then he saw Philippe again. His brother came into view led by a pair of young fauns who whispered and tittered and leered as they came. A second stone erupted from the ground to offer Monsieur rest. He took it with as gallant a grace as if he were sitting down to the card table, then held out his hands in almost the same manner as Apollo. The same nymph scampered up and gave him a lyre wrought not of tortoiseshell and cow's horn, but of silver and pearl and gold.

A half-smile curved Philippe's mouth as he spoke to Apollo. He turned to Louis then and said, "I've told him that he is too generous with me."

"What is the meaning of all this?" Louis demanded.

"It is the contest of which I told you, sire. The one which you have consented to judge."

"But—but that cannot be! You've never held yourself to be the equal of Apollo in anything!" *Or of me,* he thought. And then: *Have you?*

"It would have been as much as my head was worth if I had been so great a fool," Monsieur replied placidly. "However, you cannot have a judge prove himself worthy of his hire if there is no contest to measure his perspicacity; and you cannot have a contest if there is only one competitor."

"What manner of contest is this?"

Monsieur held up the glittering lyre and gave his royal sibling an ironic smile. "I'd hazard it had something to do with song."

"A music contest! Is this a fit employment for kings?"

"It has been so before. King Midas of Phrygia himself once sat in judgment over Apollo and the satyr Marsyas, whose instrument of choice was the pipes. The nine Muses too shared the decision of the contest, which may have been to Midas' ultimate advantage, even though he did not think so at the time. For you see, Midas gave the palm to Marsyas, while the Nine—quite rightly— overruled him and named Apollo victor. For his poor judgment, Apollo afflicted the king with a pair of ass's ears. This accounted for a whole new style of courtly headgear in Phrygia, but if Midas's ruling had been unopposed, he might have expected worse. You see, the gods are notoriously poor losers. Come to that, they're not such gracious winners either. After Marsyas lost, Apollo had him flayed alive."

Louis picked himself up from among the cushions, strolled casually up to Philippe and murmured for his brother's ears alone, "This contest . . . has only one judge?"

Monsieur's glance swept the verdant scene. "So it appears."

"Myself?"

Monsieur shrugged.

"And you are the god's competition?"

Another shrug. All this was obvious.

"My brother, what's to become of you when I name Apollo the victor?"

"*When?* Not *if?*" Monsieur's eyes twinkled with jocund malice. "So, you have turned astrologer. You can foretell the contest's end even before it has properly begun. Marvelous!"

Louis snorted. "Don't be a fool, Philippe! How can Apollo not be the victor? He is the god of music and song, while you—"

"While I am a worthless second son of France with an embarrassing addiction to the Italian vice; is this not so?" Monsieur chuckled as the king felt himself overcome by furious blushes. "Yet Apollo was also god of music and song when Midas named Marsyas the better. Your prediction may yet come a cropper, sire. Might it be that the deity will lay a spell of truth upon the judge's royal tongue? Can you say truly if the music of a god is not too exquisite for the ears of a mere mortal—albeit one of royal blood—to appreciate? (The Muses were themselves divinities, recall!) Could it not then transpire that you will give the verdict of your heart and not of your self-interest?" Monsieur's smile was painful to behold. "My skin or your ears: Which shall be the sacrifice today? Never mind, Majesty; you can always set the styles at court to hide a multitude of sins ... or just a pair of long ones."

Louis would have spoken, but he found himself dragged back to his old place by the attendant fauns and satyrs. A hush fell over the meadow and the shrine. Apollo rested his lyre on one knee, touched the cords, and lifted his voice in song.

Louis closed his eyes as if in ecstasy. He was in practice, having had the occasional mistress who fancied herself adept at the keyboard and gifted in song. Usually she was too good to be comical and too bad to be borne, but even a king knows the right amount of flattery must be paid to the ladies if they are to be amenable afterward.

To an ear pampered by the refined harmonies of Lully and Couperin, this Attic caterwauling was enough to bring down the walls of distant Troy all over again. And the king had no idea of what the god now sang. The words were foreign as the melody. It irritated Louis to be in the dark. For all he knew, the god was mocking him in song. The derisive expressions on the satyrs' nut-brown faces led him to that conclusion. He had half a mind to hand the palm to Philippe even now, without benefit of a hearing.

Then a fly buzzed near the king's head and he lifted a hand to brush it away. He touched his ear.

Heee-hanh, the fly seemed to whisper.

When the god was done, Louis's applause was as deafening as only one pair of hands could make it. He had no idea of how fatuous he must have looked until he heard his brother's knowing snicker, and subsided. Apollo received the tribute impassively, his face a golden mask. For a moment, Louis feared he'd erred.

"Calmly, sire," said Philippe. "Just because the god does not acknowledge your applause does not mean you have sinned against Holy Mother Etiquette. You of all people!"

"I warn you, Philippe, I'm in no mood for your childish taunts. Once you sing, I must judge, and then—" A chill compounded of dread shook him.

"For once, Louis dear, I could not care less about jumping windward of your sacred *moods*. And a fig as well for your opinions. You've always scorned me for what I am—as if my whole life were bounded by what I accomplish in my bed! I hear you, you and the rest who call me less than a man. Who is the true man? You, with your tally of ladies? Is that the measure? I have only slept with my wife—*and* begotten children of her, for what that's worth. Yet to your eyes, I am nothing manly. And being less than a man, you assume I must naturally be somewhat a coward, too."

"Philippe, I never said—"

Monsieur held up one hand. "Very well. Here's your opportunity to teach me how a real man—a brave man, a warrior with or without a war—conducts himself. Your words can save my skin—my life—or your ears. Show me how brave you truly are."

Against his will, the king felt his hands stealing back to caress the royal ears. The high-crowned wig he wore concealed them, but it would never suffice to hide a jackass's hairy appurtenances. "My—my dearest Philippe," he stammered. "We are, after all, in the presence of a god. Who can say whether he will let me speak my mind? Indeed, who can say whether his powers won't force me to make any choice but the just one? After all, Apollo, king of music, lord of song—"

"Tell me: Did you really enjoy his song so much?"

"What do you think?" Louis hedged.

"I think—" Monsieur rose. "I think I had better get used to going about in a *much* cooler condition."

And before the king's astounded eyes, Monsieur le duc d'Orleans stripped himself down past the smallclothes all the way to the naked skin.

"Better," he said, took up the lyre, and played.

Louis listened to his brother's playing, amazed. Philippe had never touched a lyre in his life—of that Louis was certain—but he had toyed with other stringed instruments and been dutifully praised for his prowess by his *mignons* and those courtiers who sought to reach the king's favor by currying that of his younger brother. Of course one expected such lackeys to lie, but this—!

This is impossible! thought Louis. *They told the truth, a curse on all undependable flatterers! He's good. My brother is good at this. Better than Apollo, at any rate. Ten thousand demons, now what shall I do?*

Monsieur's melodious playing was next joined by a well-established tenor voice. Louis cocked his head, but to his chagrin noted that Monsieur had chosen to sing in a tongue other than French. It was, judging by the sound and accents, the very strain of Greek which the sun god himself favored.

How can he expect me to choose him as the victor if I can't even understand a word he's singing? Louis thought grimly. Or not so grimly. A door was opening for him, a means of escape, an excuse. Who could blame him if he named Apollo the victor when Monsieur bypassed the chance to gain the lone judge's good will by singing in French? Whatever the duke's fate after the contest's verdict was pronounced, Louis might wash his hands of it. The king sat back on his cushions and tried not to smile.

Monsieur, on the other hand, did not limit himself to sitting. He stood, the lyre resting easily in the crook of his arm, and accompanied music and song with dance. The satyrs stared, the fauns gaped. What manner of dance was this to partner what manner of song? For Monsieur now minced and pranced and wiggled his nakedness most indecently. Louis felt his own mouth falling open like a country bumpkin's at first sight of Paris.

What in the name of Our Savior does he think he's doing?

Whatever else Monsieur's unspoken thoughts encompassed, he was doing *something*. As he sang on in his clear, piercing tenor, the sun god himself seemed to transform from an icon of implacable majesty to a softer being—April's sun, not the merciless blaze of August. His burnished limbs relaxed, his whole expression melted

into a wistful smile. Monsieur sang on, and Apollo took
up his own lyre to join him in yearning duet.

At last Philippe laid a hand across the thrumming
strings and silenced them. He smiled, but not at his
brother. The sun god returned that smile with all the
warmth of which he was capable—which was, undoubt-
edly, quite a bit. Apollo stood and came forward, letting
his lyre fall into the dewy grass, extending his hand to
Philippe. A flare of purest light struck Louis blind just as
he beheld the sun god pass his arm around the waist of
Monsieur le duc d'Orleans and lay his golden head down
on Philippe's shoulder with a sigh.

Stunned senseless by the assault of light, Louis plunged
into darkness. He awoke with the smell of rich earth in
his nostrils, formless blobs of green and blue and orange
swimming before his eyes. He blinked these away and
was looking up into the sky, partly obscured by a spray of
roses.

"Are you all right, sire?" Monsieur leaned over into
Louis's view. He was once more fully clothed.

"Where—?" the king began.

"No fear; we're back at Versailles. You, to be accurate,
are flat on your back beside the roses. *Are* you all right?
Would you like me to summon the servants?"

"Not—not yet." Louis took hold of Monsieur's arm
and pulled himself to sit. "What happened?" he demanded, not letting go his hold. "In the name of God,
what did you do?"

"Are you certain you'd like to know that?" Monsieur
asked archly, then laughed. "I have your meaning; I'll
tell. I knew that so long as there was a contest, there
would have to be a winner and a loser. I did not fancy being the loser—I am deucedly attached to my skin,
voyons—but I did not think you'd like what might befall
if you denied Apollo his own laurels. It's been some centuries since Midas made his mistake. Apollo has had time
to think of worse things to inflict on mortals than ass's
ears. No, my brother; the only way we both could escape

that contest whole was if there might be no contest at all. And so I simply refused to compete."

"But you—you sang. I heard you!"

"And did you know the words?" Monsieur was still pleased to play the coquette.

"You know I didn't," Louis growled.

"It was an original composition ... almost. The air, I confess, was Lully's, but the words were mine. I sang about what a lovely day it was and what a bunch of fools we were, gathered together solemn as a row of constipated owls on a branch simply because someone had laid hands on a *female*. And what was a female to the ancient Greeks? The only truly effective way of making more males. What a waste of time! I then sang of the gods' own sport when more worthy companions than mere females showed themselves willing: Zeus and Ganymede, Heracles and Hylas, Apollo and his own dear, lost Hyakinthos—!" Monsieur closed his eyes in blissful reverie.

"And then—?" the king prompted.

Monsieur opened his eyes. "And then I showed myself worthy and willing, that's all. There was no contest and here we are, little the worse for wear."

Louis looked down and saw that his clothing was restored, the scrapes and scratches of the rosebush thorns vanished. He touched his ears charily and found them still the same: human. *None* the worse for wear, he'd say.

He clasped his brother's hands. "Philippe, I owe you much. Above all, I owe you my apologies for every sneer I may have tossed your way simply because you are—" He searched for the least offensive way to say it and discovered, to his shame, that there was none.

"Never mind, Louis," said Monsieur, helping the king to his feet and brushing the dirt from his clothes.

Louis laid his hands on Monsieur's shoulders. "You are as brave and genuine a man as any I know," he said.

Monsieur smiled. "*L'amour, c'est moi.* Now let's go in."

The Tale of Lady Ashburn

John Gregory Betancourt

Based on a story by Lafcadio Hearn

When ye make to resound the stone melodious,
When ye touch the lyre or the guitar,
    Accompanying their sound with song,—
Then do the grandfather and the father return;
Then do the ghosts of the ancestors come to hear.

Do you ask me who she was—the beautiful Lady Ashburn? For a thousand years and more the trees have been whispering above her bed of stone. The syllables of her name come to the listener with the lisping of the leaves; with the quivering of many-fingered boughs; with the fluttering of lights and shadows; with the breath, sweet as a woman's presence, of numberless savage flowers—"Lady Ashburn, Lady Ashburn, Lady Ashburn." But, save the whispering of her name, what the trees say cannot be understood, and they alone remember the years of Lady Catherine Ashburn.

Five hundred years ago, in the chaos following the death of Uthor Pendragon, there lived a knight celebrated for his learning and for his piety, named Sir Pelloux. This Sir Pelloux had several sons, among them a handsome boy who for scholarship and for bodily grace and for athletic accomplishments had no superior among the youths of his age. And his name was Arthur.

Now when the lad was in his sixteenth summer, it came to pass that Sir Pelloux was given the title to the lands north of the Thames, and Arthur accompanied his family thither. Nearby lived a knight of high rank whose name was Sir Garvain, and who wanted to find a worthy squire. On hearing of the arrival of the new Sir Pelloux the noble Sir Garvain visited him to obtain advice in this matter and, happening to meet and converse with Sir Pelloux's accomplished son, immediately arranged for Arthur to serve as his squire.

Accordingly the youth made ready all things necessary for his new sojourn; and his mother, bidding him farewell, counseled him wisely, and cited to him these words: "By a beautiful face the world is filled with love; but Heaven may never be deceived thereby. Shouldst thou behold a woman coming from the East, look thou to the West; shouldst thou perceive a maiden approaching from the West, turn thine eyes to the East."

If Arthur did not heed this counsel in after days, it was only because of his youth and the thoughtlessness of a naturally joyous heart.

And he departed to abide in the keep of Sir Garvain, while the autumn passed, and the winter also.

When the time of the second moon of spring was drawing near, a longing came upon Arthur to see his parents, and he opened his heart to the good Sir Garvain, who not only gave him the permission he desired but also pressed into his hand a silver gift of two ounces, thinking that the lad might wish to bring some little memento to his father and mother, for it was the custom to make presents to friends and relations.

That day all the air was drowsy with blossom perfume, and vibrant with the droning of bees. It seemed to Arthur that the path he followed had not been trodden by any other for many long years; the grass was tall upon it; vast trees on either side interlocked their mighty and moss-grown arms above him, beshadowing the way. But the leafy obscurities quivered with bird song, and the deep vistas of the wood were glorified by vapors of gold and as odorous with flower-breathings as any wedding chapel.

The dreamy joy of the day entered into the heart of Arthur, and he sat himself down among the young blossoms, under the branches swaying against the violet sky, to drink in the perfume and the light and to enjoy the great, sweet silence. Even while thus reposing, a sound caused him to turn his eyes toward a shady place where wild apple trees were in bloom, and he beheld a young woman, beautiful as the pinkening blossoms themselves, trying to hide among them. Though he looked for a moment only, Arthur could not avoid discerning the loveliness of her face, the golden purity of her complexion, and the brightness of her long eyes, which sparkled under a pair of brows as daintily curved as the wings of a butterfly outspread. Arthur at once turned his gaze away and, rising quickly, proceeded on his journey. But so much embarrassed did he feel at the idea of those charming eyes peering at him through the leaves that he suffered the purse of money he had been carrying to fall without being aware of it. A few moments later he heard the patter of light feet running behind him, and a woman's voice calling him by name.

Turning in great surprise, he saw a comely serving girl, who said to him, "Sir, my mistress bade me pick up and return to you this silver which you dropped upon the road." Arthur thanked the girl gracefully, and requested her to convey his compliments to her mistress. Then he proceeded on his way through the perfumed silence, athwart the shadows that dreamed along the forgotten path, dreaming himself also, and feeling his heart beating with strange quickness at the thought of the beautiful being that he had seen.

It was just such another day when Arthur, returning by the same path, paused once more at the spot where the gracious figure had momentarily appeared before him.

But this time he was surprised to perceive, through a long vista of immense trees, a dwelling that had previously escaped his notice—a country residence, not large, yet elegant to an unusual degree. The bright thatch of its roof, rising above the foliage, seemed to blend into the luminous azure of the day; the deep, carved designs of its porticos were exquisite artistic mockeries of leaves and flowers bathed in sunshine. And at the summit of terrace steps before it, flanked by great stone lions, Arthur saw standing the mistress of the mansion—the idol of his passionate fancy—accompanied by the same serving girl who had borne to her his message of gratitude.

While Arthur looked, he perceived that their eyes were upon him; they smiled and conversed together as if speaking about him; and, shy though he was, the youth found courage to salute the fair one from a distance. To his astonishment, the young serving girl beckoned him to approach. Opening a rustic gate half veiled by trailing plants bearing crimson flowers, Arthur advanced along the verdant alley leading to the terrace, with mingled feelings of surprise and timid joy.

As he drew near, the beautiful lady withdrew from sight, but the serving girl waited at the broad steps to receive him, and said as he ascended, "Sir, my mistress understands you wish to thank her for the trifling service she recently bade me do you, and requests that you will enter the house, as she knows you already by repute and desires to have the pleasure of bidding you good day."

Arthur entered bashfully, his feet making no sound upon a carpet as soft as forest moss, and found himself in a reception chamber vast, cool, and fragrant with scent of blossoms freshly gathered. A delicious quiet pervaded the mansion; shadows of flying birds passed over the bands of light that fell through the curtains; great butterflies, with pinions of fiery color, found their way in, to hover a moment about the ceiling then pass out again into the mysterious woods. And as noiselessly as they, the young mistress of the mansion entered by anther door and kindly greeted the boy, who bowed low in salutation.

She was taller than he had deemed her and as supplely slender as a beauteous lily; her black hair was interwoven with creamy blossoms; her gown of pale silk took shifting tints when she moved, as vapors change hue with the changing of the light.

"If I be not mistaken," she said, when both had seated themselves after having exchanged the customary formalities of politeness, "my visitor is none other than young Arthur, newly made squire to my respected relative, Sir Garvain. As the family of Sir Garvain is my family also, I cannot but consider his squire as one of my own kin."

"Lady," replied Arthur, not a little astonished, "may I dare to inquire the name of your family and to ask the relation which you hold to my lord?"

"The name of my poor family," responded the comely lady, "is Ashburn—an ancient family in this part of Britain. I am the daughter of Lady Catherine Emarques—Catherine is my name, likewise—and I was married to Sir John Ashburn. By this marriage I became related to your knight and master, but my husband died soon after our wedding and I have chosen this solitary place to reside during the period of my widowhood."

There was a drowsy music in her voice, as of the melody of brooks, the murmurings of spring, and such a strange grace in the manner of her speech as Arthur had never heard before. Yet, on learning that she was a widow, the youth would not have presumed to remain long in her presence without a formal invitation. After having sipped the cup of rich wine presented to him, he arose to depart.

Catherine would not suffer him to go so quickly.

"Nay, friend," she said, "stay yet a little while in my house, I pray you; for, should my cousin ever learn that you had been here and that I had not treated you as a respected guest, and regaled you even as I would him, I know that he would be greatly offended. Remain at least to supper."

So Arthur remained, rejoicing secretly in his heart, for Catherine seemed to him the fairest and sweetest being he had ever known, and he felt that he loved her even more than his father and his mother. And while they talked the long shadows of the evening slowly blended into one violet darkness; the great citron light of the sunset faded out, and the moon opened its cold, bright eye in the northern sky.

Within the mansion, oil lanterns were lighted. The table was laid for the evening repast, and Arthur took his place at it, feeling little inclination to eat, thinking only of the charming face before him.

Observing that he had scarcely tasted the dainties laid upon his plate, Catherine pressed her young guest to partake of wine, and they drank several cups together. It was a purple wine, so cool that the cup into which it was poured became covered with vapory dew; yet it seemed to warm the veins with strange fire.

To Arthur, as he drank, all things became more luminous, as by enchantment. The walls of the chamber appeared to recede, and the roof to heighten; the lamps glowed like stars in their chains, and the voice of Lady Catherine Ashburn floated to his ears like some far melody heard through the spaces of a drowsy night. His heart swelled, his tongue loosened, and words flitted from his lips that he had fancied he could never dare to utter.

Yet Catherine sought not to restrain him. Her lips gave no smile, but her long, bright eyes seemed to laugh with pleasure at his words of praise and to return his gaze of passionate admiration with affectionate interest.

"I have heard," she said, "of your piety and your goodness, and that you have studied with the monks to master the intricacies of Latin to better know the words of our Lord. Although I cannot claim to possess any such scholarly learning, I will venture to lay modesty aside and beg you to condescend to examine my late husband's collection of writings."

"The honor and the gratification, dear lady," replied Arthur, "will be mine; and I feel helpless to express the gratitude which the offer of so rare a favor deserves."

The serving girl, obedient to the summons of a little silver bell, brought in a stack of papers and retired. Arthur took the manuscripts and began to examine them with eager delight. The vellum upon which they were written had a pale yellow tint and was light as a fabric of gossamer. The characters were antiquely beautiful, as though they had been traced by the pen of a master, and the signatures attached to the compositions were the names of Catullus, and Miso, and Virgil. Arthur could not repress a cry of delight at the sight of treasures so inestimable and so unique; scarcely could he summon resolution enough to permit them to leave his hands even for a moment.

"Oh, lady!" he cried, "these are veritably priceless things, surpassing in worth the treasures of kings. These are the writings of great masters who died many hundreds of years before our birth. How marvelously they have been preserved! Is not this a wondrous ink in which they are written? And how divine the charm of this composition!

"Catullus! Darling Catullus!" murmured Catherine, with a singular light in her eyes. "Catullus is also my favorite. Dear Arthur, speak aloud his words to me—the music of those grand years when men were nobler and wiser than today."

And Arthur's voice rose through the perfumed night like the voice of a dove, the words blending together in liquid sweetness. Yet after he had finished still Arthur sat, overcome by the witchery of his own voice, while the lights of the chamber swam dim before his sight and tears of pleasure trickled down his cheeks.

So the ninth hour passed, and they continued to converse, and to drink the cool purple wine and to read the poetry of Catullus until far into the night. More than once Arthur thought of departing, but each time Catherine would begin, in that silver sweet voice of hers, so wondrous a story of the great poets of the past and of the women whom they loved that he became entranced; or she would sing for him a song so strange that all his senses seemed to die except that of hearing. And at last, as she paused to pledge him in a cup of wine, Arthur could not restrain himself from putting his arm about her neck, drawing her dainty head close, and kissing the lips that were so much ruddier and sweeter than the wine.

Then their lips separated no more—the night grew old, and they knew it not.

The birds awakened, the flowers opened their eyes to the rising sun, and Arthur found himself at last compelled to bid his lovely enchantress farewell. Catherine, accompanying him to the terrace, kissed him fondly and said, "Dear Arthur, come hither as often as you are able—as often as your heart whispers you to come. I know that you are not of those without faith and truth, who betray secrets; yet, being so young, you might also be sometimes thoughtless; and I pray you never to forget that only the stars have been the witnesses of our love. Speak of it to no living person, dearest, and take with you this little souvenir of our happy night."

And she presented him with an exquisite and curious little thing—a small dagger with a hilt worked in likeness of a couchant lion, wrought from a stone as yellow as gold. Tenderly the boy kissed the gift and the beautiful hand that gave it. "May God punish me," he vowed, "if ever I knowingly give you cause to reproach me, Catherine!" And they separated with mutual vows.

That morning, on returning to the keep of Sir Garvain, Arthur told the first falsehood which had ever passed his lips. He averred that his father was ill and had requested him thenceforward to pass his nights at home, now that the weather had become so pleasant; for, though the way was somewhat long, he was strong and active, and his father had need of him.

Sir Garvain believed all Arthur said and offered no objection. Accordingly the lad found himself enabled to pass all his evenings at the house of the beautiful Lady Ashburn.

Each night they devoted to the same pleasures which had made their first acquaintance so charming: they read and conversed by turns; they composed rhymes upon the flowers, the trees, the clouds, the streams, the birds, the heavens. But in all accomplishments Catherine far surpassed her young sweetheart. Her poems were ever superior to his in harmony of word coloring, in elegance of form, in classic loftiness of thought.

So the summer waxed and waned upon their love, and the luminous autumn came, with its vapors of phantom gold, its shadows of magical purple.

Then it unexpectedly happened that Arthur's father, meeting Sir Garvain by chance, was asked by him: "What is your illness that your boy continues to travel every evening to your home? The way is long, and when he returns in the morning he looks fordone with weariness. Now that the winter is approaching, he should spend his evenings at my side, learning the ways of knights."

And Sir Pelloux, greatly astonished, responded: "Sir, my son has not visited me once, nor has he been to our lands all this summer. I fear that he must have acquired wicked habits, and that he passes his nights in evil company—perhaps in gaming or in drinking with others in your employ."

But Sir Garvain returned: "Nay! that is not to be thought of. I have never found any evil in the boy, and there are no taverns nor gambling houses nor any other places of dissipation in our neighborhood. No doubt Arthur has found some amiable youth of his own age with whom to spend his evenings and only told me an untruth for fear that I would not otherwise permit him to leave my keep. Say nothing to him until I have discovered this mystery. This very evening I shall send my servant to follow after him and to watch whither he goes."

Sir Pelloux readily assented to this proposal and, promising to visit Sir Garvain the following morning, returned to his home.

In the evening, when Arthur left the keep of Sir Garvain, a servant followed him unobserved at a distance. But on reaching the most obscure portion of the road, the boy disappeared from sight as suddenly as though the earth had swallowed him.

After having long sought after him in vain, the servant

returned in great bewilderment to the keep and related what had taken place. Sir Garvain immediately sent a runner to Sir Pelloux.

In the meantime Arthur, entering the chamber of his beloved, was surprised and deeply pained to find her in tears.

"Sweetheart," she sobbed, wreathing her arms around his neck, "we are about to be separated forever because of reasons which I cannot tell you. From the very first I knew this must come to pass; nevertheless, it seemed to me for the moment so cruelly sudden a loss, so unexpected a misfortune, that I could not prevent myself from weeping. After this night we shall never see each other again, beloved, and I know that you will not be able to forget me while you live. But I know also that you will become a great warrior and that honors and riches will be showered upon you, and that some beautiful and loving woman will console you for my loss. And now let us speak no more of grief, but let us pass this last evening joyously, so that your recollection of me may not be a painful one and that you may remember my laughter rather than my tears."

She brushed her bright teardrops away and brought wine and music from a melodious lyre, and would not suffer Arthur to speak for one moment of their coming separation. And she sang him an ancient song about the calmness of summer lakes reflecting the blue of heaven only, and the calmness of the heart also, before the clouds of care and of grief and of weariness darken its little world. Soon they forgot their sorrow in the joy of song and wine, and those last hours seemed to Arthur more celestial than even the hours of their first bliss.

But when the yellow beauty of morning came, their sadness returned, and they wept. Once more Catherine accompanied her lover to the terrace steps, and as she kissed him farewell, she pressed into his hand a parting gift—a sword sheathed in silver, wonderfully chiseled and worthy the hand of a king. And they separated forever, shedding many tears.

Still, Arthur could not believe it was an eternal parting. "No," he thought, "I shall visit her tomorrow, for I cannot now live without her, and I feel assured that she cannot refuse to receive me." Such were the thoughts that filled his mind as he reached the keep of Sir Garvain, to find his father and his master standing in the front hall awaiting him.

Ere he could speak a word, Sir Pelloux demanded: "Son, in what place have you been passing your nights?"

Seeing that his falsehood had been discovered, Arthur dared not make any reply. He remained abashed and silent, with bowed head. Then Sir Pelloux, striking the boy violently with the back of his hand, commended him to divulge the secret. At last, partly through fear and partly through shame at having lied, Arthur faltered out the history of his love.

Sir Garvain changed color at the boy's tale. "Boy," exclaimed the knight, "I have no relative of the name of Ashburn; I have never heard of the woman you describe; I have never heard even of the house which you speak of. But I know also that you cannot dare to lie to your father. There is some strange delusion in all this affair."

Then Arthur produced the gifts that Lady Ashburn had given him—the dagger with the yellow stone hilt, the sword sheathed in silver, also some vellum sheets of poetry which she had entrusted to him.

The astonishment of Sir Garvain was now shared by Sir Pelloux. Both observed that the dagger and the sword bore the appearance of objects that had lain buried in the earth for centuries and were of a workmanship beyond the power of living man to imitate. And the compositions proved to be veritable masterpieces of poetry, written in the style of the Roman poets of eight hundred years before.

"Friend," cried the Sir Garvain, "let us immediately accompany the boy to the place where he obtained these miraculous things and apply the testimony of our senses to this mystery. The boy is no doubt telling the truth, yet his story passes my understanding."

And all three proceeded toward the place of habitation of the Lady Catherine Ashburn.

But when they had arrived at the shadiest part of the road, where the perfumes were most sweet and the mosses were greenest and the fruits of the wild apple trees flushed most redly, Arthur, gazing through the groves, uttered a cry of dismay. Where the tall thatched roof had risen against the sky there was now only the blue emptiness of air; where the wood walls had been there was visible only the flickering of leaves under the aureate autumn light; and where the broad terrace had extended, could be discerned only a ruin—a tomb so ancient, so deeply gnawed by moss, that the name graven upon it was no longer decipherable. The home of Lady Catherine Ashburn had disappeared.

Suddenly Sir Garvain smote his forehead with his hand, and turning to Sir Pelloux, recited a well-known verse the local storytellers sometimes sang:

Surely the apple flowers blossom
 over the tomb of Lady Catherine.

"Friend," continued Sir Garvain, "the beauty who bewitched your son was no other than she whose tomb stands there in ruin before us! Did she not say she was wedded to a knight named Sir Ashburn? There is no family of that name, but Ashburn is indeed the name of a field not far from here. There was a dark riddle in all that she said. She called herself Catherine Ashburn. There is no person of that name, but the old verse says she was buried in a grove of ash trees."

Sir Pelloux looked nervously through the shadowed copse. "I recall the legend now. Lady Catherine died not as other women die. Her limbs may have crumbled to dust; yet something of her still lives in this deep wood— her spirit still haunts this shadowy place."

Sir Garvain paused to make the sign of the cross, his brow creased, one hand upon the hilt of the great sword he wore. A vague fear fell upon the three. The thin mists of the morning made dim the distances of green and deepened the ghostly beauty of the woods. A faint breeze passed by, leaving a trail of blossom scent—a last odor of dying flowers—thin as that which clings to the hem of a forgotten robe. And, as it passed, the trees seemed to whisper across the silence.

Fearing greatly for his son, Sir Pelloux sent the lad away at once to serve as squire for another of his brother knights. And there, in after years, Arthur tried to forget Lady Ashburn. He bent to his studies and soon mastered the sword and lance, and in time grew to learn his true heritage and to discover that his destiny was to be king of all England. But that is another story.

Whatever he did, whatever he accomplished, never could Arthur forget Lady Ashburn; and yet it is said that he never spoke of her—not even when his queen begged him to tell the story of the two beautiful objects that always lay upon his table: a dagger with a hilt of yellow stone and a sword more richly worked than even Excalibur.

Author's note

"The Tale of Lady Ashburn" is taken from "The Story of Ming-Y," a traditional Chinese fantasy, which I first encountered in *Some Chinese Ghosts,* by Lafcadio Hearn. It is a timeless story that transcends setting and character—witness the seamless way it incorporates itself into the English countryside and the Arthurian myth.

As Lafcadio Hearn's version is in the public domain, I took the liberty of borrowing some of his poetic phrases for this retelling. The interested reader might want to go back to the original version, or to locate Lafcadio Hearn's other books of Oriental fantasy stories, such as *Kawidan* or *In Ghostly Japan.*

—JGB

Changeling

Kristine Kathryn Rusch

The colored lights danced over his baptismal crib. He didn't have words yet—he was only four days old—and the world still blurred before his half-opened eyes. He had been left alone for just a moment. His pagan mother, queen in more than name, was arguing with his Christian father over the necessity for the ceremony. The nurses huddled against the strong oak doors, listening through the cracks as the queen vented her fears about the holy water to be dripped on her son's head.

The baby, whose father wanted to call him Sebastian and whose his mother wanted to call him Elric, reached toward the lights, pudgy fingers grasping with the odd strength that only babies have. By accident, he touched a blue light and pulled his hand away with a startled cry. With the smell of sulfur and a bit of smoke, the light had become a tiny naked woman, with thin wings shimmering on her back.

"Got him," she said.

The other lights stopped flickering and floated to her, each popping and becoming little naked people as well. The baby watched them, his fingers stinging with heat and turning blue at the tips. He whimpered as the little people wove a gossamer net around him, but his nurses, intent on the argument that had just missed—by the width of a poorly aimed goblet—coming to blows, heard nothing. The net was soft and warm around him. As it lifted him in the air, his fingers stopped stinging, and he could almost smell his mother's milk. The rocking and the milky scent soothed him. As the little people carried him to the window, he felt a calm he had never known before.

He turned his small head in its nest and looked down on his former bed. Another being had already taken his place, fingers curled over the baptismal blanket as if to hold it tight.

"Changeling," the baby thought, marking not just his first word, but the arrival of his conscious being, born a full adult, thanks to the fairies' magic touch.

Arianna opened the sash covering the window that overlooked the garden. She climbed on the window seat and tucked her bare feet under her long dressing gown. Sunshine warmed her, and the scent of roses filled the room. She leaned back and closed her eyes, not wanting to see the tapestry-covered walls that she had seen every morning of her entire life. The thick featherbed leaning against the wall was rumpled—no one had come in yet to fix it or to dress her—and the fire in the grate had burned to ash in the middle of the night.

But it didn't matter. The morning was warm and beautiful, just as Mother had predicted it would be. Mother had been upset each time she spoke of the coronation: her bejeweled hands clasped as if in protest and her great green eyes filled with tears. She had never liked Elric, always claiming that he was not her child, something Father had laughed at, recalling the Great Baptism Debates and before that, the Awful Royal Birth Screams that had echoed from the chambers above.

Lord, how she missed her father. His calmness had been the perfect foil to their mother's odd notions. Besides, he had always found time to spend with his children, even when their mother had not.

Mother had managed to stall the coronation for six weeks, but the Lords had finally overruled her. Mother had said nothing of it, but Arianna assumed that the lords had threatened to overthrow her if she didn't allow Elric to take the throne.

Not that Elric cared. Elric did whatever anyone told him, which should have pleased Mother, if she had wanted to retain power. All she had to do was order Elric to listen to no one but her.

Something rustled in the garden below. Arianna opened her eyes and leaned out, hoping to see a deer. She had seen one on the morning of her father's death, and Mother had said that proved she had second sight, had seen the death warning, and failed to heed it. Arianna had said that it proved there was a deer in the garden and nothing else.

The rosebushes were in full flower. Red and white flowers stood out like drops of paint against the rich green leaves. Off to the side were the hedgerows, marking the delineation between the rose garden and the rest of the flowers. A bird burst out of a copse of trees to her left and Arianna started to turn away, thinking that was what she had heard, when she realized she had seen something else.

A shiny black head of hair half hidden among the cluster of white rosebushes in the center of the garden. She made herself turn back slowly, trying to ease the beating of her heart. When she was a child, her mother used to tell stories of tribes of evil woodsmen who beheaded children and used their hair for court wigs. Even though Nurse later explained that those were tales designed to keep the children on the palace grounds, part of Arianna still believed the stories to be true.

The hair moved just a little, enough so that Arianna was convinced that it was attached to someone. She leaned out the window, careful to grip the cold stone sill. At that moment, the person stood, and she was startled to see Elric, surveying the garden as if he had never seen it before.

She pulled herself back enough to stay out of his view. Elric looked odd. His shoulders seemed wider, and his mouth had a curl to it, almost as if it would ease into a smile or snarl at any moment. His skin looked white in the morning sun and his black hair darker than it usually appeared.

But that wasn't what surprised her. What surprised her were his eyes. They had a sharpness, an alertness, to them that she had never seen before.

"Elric!" she called. "You're supposed to be in your rooms!"

He glanced up at her, expression as wild as the deer she had seen, and then he shimmered and disappeared.

Caught. Seen by a switch of a girl no bigger than his Aunt Fay. If they knew back at the Gates, they would laugh him from the Ring, and he would lose his chance to become king of them all at the Midsummer Frolic.

He crouched in the shadows of the trees. The girl still leaned from the window, searching the garden, trying to find him. She had a familiar look to her, a brightness to her eyes, that only those with a touch of Trueblood had. If she looked hard enough, she could probably see him, even now. Truebloods could not hide from each other.

She went back inside and he sighed with relief. He had been a fool coming here so close to the solstice, but he couldn't stay away. After he became king, he would never return to the mortal world. He would stay in the Ring, protected by magic, until his powers waned and a new king rose to take his place.

A shiver ran down his back. In the shade the ground was damp. He wasn't used to being in the mortal world in the daylight. Birds flitted from tree to tree just as they did in the Ring, and the sun had a warmth he had never felt before.

Something about the castle drew him. Something that whispered at the edge of his memory.

Elric.

She had called him Elric.

"Sebastian!"

"Elric!"

"Woman, I'll have none of your heathen names for my

son. He was born into a Christian household and Christian he'll remain!"

The People called him Gift. He remembered the naming ceremony around the fire. He had rested in a new cradle made of fern and twigs and the remains of his net. They had called him Gift and thanked the forest gods that they had been able to save him.

He would receive a new name, should he be crowned in the darkness.

Elric, you're supposed to be in your room.

He had been in this castle before. Flashes (*another being in his place*) had haunted him each time he stood in the garden. They would haunt him until he died.

Unless he settled it now.

She had thought him Elric. Elric he would become.

Arianna did not move as Lissa tugged on her hair. Mother had dictated the dress and the hairstyle: several long braids wrapped around her head and decorated in pearls. Arianna loved to have her hair fall free, but Mother said that was unbecoming to a woman without a husband. Mother's husband had died, but she still wore her hair long and flowing down her back. Arianna wondered if she would ever be able to do the same.

Arianna's reflection in the rippled glass showed a face white with strain. Lissa held her lower lip between her teeth as she combed. Mother had beat Lissa with a comb once when Arianna's hair had tumbled down her shoulders during dinner. Lissa had vowed never to let that happen again.

Lissa pulled so hard that Arianna's head wobbled. She would not cry out. She would say nothing. She wanted out of this room as quickly as possible. She wanted to see Elric.

If she closed her eyes, she could see him there, movements as wild as an animal's. He had shimmered and disappeared, but as she had crouched down from the window, she had thought she saw him in the trees, staring at her.

Her brother had always been odd, but his oddness had never seemed purposeful before.

"Are you almost done?" she snapped at Lissa.

"I still have half the head, Highness," Lissa said, "and it must be right for the queen."

"The queen be hanged," Arianna said, but not loudly enough for Lissa to hear. Arianna feared her mother's wrath as much as the maid did.

The castle was cold. He thought it odd that mortals would chose to live in a place colder than the outdoors. The air smelled damp and musty, and strangely familiar.

He had never seen so much activity in one place. In the large kitchen, the only warm room he had found, women wearing kerchiefs over their hair tended fires in large stone boxes. The room smelled of cooked game and fresh bread. His mouth watered, but mortal food was not what he was after.

In the larger gathering rooms, servants added decorations to the walls. Up the flat stone steps, a woman with the shine of a Trueblood allowed another woman to help her dress. The girl he had seen sat before a mirror while another girl played with her hair. Men in other chambers helped each other dress. But only one chamber drew him, one he remembered being in when he was so tiny he could not speak.

The oak door was closed, but he spoke softly to the dying wood. It answered creakingly in great pain from the metal studs someone had poked in its frame. He brushed his hand along the scarred surface, easing some of the pain, and the door slid open for him without a sound.

He slipped inside. The cold walls were covered with woven rugs, decorated with great care. Voices echoed from the inner chamber. He walked around the gilt-edged chairs and made himself shimmer like light before stepping into the carved open doorway.

His shimmer nearly left him. He froze, cold as the surface of a pond on a winter day. Standing before him, wrapped in heavy woolen robes, was the being he had last seen as a baby. Only now it looked like a waxen image of himself.

Another man bobbed and danced around the image. ". . . bit warm, Highness," the man was saying, "but lovely. Yes, impressive. The others will be pleased to see the wealth this kingdom has. You must walk firm, my Lord Elric, as if you own it all, since you do now. You do."

Elric. You should be in your rooms.

Elric! 'Tis a royal name from my people! You shall not corrupt him by naming him for some misbegotten saint!

His fingers twitched and the sharp blue pain he had felt ever since he could remember returned. Lights. Lights. He had seen lights and touched them and then . . .

. . . he was beside the fire and they were calling him Gift. He was no gift. He was one of the many babies brought to fairie because the fey had grown old and corrupt and could no longer bear their own.

His shimmer disappeared, and he had to catch the cold stone to keep himself from falling. No wonder Fay had to boost his magic when he confronted the adults. The little bit of Trueblood wouldn't carry the magic required of a full Trueblood. He was mortal. He was mortal and they had never told him.

A rustle behind him made him turn. The girl was there, looking older, the hair piled on top of her head and wrapped in pearls. Her dress clung to her chest, then widened at her hips until he could barely see her tiny slippers peeking out.

"Elric," she said, her forehead wrinkled in a frown, "why aren't you dressed?"

He grabbed the shimmer, pulled it back around him and pushed against the wall. Her frown grew. She reached out, and would have put her hand through him if he had not moved away.

"Milady Arianna?" the manservant spoke.

The girl shot a suspicious glance at his hiding spot, then walked into the other room. "Elric," she said, looking at the waxen image. "Elric? Is that you?"

The wax image didn't answer. The girl frowned, and flounced out of the room.

Because Mother had waited so long, the Lords had decided to hold the coronation in the church. Arianna arrived early, knowing she would catch her mother there.

The church was a miniature version of the castle. Made of stone and mortar, with towers on all four sides, it looked like a child's play toy instead of a place of worship. Arianna had stepped inside only once—for her father's funeral—and she had been very uncomfortable.

Inside, the church was colder than the castle's closed east wing. The back pews were made of stone and were covered, just for today, with thin red cushions embroidered with the family's crest. The front pews were wooden boxes, designed to hold and protect the gentry from the masses. The king's box, rarely used, had a small platform leading up to it, so that the king would sit higher than anyone else in the room.

Arianna stood in the door for a moment, getting her bearings. Her mother's voice echoed from one of the back rooms: high, strident, and forceful. Arianna didn't know how the bishop could argue with her. No one argued with Mother.

Arianna walked down the stone floor. A rolled-up red rug would be laid for her brother, but not until he appeared. The stone sent chills through her thin slippers, and she stifled the urge to sneeze.

Her father had lost the religion battle, just as he had lost most battles with his wife. Arianna sometimes thought he had died early, just to get away from Mother.

She followed the voices into a group of rooms of the king's box. The rooms were done in gold and red, with plush chairs and big oak desks. Mother always said the church had money. Here was the proof of it.

The bishop faced Arianna. He wore his white and gold robes and clutched a staff so tightly that his knuckles had turned white. His round face held no expression at all except for two red spots on his cheeks. Arianna knew the feeling. Sometimes a club to the head might make Mother talk sense.

Mother towered over the bishop. She had insisted on wearing her specially built shoes with the three-inch heels, making her taller than anyone in the kingdom. Her dress, made with real gold thread, and heavier than the king's coronation crown, shimmered in the candlelight.

"You will *not* touch him, nor will you douse him in holy water," Mother said with such force that Arianna knew that she had repeated the sentence at least a dozen times.

"It is part of the ceremony, Highness, and as such, I cannot skip the ritual. The foreign nobles will know."

"Foreign nobles be hanged!" Mother said. "He is not a Christian. He does not need Christian trappings at his coronation."

"He will be a Christian king, Highness, ruling a Christian nation."

Mother waved a hand and the bishop winced. "If only his father were alive. He would come up with some kind of compromise."

"If Father were alive," Arianna said, "we wouldn't be having the coronation."

Mother whirled. "Arianna!" Her voice held relief. "Show him what holy water does to my children."

Arianna swallowed. The burn marks ached. She had dipped her fingers in holy water after a ceremony held in the palace. Nurse had to put out Arianna's burning skin with her skirt. Father had warned Arianna never to show the bishop the scars. He said that would be grounds for a complete revolt against the monarchy.

"It makes us nervous, Bishop," she said, ignoring her mother's plea-filled gaze. "Perhaps you can wave—" she didn't know the term for the equipment he used—"that thing over my brother's head and pretend there is water in it. After all, we're going to pretend that he's a Christian king since none of us know the first thing about your religion!"

"Arianna!" Mother hissed.

"Quite right, Arianna, quite right," the bishop said. "A compromise worthy of your father. Then the other nations will think we have a Christian king, and I will not have shirked my duties."

Odd that he didn't worry about the reaction of his god. Arianna sighed. She didn't have time to think about that. "Mother, I need to talk with you."

Her mother glanced at the bishop, then at Arianna, as if she couldn't believe the argument had been so easily settled. "What is it?"

"Privately, Mother."

"All right." Mother shot another angry look at the bishop, then left the room and followed Arianna out of the church. As they stepped across the threshold, Mother wiped her shoes to get the stench of holiness off them. "What's so important?"

"I saw something strange in the garden," Arianna said. She explained Elric's odd behavior and the way the new image of him had disappeared twice, both times leaving a shimmer that she could barely touch.

"And you can see that shimmer?" Mother asked.

Arianna nodded. "It doesn't go away, no matter what I do. If I squint, if I touch it—no matter what, it stays."

Mother sighed and shook her head. "We need to take you home and get you tested," she said. "I should have known when that holy water exploded on you—"

"Mother, please." Arianna had been listening to that speech since the deer in the garden.

Mother smiled absently and patted Arianna's arm. "If you see that shimmer during the coronation, I want you to point it out to me," she said. "Then stand back."

A small crowd of people had disembarked from a carriage near the gate. "What is going on?" Arianna asked.

Mother's smile grew wider. "I don't know," she said, "but I think there's magic in the air."

He shimmered against the wall until the manservant left. The waxen image still stood in front of the mirror, unmoving. It appeared to be staring at itself, but he knew that it was waiting for someone to tell it what to do.

Mortals were such fools. They actually believed that lump was a real being? If he had not come back, the waxen image's reflexes would have slowed to nothing. It needed power from its home source and he knew he was that source.

He was Elric.

The name suited him better than Gift. He wiped the shimmer off his skin and went into the dressing room. The waxen image turned at the sound. Elric approached and touched it, feeling the clammy skin, shivering at the lifeless eyes.

He let the image go. So he had been home here, once. Not long, though. They had taken him young, as they often did.

He had time. He hadn't expected to find the answers so quickly. He would follow this image and see what its day was like.

Arianna sat on the altar beside her mother, staring at the bishop as he repeated his admonitions to the new Christian king. Elric hadn't moved from his spot in the back of the church. He looked normal now—a bit slow, and witless, the kind of man who would always do what he was told. Was that why the lords wanted to speed up the coronation? So that they would have a malleable king? Did that mean that Mother would have to fight for her very existence?

Arianna sighed. She didn't like thinking of the future.

The bishop finished his lecture. One of the churchmen in the back signaled Elric to walk down the aisle. Two young boys walked before him, opening the red carpet. Elric walked as he was told: step, pause, step, pause— never taking his eyes off the front of the church. Mother stood and Arianna stood beside her, feeling a strange fear in the back of her throat.

Elric knelt on the steps leading to the altar. The bishop walked down two steps to tower over his future king.

Something shimmered on the back of Elric's coronation robe. Arianna tugged her mother's overlong sleeve.

"There," she whispered, pointed to Elric's feet. "There it is."

Mother frowned.

The bishop turned and dipped his staff in the holy water. Arianna turned white. He had promised. He had said she had come up with a good compromise. She started across the altar, her mother grabbing at her skirts.

"No, Arianna!"

"... *e Spiritu Santu*—"

She grabbed the bishop just as her mother grabbed her, just as the holy water flew from the bulbous end of the staff. The water landed on Elric and splattered the back of his robe, the carpet and the people sitting in the front boxes. A drop landed on Arianna's hand, and a small fire flared, sending sharp pains through her skin.

She slapped it out. Another fire started on Elric's robe. Elric himself looked up at the bishop—and smiled, truly smiled for the first time in his life. Then he vanished, leaving only bits of clay and earth on the collapsing robe.

The nobles in front screamed. The church smelled of smoke. Mother had pushed the bishop aside and was struggling down the steps in her too-tall shoes. The fire on the back of the robe had grown until it was the shape of a man.

Elric. It was Elric. Not the one who had disappeared, but the one she had seen that morning, with his lively blue eyes and strong, quick-moving fingers.

The bishop picked up the bowl of holy water and made to throw it on Elric, but Arianna grabbed his arm. "No," she said, wincing as more water spilled on her. "It won't put out the fire."

Another flame sprouted on her arm, and she had to use the bishop's sleeve to put it out. He looked at her with such repulsion that she thought he was going to hit her.

Elric's fire was out, and he was cradled in his mother's arms. She picked up the robe and wrapped it around him, murmuring, "My son! My son!"

One of the lords stood. "I demand to know what has happened."

"There is an enchantment—" the bishop began.

"—which the bishop broke," Arianna replied. "That was why my brother was always so slow. The tears of Christ have made my brother himself again."

A rustle of voices ran through the crowd. Elric staggered forward, held in place by Mother. She wasn't going to let him go. He shot a glance at Arianna, a look filled with such panic that she felt her heart go to him. "What was that?" he whispered. His speech had an odd accent, a lilting, almost musical tone.

"Christian Holy Water," she whispered.

"Christian?" He let out air, almost like a sigh, then began to struggle.

"Don't move, you fool," Mother hissed in her best command voice. "You can't go back now. You can only stay with us. Best make what you can of it."

"This is a Christian place?" His voice, mercifully, remained low. "I can't stay here."

"You have to," Arianna said. "You're being crowned king."

"King?" He glanced at the door, then at the ceiling, then surveyed the burn marks on his skin. He looked at his fingers as if he expected something on them, but couldn't find it. "I am mortal then."

The bishop yanked his sleeve from Arianna's grasp. He looked at the crowd, then at Elric. Arianna could see the bishop make a decision before he spoke. "Of course you're not mortal, boy," he said as quickly as his booming voice would allow. "You're king—above man, above all except God."

He waved the staff over Elric and spoke more Latin. The noble sat down, and Mother relaxed her grip. The coronation was done.

But Arianna watched that lively, intelligent male face. Her true brother. The coronation may have been over, but the fun was just beginning.

Elric had fallen asleep beside the fire, listening to the coo of his newborn son. He had been awake for nearly three days now, listening, waiting. The window open, the baptismal crib decorated just as he remembered it. He had banished the nurses and guarded the child himself.

Colored lights flew in the window. The baby's coos grew louder as he saw the pretty colors. He reached for them, giggling as he did, accidentally touching one. A pop and the smell of sulfur filled the room, jarring Elric awake.

The fairy stopped her ministrations over the baby. She stood in midair and bowed to Elric.

"Human king," she said in a mocking tone.

He reached for her, his fingers still heartbreakingly normal. The blue had been gone for years. "Take me back," he whispered.

She shook her head. "You've been tainted," she said. "I'll take your son."

He watched as the fairies wove a skein of light and wrapped it around his child. He wished he could speak to the boy, tell him that the world of magic was a better world than this, that there was hope there and—

The door burst open behind them. The fairies disappeared in a halo of light. Elric had to run forward and catch his son before the baby dropped back into the crib.

"They were here," his mother said. "I smelled them."

She reached into the air, touched a remaining light beam, and winced as it popped. One fairy shook a fist at his mother and flew away. She turned on Elric. "You were going to let them take him."

He stared up at her. She was Trueblood and powerful, but she had never scared him. She had chosen to give up her life for a life with humans. He clutched the baby to his chest.

"Yes," he said. "I was going to let them take him."

"Why? Don't you remember? Don't you know fairies can never love?"

He didn't care about love. He was too fairy to know what it meant. But he remembered. He remembered the free-flowing magic, the warm nights, the wonderful spectacle of lights. They hadn't loved him, but they had given him laughter, which no one seemed to understand here.

He looked at her, and felt a sadness burn into his soul. "They'll never come back now."

"I know," she said. "And now we are finally free."

She took the baby from him and left the room. He went to the window and stared out, seeing lights flickering in the garden. He would call them back if he could, but he was mortal bound and ugly in their sight.

They would die off soon. Their line was too weak. He would never see them again.

"We're not free," he whispered to the uncaring wind. The lights around him winked out—one by one. "We're all prisoners of our destiny."

A Parker House Roll

Dean Wesley Smith

When your best friend is a four-year-old time-traveling talking oak tree named Fred, you don't introduce him around to your other friends. And especially not to a girl you are trying to impress.

So when Sally, my new girl, and I spent the June afternoon in my backyard, under a huge orange beach umbrella, talking about what costumes we were going to design for the next science fiction convention, Fred had strict instructions to not say a word.

I had a standard, three-bedrooms-down-the-hall track home, and my backyard was one of those standard subdivision square things with a patch of grass, a bunch of bushes, and about five small trees, one of which was Fred. After I planted Little Fred and he started talking, I put up a seven-foot wood fence all the way around the yard. I got too many stares from the neighbors because I would stand in the snow talking to small tree. I suppose if one of the neighbors talked to trees, I would have stared, too.

The fence turned out to have added benefits in the summer, especially when I wanted to have a girl over, but the fence didn't solve the problem of Fred. He had already cost me two girlfriends. Whenever he spoke they just wouldn't believe that what was talking was the baby oak tree. They always thought it was me playing some sort of stupid joke on them. And since Fred usually insulted them, convincing them it wasn't me had proved to be very, very difficult.

So this morning, before Sally arrived, I stood in the backyard and sternly lectured the young tree to behave himself. I even went so far as to tell him that if he said a word in front of Sally, I would never listen to another one of his stupid limericks.

The threat worked. Not one word from the tree. For two hours Sally and I laughed, drank cold, fresh-squeezed lemonade, and planned our costumes. He kept quiet. But as I came back into the yard after walking Sally to her car, Fred quickly started off with his revenge:

> There was a young girl of Oak Knoll,
> Who thought it exceedingly droll,
> At a masquerade ball,
> Dressed in nothing at all,
> To back in as a Parker House roll.

I dropped down onto the lawn chair and pretended to not pay attention to the six-foot-tall oak tree with fifty-seven leaves. Fred had told me that number one day last week just to impress me with his growth. It had now been over four years since I had taken an acorn from the first talking Fred, Big Fred I liked to call him, and conceived Little Fred.

"You do know what a Parker House roll is, don't you?" Fred asked, his voice seeming to come from everywhere around the little tree. Actually, one day Fred and I figured out that he was really projecting his voice inside people's heads. But it always seemed that his voice was coming from the air around the tree. It had taken me two days of climbing in the huge branches of Big Fred before I believed the talking wasn't just a practical joke of some kind or another.

"That limerick dates from the early 1940's. Its history is interesting."

Again I just sipped on the cold lemonade and stared at the notes and sketches Sally and I had been making. He knew I hated learning about the limericks almost as much as I hated hearing them.

"You know," Fred said, pretending that I wasn't pretending to ignore him, "that you two have no real costume sense at all."

I laughed. "Yeah, as if a tree knows anything about costumes."

"Actually," Fred said, his voice taking on a British accent and sounding very formal, "I know a great deal. Many a costumed human has reposed under oak trees over the centuries. Remember, you were dressed in a very strange manner on the night we first met."

"How could I forget?" My date and I had left a costume party and gone looking for a little fun in an outdoor private place. I was dressed as Bucky the Space Pirate and she was dressed as the Moon Queen. We ended up under the old limbs of Big Fred, down in the corner of Center Park. Just when we were getting, as they say, "down to it," Big Fred decided to talk to us with a limerick insulting a part of my date's private anatomy. She never believed it wasn't me doing the talking, even though my mouth was in a place that made talking somewhat difficult. We never went out again.

And I have hated Fred's limericks ever since.

"That is nothing," Fred said, going on as if it really mattered to me, "when we think of the humans of previous centuries. Their normal dress would function very well for costumes today. There is a long tradition of that, too, as you well know."

He paused for a moment. "If you want to see a real costume, hold onto one of my limbs and I can take you to the tree that Queen Elizabeth was sitting under when she was told her sister died and she was Queen of England. She had on a very fancy dress that day. It would make a wonderful Martian Goddess design for Sally."

"Thanks," I said, "but I think—"

"In fact, I even know what Elizabeth was reading at the time. I wouldn't mind taking you to see."

I shook my head and went back to studying the

sketches of costumes we had talked about. Oak trees had this ability to move back and forth through time along, for lack of a better way of putting it, their family trees. To prove that to me, Big Fred had convinced me to climb into his limbs. He took me all the way back to the dinosaurs, where it seemed as if one of them was trying to knock me out of the tree. Scared me so bad I had never had the courage to try it again.

"You know," Fred went on, as if being silent for the two hours had dammed up a flood of words. "Actually, what the early British kings wore would make a much better choice of costume for you. In fact, poor young King Edward VI dressed most times very much like your Bucky costume. Only with more class."

"Not a chance," I said. "If anything, Bucky dresses more like a musketeer."

Fred laughed. "As if you would know. Come on. Grab a branch and I'll take you back to see poor little King Edward. He was poisoned, you know. That's why he died before he turned sixteen."

I stared at the little tree, its leaves drooping in the heat of the afternoon. Damn him. He knew I loved a good mystery. And he knew I was interested in the history of that period of Britain. He had me. "How would you know that?"

Again Fred just laughed. "Only way you're going to believe me is if I show you."

I dropped the notebook on the grass. "Damn it, Fred. After that ride back to the dinosaurs, the last thing I want to do is have you whisk me into the past again. It isn't a normal thing to do."

"As if what you did with Sally the other night was?"

"Fred! How could you see? It was dark out here."

Fred didn't say a word, so I grabbed my lemonade and went back into the house. No way some stupid little tree was going to get the best of me.

Two hours later I found myself sitting on the ground at Fred's base, holding on to his lowest little branch.

At least Fred had the decency not to laugh.

* * *

The world went black for a full second, then the shock of cold, winterlike air slapped me. I gripped the rough, cold bark of the huge oak limb I found myself straddling and glanced quickly around at the limbs and other trees. Damn, this felt so real! Fred had always promised me that I would never really leave my backyard. Yet when Big Fred took me back to the dinosaurs, I swore I felt that dinosaur hit the tree.

And right now I would swear that I was holding on to a very large limb in a very cold forest, God knew where. My heart pounded in my chest, and the blood rushed through my ears so fast I could barely hear. All I wanted to do was cry for Fred to take me back. What the hell had I been thinking? Man wasn't made to go riding oak trees through time.

There was a rustling noise, and I glanced down. I was about fifteen feet above the ground in what looked to be a pretty thick forest. Below me were two men, one bent over working at something in the low brush. The man standing looked to be of a higher class. He wore breeches, with a white blouselike shirt and a cloth coat and hat. The man working the brush was obviously a beggar of some sort. His rough clothes were filthy, and all the way up in the tree I could smell his odor. Layers of sweat and onions. Rotted onions.

As I looked closer, it became clear that even the standing man's clothes were dirty, and his hair under his hat looked as if it hadn't been washed in a year. I guessed that both their odors were mixing, since the smells were strong this far up in the tree. My eyes were going to start watering in a minute.

"Fred!" I whispered. "Get me out of here."

But Fred didn't answer.

The man on his knees stood, his hands covered with dirt. He handed something carefully to the other man, who looked at it for a moment, then nodded and placed it in a small cloth bag. He flipped the beggar a coin and turned and walked away through the woods. The beggar quickly stuck the coin in a dark place in his coat and headed in the other direction down the path. Neither looked back.

After they were out of sight I looked around to make sure no one else was in sight, then asked, "Fred? Who were they? What were they doing? Now that I have seen this, can I go back? It's colder than hell out here."

Fred's laugh came softly, as if from a long distance. "Actually, who they are doesn't really matter. But what they were doing most definitely does. Notice down where they were in the bushes. See the mushrooms in the fairy ring configuration? That is what they were picking."

"So?" I asked.

"Those are panther mushrooms or, as they are scientifically called, *Amanita pantherina*. Sometimes they are called fly agaric, because they are used to kill flies."

"Poison?"

"Very much so. Hang on. Off to the next stop."

"Wait. I don't—" But it was too late. There was a second of darkness, and then I found myself on a much smaller limb, with much less to hang on to. And it seemed even colder, if that was possible.

This oak tree occupied a solo position on the edge of a huge expanse of lawn and hedges on the edge of a cobblestone road. The road seemed to be the main entrance to a huge palace, or whatever they were called in Britain. The same man who had pocketed the mushrooms rode up the road and under the branch I sat on. I noticed after he passed that he was the one who smelled of rotten onions.

"This is where King Edward VI is staying at the moment," Fred said. "Hang on."

Again there was a second of blackness. I found myself in another oak tree on what seemed to be the opposite side of the same huge building. The sun was brighter, and the air seemed slightly warmer.

"It's two days later," Fred said, his voice almost a whisper. "Watch."

"Why are you whispering?" I asked Fred. But he didn't have time to answer.

A small boy, white-skinned and thin, walked up and sat on a stone bench below the very limb I clung to. He was dressed in green tights, an ornate jeweled vest of a dark green color, and bright jeweled shoes, also dark green. Fred was right. It would make a great costume for a science fiction convention. But it needed a hat. The king wasn't wearing one.

A man dressed completely in black with a white powdered wig that didn't even pretend to hide his black hair walked slowly up to the boy and handed him a brown-looking drink in an ornate challis.

The boy stared at the drink for a moment, then took a big gulp and made a face. If the stuff tasted as bad as it looked, it was amazing the kid was drinking it.

"Medicine," Fred whispered. "Made up of nine spoonfuls of a liquid distilled from spearmint and red fennel, liverwort and turnip, dates and raisins, an ounce of mace, two sticks of celery, and the quarters of a sow nine days old. Of course, it also is laced with a small amount of the ground-up mushrooms."

"You're kidding?" I said, my voice almost breaking out of a whisper. The young king and his doctor didn't seem to notice.

"I'm not," Fred said. "The king will be dead by early July. Poisoned from the medicine he was taking to get better."

"But who? Who wanted him dead? Who is the guy giving it to him?"

"That is just one of the doctors," Fred said. "He doesn't know, I'll wager. But thousands want the young king dead. This is the time of the great fights between Protestant reformers and Catholics. Actually, most who know the king was poisoned think it was the Duke of Northumberland who did it. He had the young king sign a Devise for Succession right before he died to give to the crown to his wife, a Lady Jane Grey."

"But Northumberland was beheaded by Bloody Mary. Right?" I felt proud remembering that much of my English history.

"Correct," Fred said.

Below me the young king handed back the challis to the doctor and stood. "Dost thou hear voices?" he asked, his voice thin and high.

The doctor shook his head no.

The king looked around for a moment, then shrugged and moved off toward the palace at a slow walk.

"Can he hear us?" I asked. "Please tell me he can't hear us."

"Well," Fred said, "did you get enough information for a new costume? Did you notice the detail of the neckline and how—"

"He could hear us, couldn't he?"

"The king? Yes, I suppose he could. But did you also get a good look at how he did the tights with those shoes?"

"Damn it, Fred. You said I wasn't really here."

Fred laughed. "Actually you are and you aren't. If someone was to look in the backyard they would see you sitting beside me for about five seconds. That's all the time we will be gone."

"But what would have happened if I had fallen out of this tree right on his head?" I looked down at the stone bench where the king of England had just been sitting. I was going to be sick.

Fred laughed. "I suppose you would have changed history. There has been a great deal of speculation as to how things would have changed if Edward had lived. But no scenarios worked out with someone falling out of a tree and killing him." Again Fred laughed.

"This is NOT funny!" I screamed at him.

Across the lawn, both the king and the doctor turned and looked back in my direction. Then the king started back, and the doctor clapped his hands to summon someone from near the palace.

"Fred! Get me out of here."

"But this would be such an interesting occurrence, don't you think?"

"No! I don't!" I screamed again. Then in the lowest,

meanest voice I could manage I said, "Now get me out of here."

The world went black and then everything came back to light. But I was still sitting in a damn oak tree in England. And it was still cold.

"Fred!" I said, my voice as mean and as mad as I could make it sound. "I want to go home. Now!"

"In a moment," Fred said.

I took a deep breath and looked around. Across an open square from the tree was the famous Tower Hill, which I had seen hundreds of times in pictures. A crowd filled the open area, and there were three men on a raised platform, all dressed in black. One appeared to be a priest. And as I watched, one man with his hands tied behind his back kneeled and put his head in what looked to be trough. The third man, with very little hesitation, swung a huge ax and cut the kneeling man's head off.

I couldn't believe my eyes. The man's head rolled into a basket, and the executioner reached down and picked it up for the cheering crowd to see. Blood still squirted from the headless body as the heart kept pumping, and still more blood dripped from the head.

I felt dizzy and sick as I gripped the rough bark of the oak. "Fred," I whispered, "who was that?"

"Northumberland," Fred said. "Just thought you would want the entire story of what happened to the man who poisoned a British king."

"Home? Please?"

"You wish is my command, oh, master," Fred said.

The summer heat washed over me, and the second I felt the ground under my butt I let go of Fred's little limb and lay back on the warm grass. The sun felt heavenly against my face, and my hands tingled as they warmed up.

"Well," Fred said, "did you get some good ideas for costumes? You do that King Edward one and you will really impress that Sally friend of yours."

I sat up and stared at the little oak tree. "Fred, why isn't the poisoning of Edward in the history books?"

"For the same reason a lot of crimes go unpunished. No proof. You would be amazed at what we trees have seen you humans do to each other over the years. In fact, you know the skeleton that was found by the lake last week?"

"Yeah," I said, not really wanting to know what Fred was going to say.

"He was killed. Twenty-one years ago. Grab a limb and I'll show you who did it."

I scooted back on the grass a few more feet away from the little tree. "I think I will pass on that one." I could just see myself trying to explain to the police how I knew what happened in a twenty-one-year-old murder. Better in this case to just not know.

"Suit yourself," Fred said. "You want to hear another limerick? It's about costumes again."

I groaned and lay back on the grass so that the hot sun on my face would chase the cold and the picture of that young king from my mind.

"Oh, good," Fred said, his voice bubbling with happiness. "This limerick is also from the early forties and is very similar to the other one I told you this afternoon."

Again all I could do is groan.

> A nudist girl wearing three raisins,
> A masquerade prize was her goal,
> The judges said, "Lookie,
> From the front she's a cookie,
> From the back she's a Parker House roll."

"You do know what a Parker House roll is, don't you?"

No way was I going to tell the damn little tree that I didn't.

The King Who
Would Fly

Karen Haber

There was once a king, Alistasair IV, gray-haired and long-bearded, who ruled a small, orderly kingdom called Farandale. Come summer in Farandale, crops grew in neat green rows in neat green grids across the farmlands. In autumn the leaves lingered, gold and red, on the trees until they fell, almost at once and all together, and were raked into neat piles and carted away. Winter found the Farandalians rosy and plump-cheeked, savoring the goods in their well-stocked larders and skating on the small lakes that dotted the kingdom. Spring was best of all, for the birds returned from their winter exile to perch, singing, in the budding trees, and the families put away their heavy wraps and came out to stroll the village greens.

It was Farandale's only misfortune to have as neighbors several larger disorderly kingdoms: Ebbinsrule, Mulgulch, and Savanly. The kings of these kingdoms were bulky, blustering men who roared when they spoke and ruled by cruelty. King Alistasair counted none of them as friends.

The king had a daughter, the golden-haired Princess Esme, upon whom he doted. Perhaps he was overfond of the princess, but she was, after all, the only child of a late marriage, and the queen, her mother, was dead. Esme, for her part, adored her father and seemed quite content to remain by his side summer, winter, spring, and fall.

In early spring, Severin, king of Savanly, came to visit the court of Farandale. During the feast of welcoming he saw Princess Esme and was much taken by her grace, beauty, and modesty. All during the meal, and the festivities that followed, Severin found his eyes tracing and retracing a path to Esme's sweet face.

Later that night, as he and Alistasair sat alone before the hearth in the great hall, peacefully smoking and watching the yellow flames dance and caper, Severin sighed a long sigh.

"The lot of a king is a lonely one," he said.

Alistasair said nothing, merely nodded and gazed into the fire.

"So many decisions," Severin said. "So many demands."

Again Alistasair was silent.

"It would be easier with a helpmate."

Alistasair raised an eyebrow. "Are you thinking of marrying again? At your age?"

"And why not?" Severin demanded. "My wife has been gone for twelve harvests."

"Have you selected a bride?"

"A lovely girl. Well-connected."

"Well, best of luck, then." Alistasair slapped his palm against the bowl of his pipe and left the ashes on the hearthstones to be swept up in the morning. He stood. "Good night."

"Don't you want to know who she is?"

Alistasair had his mind on his featherbed and had quite forgotten what they had been speaking about.

"Who?"

"The bride I've chosen."

"Of course, of course."

Severin grinned until his sharp nose almost met his chin. "Your daughter, Esme."

"What?" Alistasair was suddenly wide awake. His blue eyes blazed with anger. "Marry Esme? No. No, it's unthinkable. Simply out of the question."

Severin's smile vanished, and his hawklike countenance flushed dark red. "And why is that?"

"She's a mere child."

"Seventeen this year. Girls younger than she have been married and borne children."

"Nevertheless." Alistasair folded his arms on his chest. "Why not choose a young widow? A seasoned woman."

"A widow for a king's wife? Ridiculous. No. I've made my choice, Alistasair."

"And I tell you it's impossible."

Severin was not accustomed to having his desires thwarted, even by another king. He glared at Alistasair, nodded curtly, and hurried from the room.

Alistasair watched him go and a flicker of apprehension warmed his chest. Severin was a dangerous man to cross. But for a brute like that to ask for the hand of his beloved daughter! It was beyond imagining, truly. Alistasair shook his head sadly and went up to bed.

At dawn Alistasair awoke to find that Severin and his party had gone in the night, departed without a word of farewell. It was a bad sign indeed when kings flouted the rules of courtesy.

But it was not Severin who shattered the peace a fortnight later.

A runner burst into the forecourt of the castle at midday, winded, gasping, dripping with sweat.

"The armies of Ebbinsrule and Mulgulch have allied and march on us," he said. "They've crossed the border at the Kinnisfree delta and are headed inland."

"Both armies?" cried the defense minister. "They outnumber us. We'll never stand against them. We must sue for peace or gain help from Savanly."

Alistasair was grim and silent at the news. He knew that help from Savanly would be long in coming; it would not arrive in his lifetime, at the very least.

"We must prepare for siege," he said.

The courtiers looked from one to another in disbelief. But Alistasair's countenance was so baleful that none dared argue. In silence, all withdrew from the court room until only Princess Esme remained.

"Father," she said, "is it truly so bad? Would you deny the young men the right to defend their kingdom?"

Alistasair shook his head. "They would waste their lives in a hopeless effort."

"Then surely King Severin would grant us aid. Why do you hesitate even a moment to contact him?"

"If you knew the reason it would pain your heart."

"What? What are you withholding? Tell me."

"I cannot."

She took his hand gently, and said, "Would you deprive me of the pleasure of helping you to bear the burden of your terrible knowledge? Come, you must share what you know with me. Say it quickly and then it will be easier for you."

Alistasair tried to pull his hand free from her grasp but failed. Ruefully, he stared down at the polished stone floor and knew that he could not spare his child the truth.

"King Severin wishes to marry you."

For a moment Esme said nothing. She seemed stunned. "When did he tell you this?" she asked.

"During his last visit."

"And how did you reply?"

"I refused him, of course."

A tiny smile lit Esme's face. "Is that why you will not go to him now?"

"He would laugh at me or, worse still, join with our enemies."

"Not if I agree to the match."

"Daughter!" Alistasair turned, horrified.

"No, don't argue." Her eyes, blue-green, filled with tears. "I can't be selfish—nor can you—when the good of the kingdom is at stake. If I marry Severin he will always be our ally against the others."

"It seems a huge price to pay, too huge."

"To save Farandale?" She threw her arms around his neck. "Kiss me and tell me you'll agree to the marriage. Hurry, before I change my mind."

Alistasair embraced her and kissed her golden head. "My daughter, you are all I have."

"You will still have me," she whispered. "I promise."

Both of them cried together for a moment. Then the king nodded, and Princess Esme took her leave of him. With a heavy heart, Alistasair called for his messengers and told them to prepare for a journey to Savanly.

Severin accepted Alistasair's offer and immediately dispatched troops. Within days, the superior army of Savanly, joined with Farandale's soldiers, had inflicted great damage upon the invading forces. But much blood was shed and many lives were lost before the enemy had been routed and forced back across the Kinnisfree River into Ebbinsrule.

The wedding of Princess Esme and King Severin took place the following spring just as the trees were sprouting their first gold-green leaves. Songbirds wheeled across the sky, pipers piped, and after dark, fireworks lit the heavens with flashes of silver, red, and gold. All assembled agreed that a finer celebration had not been held in ages—all, that is, save King Alistasair.

He brooded before the ceremony, and after it he wept. No amount of singing, dancing, feasting, or jesting would raise his spirits. Not even the sweet, solemn face of his beloved daughter Esme, glowing in the lamplight as she promenaded on the arm of her new husband, made Alistasair smile.

"That old goat!" Alistasair said to himself. "Smug and grinning as though he's found the bean in the Christmas cake. Look at him, parading like a fool in those bright red stockings. Ridiculous. He has no dignity, no dignity at all."

And, too soon, they were gone. Esme, Severin, and the entire wedding party returned to Savanly, leaving Alistasair in his castle, alone.

He sulked, he sighed, he kept to his rooms or stood in the highest tower, gazing out toward the border between Farandale and Savanly.

"The king should marry again," whispered a palace chambermaid to her lover, a footman.

"He should travel," said the footman to his brother, a guard.

"He should hold a joust and pageant," shouted the guard to his friend, the minstrel.

"Pageant, marriage, or travel," sang the minstrel to the sorcerer. "The king should do something!"

The sorcerer nodded sagely. "I'll go see His Majesty."

Now the sorcerer was an old, old man. He had been the court sorcerer for King Alistasair's father and his father's father, and he remembered the current king's great-grandfather. He was entirely bald but had a white beard reaching down past his knees, which he braided at the ends into two yellowed tails. He wore a long green coat and purple boots, and he carried a staff of polished yew wood in his right hand.

Huffing and wheezing, he climbed the nine winding flights of stairs that led to the top of the tallest tower in the castle. There, in the dim blue twilight, warmed only by a single candle's guttering flame, he saw the king sitting, dejected and alone at the window.

Said the sorcerer to King Alistasair, "Majesty, what ails you? I haven't seen you smile in all the time since Princess Esme's wedding. Surely other men—other kings—have married daughters off and yet found joy in the world."

"Perhaps," the king said. "But those were other kings."

"Come, come," said the sorcerer, as if addressing a naughty schoolboy. He was the only one in the castle who dared speak to the king in that tone. "You were never given to moping before!"

The king merely sighed and turned his head to gaze out at the darkening sky.

"All right, come along and we'll see if we can't do something to bring a smile to your face."

Obediently, almost like a child, King Alistasair stood up and followed the sorcerer back down the stairs and into the palace proper.

Once they were in the sorcerer's low-beamed rooms, Alistasair settled by the westernmost window, tapping the toe of his boot absently against the tiles of the windowseat.

The mage frowned and, beckoning to him, said, "What would you, sir? You must find your heart and center once more. Mooning about won't do it. Brace up."

A white dove soared past the window, circled, and came to land upon the sill.

"Ah, if only I had the wings of a bird," Alistasair said. "Then might I see my Esme whenever I wished."

"You wish to fly?" the mage asked.

"It's an old man's fantasy."

"Well, you *are* a bit along in years to try it."

Alistasair sat up quickly. "Do you mean to tell me you can help me? You can make me fly?"

"I didn't say I could. But I didn't say I couldn't. I won't promise miracles, Majesty. But perhaps we could give it a try."

Alistasair smiled for the first time in weeks. Color came back to his pale cheeks and his eyes sparkled. "By all means then, wizard, let us try."

The sorcerer dug around in an old trunk until he found what he was looking for: a stained hide sack of full of herbs and leaves. He tipped a handful of the mixture into a stone brazier and watched in grim satisfaction as a fragrant blue cloud boiled up and began to fill the room.

"Breathe deeply, oh, king. This is the first step."

Alistasair did as he was told. The smoke was vaguely peppery but not unpleasant.

"Now stand upon that green stone next to the hearth and say not a word."

Of a sudden the mage was blazing with white light, burning with a brightness difficult to behold. He pointed a finger at Alistasair, and the king felt as if he were being lit from within, sizzling with strange humors, as the mage intoned:

Fire, water, wind, and earth,
Leave behind the land of birth,
Go, unfettered, through the sky,
See as from a falcon's eye.

The sorcerer repeated the incantation several times, and Alistasair found himself joining him. After the fifth repetition, the mage held up his hand, and silence reigned. The faerie light that glowed within him faded, faded and was gone.

"When will I be able to fly?" Alistasair demanded.

"Not today, and not tomorrow," the sorcerer replied. "But soon, perhaps. It takes practice."

True to the old man's words, it was a week before the king could levitate himself even an inch above the green flagstones by the hearth. Two more weeks' effort and he could bound from one side of the court room to the other, his purple robes flapping like wings. He scampered up the tapestries of the feasting hall and swung across the banners that lined the ceiling. In spirit and even in appearance he seemed restored to youth, a young man again.

"Great fun," he hooted, and gamboled through the air. "Come, wizard, join me."

The mage frowned. "This is not a game for grown men," he said. "Nor for kings, save for foolish old ones who order it. A waste of good magic, and for what gain? A king's good humor."

"Fah! You're dry and old," Alistasair retorted. "Magic is wasted upon you."

"Is that so?" the mage said. "I half wish I had never taught you these spells."

"I feel young again! I could fly to the far shores of Savanly and back!"

"Better you should keep your boot heels on the ground and seek the company of old men."

For answer, Alistasair spun twice through the air over the wizard's head, laughing uproariously.

The mage sighed, defeated. "Majesty, shall we take up today's lesson?"

"But what is today's spell?"

"That of shape changing."

"And why must I learn that?"

"Surely you don't mean to go flying across the kingdom as you are," the mage said. "Imagine the people's reaction to seeing their king in the sky, flapping about in his fine robes like some great royal goose. No, no, it just won't do. It's one thing to sail across the ceiling of the grand court room where only I can see you. But quite another to go out, among your subjects, and do it. They won't like it. Not one bit."

"I see what you mean." Alistasair landed with a thud, out of breath. He sat heavily upon a mahogany bench and gestured for a cup of mead.

After he had finished it, he nodded to the mage.

The sorcerer held his staff in both hands above his head and chanted:

> By the ancient blood you carry,
> By the scores of years which shaped ye,
> Come undone from human kind,
> Be whatever you would be.
> Nothing here shall keep you tethered,
> All bonds, all ties, are now shattered
> Roam by sea or sky or meadow
> Go now as you wish to be.

King Alistasair felt dizzy. The room spun around him, the very stones seemed to dance in the walls. When his vision cleared he was no longer a man but rather a gray-tufted, black-beaked hawk. No one but a wizard would have noticed that the gleam in the hawk's yellow eyes was quite human.

Before the wizard could stop him, King Alistasair, wings and all, had hopped up to the windowsill and flown straight out into the blue sky in the direction of Savanly.

"Wait!" the mage cried. "Come back, sire. You're not ready." But his voice ebbed, fading on the breeze.

The castle and its grounds shrank to dollhouse size behind the transformed king. Soon Alistasair was soaring above open fields. In fascination he gazed down on the mite-sized humans that were urging doll-sized oxen to drag plows over the brown earth, cutting fresh ruts. The roads that lined the fields were gray ribbons left behind by some giantess. Townships became children's toy blocks; even church steeples were mere toothpicks below him.

With each stroke of his powerful wings he was that much closer to Savanly and his daughter, Esme. And, so thinking, Alistasair put every ounce of his energy into making the court of Savanly before nightfall.

When Alistasair arrived at Severin's castle he was cold, sore, bone-weary, and ravenous. His hawk body, being illusion, could take no nourishment, but he dared not revert to his true form in order to go grubbing about the kitchen. Imagine, he thought, the look on the cook's face as the king of Farandale came among the pots and cauldrons hoping to cadge some crusts of bread.

He rested on the highest rim of the castle's battlement and gazed down at the town twinkling golden lights in the gathering dusk. On the level just below him the guards were changing their watch, calling challenges, exchanging passwords, nodding and passing.

Alistasair was too tired to remain perched on the cold stone. He glided down to the nearest arched doorway and said the words which unmade the spell. Immediately the hawk vanished, and a weary old king sprawled, inelegantly, on the flagstones.

He got slowly to his feet, thinking, I must rest and eat. But his feet became tangled in something and he nearly fell before he caught his balance. He had stumbled across an old rag which someone had left in the passageway. It was a tattered homespun cloak: perhaps a forgetful guard had misplaced it. Alistasair whispered a blessing upon whoever had left it and wrapped the homely thing about his head and shoulders.

"You there! Old man!"

A guardsman had come upon him unawares. Hastily

Alistasair improvised, hiding his face in the cloak and holding out his palm. "Alms, kind sir. Food or drink, I beseech thee."

The guardsman looked more puzzled than put out. "What are you doing up here, old beggar? You belong in the kitchen. Go on down there and see Marsie. She'll give you some scraps."

"Much obliged. Thank ye, sir." Nodding, keeping his face out of the torchlight, Alistasair ducked down the passage that the guard had indicated. It led to a narrow, spiraling staircase carved into stone wedges barely large enough to hold a grown man's foot.

When he emerged several floors down, he was quite dizzy. After a moment his head cleared. He heard voices raised in revelry and the sound of cutlery, of food and drink being consumed. Peering around a corner, King Alistasair spied a feasting hall whose grand table was lined with nobility in fine silks and embroidered robes.

At the far end of the table were two tall golden thrones festooned with carmine tapestries. In one sat King Severin. In the other was Esme, a jeweled crown upon her yellow hair.

Alistasair's heart rose up into his throat. He opened his mouth to hail his daughter but closed it again. Silly old man, he thought. Would you create a scene? Stay hidden, unobserved. You may watch but make not a sound.

He found the shelter of a curtain from which he could peep out at his daughter. She looked pale, her face seemed thin, and she ate with quick, nervous motions. Occasionally, the king would address a comment to her, and she would respond with grave courtesy. Never once did she smile.

I knew it, Alistasair thought. She is pining, unhappy. I should never have sold her freedom, not even to secure the safety of Farandale. Tears filled his eyes as he watched his daughter.

He strained his ears to listen to the fine folks' chatter. From what he overheard he learned that the feast was in honor of a party of ambassadors from a distant land across the sea.

The leader of the foreign party was called Gareth, a tall man, broad-shouldered and dark-haired. When he smiled, the firelight flashed upon his white teeth. His dark eyes sought out Queen Esme, and only to his comments did she respond with a smile.

As the dinner ended, King Severin suggested that the group repair to a smaller room for musical entertainment.

Ambassador Gareth hurried to offer his arm to Esme. The look that passed between them was quick but unmistakable. Alistasair had once looked upon his own wife in a similar manner. Strangely, King Severin seemed unaware of the silent communication taking place between Esme and the handsome stranger. Alistasair felt his chest contract with fear for his daughter.

He wanted to follow the party but could not find a way to do so without drawing attention. What's more, he saw that the table was unattended. His stomach, long-neglected, growled repeatedly. So he waited until the sound of footsteps diminished and the hall was quiet save for the snap of the fire in the hearth. Feeling like a beggar, he scurried out of his hiding place; and grabbed a heel of bread and some scraps of meat. He was tempted to take more, but the sound of servants' voices made him rush back to his hiding place.

Once he had eaten, he grew sleepy and made a bed for himself out of the cloak he had found. Lucky for him, no servants neared his hiding place; if they had, they would have wondered how and why a drapery could come to be snoring fitfully.

Alistasair awoke before dawn with a start. Where was he? Why was he curled on his side behind a velvet curtain? His mind cleared and, in wonder, he recalled the events of the previous day.

He peered out and saw that the hall was dark and quiet, lit only by a small torch which guttered in its sconce. It was too early for anyone to be about. Alistasair stood up and stretched. His old bones were stiff after a night spent on the cold stone floor. Perhaps a quick flight would loosen him up a bit.

Whispering feverishly, he worked the charms which the wizard had taught him. The king disappeared, and where he had stood moments before now perched a gray-winged hawk. He leaped to the window, and from there he sprang out into the misty purple sky.

Below him lights flickered, here and there, like lightning bugs, marking a farmer or merchant beginning his day. Alistasair swooped low over a group of homesteads and caught an updraft which flung him up and out, past the shoreline and over open water.

The bay of Savanly was smooth as green glass in the early light. One great ship, three-masted and dark, rode the swells at anchor. Its flag was unfamiliar to Alistasair, and he flew closer to get a better look.

There were a few men on deck, setting riggings, keeping watch. One of them looked familiar. Alistasair peered at him uncertainly. Yes, it was the tall and handsome ambassador, Gareth, who had smiled upon his daughter.

"I don't think we should risk it," said the ambassador, shaking his head.

"Gareth, you know what we do here."

"Yes, but that was before I saw *her.*"

Alistasair didn't require telepathy: he knew of whom the man named Gareth spoke.

"Don't be a fool. The invasion has been planned for months. We've tested his mettle: the king is old and easy. The army is strong, but we'll win in the end. All that's left is for us to give the word."

"Not if she'll be hurt."

"Are you mad? Disrupt our plans over a woman?"

Gareth grabbed his companion by the breastplate. "Not just any woman. She's the finest thing I've seen in this or any land. I would kill a legion for her. And if I can't protect her, then I say to our fleet and to our plans: be damned."

"But—"

"I will have her for my wife."

"Yes, Prince."

Alistasair's head swam with new and unwelcome information. An invasion fleet led by this Gareth, who, it seemed, was a foreign princeling!

Spreading his wings, Alistasair took to the air once more. But he had lost his bearings, and rather than flying inland he flew far out over open sea until he seemed the only solid thing in existence, one single speck of man-bird above the eternal ocean. Just as he began to tire, he spied a ship—no, a fleet of ships—dark, mysterious, and all bearing the same flag as Gareth's ship, sitting motion-less in the water. Ranks of men stood at attention on the decks of each ship. They wore full battle armor.

Without meaning to, he had found the invading fleet. But what to do? Go back, back to Severin's palace, he thought. Warn Esme to flee.

He wheeled in the brightening sky and desperately made for land. By the time he saw the castle, it was high morning and the sun was climbing behind him.

Winded, his wings aching, Alistasair circled the castle, over the battlements and courtyards, peering in this win-dow and that until he found the queen's bedchamber.

He perched in her window, wondering whether he should unmake the spell of changing and unceremoni-ously tumble onto the rushes by his daughter's hearth.

But whispered voices made him sit upright rather than sag. He listened closely and heard his daughter's own sweet voice, saying, "No, no. I can't. Please, he must understand—"

Again the whispering, and then Esme sighed. "All right," she said. "All right. Tell him yes. Yes, I'll come to him."

She moved into view. There was a look of hope on her face so vivid that it nearly broke Alistasair's heart. Bright spots of color flared in Esme's pale cheeks, and her mouth curved in a full and willing smile. It was the face of a woman in love. Alistasair stared for a moment: he had never seen her this way. And he knew suddenly that he dared not reveal himself to her or warn her: he must remain a spectator in whatever was to come.

In the days that followed, Alistasair grew skilled at snatching bits of food and catnaps when he could. He favored the roofs of churches and towers of castles, any high place with shadows in which he could hide. He grew leaner and harder through his daily exertion. And what he saw left him chastened and changed.

He saw his daughter steal from her husband's castle to meet her lover on his dark ship, heard her exchange vows of devotion with him and even promise to help him in his treacherous quest.

Woe, he thought. Woe to see this. To witness my own child committing treason, turning upon her lawful husband and welcoming the enemy to the very gates of her castle. Woe to the people of Savanly, to all of King Severin's subjects. Most of all, woe to him who foolishly took my only child in payment for the safety of my land. Woe to Severin.

I must warn him. Though it doom my beloved child to death, exile, or a loveless marriage and a lifetime of misery, I cannot stand by and watch her betray her husband. After all, he is a king like myself. I have no love for him. But I owe him warning.

How she will hate me for what I do. And how I will despise myself. Oh, how I wish I had never come here! No matter which way I turn, all paths lead to hard and bitter choices.

Alistasair wept long and hard. Many a man would have been astounded by the sight of a mighty hawk weeping as it wheeled through the sky.

He waited until the king was alone in a private garden. Gliding silently down, Alistasair lit upon the dewy grass and quickly whispered the spell of unmaking.

"Ho, Severin!"

His son-in-law spun about, hand upon his sword. "What? Alistasair, here? How did you come? Why were you not announced? I'll wring the neck of that page!"

"Peace, brother. Please, I traveled alone and thought to announce myself."

"Alone? On the long road from Farandale to Savanly? Are you mad?"

"Not quite yet," Alistasair said. "But I have hard news. Is there somewhere we can speak in private?"

"Right here and now. Tell me what you know."

So Alistasair told Severin of the plot against him and his kingdom. Severin said not a word until he had finished.

"But how did you learn this?" he demanded.

"I cannot tell you."

"It's impossible. Esme turned against me? She, who cries when flowers die, plotting my end?" Severin laughed harshly. "I'd say your mind has been wandering, Alistasair. You came all this way for nothing."

"But—"

"Why are you so eager to sow discord between my wife and me?" Severin scowled and reached once more for his sword, checking his gesture at the last moment.

"Old fool! I know you've never approved of our marriage, but married we are, and married we'll stay, despite your laughable attempts to part us. If not for your daughter, I would have you thrown out right now. But you may stay the night, provided you don't try to see Esme. You would only upset her. Go, now, while my temper is still under control."

Silent and astonished, Alistasair bowed slightly and hurried out of the garden.

That very night, Alistasair watched grimly as the invasion forces made landfall before dawn. High in the air, safely in hawk form, he looked down upon the rows of soldiers, fifteen abreast, heavily armed, who marched upon the king's castle, swarming like ants over the countryside.

As he watched, the soldiers kicked in the door to the royal bedchamber. Severin was pulled roughly from his own bed, dragged into a courtyard, and run through with a sword.

At that terrible sight Alistasair could bear no more. Crying "Enough! Oh, woe, woe," he turned and sped, with heart breaking, for home.

The sorcerer smiled with open relief when Alistasair lit upon the worn and ragged rug by his workbench and bird became man once more.

"So, Majesty, you have been gone for some time. To Savanly?"

Alistasair nodded.

"What news?"

"Much, and none of it good."

"So?"

"I would rest a while," Alistasair said. "And then I would have you read the cards for me, mage."

"Your fortune, my liege?"

"No. That of my daughter."

Without another word the sorcerer went away to summon food. When King Alistasair had eaten and rested and eaten once again, he returned with his tarot and cast Esme's fortune. As he set down the cards, the mage clicked his tongue in surprise.

"Tch. Severin—and Savanly—have fallen. I see a prince who will be a king now, and a princess who has been queen and will be queen yet again.

"Gareth and Esme will rule together, and with time their kingdom will spread beyond the borders of Savanly. Upon your death, Liege, Farandale, and Savanly will be ruled jointly by Esme and her king.

"Shortly will they come to you making gifts and talking of treaties. Your daughter will be no stranger here."

The sorcerer heard an odd sound and looked up from the cards to see the king weeping.

"But this news should please you! Why do you weep?"

"My daughter will ever be stranger to me now! I have seen a side of her that no father should ever spy in his daughter."

"Yet you love her none the less."

"Still, I would have her back here with me, a little girl again, and innocent."

The sorcerer made a sound that might have indicated sympathy or impatience, gathered up his cards, and let the king cry until he had no tears left.

Presently, the mage saw that the king had arisen and was idly pacing the room.

"What is it, Majesty? What else do you wish? To fly once more? To become a fish and swim the ocean deep?"

"No, no," Alistasair said. He paused, looking both disgusted and weary. "I'm done with all that."

The sorcerer nodded. "I see."

"You were right, old wizard. Flying is not a game for kings to play."

The sorcerer said nothing.

"Why didn't you tell me, warn me, that we must relinquish the most cherished of our possessions, our illusions, even our children?"

"I tried, my lord. But life—with a bit of magic thrown in—is sometimes a better instructor."

Alistasair sat down hard upon the mage's wooden bench. He laughed with strange and silent mirth, his shoulders shaking. Then he sighed.

The mage leaned forward. "And now, sire? What's your pleasure? What shall it be?"

The king of Farandale looked once out the window and then met the wizard's gaze. "A game of whist," he said. "A cup of mead. And the company of old men." And he smiled a sad, knowing smile.

The Kiss

Alan Dean Foster

Crisp, small memories of autumn, a few leaves clung to the naked branches of the trees, dry and brown as stale oats. Whiteness blanketed the park, silent snow dancing in tiny pinwheels across the shoveled walkways like tenebrous toys exhaled from some spectral workshop. Tapered icicles parasitized the bright, hard metal of a water fountain, bearding chrome. Over everything the first week of January lay, pregnant with chill.

Jenny blinked away the snowflakes that swirled about her like stoned white mosquitoes as she sighted a path through the open places, taking the shortcut home from work and disdaining the bus stop immediately outside the office. The short walk would allow her to avoid a connection in a less congenial section of town. After eight hours in the limpid atmosphere of the sterile cavern in which she worked, the air outside rejuvenated her lungs as well as her legs.

This morning the weather pundits proclaimed the storm arrived, but it had taunted them by stalling just outside the metroplex, teasing the inner city with gusts and cold laughter. Just for me, she thought. Just to save me fifteen minutes I don't have to spend now waiting in a bus shelter rank with the scent of slept-upon newspapers and clotted urine. Grateful for the respite, she lengthened her stride, not wanting to miss the crosstown. Bucking the wind, trifles of ice as beautiful as they were capricious tickled her exposed cheeks, only to be turned to simulacra of tears as they were instantly metamorphosed by the bundled furnace of her body.

A little louder the squall sang, urgently warning. She shielded her eyes as she searched for the bridge that spanned the central pond, blinking against the rising blizzard. There it was—a russet arch of brick and mortar spanning the gray water, solid and familiar. Careful there on the tricky rise, lest she slip in her slick black boots, the tops feathered with damp fake fur.

She had only just started across when she heard the soft croaking.

Why she paused she never knew, but pause she did, to shove snow from the railing with a gloved hand as she turned to peer over the side. Nothing to be seen below but liquid as hard and gray as old slate shingles. Frowning, she started to turn, to go, when it sounded again.

Hesitating, despite nothing near save snow and trees stark as tombstones, like brown lightning rammed into the earth. Uncertainly she retraced her steps from bridge to pond's edge, her boots leaving behind in the snow deep, oval echoes of her passing.

A small shape crouched on an exposed ribbed slab of weathered granite that protruded out into the slushy surface. She bent, then crouched.

"Why you poor thing, what are you doing out this time of year? You're shivering!"

Ordinarily she would have walked on, would have ignored the small, insignificant blob of drab flesh. The sticky, moist mass, resembling a sock soaked in cold phlegm, repulsed her. But she had on gloves thick with plastic and fleece, fashionable artificial skins that would keep her fingers inviolate. She plucked the baseball-size creature from its perch and cradled it in one palm, sheltering it from the wind with the other.

Bulbous eyes visceral with anger rose to meet her own and so startled her that she almost dropped it. After that, the voice was almost anticlimactic.

"I am a prince, real and true. If you will but kiss me, I will whole again become."

Snow crowded her cheeks, seeking crevices to chill within her layers of clothings, pinking her cheeks and nose. She looked around, was still alone. Twilight served notice on the approaching storm. Or perhaps not quite alone.

Ridiculous, she told herself. Ridiculous and absurd!

Within her cupped, sheltering fingers the amphibious lump lurched clumsily forward. "A single kiss and you will see the reality that is me."

Kiss that blob of mucusy flesh? Press her own sensitive lips against that thin, blubbery slit? Still, her lipstick was on heavy, a wind prophylactic applied prior to leaving the office. What better time and place than here and now, isolated and unobserved, to indulge just once in a brief, lunatic folly?

Suppressing the rationality which normally mapped her waking hours, she inclined impulsively forward and touched the flabby face, withdrawing almost immediately and wrinkling her mouth. Enough of a witless winter's dream! If she didn't hurry she was going to miss her bus. Not ungently, she returned the creature to its rock and turned to leave.

In the center of the bridge, at the apex of its arch, a twinkling made her turn, tempest glow silhouetting a presence that was now where a moment before had been nothing. Flakes of black silver, tarnished by time and circumstance, shaped a massive bulk behind her. It had arms and legs and it moved with purpose in her direction, clad in thick coat and pants, heavy shoes laced with dead snakes and a wide-brimmed hat that shadowed the face.

Her mouth opened when she saw the knife, long and lean as its master. Edge keener than her deepest fears, blade brighter than the luminant snow, which fell anxiously now, as if embarrassed at its delay, it rose toward her like a live, twisting, animate being. A coldness that was not of isobars and pressure fronts congealed within her gut, a ball of frozen jelly heavy as hopelessness.

Thick and gnarled and powerful, his hands were upon her, freezing her as effectively as if she'd been overrun by a glacier. The knife described a Gothic arc and blood bright as pomegranate juice shocked the pristine snowbank in which they stood locked in unholy embrace. She blinked and expelled a querulous trauma.

"*Why?*"

His gaze and expression were as one, as cold-clammy and pigmentless as the queasy flesh of a cave salamander wrenched up suddenly from the abyss and left to shrivel in the sun.

"*Never kiss a dark frog. . . .*"

Later, when he was done and fresh snow tenderly went about blotting up the crimson bloom, he abandoned the park and headed deeper into the city, knowing there would be other princesses. Real and true.

Divine Right

Nancy Holder

Dressed in his finest battle armor of mail and plate, Alfonso reeled out of the room that reeked of agony and defeat. Tears and incense choked him, and as he fought for control, the chanting of the black-robed friars who lined the walls of his Moorish castle filled his brain to bursting. He panted, hard, forcing back his grief. Louder the chanting swelled, sobs mingling with it, and Alfonso was humiliated and enraged. He roared down the torchlit horseshoe arches of orange and blue mosaic; he shouted his fury; and courtiers, having hastily donned their most somber houppelandes and robes, fell to their knees, heads bowed. All Castile knew of his despair, and of the failure of his line. There was to be—finally, certainly—no heir.

His only child, his daughter, was dead, gone to join her mother, the lovely Portuguese, and her English husband, King Eduardo, who had perished from a fall in London scant weeks before. Holy Santa Maria, his loves, his beautiful ones. His *amorcitas.* Alfonso was cursed. He and his fathers, and his fathers' fathers—they would all be forgotten. It would be as if they had never been.

The courtiers dropped to their knees, the men sweeping hats to their chests, the women pressing the edges of their linen veils to their lips as they wept. With their horned headdresses, they looked like devils, and his mind saw them for a moment as evil witches who had put spells on Beatriz out of jealousy of her beauty and piety and extinguished the life in her womb; warlocks who wished to see the line of Castile's greatest heroes die out, after all he and his fathers had fought and died for—to wrest Castile from the heathen Moors, and to husband and protect the kingdom as lord and master.

He slammed through the palace, through archways of mosaic and corridors of stone lace, and strode into the large, dark chapel. A huge fresco of the Holy Son of God gazed sadly on him with wide brown eyes. Two monks knelt at the chancel rail; clearly shocked by the sight of the king, they rose and scurried away like little black terriers.

"Father! Father!" Alfonso shouted. "Come and confess me, for I mean to do violence this day! There are witches, and devils, and all shall die. This I—"

"My lord king." Alfonso's Dominican confessor, Father Fernando, glided like an angel from the shadows in his white habit and black hood. "In time we will learn God's will in all of this," he said, lifting a hand in benediction. "But not today. Today we must pray for the soul of your dear child, and of her unborn child."

Alfonso roared. "Pray to God? Why has He tormented me so, unless it be to spur me to action? I have been too lenient; I have been weak. It is the Jews—"

"Please, sire. That is as may be." The priest lowered his hand as the king sank to his knees. "Please, for pity of her who loved you, today let your mind rest on salvation."

Alfonso folded his hands, but his heart seethed with rage. He did not pray. He could no longer even think. After a time, the priest said softly, "Would you like to confess what is in your heart, my king, and savor the comfort of the Eucharist?"

Alfonso shook his head. "Later," he growled at the man, as if he were a lackey.

Unoffended, Father Fernando said, "Then bless you, my son," drew the sign of the cross over Alfonso, and withdrew.

Alone in the chapel with its smoky incense and the

flickering lights on the faces of the saints, Alfonso of Castile wept. He was too old to get children on another wife. His daughter had been his last hope for his proud line. His name would die out, to be spoken of only by cloistered scholars and in requiem masses.

Sobbing bitterly, he pulled out his sword and held it hilt upward, like a cross. In the distance, he heard the death chant for his daughter and grandchild. They would want to lay her out here in the chapel, under the protection of God and all the Saints—whose protection she no longer required, for surely a rose such as she was in heaven already. He stood, and dared to walk around the elaborate gilt rood screen to the high altar. Beneath the face of the Holy Christ and a huge crucifix carried all the way from Jerusalem sat the golden reliquary that contained the thigh bone of San Francisco de Sales, who had long honored and protected Alfonso's family.

"I shall not die without a successor," he whispered. An oath spoken over the bones of a saint bound one's soul for eternity. "In the name of Saint Francis, I shall not have lived and reigned in vain." He closed his eyes, thinking of the turmoil and suffering that would erupt if he were to die without naming him who would come to power next. The blood and death of civil war would not hang upon his head. That would not be his legacy.

But whom could he choose? He had no one he trusted. With no living children, he had no sons-in-law. Without brothers and sisters, he had no nephews. Nor did he have dukes or barons he could count upon. He had always been an island in the river of treachery around him, and he had known it.

He sheathed his sword and looked up at the sad face. Everyone he loved was dead. All that was left to him was his kingdom, yet he loved Castile with the fervor due Blessed Mother Church Herself.

"I swear again," he murmured, closing his eyes and laying his sword tip on the box. "*Santa Maria, Madre de Dios,* protect me this night, and I shall proclaim my heir by the dawn of the morrow."

He lifted his head and opened his eyes, filled with a holy purpose. "I will know him by a sign." He paused, as a lightness flooded into him, uplifting him in his sorrow. And he knew what he would do. "Whoever enters the castle gates in the last moment of this night shall be my heir. This I swear, Most Holy Mother."

The sad eyes seemed to brighten, and a small measure of peace entered his breast. In thanks, he sank to his knees and folded his hands.

And heard the retreating sound of footsteps across the chapel threshold. He looked up and saw no one.

"Stop!" he shouted, but the runner was gone. Rising, he flew to the door. A guard stood just outside, dressed as he, in heavy armor. He wore a helm with no visor, and his dark Castilian brows raised as Alfonso cried, "Who left this place just now?"

"A nun, my lord," the guard said.

"Nun?" Alfonso glowered at him. "Which nun?"

The guard gestured helplessly. "One looks the same as another, sire."

Alfonso exhaled heavily. "Which way did she go?" The guard pointed to the left. "Follow her!"

He clapped his hands, and the guard on the right hand of the chapel entrance bowed from the waist and saluted him. *"Sí, mi rey?"*

"Gather your men and go to the convent. Tell the Mother Superior we are coming to question the sisters. Hurry."

Watching the two men hurry away, each to his task, Alfonso frowned. That someone had heard of his plan altered everything; where he had sought divine intervention, now the court would begin the maneuvering and treachery he had sought to avoid. It would be disaster if the nun told what she had heard, and it would be safest to assume she would. But he could not forswear himself. He had pledged on holy relics, and there was no way to undo what he had done.

Another guard appeared, rushing smartly toward him. It was ever thus, for the person of the king was never without protection. His hand was at his sword. "Your Majesty, may I be of service?"

Alfonso nodded. This man was young but very tall and broad-shouldered. He had eyes the color of the sky and very strong features. He carried himself well; there was an elegance about him that spoke of bloodlines higher than his station. "Stay by us. Call fifty men to guard us. We are to be surrounded at all times this night."

The young man looked confused. "But it is ever thus, my lord."

"Tonight is different," Alfonso told him somberly. "Do as we say, and we shall raise you up."

The guard bowed low. "Sire, your wish is ever my edict."

And Alfonso thought, *I could do worse than this one. Truly, he has the bearing of a king.* "Do you walk with us, young man," he said. "What is your name?"

"Ricardo, sire," the man answered. His voice, while courteous, was not servile. He served his master, but he also thought well of himself.

El Rey Ricardo, Alfonso mused, and began to pull off his right gauntlet. "Tell us of yourself. Tell us everything, and spare nothing, for we have many hours together tonight, and we will know who keeps our kingdom safe."

"Yes, my lord," replied the man, obviously dumbstruck, but maintaining his composure nonetheless.

Alfonso was pleased. "We are due at the convent."

The hours dragged past. The fires guttered; smoke filled the halls of the beautiful Moorish palace, rolling along the floors like sea fog. The castle grew quiet, and quieter still, the chants for Alfonso's daughter distant and ghostly; Alfonso more and more apprehensive. No nun had come forward and confessed she had been in the chapel, though all had wept at the news of the Princesa's death. She had been their patroness and favored them with many gifts of gold and food. No gossip spread about the king's vow—at least, none that reached the king's ears. Alfonso possessed many sets of ears all over his castle, his kingdom, in foreign lands. But no one talked, he was informed, of anything unusual—merely the same plots to grab power among the nobles, to cuckold another man, to usurp the lands of another.

Ricardo and the guards accompanied him everywhere that night, though Alfonso kept the one named Ricardo closest by him. Ricardo would not eat when the king would not, and would not drink when the king would not, and at length Alfonso told him, "Go in a little while outside the castle walls, and when you hear the crier begin to call the end of night, walk inside at the last." Alfonso touched Ricardo's arm. "Though this seems a whim of an old man, do it, and you shall be glad."

Ricardo saluted Alfonso and said, "I shall obey, sir."

Alfonso, wondering if he was doing the correct thing, and having no idea if heaven would condone his intervention, patted the youth on the shoulder and said, "Good lad."

They walked, and Alfonso wished for a cloak; it grew very cold. At length he said, "It grows late, young Ricardo. Get you outside the castle, as we told you, and if any try to stop you, show them this ring." He took from his hand the ring he had given the queen on their wedding day. "It is well known."

"My lord—" Ricardo demurred, his eyes widening as the king dropped it into his palm.

"We shall be in the chapel. We shall await you there." He raised a hand. "God be with you, Ricardo, for you are serving His holy duty tonight."

Ricardo, his bright young face blank with bewilderment, sank to one knee and murmured, "It is enough that I serve you, my king."

"Don't blaspheme," Alfonso said approvingly, and waved for the man to leave him. Then he said to the guards, "Take us to the chapel," and slowly they all massed around him like a Roman phalanx. He felt vulnerable, and old, yet hopeful.

And terrified.

He blessed himself with holy water from the font. His

monks knelt in dark black rows, hooded heads bowed as
they prayed for his beautiful daughter. His heart caught as
he saw her lying on her bier in her robes of state before
the altar, her hands clasped over her breast filled with
roses. He came to her, and knelt, and touched her blood-
less lips. Recoiled. She was so cold. Her beautiful black
hair was gathered around her shoulders; she wore her
gold wedding gown and her English crown. Alfonso held
back a sob and crossed himself. One night would she pass
here, and then she would be consigned to the earth. The
thought was ashes in his mouth.

He turned on his knee to the monks and the guards.
The monks sang mournfully; some of the guards began to
kneel, while others made a wall between him and the rest
of the chapel.

"Sirrah, fetch our confessor," he said to the nearest
man, a rough, Moorish-looking youth with a short beard.
"And you, get you to the watch. Observe who comes late
into the palace, and latest of all; and if it is not your fellow, Ricardo, inform whoever it is that he must come at
once to the chapel." There, the king would swear before
man and the Church that this man would be his successor.
But of course, no one knew of this, save for the nun—or
witch, or spy—who had still not been found.

The men left; and with his other men around him, and
the singing monks, Alfonso walked behind the screen
again and knelt facing them all, his hands on the holy
relic box. The guards stood awkwardly, clearly wishing
likewise to kneel, one coughing into his fist now and
then. Swords clanked against surcoats and vambraces.
Leather squeaked.

In silence they waited. His daughter slept.

Father Fernando came, roused from sleep with the
smell of wine on his breath. Alfonso almost found it
within himself to smile. He said, "Good even, Padre.
Tarry here with me, for I shall have need of you tonight."
He should get the bishop, but that one he did not trust.

"In what office, my good king?" the priest asked solicitously. He glanced at the body of the princess and made the sign of the cross over her.

"In your holy office. I beg you, pray for me." And the two men knelt once again, beside the dead girl.

"For your soul, my son?"

Alfonso swallowed. "How often do you pray for my father?"

"You have paid for masses, my lord," his confessor reminded him.

"And for my grandfather?"

"Your father paid for those."

Alfonso closed his eyes. The priest regarded him. "My son, God never forgets us."

Alfonso fell silent. He almost said, *That is not enough for my house and for me.* But he kept his silence.

Time passed. Alfonso asked softly, "What is the hour?"

"The evening is nearly done, sir," his confessor answered.

Alfonso said to one of the guards, "Take ten of your fellows and watch the castle doors. Make sure that no harm comes to anyone who crosses our threshold, and take note who it is who comes into our house at the calling of the night."

"Aye, sire," the guard replied, and did as he was asked.

Alfonso said, "All the rest in this place, leave us. Wait outside until we call you." He touched the priest's sleeve. "Save you, Father. I beg you to hear my confession."

Father Fernando looked concerned. He said, "As you wish, my liege."

The monks abruptly stopped singing and filed out of the chapel. Noisily, the guards followed them, and the two men were alone. Alfonso sank to his knees. "I have made a vow to Christ and Our Lady, and soon it will be kept. For that, I must bear the sin of pride. I believe that witches and Jews killed my child. For that, I carry deep hatred in my heart. I have slept with no woman since the death of my wife. I have not eaten to excess. But surely I am a wicked man, for God has driven me to desperate measures to ensure the safety of my realm."

The priest said nothing. A silence grew between them. Finally he murmured, "And what measures are those, my son?"

"Soon you will know. But bless me now, and excuse me, for I can say nothing of it until it is done."

"Do you confess that pride and hatred are sins you must strive to dispense with?"

In Alfonso's heart he answered, *Not in this case.* With his lips, he replied, "Sí, Padre."

"Then I absolve you, my son, in the name of the Father, and the Son, and the Holy Spirit."

Alfonso exhaled slowly. He kissed the priest's hand and got to his feet. "I'm so tired."

"It is late, my son." Father Fernando gestured to the painted wooden statue of the Holy Virgin. Her arms were outspread as if to embrace and comfort all the souls in the world. "Have you lit a candle in honor of your vow?"

"No." Alfonso moved to the banks of candles and lit a stick with the flame from the nearest one. He heard the flare, smelled the wax, and he touched the wick of an unlit candle near his elbow. The glow made a tight fist of his heart. "Beatriz," he whispered, "as long as I live, I shall never forget you."

"She rests with the angels, King Alfonso."

"Who sing her praises eternally."

"Indeed, my son."

"Ay," Alfonso moaned, and crossed himself. He spoke more brightly. "I met an amazing young man today, Father. His name is Ricardo. He's in my guard. Do you know him?"

Father Fernando made a gesture with his hands. "There are many named Ricardo in your guard, *mi señor.*"

"Ah, but this one. This one is different. He's a torch among candles." He gestured at the flames. "I'm sure his heart is on fire. He could be a lion for Castile."

"Then he will prosper in this life, and perhaps in the next," the priest said, clearly striving to discern what the king was about. He hesitated. "I sense you wish to be alone, my son."

"Perhaps for a few moments. With God."

Father Fernando rose. He bowed. "I have confessed you since you were a boy, my lord. None love you as I."

"Then perhaps it should be you," Alfonso murmured, but knew that could not be so. Kings and priests must keep to their own places.

"My lord?" Father Fernando queried.

"Idle chatter. Idle fancy," Alfonso said. "Go with God, Father."

"Be with God, my son." Again the priest made the sign of the cross over the king. "Your ancestors delivered this land from the heathen Moors. God smiles always on your house."

"Then why has God ended it?" Alfonso blurted.

"God may have a plan."

"We both do."

The priest paused, as if waiting for Alfonso to explain. When the king did not, the man sighed and walked the long way out of the cold, dark chapel.

Alfonso waited alone beside the bier of his child. He heard the crier. " 'Tis the witching hour! Bless all who are in their beds." He crossed himself. The time had come. *Let it be Ricardo,* he thought, *or one even better. Let it be a lion for all Castile, who would rule in my name.* And he realized how foolish his vow had been, unless one trusted in God.

He waited. And grew tense, for no one came.

At length he stood and whispered to Beatriz, "Pray for me, princess of the angels." He could see his breath as he moved and paced. The linked plates of his sabatons rang on the hard stone like the strokes of midnight. His heart beat in time.

He heard someone rush into the chapel, and murmured, "Blessed Mother."

In the cold night, a figure in plate and mail staggered toward him. It was the young Ricardo. Blood gushed from his face, his hands, his neck. His skin was mottled; pustules rose, formed, burst, and gushed pus down his face. The youth's blood ran onto his armor and steamed in the frigid air.

Alfonso gave a shout. He stared into the face of the youth and lowered him to the ground. Ricardo was dead.

"Guards!" Alfonso shouted. "Guards!" He ran out of the chapel, and froze at what he saw.

His guards lay in death heaps, their faces covered with boils, their flesh erupting even as he looked; Father Fernando sprawled among them, his face a demon-hell of blood and ruin.

A hooded figure appeared at the end of the passage, dark and looming, cloaked in black. It carried a staff, and it did not walk—it floated. Alfonso's bones turned to ice as the figure came toward him; the air grew winter-frozen; his breath streamed like dragon's breath. The corridor fell into utter darkness, save for a red glow surrounding the figure. It advanced, a black shape in crimson darkness. The icy air became a wind that howled around it.

The corridor stank of rot.

Alfonso backed away, into the chapel, stationing himself between his daughter and the young guard. He drew his sword. He was shaking.

The figure followed, bringing with it the blackness, the glow, the stench. "You called me, you promised me," the figure said in a strong, inplacable voice.

Alfonso shook his head, extended his sword. "No."

"I am the heir of your dead loins."

His sword arm shook. "No."

"You swore."

Alfonso crossed himself with his free hand. "By the Blessed Virgin, I did not. The little nun . . ." As he spoke, his face grew hot; his hands burned. Sweat poured from his brow. He shook wildly.

"She is dead, and therefore my first subject. But I shall rule over all your kingdom. You have ordained it."

"No. My God, no!" Alfonso lunged. His sword missed the figure. Could not have. Yet still it stood before him.

"Not your God, no. Your foolish pride, King Alfonso,

which you would not truly release. That is what called me."

"No, for Castile did I vow!" Alfonso staggered backward, sending the banks of candles to the Holy Virgin crashing to the floor. His sword followed. Bile spurted into his mouth, spewed out. Wrenching pain shot through him. Blisters formed on his hands, rose, burst and ran. His flesh melted; his face dripped onto his chest.

"Then you must be the hand of death, not I, and whatever you love you kill." The figure chuckled grimly. You cannot lie to me, Your Majesty, even if you can lie to yourself." It put its gloved hands to its hood. "All you wish is to be remembered." The hood dropped back, and Alfonso saw—even as his heart stopped—

The Black Death spread over Castile, over every fortress, every demesne, every village. It raged for three years; it killed thousands and thousands of people.

And in troubadour's song, and monk's book, and peasant's curse, Alfonso of Castile was never forgotten.

With special thanks to Judy Tarr and Lois Tilton.

In the Name of the King

Judith Tarr

Far in the east of the Field of Flowers, in the country west of the horizon, in the land of the blessed dead, the King's Architect Senenmut paused by a stream so that his mare might drink.

She was only a little mare, not even thirteen hands high, delicately graceful like a gazelle, with a sweet dark eye and a soft gait. She had drawn his chariot while he lived. Now that they both were dead, she was his companion and his friend. She had guided him in his journey from the tomb and stood beside him in the courts of judgment. Her heart weighed with his against the feather of Justice had swayed the balance and gained him entry to the fields of peace.

While she drank her fill from the stream that wound among the lotus blossoms, he rested against her, arm over her back. Although she was dead, she felt like a living thing, warm and breathing. She ate, she drank, as he did, as did all the souls in this realm beyond the horizon.

Even the sun came here, the boat of Ra sailing from the dusk of the living world to be the dawn of this one. His light paled the stars that did not fade, and brought splendor to the dry land, and set the beasts of the dark to flight—terrible beasts, demons, devourers of souls. They flocked the borders of the Field of Flowers, moaning and gibbering, dragging the tattered rags of less fortunate souls. But they never passed into the Field. The blessed, once judged and found worthy, were free of them.

Day was passing in the land of the dead, just as night passed in the Two Lands of Egypt. Senenmut's mare raised her head, shedding water from her muzzle. Shouts rang faint through the shimmering air: the boatmen readying the bark of Ra for its journey. The god's radiance moved slowly among the flowers, touching now one, now another, with molten brilliance.

A throng of souls walked with him, kings and queens among the dead, or high noblemen and loyal servants who had won their way to this place. It was a long way and perilous, and its paths open only to those who knew the words, the magic of true names. Such magic in old days had been given only to kings and to kings' children. Now kings bestowed it on lesser mortals—bringing in a pack of commoners and low rabble, to the disgust of the most ancient. But the gods, even golden Ra, offered no objection.

Senenmut, born a commoner, son of a scribe and a simple lady of the household, had grown to suspect that the gods were considerably less inclined to snobbery than the gods' children. Perhaps the gods were even amused. Was Ra smiling above the throng of heads in their lofty double crowns? So much royalty, perhaps, might seem common to divinity; the god might find it refreshing to look on a head that had never worn a crown, nor ever wished to.

One figure sat a little apart, watching, saying nothing. The high cone of the White Crown, the lower squared helmet of the Red Crown in which it nested, were laid aside. The crook, the flail lay beside them. The false beard was nowhere that Senenmut could see.

He approached without servility, with the mare walking at his shoulder. Her ears were pricked; she was looking for the bit of sweet that this of all pharaohs always had for her.

This pharaoh smiled at him, a smile unmarred in sweetness by the death that was still so new, the courts of judgment just lately passed, the scars of ordeal still faintly evident in the shadowed eyes. He knelt because it was his pleasure, and took the slender hands in his, and smiled himself. "O my king," he said.

"Senenmut," said his king. The name throbbed like a drum, as all names did here, where names were the greatest of powers. The king started a little: it was still new, that magic, and still strange. Magic in the mortal world was a much lesser thing, muted and blunted by the power of living earth.

Senenmut spoke with care, knowing what power he invoked, what strength he imparted. "Maatkare," he said. "Hatshepsut."

The king's hands clenched in his. He was braced for that. One gave a name as a great gift, for it brought life and continued existence to the soul—and to one as new as this, an increase of strength.

"There, love," he said, soothing. "There. It gets easier, the longer one goes on."

"I do hope so," said Hatshepsut. That was closer to the voice he knew, briskly practical, with the crisp edge of one accustomed from childhood to command. One who, born a woman, meant to be a queen, claimed the right and title of a king—because a woman, even a queen, must defer to a king, and a king defers only to the gods.

"And," she said, since his thoughts were as clear here as if they had been spoken, "no one else could do it as well as I." She rose. She was a small woman, but she stood very straight and walked with a firm stride, not mincing like a silly female. She kept a hand in his.

They watched the Sun-god embark on his boat. The boatmen cast off from the strand onto the river of light. The oars swung to the beat of the drum. A sigh escaped the flock of kings left standing on the bank. None, however he strained, whatever magic he invoked to sharpen his eyes, could see past the god's brilliance to the lands of the living.

As the god passed, his light faded. The stars came out one by one, white and motionless in a sky blacker than any mortal night. The beasts of the darkness, rousing, began to howl and gibber.

Hatshepsut stood bravely still, but her hand gripped Senenmut's to the point of pain. He tugged gently. She did not move. "It's morning there," she said. "The bread is baking. Can you smell it? Can you remember?"

Senenmut nodded. The memory could pierce like pain, if he let it. They did not bake bread here. Bread appeared when one was hungry, and beer, and whatever else one desired. Or servants brought it, silent images without life or volition. The simple homely acts of grinding the flour, mixing the dough, baking the bread, had no place among the royal dead. Kings did not do such things, nor did many of them seem to care how it was done, as long as they ate when they were hungry, and drank when they were thirsty.

Hatshepsut would forget. They all did. The shadow of life that was here would be enough. The magic of the Otherworld would engross her, the gods' presence console her. She would become one with the blessed dead, even those who looked at her askance for what she had done: named herself king and in the naming become the thing.

Once more he urged her to come away. This time she yielded, walking with him to the palace that he had built for her of magic and bright will. The greatest joy of his death had been the moment when, after the jackal-god had guided her into the Field of Flowers, she had seen who waited for her, and what he had done to bid her welcome. Her face had lit like a lamp in the gloom of the Otherworld. The shadow of sorrow had vanished, the veil of forgetfulness fallen. She had been his Hatshepsut as she was in life, vivid, joyous, splendid.

Her servants now were waiting, her noblemen who had gone before her. They sat to the feast with which they held each night at bay, in music and in dancing, and in prayers to the gods who were more clearly present here than ever in mortal Egypt. Here she was content. Here she could forget that she was dead.

Senenmut remembered, and never forgot. But Senenmut had no care for life or death, only for her presence. Death had been grim punishment while she still lived. Now she had come to him; now he was whole.

The dead sleep when it pleases them. As the living dream of the Otherworld, so do the dead dream of mortal things. Often they find themselves in their own tombs, winged and human-headed ba-spirits fluttering in the dusty stillness, or mute motionless bodies lying stiff and emptied in stone sarcophagi. But sometimes, if they have great will or great power, they wander the world in spirit-shape, and watch what passes there.

Senenmut, lying beside his king in the bed that they shared in death as they had in life, dreamed that he stood beside that bed with its head and feet like a lion's and its coverlet of soft scarlet wool. The figure in it in his dream was small as Hatshepsut was, slender yet sturdy, with the oval face and the arched nose and the wide-set eyes. But it was not his king whom he loved, though for a fact it was a king: none other would dare lie in the king's bed.

"Thutmose," whispered Senenmut's spirit. The queen's stepson, the king now that she was dead, stirred and woke and looked about. His dark eyes glittered, but only a little with fear. He was brave, was Thutmose, like the lion he so loved to hunt.

He saw nothing, although Senenmut stood close enough to touch. He sighed faintly and shrugged. After a moment he rose.

It was dawn beyond the walls of the palace. Bread was baking: its fragrance wound through the shuttered windows and made Senenmut want, all but irresistibly, to weep.

Thutmose yawned and stretched. He was not the supple boy that he had been while Senenmut was alive, but he was a slender, compact man, well honed in the hunt and in exercises among his soldiers.

Brat of the armies, Hatshepsut had called him, half in scorn. Hatshepsut had had little patience with him. They were remarkably alike in looks, in temper, in quickness of wit—but he was young and male and inclined to fight his way out of difficulties. Hatshepsut preferred the subtler way, the woman's way: words and wheedling and, in extremity, threats.

She had always won their arguments. Thutmose was too easily driven to speechlessness, and thence into violence; violence that he had never gone so far as to turn against the king. Even though he knew, everyone knew, that had Hatshepsut not stood in his way, he would have been king, sole and absolute. The gods had chosen Hatshepsut. Thutmose was the gods' child and their servant. He yielded to their will.

Now he was king. He ruled well, Senenmut perceived, watching him as he performed the rites and offices of the day. He had learned to negotiate, or to choose advisors who had mastered the art. He was not resolving every quarrel with a sword or a bow.

Hatshepsut would be pleased that her stepson had turned out so well. She had never faulted him for being what he was, nor hated him for all their quarrels. "He's sensible," she had said often enough. "He knows which of us is best fit to rule." She had reckoned herself fortunate in her successor.

A shriek tumbled Senenmut out of his dream and into waking death. He was on his feet, looking about wildly for the demon that must have pierced the veils and the ban and fallen on the servants.

No demon prowled and gibbered in Hatshepsut's palace. The scream was Hatshepsut's. She writhed on the bed, twisting in torment. He sprang to clasp her in his arms. Nightmare, he thought. Memory of the ordeal through which she had earned her place among the blessed.

He held her and stroked her and soothed her until at last she quieted. She lay gasping, clutching him with blind strength. He rocked her till her grip loosened and her breathing slowed. When she stiffened against him, he

let her go. She would not thank him for being stronger
than she, or calmer.

No more would she speak of the dream that had waked
her screaming. He could not ask. In most things she was
his beloved. In this she was his king.

Senenmut dreamed again of the living palace that was
the image of this one in the land of the dead. He dreamed
again, and yet again, of the king who lived in that palace.
Simple dreams, harmless dreams, dreams of the king at
rest and at the labor of his rule. They were rather dull, as
dreams went.

Hatshepsut, as if to counter that dullness, dreamed hor-
rors. She could not elude sleep. If she tried, it came on
her while she sat listening to the singers or watching the
dancers or hearing the gods' praises.

She did once, in a moment of great weakness, betray
to Senenmut a little of what she dreamed. "Darkness,"
she said. "Darkness absolute. Nothingness. To be blind,
deafened, sunk in oblivion—not to *be* . . . to be nothing.
Nothing at all. That—is what—"

He stopped her before she said more. She was dreaming of death. True death. Death of the soul, with no life
after. It was a horror of most peculiar potency in this
place to which her strength of wit and will had brought
her. Her body was preserved as it must be for eternity.
Her name was written everywhere that a name could be
written, that no one might forget it. Her self was safe, her
soul secure in its palace in the Field of Flowers. She had
nothing to fear.

And yet she feared. She dreamed, and woke raw-
throated with screaming.

The wise among the dead knew no cure for ill dreams.
Such were not a malady of the dead. Senenmut, in the
company of his faithful mare, sought out the most ancient
of them all, one by one, even some so ancient that only
the loremasters remembered their names. None had any
help to offer.

Hatshepsut was sinking. Preposterous to think that of one who was dead and therefore, one should imagine, free of such mortal frailty, but there was no other way to perceive it. She was like a woman dying of a nameless malady.

Her strength was fading. Her eyes had grown dull. She seemed somehow transparent, as if the fabric of her being had frayed. Invocation of her name strengthened her for a little while, but it was not enough.

"There is one thing," said a king of vast antiquity and remarkable freshness of face, like a youth just come into manhood. Senenmut had found him tilling a field of barley by the banks of a river of light, with a white ox yoked to his plow, and a golden goad. It seemed to be a kind of ritual, or a habit of such long standing that even he could not remember why he did it.

He was not displeased to pause, nor unduly perturbed to be approached by an obvious commoner, a soft-bodied, shaven-headed scribe dressed in the fashion of the most recent dead. "It might be," he said when he had heard Senenmut out, "that someone in the land of the living is casting ill fortune on your king's memory."

"But," said Senenmut, "what mortal is strong enough to touch her even here, among the dead who are blessed?"

The ancient king shrugged. "The gods know. You could ask them."

Senenmut shivered. He had never approached a god here. It was not that the gods discouraged petitioners—quite the opposite. There were throngs of souls about every divinity who wandered in the Otherworld. But most of those souls were royal souls. Senenmut was a commoner. To approach a god, even on a king's behalf . . .

While Senenmut pondered, the ancient king had gone back to his plowing. Senenmut thanked him as was proper. He did not seem to hear, or to remember that Senenmut had spoken to him.

The land of the dead was full of gods, now that Senenmut took time to notice. They seemed to be everywhere, surrounded by sycophants, doing nothing in particular, except for those whose task it was to rule the dead.

Osiris sat in his grave-wrappings in his hall of judgment. Senenmut watched him oversee the weighing of a man's heart. The heart weighed far too light on the scale of Justice. The man's soul, appalled, shrieking curses and prayers and promises of anything, everything, if only he could escape, was fed feet first to the Eater of Souls.

The great beast belched thunderously and eyed Senenmut as if it might fancy a final morsel. He fled.

Anubis the Guide, jackal-headed and jackal-quick, was herding a flock of souls to the judgment. Senenmut could not come close enough to ask his counsel, let alone to win an answer.

Great Ra in his mantle of light was walking by the river, as he did every day of this afterlife, resting from his journey through the lands of the living. Surely he of all gods would know best what mortal man worked spells of torment on a king who was dead. But kings surrounded him. Queens waited on him. Senenmut despaired of ever gaining his ear.

Senenmut wandered away up the river, with his mare walking dejectedly at his side. What god would ever stop to listen to the likes of him? What god would care, even if he heard what Senenmut had to ask?

Out of sight of the bark of Ra but still in the sphere of his light, Senenmut stopped and sat on a stone. The mare dropped her head to graze. He gazed blindly at the river, at the bright fish that leaped there, pursuing dragonflies that were spirits of the dead.

A cat came walking out of the tall grasses. At first she was only a movement in the corner of Senenmut's eye. He glanced at her without thinking. She was a sleek cat, small as his mare was small, with delicate feet and a long, elegant tail. She stalked directly to Senenmut and sprang into his lap and began to wash her paws.

He was not ready, quite, to see her as a portent. Cats were their own creatures here as in any other place. He smoothed her fur with his hand, finding it soft, like sleep. But she was very wide awake. She left off bathing to lean into his hand. He rubbed her ears. She began to purr.

After a while he wearied of stroking her and let his hand fall. He sighed. If the dead could die, then Hatshepsut was dying. "And I don't know what to do," he said. "I don't know at all."

"You could," said the cat, "finish scratching my left ear."

Senenmut started. Of course animals could talk here, if it suited them. It did not suit his mare, but clearly it suited this cat.

He did as she bade him. Cats, as every Egyptian knows, are all goddesses, all faces of Bastet. One should always oblige a goddess.

"Ah," she said, "that's better." She yawned and stretched. Her claws just pricked his thighs under his kilt.

He expected her to leap down then, since she had got what she wanted. But she stayed in his lap, blinking her big yellow eyes at him, until he said, "If madam has any further wishes, madam has only to ask."

The cat yawned. "I know a thing," she said.

Senenmut's brows rose.

"You could ask," said the cat after a while, "what it is that I know."

Her claws had tightened on his thigh. He drew a careful breath. "What does madam know?"

"Madam knows," said the cat, "that a certain king is ill, here where no illness should be. And madam knows that the king has cause to be ill."

Senenmut's breath had begun to come faster. If his heart had been in his breast and not in a jar beside his body in its tomb, it too would have beat a quicker rhythm. "Would madam please to name that cause?"

"I might," said the cat, leaping from his lap. His leg stung where she had sunk her claws. She walked away from him, tail high and delicately curled at the tip.

Almost he failed the test. Almost he let her go. But she was walking, not bounding through the tall grass as a cat might who goes about its own business. She meant, surely, for him to follow. He thrust himself up from the stone and hastened after her. The mare trotted after him, snatching a last mouthful of grass for the journey.

The cat did not lead them far. She followed the river's bank, then turned somewhat away from it, toward a hill of stones that might, in time long past, have been a king's palace. Now it was only rubble and broken walls with grass growing on them.

A falcon perched on a crumbling jut of wall. Senenmut's eye met the falcon's. The bird blinked once, slowly, and spread its wings.

Senenmut bowed low, even to the ground. Lord Horus mantled and took wing into the vault of the sky.

Much heartened and a little afraid, Senenmut looked back toward the cat. She was gone.

His heart sank. Then he saw the flick of a tail, the passage of a supple sand-brown body among the sand-brown stones. He scrambled after her.

Just as he came level with her, she halted, so quickly that he tripped and fell sprawling. The world spun away from him. As in a dream, or an image painted on a wall, he saw the cat, and the mare standing stiff with alarm, and the hard flat vault of heaven beyond the stones of the wall.

He fell, and fell without ending—fell down and down into a swooping dark. There had been an opening in the wall, he remembered dimly, and perhaps a stair. He spared an imprecation for the treachery of cats.

He struck bottom at last with force that would have shattered bones if he had been a living man. Even as it was, it was a whirling while before he could see, and longer before he comprehended where he was.

Walls. Pillars. A mingling of deep gloom and sudden brightness.

The gloom was shadow under a lofty roof. The brightness was sunlight lancing through the pillars. He knew the shape and placement of them—knew them as he knew his own hands. He had built them, he and all the king's workmen, raising her temple to the glory of her name.

He was lying on his back. He was not, as he had half expected, in the form of a ba-spirit, human-headed, bird-bodied. The shape he wore was his own, kilt and all—his ka, the strongest of his spirit-selves. He rose slowly, prepared to count bruises, but there were none. Of course. He was dead. The dead could not suffer the ills of the living.

Unless the dead were Hatshepsut, and were dying in the place where death, once having come, did not return.

Voices rang beyond the pillars. Senenmut knew the sound of chisel on stone. There was a crash, a chorus of shouting.

What, were they building anew in the temple that he had raised for his king?

"Go and see," said the cat.

She was sitting at the base of a pillar, tail curled neatly round her paws. She seemed a solid creature, a living cat, with even a ring in her ear, a gleam of gold in the gloom. But he saw the light of the goddess on her. He bowed to her. "I regret," he said, "that I thought—"

"Oh, I am treacherous," said the cat. "That's true enough. But not now. Go and see what they do to your king."

Alarm blared in him at that. He ran toward the light.

It was splendid. Blinding. Sheer raw sunlight in the land of the living, unsoftened by the magic of the dead. He blinked in it, dazzled, weeping with the splendor of it.

But even as he wept, he strained to see what he must see.

There were men swarming on the outer face of his temple, men with hammers, with chisels, with ladders. Even as he stood on the edge of the light, one scaled the mighty image of the king that stood nearest to Senenmut, and set chisel to the carved and painted eye, and with the hammer drove it home. He struck out the eyes of the king, as one below effaced her name.

They were doing it all through the temple—all through the Two Lands. They were putting out her eyes. They were casting down her images. They were hacking out the name of Maatkare Hatshepsut and carving that of Menkheperre Thutmose.

A low wail wound about Senenmut. It was his own voice, his own cry of horror and despair. Terrible things he had expected; cursings, ill-wishings, pure mean human envy of the woman who had dared to call herself a king.

But this.

This was more than hate. This was murder. This was destruction of all that Hatshepsut had been. In blinding her images, in effacing her name, they were unmaking her. They were destroying her soul. They were slaying all that she had ever been, even to her memory.

The doer of it, the unmaker, sat on the palanquin that had been hers, wore the Two Crowns that she had worn, held the crook and the flail as she had held them, in strong, small hands. His long eyes, drawn longer with lapis and malachite and kohl, were smiling as he watched his workmen. They swarmed as locusts will, destroying all they touched—all that had been Hatshepsut.

Senenmut sprang upon the workman nearest him and seized the hand that held the chisel. The man never paused. Senenmut's strength was no greater than a whisper of wind, his voice nothing to these living men, not even a fly's buzzing. He was spirit only, bereft of flesh. He was powerless.

He raged and wept. He whirled about Thutmose's palanquin. The wind indulged him, raised a flurry of dust, but the king's servants merely raised the screens to keep it out. The king knew nothing but a moment's inconvenience.

"Why?" Senenmut shouted at him—for all the good it did; for all the power he had to make anyone hear him. "What did she ever do to you?"

"She was king," said the cat.

Senenmut spun. The cat had followed him into the sunlight. People could see her: the servants eyed her askance, but did not drive her off.

She ignored them. "She was king, and he—though she let him hold the title—was not."

"But," said Senenmut, "twenty years . . . he never tried . . ."

"No?" said the cat. "She died rather young, when you think about it. He might have helped her. He's a brooder, you know. Twenty years of waiting for her to get tired of playing king and let him have what was his to begin with—that was twenty years of deciding exactly how he was going to avenge himself on her when he was king."

"Cowardice," Senenmut said fiercely. "If he had faced her while she was alive—if he had dared—"

"He didn't," said the cat. "He's going to kill her now—or finish killing her, if you prefer."

Senenmut had gone beyond horror. He was almost beyond anger. "But what can I do? I have no strength. I can't even make a workman hear me when I bellow in his ear."

"Well," said the cat, "that's Ra for you. He's a terrible sapper of strength when one's a spirit, and dead besides."

"I wasn't any stronger inside," gritted Senenmut.

"Weren't you?" said the cat.

"I—" Senenmut stopped. Had he been stronger within, away from the sun? Or was it—

"There," said the cat. "Now you see."

He turned away from the smug, smiling, murderous king. He turned his back on the sun, and on the workmen unmaking Hatshepsut in her own temple that Senenmut had made. He darted into the depths of that temple, through the crowding pillars, across the first of the broad and splendid courts, from shadow to sun and into shadow again.

There on the sunrise side, beyond the temple and the road that led to it, was the secret place that was Senenmut's alone. There his body lay. There, in a place that none but Senenmut and the king and a few loyal servants had ever known, was haven.

Yes. He was stronger here. He had strength deep within the temple, where he had made magic in his own name and with his own face among the manifold images of his king and her gods. But in his own tomb he was strongest of all.

And in his tomb, Hatshepsut's name and her images endured. He felt as in his own body the cutting away of her name and soul and self from the temple—but here she was safe. Here she was remembered in stone, and in the heart that rested in its jar beside his body.

He sat cross-legged on the sarcophagus, as a scribe sits, although he had no papyrus, no reed pen, no inks to draw the figures that shaped her name. He spoke it in the darkness of the tomb. "Maatkare," he said. "Hatshepsut."

Far to the west of the Two Lands, in the land beyond the horizon, he felt a stirring, a welling of strength. With the eyes of the spirit he saw her sit up in the bed to which she had fallen. With the ears of the soul he heard her call. "Senenmut!"

His spirit quivered, yearning toward that name, and toward the one who spoke it. But his heart held him fast.

They were hacking at the door of his tomb, destroying her name here as in the temple. But they would not come into the secret chamber. He wove great spells of guard and binding, sitting atop the stone that held his body. He set her name in them, and his own, and all the power of will and love and memory.

It was a mighty working, mightier than any he had ever done. He was strong—strong with the power of the blessed dead. But even they must weaken at last; must know the failing of their strength, the limits of their magic.

It was a dim and guttering spirit that sank down upon the sarcophagus and lay there, powerless even to raise its head. The dead could not die, nor could Senenmut sink into oblivion while his name remained in the temple and in the tomb. Yet he was very weak.

He heard the whisper of a step, the faint rumble of a purr. The cat's cheek brushed his foot, marking him with her scent. "That was well done," she said. "Except for one thing. You should have thought to leave a little for the journey back."

Senenmut shifted a fraction. He could see her even in the black dark, a sleek shape with the shimmer of the goddess on her. "Back?" he whispered, for that was all the voice he had.

"Back," said the cat. "To your king. In the Field of Flowers."

Senenmut's eyes closed. It did no good. He could still see. "I can't go back," he said. His voice was a little stronger. "I have to stay here. To guard. To remember."

He had not known it till he said it. It was knowledge of the heart, on which he happened to be lying, under the carved and painted stone.

"I must remember her," he said, "and guard the memory. Else—else she dies, and he has the victory. I won't have that, goddess. By your own divinity I swear it."

"Ah," said the cat. "Well. If you put it that way. It's true, he's a vindictive little man. He could be a cat, don't you think?"

"That's an insult to your kind," said Senenmut.

"There, now," said the cat. "I wonder what he'll say when he comes to the Field of Flowers and finds her there, hale and strong and missing you rather terribly?"

Senenmut's heart panged—strange sensation, since it was in the stone and he was lying on top of it. "If he comes so far, with the weight of evildoing that's on him, then he deserves any shock he gets. I'm staying here. He might take it into his head to do something once he's dead—haunt his heir till the young idiot finishes what he began, or come here himself and wipe her name from the earth. He could, you know. Once he's Osiris. If he keeps his grudge so long."

"Oh, he will," said the cat. "He's tenacious, is Thutmose." She shrugged, an arch of the back, a fillip of the tail. "But then, so are you. It's going to be a long watch. I don't think you know yet how long."

"Thousands of years," said Senenmut, though his heart

grew cold in its jar. "Tens of thousands, if need be. My king will live. I'll see to that."

"You always were a vain man," said the cat. She did not seem to regard it as an insult.

She did not bid him farewell. Such was not the way of cats. One moment she was there, regarding him with lambent eyes. The next, she was gone.

Senenmut was alone. He had never been so, not even when he died: his little mare had been waiting for him when he climbed out of his tomb and began his journey among the dead. She would wait, he knew, until he came back again. She loved him. She would not forget.

He would come back. When his task was done. When his king was safe, her name alive again, her memory made strong in the hearts of the living. However long it was. However many years he must endure, defending her against her enemies.

It was dark in the tomb. His heart was still, slumbering again in its jar. No air moved. No living thing stirred.

And yet there was a whisper on the edge of hearing, a shimmer on the edge of sight. Magic; power; guard and binding. And in their center, the thing that mattered most in the world. The name that he loved, which was the essence of his king. While it endured, and while he endured to guard it, she would live. The dark would not take her. Her soul would not sink into nothingness.

Maatkare, the whisper said. *Hatshepsut.*

The Feather of
Fatherhood

Lawrence Schimel

Night and day Zál paced the halls of his palace. The nurses whispered that, had his hair not already been white, it would have turned so from worry. But Zál had been born with hair as white as a goose's wing; thus his name, which meant "The Old One." Zál's father, Sám, had feared his son's white hair was an aberration, and had abandoned him to the elements at the base of Mount Alburuz. But the Símurgh had found him, rock-cradled at the foot of her mountain home, and took pity on him. She'd raised Zál as her own, teaching him ancient lore and the languages of man from her vast wisdom, until that day when she returned him to the world to reclaim his heritage as ruler of the lands of Rúm, far encompassing Byzantium.

Thinking of the events concerning his own birth reminded Zál of his present worry: the birth of his son. Rudába's belly was taut, as if the skin were stretched over a stone, but she was unable to give birth to the child. Though he had summoned all the aid of his kingdom, Zál knew of no further way to help her. He felt as if he was betraying his own son, even before he was born, just as Zál's father had betrayed him. Zál had been fortunate enough to receive the Símurgh's aid; his own son lacked similar protection. Unless . . .

Zál rushed into his sleeping room and searched the

items on a shelf for an ivory casque. Finding it, he pushed aside the loose veils surrounding his bed and sat cradling the casque in his lap. He ran his fingers along the exterior, carved in the likeness of a majestic bird, then opened it. Inside, cushioned on white silks, lay a large blue feather. Zál could hear again the Símurgh's words at their parting, when she gave the feather to him: "Bear this plume of mine and so abide beneath the shadow of my grace. Henceforth, if thou shall need my aid, burn this feather and behold my might."

As he took the feather from its casque, Zál reflected on the irony of the situation. He had imagined, after she had given him the feather, that he would save it until a war against the direst enemies of his kingdom and burn it then to rout them epicly. Or perhaps he would be engaged on a quest and need to fly over a vast chasm, or an ocean. He would burn the feather, and she would appear and aid him in an impossible feat.

But to summon her because his wife could not give birth? He was calling the Símurgh, essentially, to play midwife. Was this misfortune enough to deserve his using the feather now?

Zál did not need to deliberate long. He stood and called for servants.

A brazier filled with sandalwood coals and jasmine was set in the center of Rudába's room. Zál glanced at his wife's sweating form straining on the bed, and dropped the feather into the fire. Blue smoke billowed from the brazier. As it swirled around Zál, he felt lightheaded, recalling suddenly the exhilarating sensation of flight from the days of his childhood, when he soared over the world on the Símurgh's back. In his mind he saw her before him once again, as she pulled the feather from her wing and handed it to him.

Suddenly, surging from the coals, the Símurgh emerged. She filled the chamber with her grandeur and might, her wings easily spreading across the vast hall, her tall neck arching up to the ceiling, then down again to bring her familiar head to rest before Zál. She spoke softly, but her voice filled the chamber with resonant power. "I have cherished you beneath my wings and raised you as my own. You have summoned me, and I have come. What ails thee?"

Zál could not speak, his heart overfull with joy at seeing once again she who was his mother, nurse, and first friend. He pointed at the bed where Rudába strained against the sheets as the child inside her strained against her skin. The Símurgh understood at once.

"With musk and milk a poultice make, from herbs that I will show you." Zál could almost smell each herb as she said its name. He wished Rudába could breathe in the vapors and let them mingle in her heart to make her well. "Ply her with wine to dull her senses, then slit her side with sharp steel. Take the lion from its lair and apply the poultice to the wound." The Símurgh stretched her wing and plucked a feather from it with her beak. "With this feather, close the wound, pressing both sides to it as you seal her flesh. Thus shall your child be born, a palladin to rival his father's fame and glory."

She stretched her wings again, as if to burst through the ceiling of the palace into the sky. Zál yearned to go with her, to go flying once more, to sit curled beneath the shelter of her wings and talk of all that he had seen and learned in the world since leaving her nest. They had only just been reunited; surely there was time to talk for a while. Time to simply look at each other.

Rudába moaned as she thrashed on the bed, and Zál knew he could not go as the Símurgh surged upward into clouds of blue smoke. He would not abandon his own son the way his father had abandoned him.

Rudába lay before him unaware. Zál held a blue-steel dagger above her side, poised like a hawk about to strike. He had killed men before, but could not force himself to press the knife into his wife's flesh. Could he ask one of his men to do it? Of course, but could he trust so delicate a task to one of them? Not only was his wife's life at stake, but that of his unborn son within her. Zál glanced at the large blue feather lying at Rudába's side. He trusted the Símurgh's promise of aid, but to cut into his wife's flesh felt as if he gashed his own side.

He must do something. His son lay inside her womb, waiting to be released. With a swift, clean stroke he pressed down with the blade, splitting Rudába's taut flesh like silk. Blood poured over her side like a river overflowing its banks. Zál reached inside her womb and pulled the babe from within her. He was a large boy, who kicked as he was withdrawn. Zál laid him on the bed next to his mother, and the midwife pulled the caul from the babe's mouth. The child's lungs filled with air, and he cried out lustily. Zál smiled and called to the servants to bring him the ointment, which had been prepared exactly to the Símurgh's specifications. Staring at the blood which flowed from Rudába's side, Zál's heart felt drained of blood, as if it pooled in his stomach ready to pour forth in sympathy. He spread the ointment over the wound and folded the flesh together, running the feather's barbs between the edges. He pressed the wound closed and ran the feather atop the cut once more. As the Símurgh had promised, the flesh grew whole as if no wound had been made.

Staring at his wife and son, Zál felt as lightheaded as when he was flying on the Símurgh's back and staring down at the world so far below them. He wished he might have gone flying with her, might have sat beneath her wings and listened to her tell tales from her vast lore. But it was not to be. He had also wished for a family, for a son of his own to care for as the Símurgh had cared for him. At present he could not have both desires, and he had been forced to choose. The choice, he thought, smiling down at his wife and son, had been the right one.

But one day, he vowed, he would take his son to the foot of Mount Alburuz, and together they would fly over the world on the Símurgh's back.

Rudába woke momentarily. "Birastam," she said, smiling with relief. *I am delivered.* She closed her eyes again and fell into a peaceful sleep.

"That is what you shall be called," Zál told the child,

as he tickled the babe's bare stomach with the tip of the feather. "Rustam."

The child opened its eyes and smiled as he regarded his father. His eyes were the same blue as the Símurgh's feather.

Blind Sceptre

Brad Linaweaver

"There are no good emperors," said the king. No emperors being present at the banquet table, there was general agreement. The absence of any emperor on the continent of Ir contributed significantly to the nodding of noble heads and the murmuring of assent in support of the king's words, even by those lords and ladies whose grasp of history was tenuous at best. The queen forced herself to smile.

Only the Lady Cynthia remained impassive. In the privacy of her chambers at court she had become a student of history. More than five hundred years had passed since the countries of Ir had suffered under an imperial yoke. Only the intervention of supernatural powers had put an end to that broad and indiscriminate tyranny. At least that's what the common people believed. Official, and officious, court historians explained the fall of the emperor in terms of economics and politics.

Lady Cynthia preferred the notion that the gods would judge harshly one who would presume to own all They had created. Lady Cynthia was the lover of the king and wondered if a man of his appetites could ever be satisfied. Too often he had referred to the magic sceptre that had absorbed all the power of the empire. Too often he had made bad jokes at the expense of the priesthood, which hid the sceptre in one of its monasteries, out of the reach of ambitious kings.

There had been a time when she had loved her monarch. Tired of the courtesans, he had wanted a more refined adventure. The lady and the king had caught each other in an artfully spun web. The queen was too much like the king to offer him love. Most women at court put on excellent performances, but he could see through their intentions as easily as the revealing night garments they wore to his bedchamber. But when the king looked at Lady Cynthia, he received her steady gaze from strong brown eyes in place of the meekness and deceit that were the norm. When he reached out and touched her long face with its high cheekbones and caressed her night-black hair, there was no pulling back on her part; her eyes never turned away from him, as she would have been trained to do from childhood.

She still fondly recalled those days as she picked delicately at her vegetables in the banquet hall and listened to the king lecture his unfortunate guests. He was going on and on about a monarch's responsibilities to his people as she remembered the first words he had spoken to her: "You're a brave one!"

When he had complimented her courage on that day so long ago, her cool reserve had almost cracked and the little girl she carried deep inside almost broke free of all restraints. She had never gotten over the death of her father, and at that moment the king made her remember how much she still longed for parental approval. But she had learned to suppress all genuine gaiety at a very young age. A typical male despite the crown he wore, the king had redoubled his efforts to elicit her approval. Female ice is said to inspire the hottest male flame.

The early days of their romance had been the happiest period of her life. At first there was the almost childish pleasure of sneaking around behind the matronly queen's back; but all ladies at court were sophisticated enough to know that the queen had spies everywhere. She was ten years older than the king when their marriage had been arranged. As such, the queen entertained no romantic delusions. Her central interest in life lay in organizing the minute details of everyone's life at court. Every new mistress of the king's could count on a brief holiday from meddling until the king's ardor had cooled. After that, the latest love interests would be assigned some level of significance by the queen and stay under her charge.

The Lady Cynthia had been the king's mistress for over a year, and there was still no sign of flagging interest on his part. "I don't understand it," the queen had told the alchemist. "These affairs of his rarely last a month. Is there some kind of anti-love potion you could make for me?"

The alchemist was so old that everyone assumed he must have wisdom to match his years. "I can poison people and not leave a trace," he said. "I can make people fall in love. But falling out of love is something beyond my humble powers."

With a sigh, the queen surrendered. She considered routine murder unbecoming to her station. Nature would have to take its course. What she didn't know was that the alchemist was playing his own game with the king and wasn't about to jeopardize it.

Nature was in no rush where love was concerned. The king found Lady Cynthia fascinating for many reasons. She didn't hide the fact that she could read. The queen would never understand this sort of attraction. The physical attraction between king and lady was made all the stronger by the growing closeness of their minds. Entire evenings had passed in which Cynthia forgot that she was making love to her king, and the only authority he held over her was his power to make her feel both wanted and satisfied.

She never dreamed a day would come when she could sit at the king's own table, among his inner circle, and be mind-numbingly bored. But such was the case as she listened to him intone: "Everything must be in its proper place for a well-ordered society to function. Empire throws the natural order out of balance."

This latest platitude won the approval of no less a substantial presence than Lord Bottoum, far gone in drink. Empty wine glasses were lined up in front of his stout frame like so many conquered soldiers, the last glass having tipped over and its red tide coming within an inch of staining the Lady Cynthia's lavender sleeve. The man could always be counted on to provide entertainment by virtue of his indiscretions, which were so finely wrought that no court jester could hope to compete.

Even the Lady Cynthia was roused from her gray mood as the entertainment began. "My liege," Lord Bottoum addressed his king, "no emperor could possibly equal your steady hand at the tiller of the state." At this point, most speakers would have detected the sudden silence settling over the room at the inappropriate comparison. A king reigning in his properly ordained sphere was not to be thought of as in any way similar to a world-aggrandizing emperor, but such was Lord Bottoum's turn of mind that he could only imagine the silence to be respectful awe over his rhetorical blasts of air.

The king played along. "Is this flattery, Lord Bottoum?" asked the man who held the power of life and death over everyone in the room but would never confuse such authority with imperial powers.

Lord Bottoum was immune to irony and sarcasm, and with another glass of wine already in his hand, he bravely sailed on: "What I mean to say is that if any man could avoid being corrupted by the nature of imperial institutions, it would, of course, be Your Majesty."

The high priest chose that exact moment to have an attack of hiccups. Lady Cynthia raised a long-fingered hand to her mouth to suppress a laugh. This was definitely better than being bored. She snuck a look at some of the other women and detected no change in their demeanor. They obviously had no idea about what was going on.

"What is your point, Lord Bottoum?" asked the king.

Now, finally, the impolitic lord got the general drift of the situation. The last time he'd been in equivalent hot water was when he reminded everyone of how the queen would not allow her grown children on an outing because the alchemist had predicted a rainfall that never happened. Bottoum had almost lost his head over that one.

"I have no point, my liege," he said. The king frowned. The queen remembered just how annoying Lord Bottoum could be. Lady Cynthia wished court etiquette would allow her to express an opinion. The alchemist carried on an inner dialogue over whether overweight bodies were easier or harder to resurrect from the dead than bony, thin ones.

"You have no point?" echoed the king.

Legs quivering beneath the leather gaiter that came to his knees, Lord Bottoum provided the denouement of the evening's entertainment: "The only point I ever dare to make in your august presence would be to your honor and glory, my liege. Any problems that my ill-fated tongue might precipitate are never to be thought to arise from authentic sobriety. By which, I mean to say that any perceived incongruity is, in fact, a mere counterfeit of an actual blunder—or something very close to it."

The youngest woman there, a girl of surpassing beauty and golden-blond hair, giggled out loud. Cynthia had her first positive feeling for the younger woman.

Lord Bottoum finished his soliloquy at last. Even so, his mouth was still open in an excellent impersonation of a beached whale. He waited for the king to respond. Everyone waited.

With great theatricality, the king lifted a glass of wine and toasted the unhappy lord. "I thank you for clarifying your position. Are you sure you're not the reincarnation of an advisor to the old Emperor of Ir?" The priest in residence wrinkled his brow in thought as he wondered how close the king himself was venturing toward heresy with such a remark. But when the king laughed, and Lord Bottoum nervously joined in, and then everyone else except the Lady Cynthia added to the chorus, the priest decided that the gods must have a sense of humor and added his own good-natured laughter to the merriment.

Things could have been worse. Lord Bottoum might have mentioned the emperor's sceptre. But not even a drunken buffoon was likely to do that. To speak of the emperor's sceptre merited the death penalty by slow torture.

The candles were burning low, casting long shadows on the gold and red tapestries decorating the king's bedchamber. The Lady Cynthia and the king were playing a game of dragon board. In the beginning she'd been flattered when he told her that she was his first lover with the strategic sense to play this particular board game. But as she had become more proficient at the game, the king had become less interested in playing it with her.

Tonight he was strangely eager to have her play. When she'd won the second game, she was sure that would be the end of it; but he happily rearranged the fine obsidian pieces for a third contest. "You're in fine form," he said, smiling, without the least hint of a lewd suggestion about her figure. She concluded that this would be one of those rare nights when sex was not required of her.

"Robert," she said, becoming intimate, a privilege only granted to her in this room, "you seem unusually cheerful tonight."

"They're such fools," he said, "so willing to agree or disagree upon my pleasure."

"What choice do you give them?" she asked.

He responded with another question: "Do you know why I enjoy being with you?" He didn't even take a breath before continuing: "Because you speak from your conscience. You are my better half. But I know you have the same contempt for the great mass of mankind that I have myself."

"Do I?" she asked, a mocking tone creeping into her voice, accompanied by a raised eyebrow.

"You know, my little raven's wing," he said, idly stroking her hair, "there's something a little funny about calling the people my subjects."

"What is that, my liege?" she replied, and he noticed her return to formality.

"They're only objects, when you come right down to it. What difference would it make if the hand that guides them in their daily affairs is that of a king or an emperor?"

Books she had read long ago came back to her now and prompted her to say: "Perhaps there would be no difference to the people. But what of the character of the leader?"

He took up the challenge. "Why should authority over more subjects be a corrupting influence on character?"

"You were calling them objects a moment ago!"

The king looked long and hard at his favorite lady. "Are you arguing with me?"

She let herself think about the royal brothel as a possible destination for an imprudent lady. A momentary concern for dungeons flashed through her mind as well. "I suppose I am," she answered.

"Good! I need you tonight, Cynthia, as I've never needed anyone before. How would you like to be my empress?"

The words struck her as if a physical blow. Treason, heresy, blasphemy, and a bad jest all rolled up in one might be expected to break down the most carefully maintained composure. She gasped.

"Thank you," he said. "A reaction from you is always gratifying." Rising to his feet, he went over by the ornate bed, where they had played games more interesting than dragon board, and poked at the impish cherub that hung from the beautifully carved headboard. His hand was doing things to the little statue that made Cynthia vaguely uncomfortable when suddenly there was a creaking sound.

The wall behind the bed moved. The Lady Cynthia wasn't sure if she was more disturbed by the realization that every time she had made love on that bed the wall behind her had been an insecure barrier ... or if the presence of the wizened alchemist now stepping through that opening might be cause for greater alarm.

"My liege," said the alchemist, bowing to the king. "My lady," he said, bowing to her next.

"I know this is a night for surprises," the king announced airily as he put his arm around Cynthia. "I wanted you to hear my speech at dinner because as a student of classical rhetoric, you would recognize every argument."

The alchemist was carrying a long tube in his clawlike hands. He stood in the corner of the room, his head slightly bowed, and waited for authority to be exercised.

"I have no secrets from my alchemist," the king continued. "He knows of your literacy and penchant for self-education."

She bowed to her king. "The ancient world's halfhearted belief in one god led to decadence and atheism," she recited the conventional wisdom. "We are fortunate to be living in the age of faith and the certainty of a multiplicity of gods. Even so, we can learn much from the older world. Their philosophers understood the need for moderation and balance."

"What say you to that?" the king asked the alchemist.

"Admirably put," came the predictable reply. "You have chosen well."

Uncertain of the direction the men's conversation was taking, Cynthia thought it best to continue: "Kings are ordained to protect the common people from fine lords and ladies, such as my family. That's what my books say. The king is a custodian of the common interest. The king holds society together in a kind of equilibrium. And even if the king is not just and good on a personal basis, the institution of the monarchy has built-in protections to maintain civil order. As one critic of the old empire once concluded, 'Monarchy is the worst form of government, except for all the rest.' "

She took a deep breath and hoped her presentation would prove sufficient. The king applauded her. The alchemist merely smiled, a disconcerting sight with his bald head and narrow face giving the impression of a living skull.

"You have defended the hierarchical order," said the king, "even though you are living proof of what an absurdity it truly is!"

If there had been surprises before now, they could not compare to this latest remark of her sovereign. It was as if he had reached into the deepest recesses of her heart and plucked out her most secret thoughts. She looked at his large, strong face with its fierce, black beard and saw him as if for the first time. Gone was her boredom as if burned away in a furnace.

"Didn't people suffer more under the empire than in all the centuries since?" she asked in the cautious tones of a student.

"Yes," he said. "What of it? The small wars we fight now are hardly worth the bother. Every king worries over the rules of warfare so as not to offend the high priest. There's no reward in that. War should be fought to decide on the rules, not to abide by timid restrictions foisted on us by a benighted clergy."

A year of close personal contact with the king had taught Cynthia to expect him to work himself up at times like this. With a florid gesture, he motioned to the alchemist to step forth and deliver. The man did so. Theatricality was catching. The alchemist struck a dramatic pose and then opened the tube.

Her self-control back in place, the Lady Cynthia showed no expression at what was revealed; but something cold grew in the center of her stomach, as if something had just died in the castle.

The alchemist held in his hand the forbidden sceptre of the emperor. His withered hand could not activate the magical powers that lurked within the seemingly innocuous white cylinder with a plain ball on the end. But contact with a royal hand was quite another matter. The king's hand seemed a small and insignificant thing, despite the ruby ring on the middle finger, as it reached out for the forbidden sceptre.

"Robert!" She surprised herself by speaking his name in front of the alchemist. Neither seemed to mind. Today's protocol was about to become tomorrow's quaint memory.

"Women had more power in the empire, you know," said the king.

"Only the priestesses!" she cried. "And what they did to children was wrong. They ..."

She was cut off the moment his fingers came in contact with the smooth white surface of the sceptre. A sound like the rushing of a thousand winds filled the chamber. The Lady Cynthia didn't mind the noise nearly so much as what was happening to the ball at the end of the stick. The ball was becoming a recognizable human eyeball the size of a fist. The pupil, as large as a normal human eye, moved in the direction of the only woman in the room.

A light stabbed out and bathed her in its radiance. At the same time the light was reflected back on the king. The alchemist cowered in a corner, covering his face. Pictures began to flow into Cynthia and, reflected from her, into the king. They both saw the same thing, the same vision, since sight had been restored to the oldest magic wand on the continent of Ir.

First they saw Cynthia standing naked on a cliff overlooking the sea. In her hand she held a primitive stone knife. At her feet, equally naked, was a squalling infant. Far below, on the beach, surrounded by a vast army of soldiers clad in golden armor, the Emperor Robert stood as if waiting for a command. He held the sceptre high against a red sky.

His eyes met hers. She plunged the knife into their firstborn son and ...

"No!" screamed the Lady Cynthia back in the world, back in life, back in the king's bedchamber; but the relentless light would not cease its probing. Now there were new pictures for man and woman to consider.

The same scene was repeated as before. Only this time there was a change in the people on the cliff. Down below, on the beach, nothing was different. But on the cliff, the baby was gone, replaced by Cynthia, naked and bound at the feet of another woman—also naked, standing there with sagging breasts and spindly legs and wrinkled arms. The stone knife was held in the hand of the queen ... and she did not hesitate to cut out the beating heart of the king's true love.

The sceptre didn't stop there. Next came a vision of dominion. All the nations of Ir surrendered their rights to the new capital. The old castle of the king was razed to make room for a sumptuous palace in its place. All the king's old enemies pretended to be his friends, while all his friends became new enemies.

There was no end to war. But now all was insurrection. The power of the sceptre was sufficient to turn the tide, should the new emperor make a serious miscalculation, either political or military. Although not even the sceptre could promise absolute security, the probabilities were all in favor of the new despot, clad in imperial purple and green.

A chorus of voices could be heard singing the praises of the new emperor, all across the continent of Ir. Great wealth was sent to him across the ocean from countries far enough away to be allies of the new regime. Their praises were added to the domestic voices, with just a hint of caution underlying the diplomatic flatteries. Could even great distances be a safeguard against the leader with a vision so vast as this new emperor?

More and more voices could be heard, accompanying the splendid pictures of ostentatious wealth. No one was more clever than the emperor at playing one faction off against the other. They could never trust each other for one second, and in that one single fact the strength of the empire could grow and grow, as the voices sang the praises higher and higher.

During all this, the Lady Cynthia stared dumbfounded, riveted by the image of her own bloody sacrifice. Her heart sank as she realized the death sentence she had pronounced on herself with the uttering of one little word. The chanting voices seemed a funeral dirge when suddenly she heard a deeper voice, a voice with substance. Someone else was speaking for real in the king's bedchamber. Someone else was saying the same word she had spoken but a moment before. This voice was saying, "No."

As if waking from a dream, she saw the king through the light and the pictures that for all their splendor had an ephemeral quality. The king had raised his free hand as if to stop the torrent of pictures and sound while his other hand continued holding the sceptre. He was looking straight at her at the very moment the pictures became a procession of beautiful young women from all over the world, all waiting their turn to be consort to the emperor. The queen was no more of a problem to him as empress than she had been as his queen. She watched the young women with a curious pleasure, as if they all belonged to her somehow.

"No," the king repeated. His voice was softer but somehow stronger than before. There was certainty in it. Slowly he placed the sceptre on the floor. Very gingerly, his hand opened and his fingers pulled back from the smooth white surface. As he did so, the staring eye became opaque.

"What are you doing?" screamed the alchemist. "Do you know how many people I bribed, how many murders it cost to bring you the sceptre?"

"Yes," said the king, unsheathing his sword from its scabbard, where it lay propped against his chair. The alchemist's eyes grew very wide before the light in them went out. The king wiped the old man's blood on the old man's robes.

Wrapping his hands in a towel, the king carefully replaced the sceptre in the tube. "The alchemist was part of a plot against the kingdom," he told Cynthia. "Clearly he wanted to be the emperor, but he knew that only a royal hand could bring forth the forbidden magic. Everyone knows how I feel about empire. We can make them believe that's what happened."

"Why?" she asked.

"Why did I want to restore the empire?"

"No. Why did you turn down all that power?"

He came over to her and held her in a strong embrace. "Don't you know?" he whispered in her ear.

"You care for me . . . that much?" she asked. She couldn't believe this was happening.

The king sighed. "What good is an empire if I don't have anyone to talk to?" he asked of the universe at large. "The sceptre's price was too high the moment you turned down the offer."

"Thank you" was all she could think to say. He kissed her hard. She tried to make herself feel something.

Gone were the days when the Lady Cynthia had loved the king. But all the peoples of Ir could be grateful that the king still remembered how to love.

The King of Galilee

Billie Sue Mosiman

We lived in fear and trembling, holding our tongues when beaten or shoved aside by the policemen, surviving on garbage live with maggots from the heat, hiding out whenever the plagues swept through the city to take off more of our young, weak, and decrepit.

I believed Jerusalem would stand, that its people would defend it with their last drop of blood. I believed that God would spare this holiest of holy cities. No one would have believed the world could erupt again into true holocaust, this time destroying all that man had achieved in more than two thousand years. But the tensions rose to a crescendo between nations, between peoples and belief systems, and it was inevitable, something we would have foreseen had we not been blind and deaf to history, arrogant in thinking we might be spared.

Hordes of invaders swarmed our defeated Israel and turned those left living into the streets. I lost my family through bombings, starvation, disease. Disease has been worse than any modern nuclear weapon. It carried off whole populations, not just families. They say that the African and South American continents are swept free of mankind and that the North American continent has no more people alive there than before Europeans forged the New World.

In that sense Israel was spared. Buildings have toppled and streets are pocked with craters, but we were preserved from the global biological warfare that decimated most of the planet. It was thought we were preserved because this land has been claimed as holy ground, the last bastion, and so we have died slowly, for the most part, in bright agony.

There has been some talk of a resistance movement—mumblings in the dark among the fires in crumbled buildings, snatches of conversations whispered on passing in the streets. If this is true, I want to record here in this book the events for future generations, if any survive. It is probably my delusion that it matters, but I must have some purpose for living, and keeping a record is as good as any other. It passes the time and rewards me with long hours where I forget I am hungry, I am dirty, I am alone and unloved.

Before the end came, I wrote some fiction in my spare time and for a living worked as the secretary to a government official, not a high-ranking one of note, just a man in charge of "internal affairs," but to be truthful he was a lazy fool who did as little as possible to draw a salary and to stay out of trouble. He dreaded intrigue and knew if he let himself be caught up in it, his head would roll. Unfortunately, he was one of the first to be executed as a political prisoner. I was in the crowd behind the barricade, watching, and I heard him cry out, along with others, "I did nothing! I had no power!"

What he said was true, but it did not save him. He fell with a host of others that day, and the marksmen left the bodies lying scattered at the base of the wall for a week before they were removed. Each day I'd scurry past the stench, averting my gaze, wondering how I would keep my sanity if I had to look into those staring faces again.

I have no permanent place to stay; not many of the survivors of the war do, so we congregate in little groups each night in different alleyways, bombed buildings, and burned factory sites. We seek company, share news, dream of our past lives when we all lived as if tomorrow would repeat today and nothing would change, ever.

I have taken a lover. It is not unusual for strangers to exchange a night together, a clutch and fumble, over quickly and then avoidance of one another. Attachment has its penalties. Despite that, Brad and I still cling together; it feels good to have someone to depend upon, if only for a comforting voice and a warm body to cuddle near in the deepest part of night. He admires how I will write in my notebook for hours, but he has not asked to read it, nor would I let him at this point. This is not for me or for Brad. It is for some other time and some other place that is happier and more civilized.

Last night he said to me, "We have found a leader."

When I gasped, startled, he put his finger to his lips and cut his eyes to the side to indicate this was not something I should let the others hear just yet.

"Who is it? And where will he lead us, anyway? There's nothing we can do about the way things are." I couldn't imagine any ragtag band of Israelites successfully going up against the ruling military junta.

"His name isn't important. He's young, hardly more than a boy, but already some sources are calling him the 'King of Galilee.' "

I shook my head, and my shadow from the firelight danced across my knees and the notebook lying there. I could smell the rancid odor of the burnt pork fat and bones we had thrown into the fire, and I knew if I lifted my hands to my nostrils, I would smell smoke and the grease from the slimy meat of a pig's haunch Brad had salvaged from a bin behind a butcher shop. "It's so ridiculous."

"That we might take back our country?"

"That anyone would think to nickname a rebel leader after the Messiah."

"You don't understand. Some are saying he *is* the Messiah, finally come to release us."

I didn't mean to laugh and humiliate my new lover, but I couldn't help it and couldn't stop either, until I saw the look on his face. He was serious. This was no folktale told to keep nightmares at bay. I sobered and leaned forward to touch his hand. "You really mean it, don't you? But have you thought people might be deluding themselves because they're so desperate? They might wish so hard to be saved from this ... this purgatory ... they have latched onto some charismatic charlatan in a last-ditch effort to believe in the future."

"I don't think that's it." He had turned his back to me now and was arranging a blanket on the ground to lie down. "What I think is you've moved so far from God, you wouldn't recognize the truth if it stood before you."

It felt like a slap, and my cheeks burned. I stared at these pages, waiting for my blurred vision to clear before writing again. His barb had stuck a sensitive chord. It was true I had wandered far from early religious training. The events of the world holocaust had destroyed some of my lingering certainties concerning man's place in the scheme of things. When you lose everything and are brought down to living like a rat in a crevice, you either turn to your God or you turn away.

I had turned far into myself.

But the Messiah? King of Galilee? I looked up at the multitudinous stars overhead and wondered at the immensity of this rumor. And the broken souls it would cause if a king did not appear.

He was not tall, perhaps five-nine, nor particularly handsome, though he was striking in the peculiar way he held himself and gestured with his hands. He was a commanding presence despite a lack of stature or beauty, and his speeches were music in the ears. He was young, younger than most of us who were left, but his wisdom knew no age or inexperience. If he was not the Messiah, he might as well have been, for all of us grew to worship him, even me with my misgivings and bald cynicism.

I think now the quality that drew us most was his air of optimism. He thought we would be a great people again and that one day we would retake the land from the infidels, not by battle but through simple patience. Time passing. The earth revolving a certain number of years.

He taught benevolence, peace of spirit, trust that good triumphs over evil and nonviolence over the spilling of blood.

I interviewed him at length about the danger he represented and warned that even some of our own people were not fond of his methods, but he waved that away with one of his slim hands and said, "There has always been and always will be opposition. I'm not afraid." And it was true that we all live so precariously, hardly finding enough food to maintain the skin on our bones, that the worries I brought up were not really the worst any of us faced in our daily lives.

Brad adored him and became a devoted disciple of his teachings. I hardly saw Brad during the day anymore; he was so often moving around the city gathering more followers, bringing them back to the edge of town near the desert for the nightly discussions. When groups lay down to sleep now, there were none of the clumsy embraces and sweaty grunting in the dark that there had been before. It was as if, out of respect, they let go their lusts until they were away from the man they considered sacred.

When asked, "Are you the Messiah prophesied?" he would smile sadly and say, "I have an earthly father and mother just as you. I'm only trying to give you back your souls."

He made no claims. That's what convinced me he might truly be who they said he was. He led by example, not just by words; he judged no one, he proclaimed no laws, he showed no fear or pride. He was reluctant to tell us what to do.

It was not long before his name was turned in to the military and they came to search him out. I knew it would happen. For weeks we hid him, risking our own lives if we were caught doing it, and then one night after he had been in solitary prayer longer than usual, he said, "We need to leave. All of us together."

"And go where?" I asked, feeling my heart step up in rhythm at the thought. "There's nowhere to flee. They'll track us down."

"Then let them do it. We've nothing left to lose."

We had our lives, paltry as they were, but then I wondered about the retribution that would come against us for harboring this prophet, the firing lines along the wall, the corpses left to rot in the sun, and I knew he was right. We had already gone too far to turn back. By meeting with him and protecting him, we were marked for death anyway. There could be no leader of the Jews ever again. If it meant killing us all, it might come to that. It had nearly happened so many times before. This time there would be a final resolution.

We left under cover of darkness, in small contingents, by twos and threes. They had never put up a barrier, since escape to the desert reaches was a death sentence of its own. More than half the cities in Israel and the surrounding countries had been flattened to the ground. There was no longer anything as modern as automobiles, jet airplanes, or railways. All transportation centers had been destroyed, and with so much chaos, there was no production of oil or delivery of gasoline. Cars and trucks sat rusting all over the land. We had dropped back a thousand years, to a time before modern machinery changed the face of the world. What we walked toward was oblivion, without even a sack of supplies or canteens of water to keep us alive.

"Why are you going?" Brad asked me when we reached the edge of Jerusalem. "I didn't think you believed in him."

I shrugged my shoulders. "They'll kill me anyway if I stay. I might as well die among friends."

He took my hand then, and I felt tears threaten. Ahead of us I could see silhouettes against the distance. We were being led into the wilderness to die in the arms of God.

We walked toward Jericho and from there north along the Jordan River toward the Sea of Galilee. In Jericho, skirting the demolished city, we picked up more followers, men and women and children who had somehow heard that we were coming. They shared with us their meager food and drink, and on we walked through the boiling sun.

It was in the Galilee Mountains, with Har Meron looming in the distance at his back, that our young leader performed his first miracle. I witnessed it and therefore record here that it happened, that the event took place and was as real as the paper you now hold in your hand and read.

We were hungry and had begun to bicker. We were thirsty, temperamental, blistered, aching. We were on the verge of losing any hope that what we were doing was rational. I said to Brad, "Maybe we're all maniacs. Maybe our *Messiah* is a lunatic and we're committing mass suicide."

He looked at me as if I were a traitor and stomped off. I didn't really care. We had been thrown together by fate, and now it seemed we would be separated by my coming to my senses. Here on this dry, desolate ground in the shadow of mountains facing starvation I felt fevered with a desire to flee south again, to the cities.

Suddenly there was a rustle through the crowd, like wind through trees, and people began to move forward all of one body, and I went with them, curious to see what might be going on. Was there a fight? Had someone died?

It was wine. From the rocks. It flowed down barely a hand's reach from where our Messiah stood, his face shining like a moon in a black heaven. "If you believe," he shouted, "then you will be delivered." Red wine the color of blood came in a rush, in a river, and it streamed down from the slope toward all of us waiting with our faces upturned into the light of the sun.

He turned to the side and held out both hands to the pathway below him. As he slowly lifted his outstretched arms, there appeared bread loaves and rounds of cheese and heaps of olives and fish flopping, still alive, dozens of them everywhere.

People fell to their knees. I stood transfixed. Could it be? From the rocks and the very air this man had created sustenance for life? This was no magician's trick. I stooped and picked up one of the fish. It was still cold, as if it had just been freshly plucked from the sea.

He really was the Son of God, the King of Kings.

He sped down the hillside, slipping through rockfalls, and he was *laughing*. Laughing straight into the cloudless blue sky.

They killed him in Gesher ha-Ziw on the Mediterranean Sea. Unlike the Christian Jesus, they did not take the time to construct a cross from the wood of a dogwood tree. He was gunned down in the street by a sniper as we entered town, the word having traveled before us that we would come there to gather more believers.

I was back in the crowd, for we numbered in the thousands by then, and the ripple effect of the murder came through us like an ocean wave rolling up a pebbled beach. Some of those around me beat themselves on the back of their shoulders, some fainted, some wept, while others turned to run back to the desert. I stood there, buffeted by people in panic, and thought simply this: What happens now, Lord?

My answer was not long in coming. Even as I write these last words, the world is tearing itself apart with earthquakes. It is splitting asunder beneath our feet. There is an eclipse of the sun, animals and birds have vanished into hiding, the wind howls all around me.

I do not know where we will go, what death has in store, or if anyone will survive the cataclysm to read these pages.

I only know I have done what I could to make sure a record is left behind. I'm sealing this in a metal box I found in a tinker's shop. The walls are shaking all around me, tools have fallen from shelves, lamps are overturned.

Darkness is here and the King of Galilee beckons that I come.

Virolec and the Beast

Rick Wilber

I

Darkness grew from the shadowed hills while the gloaming sky faded. The loch's black water held a low, thick mist that hugged the shoreline, but out where the boy's small curach sat motionless, the fog had cleared and there was a splash of evening star reflected beneath him.

Young Virolec sat as quietly as he could in the frail skin boat. Any movement set it bobbing, and ripples would course outward when that happened. He wanted the water absolutely still.

His withered left foot ached, as it did most nights when he crossed his legs to sit in the curach, and the sole finger on his left hand itched terribly, but he dared not scratch it. He badly wanted to cough.

Instead, he waited. Quietly. When the great beast came, it was always as darkness fell.

There was a sense of movement from below, a slight upwelling, a vague sensation of its approach. He knew what he knew, no matter what his father said. It was there. It was coming.

There was a bump, small but startling, against the curach's bottom. Then, for a long minute, nothing.

Then another bump, and from behind came the sound of the great thing's emergence, a low exhalation. Virolec turned quickly, hoping to see the great head, but the steep hills on the far side of the loch cast a black background and, in truth, he couldn't see whether it was there or not.

"Are you there?" he asked, his voice cracking with excitement. "Have you come this time?"

There was, of course, no reply, but the boy thought perhaps he could see the dim outline of the thing, a huge horse's head, great round eyes open and staring at him.

"I have brought you some more fish," he said, and with his good hand reached down into the basket he had struggled to get aboard the curach. The basket was filled with the fruits of yesterday and today's labor, brimming with fish.

He tossed the first one toward the dim shape that was perhaps there and perhaps not. The fish splashed in the water. Virolec couldn't tell if the shape moved or not. He tossed another, and then more in a few minutes of hard labor so that only a few were left in the bottom of the boat. Then he sat back to let the bobbing curach calm for a moment so that he could watch to see if the Beast would come closer, in a kind of thanks.

It may be that the vague shape moved. It may be that it dove and ate and dove again and then, as the rain of fish finally ended, rose again to stare at the boy who had spent so much time with it on this task. Perhaps.

But Virolec couldn't be sure, and the darkness was full now. His father would wonder where he was. Virolec was forbidden to take the curach out on the loch after dark, and though he snuck away to do exactly that as often as he could, he had seen his father angry and wanted none of that for himself. Quietly, so the watchmen would not hear his rowing, he headed back toward the slate beach at the foot of the castle walls.

Virolec coughed as he worked at the rowing, the phlegm rattling in his chest. He tried to smother the sound, but coughed again and then took a long, labored breath. The night air was always bothersome.

The curach scraped against the beach. He clambered

clumsily out using the good hand and leg, then tugged at the little boat to bring it up onto the beach.

He started the hard climb up to the castle. Behind him, as he left, there was a light splash. He turned to look, but could see nothing in the fog.

II

Emchath, king of Airchartdan, stood behind the vitrified wall of the castle's northwest corner and peered into the night to watch for his son as the boy struggled up out of the curach and into the thin light cast by the castle's torches.

So, the boy was safe. Emchath waved to his watchman and old friend, Ewan, who stood hidden behind another stone rampart. Ewan returned the wave.

They let the boy think he roamed free as often as they could, but he needed protection, and so they practiced this little deceit.

Ewan had his own curach ready to take out on the loch if they thought the boy in danger. And Ewan had actually learned to stay afloat in the water by himself, could splash and keep his head above water for half a day if he needed. He had vowed to watch over the boy, take care of him as best he could, and so had learned this trick of staying afloat.

While the boy snuck in through the castle's open main draw, Emchath walked back to his bed so that young Virolec could come into the room in a few minutes and awaken his father from what seemed to be his evening nap. This small duplicity was a happy ritual that the two had practiced for years, the father feigning sleep while the boy came in with squeals of laughter to wake him up.

Emchath, as king of this small domain, did what he could do to make Virolec's tenuous life a happy one. The boy had surprised everyone by surviving into his twelfth year despite his ruinous lungs and frail body, and that survival itself made him all the more precious to Emchath.

Emchath, truth be known, had his own health to worry about. The small pains in his chest had grown stronger, his shallow breathing ever shorter. He hid this pain from all but his friend Ewan, but Emchath knew his own time was coming, as the time had come to his father and his father's father before him. One day there would be a huge pain, and then there would be no one to lead these people save that coughing, thoughtful boy of his.

He shook his head and started walking slowly back toward his bedchambers. With Ewan to guide him, perhaps the boy would do fine once Emchath was gone. The king hoped so. If not? There was no one else in succession, and King Brude to the north had envious eyes watching this castle on the loch. Old stories of lurking beasts, and the tricks that kept those stories alive, weren't likely to dissuade Brude from attempting a takeover.

Those stories began in the time of Emchath's father. Marauders from the north had come viking this way in the second year of his father's reign. A longboat full of death and fear had been trundled over logs across the narrow passage between the firth and the loch and then had come sailing down toward the small castle.

Some had fled, but the bulk of the glen's men and women had remained within the castle walls, ready to fight and die for their land.

But there had been no need for battle. As the myth remembered, in full sight of the castle's defenders the longboat had shuddered and come to a stop, as if foundered on hidden rocks. Then a great geyser of water had risen, the longboat broke in half, and the marauders were thrown into the water.

Some had drowned, disappearing suddenly into the black depths. Others had been slain as they struggled ashore. A few had begged mercy and been spared. Several of them had even become part of the village as time passed.

And the word of the great beast that destroyed the Viking party had spread through Pictland, growing in the passage.

Emchath's father, taking full advantage of the occurrence, had claimed he controlled the beast in the loch and had begun to exact a toll from those who passed by the castle on their trading voyages.

The threat of the thing had meant safety for the people of Airchartdan and a steady income as well. The village prospered.

Emchath held no belief in the original story, or in the existence of the beast, though his father had sworn the tale true. Emchath was far too pragmatic to believe in monsters, fairies, or the gods, for that matter.

He was, on the other hand, quite glad that so many *did* believe. And he was happy to keep up the pretense. His father, though he made outrageous claims, was pragmatic, too, and had started a small group of stealthy men whose job was to become the beast from time to time, to keep the myth alive.

Those men—and now their sons and grandsons—rowed a low-slung barge with an ornate wooden head fitted at the prow. They made their fog-shrouded attacks as frightening as they could, avoided unnecessary killing so that there would be survivors to spread word of the vicious beast.

All of this was a sham, a fakery. But the tolls were paid, and the glen safe for all these many seasons.

Now all that might change. Emchath climbed tiredly into his bed, waited patiently for his son's arrival, felt his breathing ease as he lay there, and thought of the newest threat.

There was word from the south that a party of Scots traveled this way up the Great Glen, bringing word of their new god and promises of peace and prosperity. Their leader, Emchath suspected, would be the famous Blessed Columba himself, coming north from Iona at last to work miracles for the heathen Picts.

Emchath chuckled at that. He found all religions foolish and over the years had been baptized in several different ones when that seemed to keep the peace. This new

Christianity, he thought, sounded just as outlandish as the rest of them.

Still, a religious zealot was unlikely to want to pay the requisite toll. And, Emchath thought, these Scots had already traveled north from their own lands to the western isles in just a few years. They were a hardy lot, and pushy, not like the Romans, who had been content to venture north, fight, lose, and leave. Emchath knew that even if the Scots came this way in peace and were met with friendship they would keep coming and keep coming.

That would be fine with the people of Airchartdan, who would happily take tolls from the travelers. But, Emchath sighed, to the north was the ambitious Brude, who had united the Pictish nation under one leader for the first time in generations. Brude was more likely to welcome the Scots with battle than with friendship.

Brude was a quarrelsome, demanding king. Though he would have preferred to do otherwise, Emchath had sworn fealty to him, trying to avoid conflict. Brude, in turn, had agreed to pay the tolls on the loch, but had grumbled excessively about them. Emchath expected more trouble as Brude's power grew.

So, Brude to the north and now to the south these pushy Scots. In between, Emchath thought sourly, were the few hundred people of Airchartdan and their fictitious beast. There would be difficult times ahead.

Poor, dear Virolec. Emchath worried mightily for him, fragile thing. Could he lead these people? The boy had shown no signs that he could. He was quiet, withdrawn, cursed with a vivid imagination. The boy thought he could commune with the beast, for instance, even claimed to have seen the thing, to have talked to it.

He was bright enough, to be sure. Even brilliant, perhaps. But he was physically so frail and emotionally so dreamy. The king doubted whether Virolec would be able to rally the people to him should the need arise.

He remembered the day the boy was born. The birthing had been difficult, Rhiannon so weakened by it that she had died within the month after bearing him.

The old Druid in attendance had recommended killing the baby immediately.

"He brings great change," the old fool had said. "He is not of our ways, he will bring ruin on the glen."

But the baby squalled and kicked lustily, and Rhiannon had smiled so to hold him. Emchath hadn't the heart to kill the fey little newcomer. And now, after watching the boy play on the slopes and row his curach on the loch, Emchath knew he had made the right choice, Druid priests be damned.

The door to Emchath's chambers opened and a small head peeked through. Emchath sank low into his woolen blanket, eyes closed, and waited for his son to jump on the bed with glee to awaken him. A brief wrestling match ensued, complete with a great host of young giggles and old laughter. Finally, the blanket over him and the boy over that, Emchath admitted defeat and begged for mercy. Virolec, giggling, granted it, and the two decided it was time for the evening meal.

Walking down the long hallway to the kitchen, where the two chose to eat most often, Emchath sent word for Ewan. After he broke bread with the boy, Emchath thought, he would have to gather the men and make plans. With this Blessed Columba fellow coming, the beast had a bit of its work to do.

III

The Blessed Columba did not feel particularly blessed by the miserable evening weather they rowed through. Pulling hard at the oars, he thought of his homeland to the south and west, where the rain was gentle and followed by warm sunshine. Here, the cold showers lashed him, and there seemed no respite from them for days on end. He found himself taking a turn at the oars more often than was seemly, just in an effort to keep warm.

He came unannounced to these Pictish lands, hoping to win converts to the true faith. In some parts of Britain he had spread the Word easily and won many to his side, but here he held no false hopes. These Picts had held to the old ways for centuries, had defeated the Romans, the Vikings, and anyone else who'd ventured into these lochs and mountains. Columba knew his work here was important, but he realized it would be difficult and dangerous.

Still, fingers stiff on the oars, he looked forward to reaching his first stop, at Airchartdan, and beginning his efforts. Airchartdan, with the wily King Emchath, was the key to the northern lands, Columba knew, and, he added to himself, a stop at the castle there would get them all out of this awful weather.

He smiled broadly at himself for having such a thought, an admission of his own weakness. He was glad the grin was hidden from the view of the others by the cowl of his jerkin. Some sainted philosopher, he, worried about the rain as he traveled to spread the Word and bring the Christ to these Picts.

He allowed himself a low chuckle. Some of the brothers thought Columba a miracle maker, probably thought he could control the very weather. Young Adamnan—he of the dour attitude and the constant scribbling—was at the lead of them. Adamnan no doubt thought this miserable rain to be Columba's idea, to hide them from enemies until they reached their destination. He would probably write the rain down as another miracle in that journal he kept.

"Blessed One, are you ill?" the scribbler asked from his perch in the stern of the long, narrow boat. He had heard Columba's chuckle, thought it a cough, and worried for his master's health.

Columba waved the worry away. "A slight cough, young Adamnan. Nothing more. A clearing of the throat."

"This terrible rain must be chilling you to the very marrow," Adamnan mused. "Perhaps we should put in now and make camp for the night."

"No, no. Another hour or two, Adamnan. We may find our way there yet this evening if we press on. And I, for one, am fine as long as I stay at the oars. It is you, sitting there in the wind and the rain with no exercise to keep you warm, that I worry about."

"Me, Blessed One? Worry not about me. I have the strength of ten men in me while allowed to accompany you."

Columba sighed. The poor youngster. Such zeal. Admirable in its own way, true, but the young monk was much too serious, did not know how to laugh or enjoy himself, took too much stock in Columba's supposed powers and not enough stock in his own skills. Columba had little patience with awestruck acolytes, even ones who could write. He wished the best for Adamnan but hoped that he would come in time to see Columba as a man, not a prophet. Save the worship for the Lamb.

Columba knew the power he held—and the power he didn't hold, as well. He let the brothers think what they might when such belief was useful to the work. But Columba knew himself to be only a man, and a cold and wet one at that. As far as he was concerned, his successes came from the Word working through him, that was all. He heard the Lamb speak to him, took those words for his own, said them aloud so that all might listen, and so the Word was spread.

It was that simple. There was no magic (though his enemies within the Church and without had accused him of that), no miracles. Just the Word.

Columba shivered and bent to the oar with a vengeance as a gust of cold rain whipped past the cowl to blow against his face. He wished the clouds would break and the rain ease, or that the wind would turn to blow them north, or that he could row faster and the others with him.

Now that, he thought, would be a miracle worth having, the sudden strength to row faster. The sooner there, Columba thought, the sooner dry and warm.

IV

In the prow of the royal barge, Brude, the first king of all Pictland in generations, stood alone. Dressed in thick tanned leather from armpits to waist, he carried a long sword, two daggers, and a throwing spear. At his side lay the curved shield with the sharpened rim and the family's pride, a burnished Roman breastplate won in battle generations ago. On the morrow, he would wear that protective breastplate and carry that deadly shield into combat.

He was tall for his time, and sturdily built. His body bore the marks of his success—long, slashing scars on forearms and calves, a cruel scar, too, down his right cheek.

And there was a new cut, healing now, nearly hid by his full moustache. He had won this latest scar and his crown in the struggle with Tavish that finally brought him full control over the scattered dominions of Pictland. But Tavish was all the warrior that Brude would ever want to meet. Two weeks had passed since their champion struggle, and only now had the pain in Brude's head and neck begun to recede. For Tavish, of course, the pain ended that day.

Brude fingered the gold torque that encircled his neck and thanked the gods the torque was there. It was meant to be an ornament, nothing more, but at the end of the fight Tavish's small blade would have slit Brude's throat save for that torque.

Brude spent the past few days in the standing stones of Clava to thank his ancient gods for that small favor. Going to that place unattended was foolish, perhaps, but Brude felt the need, and if answering such need with action was not his choice to make, why be king?

The ancient standing stones of the place called to him. Set in circles around two facing cairns, they spoke of an ancient and powerful past, a time of glory, a time long before the Romans, long before even the Druids.

Brude was a simple man, really, and not one prone to dreamy mysticism. But he did think often of the past honor his people had known, and he thought himself the one to lead them to that glory again, though there had been many generations since the Romans, the needed enemy, faded away. For ten long years he fought, clan to clan, to consolidate the Pictish people, to make them one, to make them ready to regain their rightful place.

And now there was a new enemy, one that closed in as he traveled south down the loch to meet it, one worth fighting.

The Scottish Celts were coming, the same Christian invaders who had come from their island to the south to occupy Dalriada and the Western Isles. They brought their own strange god with them, and their greed for more land, more power.

Brude had known for the past several years that, in time, the Celts would come here too, up the great glen from Iona, along the lochs, past Airchartdan, and then on to Inverness.

He had hoped to have more time to get ready for them. Another year, perhaps two, and he would have an army that could withstand anything from the south.

But this enemy was not going to wait. A party of them came this way now, no doubt to parley, to negotiate.

Instead, thought Brude, he would slaughter them. He had learned early in his campaign to unite the Picts that the best action was often the quickest. Attack early, attack hard. By the time word got back to Iona and the Scots could pull together a force to come back north for retribution, winter would be arriving. The Scots would wait for spring, and then the plantings, before they came. By then, Brude thought, he would be ready.

What a battle that would be, a glorious thing, one that the scops would make into a song that would last for all time.

So today he traveled down the River Ness to the loch, and on the morrow at first light the barge would row down to the old castle at Airchartdan, the vitrified walls of the ancient place a testament to a bloody past. There he would meet the Celts while their numbers were few, and sack the troublesome Emchath's little castle while he was there. Brude needed to control that passage himself, and this coming battle was the perfect excuse.

Brude had no fear of the great dark beast said to guard that castle. Brude had never seen the thing, knew no one who had, and didn't much worry whether it existed or no. He pulled his sword from the leather scabbard and held it up to see his face reflected in the burnished sheen of the blade.

This existed, this blade and its sharpened edge. And the face within it existed too and now ruled. For the rest? He would deal with it as it came.

V

His father hadn't wanted Virolec to hear, had shooed him from the room when the men came in, but the boy, like his father, had a certain flair for the surreptitious, and he knew this castle's crannies better than anyone. Ten minutes, no more, of crawling through a narrow passage and sidling silently sideways behind a hung tapestry, and he had heard every word.

The Men of the Beast would travel this night down the loch to meet these Scots coming north. There would be an attack from the beast, the Scots would flee south, carrying word of the creature back to their homeland, and Airchartdan would be safe again for a time.

The boy was not surprised to hear this. He knew of the men, had known since his fifth year, though he'd never admitted as much to his father. In fact, for months now he had thought of how he might go along on such an adventure, though he knew his father would never let him. The raids sounded very exciting.

Knowing that such a time would have to come again, he had made plans of his own. Now, while the men talked, he left, edging out from under the tapestry and back through the narrow passage before hurrying to his

room. A warm cloak, his dagger, the spot he'd found in
that corner of the barge. Tonight, the hero.

VI

For a brief time there had been clear skies, the gloaming above, a hesitant moon rising over the hills. Columba,
standing at the prow to take a rest from the weary work
of rowing, had for a few minutes enjoyed the sight of the
rising moon's reflection on the loch, the silver path reaching across to them on the boat.

The scene was beautiful, as picturesque as any in his
homeland or around Iona. Steep hills rose on both sides
of the water, with their destination, the castle at
Airchartdan, ahead in the far distance on a point of land
that jutted into the loch, narrowing the passage north. An
easy place to defend, a difficult one to attack. The castle
had a reputation for strength that brought profit in the taking of tolls as trade moved up and down the lochs.

And, of course, there was that heathen monster that
was said to inhabit the water. When the tolls weren't paid,
the stories held that the monster attacked the boats, de-
vouring those who fell into the black water.

The devil's work? Columba doubted it. His experience
held that man was devil enough without needing Satan or
his creatures to add to the misery. The monster, he
thought, was more likely one of the imagination than a
fearsome beast that sank ships that paid no toll. Perhaps
there was *something* in these waters—an ancient creature,
some very large fish. But whatever the thing might be,
Columba was sure it was nothing that strong arms and a
stout hull couldn't manage.

All of which was not to say that one couldn't believe in
all manner of strange creatures in a climate like this. In
almost an instant, it seemed, the thick fog returned, and
they again rowed through cold, spitting rain and thick
gray mist. Staring ahead, he could see nothing but
swirling tendrils of fog. He'd be happy, indeed, to finally

reach the castle at Airchartdan and begin the Lamb's work.

VII

The fog was patchy, and Virolec, hidden in the hides of a curach set toward the back of the barge, could hear the men grousing about that. They needed the mist; without the fog to help them, the Men of the Beast could not perform their work.

Soon they would put the scouting curachs over the side, and those small craft would seek out the Scots. Once they spied the other boat and signaled by tugging on the small ropes that connected them to the barge, the Men of the Beast truly began their work, rowing with muffled oars to the other boat, then ramming it in a sudden charge. A backward row with the well-trained crew, another ram from the other side—and all of this in dead silence. No commands need be made, no shouts of joy or success, just the deadly, frightening silence.

Always by the second ramming the other boat's crew was over the side. The fearful blindness of the fog, the myth of the beast, the reality of the shocking attack—it was all too much for the simple traders who came this way.

Virolec peeked through the hides and saw the shadowy shapes of the men preparing for the ramming.

At the last possible moment, the men would light the torches set in pitch that glared through the eyeholes of the great head that sat on the front of the barge.

Scouting alone in the curach, nearly awash in the tiny thing, searching out the enemy, was a position of great honor. Those men who knew the loch best served there.

Now, knowing they were approaching the Scots, the men launched the curachs, carefully easing them over the side, avoiding unnecessary splashing or talk. In the corner of the first one, the one rowed by Ewan, the king's man, hidden under a blanket, was Virolec.

VIII

Columba was turning to speak to Adamnan when there was a bump beneath them, a movement that began at the prow and rapidly traveled the length of the boat to the stern, scraping along the bottom of the hull.

A log lying low in the water? Hidden rocks?

Columba said nothing. Adamnan, eyes wide, waited. The other monks shipped oars.

For a long minute there was nothing more. Columba, finally, spoke, his voice strong, the tone stern, commanding: "A log, that was all. The Lamb protects us, brothers. Let us move on."

He wished he felt half so confident as he sounded. He turned to stare forward into the mist.

The men put their oars back in, but slowly. Adamnan, seeing their hesitation, chided them: "The Blessed Columba is with us, brothers. What could we have to fear?"

And as he said that, the water erupted before Columba's very face, a fountain rising in an incredible spray.

There was a head, huge, in front of them, and then a deep shudder and the splintering of shattered wood as the head met them. Their boat rocked and rocked again as the beast's head pulled back from them and disappeared into the fog.

The monks cried out in fear that first moment and scrambled to avoid the jaws of death. Several leapt overboard, but now, more fearful of being in the water than in the boat, they clambered back aboard.

Adamnan pulled his cross from around his neck and raised it high to ward off the beast. "Away, devil! Away!" he cried.

Columba, against his own common sense, signed the cross himself, then went to the more mundane task of assessing the damage.

Their prow was stove in, but the damage was mostly above the waterline. There were in no danger of sinking immediately. The one leak could be blocked with a robe, and that would buy them the time to reach the shore.

He dropped his own robe from his shoulders, turned to ask Adamnan for help, and saw the look of terror on his scribe's face.

Adamnan could only point the cross at what he saw. Columba turned, and there, coming again, was the head of the beast, its mouth open to take them from the very deck of their boat, to consume them, devour them.

"The beast!" Adamnan screamed. "The beast returns!"

There was a violent shock as the head of the thing hit them again. The men screamed in fear, some signing the cross, others flailing with the oars, striking out in terror at the apparition.

Columba grabbed the bow stanchion and held on for dear life as the ship rolled side to side. The water poured in the prow now through a large hole.

There was a surreal moment of calm, the only sound a low moan from the terrified Adamnan and the gurgling of the water pouring into the boat.

Columba gathered his wits, wondered if this was all, if they could swim to the nearby shore, when there came another, final eruption in the water, and the great head of a beast rose over the sinking prow of their boat. There was a screaming, an almost human cry, and then a deep shudder from beneath them and the boat, in a moment, turned turtle, throwing all of them into the frigid water. Columba, hanging dizzyingly to the cross on the prow, was whipped through the air, his hands torn from the wooden cross as he flew head over heels into the mist.

IX

Ewan had discovered the lad after just a few minutes' rowing. The balance was wrong in the curach, and Ewan moved to shift the skins around on the bottom. A pale face stared up, worried.

Ewan had laughed. Perhaps this boy had some courage, after all. He shushed him, promised not to tell the king, and then put the boy to work, staring into the night.

So he and the boy had seen the Scots, tugged on their rope, and then rowed the frail curach to a safe distance to watch. They could see the dim result of the ramming in the thinning fog. Once, twice, three times, the barge had rammed the boat full of Christian monks, and there had been great terror and screaming from the Scots.

Now there was a low cry of fear from many of them, and a great deal of splashing. Unless they were utter fools, though, few of the monks would drown. The ruins of their boat floated everywhere, and the shore was only a short distance away. Surely most of them would grab onto a plank and then paddle over toward shore. That, as ever, was the plan. The more survivors, the better, to spread the word of the beast's attack.

There was a splashing nearby, a sputtering of water blown into the air, a gasping and some curses.

Ewan himself cursed. He didn't want to have to save someone, not with Virolec in the curach with him. But he couldn't let the man drown. He rowed in the direction of the sounds.

Virolec, peering into the mist, was the one who saw the flailing hand above the water just before it disappeared.

He pointed, and Ewan was over the side in a moment, swimming under the water toward the spot where the man had gone down, reaching out to find him.

A thick wool shirt. A head full of hair. Ewan grabbed, caught, and tugged with both hands, straining to reach the surface.

He managed, barely, to break the water with his own face and gasp for air and help from young Virolec.

Between the two of them they wrestled the fellow into the curach and began to row toward the shore. They would, no doubt, pick up one or two others on the way.

The monk lay there for a few minutes as they rowed, then rose to his knees, shook himself like a great dog fresh from the water, and sat.

"Bless you," he said to Ewan and Virolec. "You've saved my life." He looked around. "What of the others? There are nine of us."

"Most will have made the shore, by now, I should think," said Virolec before Ewan could answer. "But keep a sharp eye out; we'll pick up more on our way in if we can."

The man nodded, looked out into the darkness, spoke: "It is the Lord's blessing that you were here in this craft. Our boat was," he hesitated, "attacked. By that beast they say lurks here. Rammed us. Attacked us. A beast."

"We were fishing," said Virolec, "and heard your cries. We saw nothing of a beast, though. Are you sure?"

The monk nodded. "I would not have believed the stories myself until this night. But, yes, a beast. A great huge thing, it was."

Virolec smiled, but to himself. Emchath would be happy to hear this story spread.

The fog had cleared here, and they could see dim shapes in the distance as they approached the shore. Then, a few minutes later, the curach scraped bottom and they were there.

Several of the monks came splashing out to meet them, and that was how Virolec and Ewan found that the Blessed Columba himself had been in the boat with them.

There were great exclamations of joy at Columba's survival, and many hugs and warm words all around as the monks, one by one, knelt at Columba's feet for his blessing at their all being alive.

In this way, Columba came to realize that one, only one, was missing. Adamnan the scribe.

"Where is he? Who saw him last?" Columba asked of the other monks. But none could answer. Adamnan had disappeared in the same general melee that had pitched them all overboard.

"We must search. Can you take me back out there?" Columba asked Virolec and Ewan, who had watched with some amusement as the monks had sought Columba's blessing.

Virolec nodded, "Certainly, Blessed One. He may well be out there, floating on a piece of wreckage. But we need to act quickly, before the beast returns to consume your floating scribe."

Ewan smiled at that, but said nothing. He would be happy to tell Emchath of how well his son had done here, taking charge like this, and even gently mocking the Celts.

They shoved off, and in moments were out onto the loch. The night was clear now, and the stars threw down a thin light onto the water's surface. But there was no Adamnan. Virolec, with the best eyes in the threesome, thought he saw a floating form once, and a pale face in the dim light, but there was nothing there at all when they reached that spot.

Columba was silent as the other two rowed. Poor Adamnan, poor, gentle Adamnan. To be lost like this, in the very jaws, perhaps, of that wretched beast. Ah, the story that he might have told. This was exactly the sort of thing that Adamnan loved best, something with a sense of adventure and courage, filled with dangerous beasts and terrible danger.

There was a bump from beneath, a scraping noise. The beast returned.

Then, to their left, there was another great fountain of water, a showering of cold darkness from below. And there, in the very midst of spray, rising as if catapulted from the depths, was the ragged, chubby form of Brother Adamnan, his eyes shut tight against the terror, gasping for breath.

He rose a full body's length into the air and then came down into the water in a sloppy, flailing dive. There may have been a huge rippling in the water beneath the monk as they approached.

Columba scrambled over the side of the curach and swam to Adamnan, grabbed him by the cowl of his robe and began to pull him toward the curach. The scribe was draped in ropes from their shattered boat. Perhaps those ropes or debris from the boat attached to him had eventually dragged him under. When the debris floated clear,

Adamnan came to the surface. Columba pulled and tugged on the roping, brought some of the wrappings free, and floundered with Adamnan toward the curach.

As they reached the small boat, Adamnan slowly opened his eyes, saw Columba in the water with him, and wept for joy. "My blessed, my blessed," he whimpered. "You saved me from the beast." And he clasped the tired Columba around the neck.

Virolec and Ewan looked at each other, rolled their eyes, and helped bring the two monks aboard. Within minutes they were rowing again toward the shore, all the monks now accounted for.

Blessed Columba sat tiredly, cross-legged, in the bottom of the curach, and shook his head in wonder. To think that the beast was real. It was amazing, a miracle. He would have to try and tame the thing with prayer, he supposed, and sighed. This was not a welcome task; the thing was fearsome.

There was a moaning in the distance, and Columba looked up to see that they were not yet at the shore.

Another moan, a keening, crying in the darkness, and then the head of the beast loomed not twenty yards away, coming toward them.

Virolec and Ewan cursed together, seeing the same beast, and rowed mightily to get out of its way. They were nearly clear when the beast turned to come again toward them, and from behind the beast's head a voice sounded. One of the men of Airchartdan.

"Ewan. Young Virolec. Is that you? The king, he needs you. Quickly."

Emchath's heart was finally giving out. The excitement of the ramming had brought him first to his knees, and then onto the skins at the bottom of the barge, his face contorted with the pain, his left arm seemingly afire, his chest exploding.

Virolec and Ewan came to him.

"My son, my son, do I dream that you are here?" he struggled to say.

"It is I, Father. Rest easy. We travel home now. You'll be better with rest."

Emchath managed to shake his head. No. Not better.

"My time ends, son. Yours begins." He turned to stare at Ewan. "You'll help him?"

Ewan nodded. He had never cried until that moment.

Emchath said no more. Together, side by side, Ewan and Virolec watched him die in quiet, final passing.

X

A misty, cool dawn slowly brightened the loch as the beast's barge traveled slowly toward the castle. Aboard were the Celtic monks, the new king, Virolec, and Ewan his advisor, and Emchath, hands across his chest, guardian of the glen of Airchartdan for these forty seasons and now gone on to calmer times.

"So this has all been a sham," Columba said to Virolec as they neared the rocky shore at the south base of the castle. "The great beast, the sinkings, all just trickery."

"Yes. The sinkings. But there is a beast, Columba. It lives here. I've seen it," Virolec said.

Columba nodded. Of course. The poor lad, his father gone like this. And now at this tender age, and such a fragile child, he assumes command. Sad.

They were beached on the rocky shore, and carrying Emchath's body from the barge, when a watchman hailed from the tower. The fitful fog had lifted to the north, and the man had seen a barge approaching, pennant flying. King Brude and his men. Armored.

An attack! And at such a time.

Ewan took command, ordering the men to carry Emchath's body into safe haven within and then sending the men to their places on the castle walls. They were few enough, and tired, and poorly armed, but they would fight.

* * *

Brude, aboard his barge, watched as men scrambled from Emchath's beached barge to clamber into the castle. There might be thirty of them, perhaps a few more. The mist closed down his sight again, but he'd seen enough to smile.

Brude, with his fifty stout men, all veterans, all well-armed, would take the castle in a few minutes' work. With luck, the Celtic monks would already be there. If not, he would handle them next. Either way, his problems were about to be solved. Standing at the prow of the barge, wearing the Roman breastplate that had been handed down from father to son for six generations, he raised his sword and pointed toward the castle. Behind him, keen for the fight, came shouts from his men and the clatter and thud of metal to leather as they donned their armor.

XI

Virolec had been the first off the barge, and ignoring his withered leg as best he could, had struggled over the rocks to his curach in just those few minutes.

There he shoved the little boat into the water, climbed in after, and started rowing. There was a way, he thought: If the beast was as he believed it to be, there was a way.

Brude saw the little curach in the mist, bobbing along in their path, floating directly between the barge and the castle. He waved at the helmsman to go right over the fool. Some trick of Emchath's, he supposed, something to get them to turn. Well, he wouldn't fall for such blatant trickery. They rowed on.

Virolec could see the barge bearing down. He slapped the water with his good hand. Slapped again. And again.

And there came a bump from beneath. And that stirring, that upwelling of water.

Virolec looked over the side and thought, perhaps, that

he could see, dimly in the peaty water, those open eyes staring back, that vast bulk beneath.

Virolec took the single fish and threw it toward the approaching barge. Perhaps, perhaps.

The face disappeared.

The fog closed in thick. There was a bump beneath the barge. Had they run down that curach? Brude supposed so, but wondered for a moment if they had somehow run aground, here in the middle of the loch, with the castle in sight just ahead.

Another bump. Had others felt it?

Brude turned to look at the crew and his warriors who traveled with him. They all stood, the oars raised, the barge drifting with its momentum, waiting.

A bump and then a long slide down the length of the barge, and then, just ahead of the craft, a great upwelling of water, a sudden spout and fountain of cold, black loch and then there was, staring at Brude, king of all the Picts, the first in four generations to unite the clans, a monster, the beast itself, rising from the water, a man's length of neck, more, twice that, still rising.

And looking down on him, eyes open, staring.

Spears flew toward it. Most missed, two hit and bounced off, another struck the neck and went in, hung there for a moment, and then dropped into the loch.

The beast opened its mouth as if to roar in pain, but no sound emerged. It came toward the barge, lowered the head toward Brude, as if charging him.

Behind him, Brude could hear the rustle of movement, then the splashes of men abandoning the barge, choosing the loch over waiting for the creature to ram the barge.

Brude stood his ground—alone, he guessed, though he didn't dare turn away to look.

The beast slowed its advance. Stopped. Let the barge drift slowly toward it as it stared. Brude could sense a hint of the thing's huge bulk beneath the water, a disturbance in the water more than anything else, certainly nothing you could see in the murky loch.

Brude drew his sword. Held the blade toward the beast as the barge bumped against the neck, stopped.

He slashed out, cut the thing across that long neck so that the skin parted and he could see a whiteness within before red, red blood welled up. But there was no spurting, nothing vital had been cut.

He slashed again, and those great eyes watched as he took both hands to the hilt and brought the shoulders back to start a full turn.

Another bump from below, the great bulk of the thing pushing against the bottom of the barge, threw him off and the slashing cut fell short.

Another bump, stronger, and now the barge began to rise at the prow and tilt ominously.

It rose again, higher, and Brude dropped the sword to grab at the nearest post and hang on.

Higher, the barge twisting to shake them all out into the loch's cold water. Brude fell, and in that fall remembered that he still wore the Roman breastplate, the family's pride, the mark of his kingship, that bore him heavily into the depths as he struggled with the clasps.

The battle was over in moments. Brude's men either shed their armor and swam for the shore or sank beneath the dark water. Those who reached the shore were captured. A few clung to bits of wreckage. Most died.

Virolec watched what he could see of the fight through the fitful mist. He saw the king slash at something, then slash again.

Then Brude's barge rose, rolled, and collapsed, spilling men and weapons into the loch in a chaotic jumble.

In a moment the action was done, and the small boy, king of Airchartdan, coughed once or twice and then took up his oar to head back in to shore.

On the castle walls and lining the shore there was as large a host as Airchartdan could gather. They, together with the monks from Iona, watched in the fog, seeing the barge come to a stop, watching as the boat rose and seemed to pour their enemy out into the cold water. There may have been a long neck against the prow as the barge rose. There was, perhaps, a body pushing against the hull to make the barge turn turtle. Perhaps.

But there was no question about who rowed back into the small, calm bay at the base of the castle. They raised a great cheer as their new king paddled his humble curach back toward them. The reign of their new leader was off to an auspicious start. The king of Airchartdan stood shakily in his curach to accept their adulation.

A week later, negotiations successful, a small group of men stood on the shore of the loch. One, the tallest, spoke, then splashed water onto the smallest, baptizing Virolec in the name of the Lamb and welcoming the young king into the Kingdom of the Lord.

In return, the Scots would pay their tolls as they passed by, and honor the peace they now enjoyed with Airchartdan.

Virolec, the first Christian king of the Picts, felt about such things as his father might have. One god was as good as the next, and as long as the beast was out there on the loch, the glen was safe enough.

Signing the cross for the first time, he looked out onto the water and thought perhaps he saw there, just rising, the head of the thing, watching the ceremony, watching young Virolec. Later that night, and for many more to come, Virolec rowed out in his old curach and threw fish into the water to give thanks.

Author's Note

In 624 A.D. Adamnan was born in Tirhugh, Ireland. Later a sainted holy man in his own right, as a young monk Adamnan accompanied Columba up the Great Glen to Airchartdan (modern Glen Urquhart) and recorded the travels in his famous *Life of St. Columba.*

Adamnan records in those annals the first mention we

have of what we now call the Loch Ness Monster. Adamnan, writing in Latin, calls it the "*aquatilis bestia* and tells us the story of how a young monk was rescued from the very jaws of the beast by Columba. Later in the same journey, Adamnan reports, Columba baptized an aged Pict, Emchath, and his son, Virolec. The text seems to indicate that Emchath was a powerful local lord.

Brude was a powerful Pictish king of the period who united the various clans for the first time in generations. He is reported in various sources to have met with Columba.

The current Urquhart castle ruins date from the sixteenth century, but archaeological digs at the site indicate it has been fortified since at least the time of Christ. Several miles away is the site of the standing stones of Clava, which I have Brude visit. These upright stones and accompanying funeral cairns date from about 2500 B.C. Visitors to the famous Culloden Moor battlefield (where Bonnie Prince Charlie and his Highlanders suffered defeat at the hands of the English) will find a visit to Clava, only a mile or so away, well worth the small effort.

The Picts were at their apex from before the time of the Romans (who gave up trying to conquer Scotland and built the Antonine Wall to stop Pictish incursions) to not long after Brude's time. Eventually, intermarriage with the ambitious Scots and their own relatively small numbers led the Picts into decline, and they disappeared.

Some of the actions described here are my own inventions, but most do seem to have occurred. The principal historical figures in this account are, as nearly as we can tell, quite real. Adamnan, Columba, Virolec, Emchath, and Brude really lived in that place and at that time.

As to the beast in the loch, who can say for sure?

R.W.
August 1993

Please to See the King

Debra Doyle and James D. Macdonald

Aelwulf of Ruxton was not a far-traveled man; he tended his garden and tilled his share of the common land and never ventured more than a half-day's journey from his own fireside. When he saw the great war-horse cropping grass at the forest margin, its trappings of blue and gold spoke to him only of rank and wealth, and nothing more.

The horse's owner sat resting beneath a nearby tree. The man was dressed in metal, shining in the setting sun, underneath a cloth surcoat. From where Aelwulf stood, he could see part of an armored shoulder, and a shield lying half on the ground and half on the stranger's knee.

High above in the tree, a crow cawed. The horse grazed, unconcerned, its bridle dragging on the turf.

Aelwulf began to circle wide, out of the stranger's sight. The less that common men had to do with noble folk, the better for everyone. But even in Ruxton, the villagers had heard talk of rebellion and war, and this morning had brought a smell of smoke on the east wind. Now curiosity, as much as anything else, prompted Aelwulf to glance back over his shoulder.

The man hadn't changed position. He still leaned against the tree, and his face was all red, the red of dried blood and torn meat.

Aelwulf stopped for a moment. "That one's in trouble," he muttered, and crossed himself.

He thought about going on and leaving the man to his

fate, but then thought better of it. Perhaps his fortune lay in helping out rather than holding back. Charity is a virtue, and rich men give rich rewards.

He stepped out of the woods. "Hallo, master," he called, but no answer came besides a flapping and a cawing from the crows that perched on the tree limbs.

Aelwulf moved nearer. He could hear the bluebottles now, a great buzzing cloud of them, and he could see where carrion birds had been at work on the stranger's face, everywhere that the mail coif and the helmet hadn't covered. The dead man's eye sockets were empty, the lips and tongue were gone from his gaping jaw, and bloody skin hung in tatters over the rest.

The fine cloth of the man's surcoat was torn and cut about and stained all over with blood. An arrow protruded from the man's left side, and his right hand still rested on the shaft where he had been trying to pluck it out.

The smell came to Aelwulf as the summer breeze shifted. He crossed himself again, but stepped closer. Rich men carried gold, and this one had no more use for any of his.

The body had been there for more than a little while, and it was no longer stiff. Aelwulf pulled off one of the dead man's gauntlets, a cloud of flies rising in protest as he moved the corpse. The man's hand inside the mail-and-leather glove was swollen and mottled blue. Gold and iron rings had sunk deep into his swollen flesh.

"Begging your pardon, my lord," Aelwulf said, and set to work with his little knife.

The dead man's surcoat was of blue and gold, and blue and gold were the designs daubed on the battered wooden shield. He had a leather sword belt and a sword in a wooden scabbard, with twisted wire on the metal hilts. Aelwulf looked at the sword and thought of the blacksmith in Ruxton village, and how much trouble he had getting iron.

"The plough's in need of a coulter," he said, and drew the sword out of its scabbard.

The pouch at the man's belt held three silver pennies and a little cut stone which shone with red fire. The stranger's boots of good stout leather fit Aelwulf well enough; the spurs, though, he did not need. He cast them aside and turned to the dead man's horse—too fine a beast for plow or cart, but sure to bring a good price at Saint Mary's fair. The saddlebags held fine woolen blankets and a blue cloak, and some sheets of parchment like those Priest Martin had in his mass-book, all covered with dangling seals and with writing in black and red.

Late that night, under the full moon, Aelwulf buried the dead man, and with him buried those things—the helm with its circlet of gold pried off, the coat of mail, the spurs, the seals and writing—for which he had no use. The gold and silver he carried home and buried beneath a loose stone in his hearth, with the sword lying on top. He resolved—for he was not a bad man—to have Priest Martin say a Requiem for the stranger and to pay for it with one of the silver pennies.

Aelwulf never got the chance to have a Mass sung for the stranger who had brought him wealth. Before sunup the next morning a troop of armed and armored men rode out of the Ruxton Wood with blazing torches in their fists— trampling the crops in the fields, firing the thatched houses, and putting pigs, cows, chickens, and men to the sword.

Aelwulf died. His cottage, burned and roofless, crumbled and fell in upon itself like all the others. Far away in the high castle, a rebellious lord proclaimed himself king by right of arms. And if he ruled no better than the man who had been king before him, at least he ruled no worse.

Time passed. The new king grew old, and the son who would have been king after him died before his time. The great lords of the blood royal waited for the king to name another heir, or to die without one. And late on a cold and windy night in the autumn years of the usurper's reign, a young man who called himself Diccon came for shelter to the place of ruined walls where Ruxton village had once stood.

Diccon was a singer of the common sort; he lacked the true bardic gift that would have made him welcome everywhere, even among the great lords. But he had a fair ear for a tune, and a good memory for stories and gossip, and those were enough to gain him a place in the warmth whenever there was a fire to be had. On this night, though, and this near to the king's high castle, he was a long way from any house where he might be welcome.

But the wind was blowing hard and chill, so when Diccon came to the ruined village he gathered sticks of woods and laid them in the hearth of one of the broken buildings. He struck sparks from the flint he carried in his tinderbox and built a fire to cook a rabbit he had snared that day in the Ruxton Wood.

He'd just finished pulling the half-charred meat off the rabbit's bones with his teeth when he heard the silvery clink of a bridle out in the dark. He scrambled to his feet and stood with his back to the crumbling wall and one hand near the staff he had propped against the stones.

"Who's there?" he called out.

No answer came back out of the darkness, and he did not hear the chiming sound again. After a while, he rolled himself up in his woolen cloak, with the staff near to hand, and slept.

In the middle of the night he woke and thought he heard the sound of footsteps moving through the brambles and the dry grass outside the broken cottage. He sat up, with his cloak still pulled around him against the night air.

"Who's there?" he said again and, because he was a kind-hearted young man, "If you need shelter, come up to the hearth."

But no answer came from the darkness outside the low firelight, and after a while he lay back and slept once more.

Along toward morning, when the wind died and the stars began to fade, Diccon woke again. This time he heard no sound, but when he opened his eyes a woman stood inside the ruined cottage. The coals on the abandoned hearth threw a dim red light onto her silken gown and her long dark hair.

"My lady," said Diccon, for he had been well brought up before he took to the open road. "Be welcome. What I have is yours also."

"What you have here, I don't require," the lady said, but she smiled as she said it, and her voice was kind. "But tell me truly: Will you come away with me, or take what lies beneath the hearthstone yonder?"

Diccon smiled back at her—but he had learned caution almost as early as he'd learned his manners. "Now that's a fine and dangerous question," he said. "Who knows what a man like me might find, in one place or the other?"

"Your heart's desire," said the lady. "Or your rightful place in the world."

Diccon looked thoughtful. "Do you know who I am?"

"I do. Do you know me?"

"I think so." He saw a green stone on a fine chain about her neck.

"Then choose—and quickly, too, before the sun rises."

"Alas," Diccon said, looking more thoughtful still. "It's not as simple as you make it out to be. I'm a fickle man, and my heart's desire changes more often than the phases of the moon. As for my rightful place in the world, why should I not be content to stay as I am?"

The lady shook her head and laughed. "You may be a fickle man, Diccon, but you aren't a foolish one at all. Come then, and bide with me, and tell me merry stories and all the gossip of the lands of men."

"Now, that's not so bad an offer," Diccon said. "I'll take it and be thankful."

"So let it be," said the lady. She took him by the hand and led him thence, and the fire died unattended.

Underneath the hearthstone, the dead king's sword lay untouched in its hiding place, while the usurper died in his bed and the great lords chose one of their own to rule after him. The sword rusted away with the passage of years, and the silver coins corroded. The gold circlet remained fine and pure, and the red stone as well, and both are buried yet.

As for Diccon—who on a morning long before had seen his father wear the sword and the golden circlet off to battle and never return—he lives on to this day in his lady's country.

The Name of a King

Diana L. Paxson

"*Seeker, why have you come here?*"

The boy turned to face the Gateway whose pillars glimmered in the deep shade beneath the fir trees.

"I come to seal myself to the Covenant of Westria."

"*What is your name?*" The voice came from that darkness.

"I have no Name," said the boy who had been called Stone, "until I get one from the Namer of All Things."

Stone waited, the muscles in his neck cramping as the silence lengthened. He had never known who his parents were. More than most, he needed a name of his own. As if in answer, the darkness spoke again.

"*Enter, then, oh, Nameless One, for the sake of that which you are and that which you will become . . .*"

Stone squared his heavily muscled shoulders, took a deep breath, and stepped through the Gate.

"No, I will not give up this bed!" Stone said levelly. "I was here first."

The other boy took a step forward. His sleeveless tunic of undyed cotton fell in sculptured folds as if it had been tailored. They were all supposed to be dressed alike, but the rough tunic Stone had been issued did not fit him that way. The afternoon sun, slanting through the open side of the lean-to, seemed to gild the other boy's brown curls.

"You would do better to make a friend of me," he said softly.

"I don't know who you are or where you came from, but we're supposed to be equals here," he answered stolidly, though his pulse was beginning to pound. He saw eyes gleam around them, as if some of the others hoped that the two would break the law of the Initiation Encampment and come to blows. After a moment the young noble shrugged disdainfully and turned away.

"You should've let him take th' bed—" one of those who had remained said finally. He was tall and limber as a young pine tree. "That's Buck. He's th' younger brother o' the Lord Commander—the lord o' the Ramparts. Did ye not know?"

Stone stared at him. "My foster father works a stone quarry on the road to the sacred valley of Awahna. The first time I saw Rivered was when we passed through, coming here." He laughed ruefully. "I'd hoped to take service with the Lord Commander someday. If Lord Philip's like his brother, best learn it now."

"There's little law in th' other Marches since th' death o' th' king, but Lord Philip tries t' keep peace in th' Ramparts. Likely he's been too busy to bring up his brother," said a smaller, redheaded boy.

"Busy! I guess so—myself, if the Commander spends his time huntin' slavers I won't complain!" said the first boy, whom Stone found himself thinking of as "Pine." All three found their eyes moving toward the blue ranges that rose to the east of the Initiation grounds.

Stone heard Buck and his friends settling in at the lean-to next door. More noise came from the others, where boys and girls from villages and freeholds all over the Ramparts were choosing places, ready for this summer's Name-taking and Initiation into the rites of Westria. In the other four provinces he supposed young people on the edge of adulthood must be doing the same.

A trick of the breeze carried Buck's words clearly—something about primitive conditions and low company. Stone stiffened, then sat down heavily. "He who would command others must rule himself first of all," he muttered. Pine looked at him and lifted an eyebrow.

"Just quoting . . ." Stone smiled. "An old man who used to come by our holding said that once. I called him Master, though I don't know if he's from the College of the Wise." *And sometimes I thought he was preparing me to follow the Adept's Road. What vision will lead me? What name do I deserve?*

His master was only a little bent old man, but Stone winced, wondering what he would have said about that quarrel with Buck. *I am as proud as any Lord Commander's son,* he thought sorrowfully. *But it won't happen again!*

Stone pulled absently at his sandal strap, trying to stretch it, while the lecturer, an old priest from Rivered, droned on.

"You may find it hard to understand how men could misuse the earth from which they sprang," the old voice quavered. "We can only try to imagine how an entire race could endanger its own existence and destroy whole kindreds of its brethren. But the ruins of the cities those people built can still be seen . . ."

There was a giggle behind him, and he glimpsed Buck sliding a large red ant from an oak twig onto Pine's bare leg. Without thinking, Stone reached and flicked it away. At that moment Pine finally realized what was happening. He squawked, and the priest glared at Stone. Buck stifled a laugh.

"Now, who can tell me how the earth reacted to this mistreatment?" the priest asked repressively. Buck raised his hand.

"There were earthquakes, and fire from the mountains . . ."

Stone glowered at him, wondering if *his* sandals pinched.

"Too much rain fell," said a girl whose skin glowed like polished walnut wood in the hot sun.

"And all the animals began to attack—" said the red-haired boy.

"But does anyone know *why?*" the priest asked then.

There was a silence. The legends they had all learned as children told only the events of the Cataclysm. Finally Stone lifted his hand.

"I have heard that the people dug into the ground and cut down the trees. The sky was darkened and the seasons disordered. The plants could not grow. And the Guardians of the plant and animal kindreds stirred from their long sleep and took counsel how to save their people, and they decided to do away with Man."

"And so for a ten-year the beasts killed men—" the priest sounded suddenly tired. "And when those years were done and men were few upon the earth, the last of them met with the Guardians in Council, and by the mercy of the Maker of All Things a Covenant was made. May the Maker grant that we do not forget what they learned with such pain." The old man nodded. "Little brother, you have answered well."

Stone saw Buck shrug disdainfully and turned away. He was no lord's son, but he had had a good teacher. For a moment he seemed to see the Master's deep eyes upon him, and then he buried his head in his arms. *Again? Will I never learn that it is not what I know that matters, but what I am?* He heard the rattle of a pebble and a girl's squeal, and then Buck's laugh.

Stripped to their clouts, a dozen boys and girls were playing stickball. Stone dragged off his tunic and folded it carefully over a low-hanging branch of the great live oak that shaded the field.

"Stone-shoulders!"

Stone whipped around, saw that the speaker was Buck, and looked away. But he could not close his ears as the other boy went on.

"You can see he comes from a rock quarry—slow as stone too, I'll wager—" There was an echo of laughter from the youths that surrounded him.

Stone stalked away from them, too proud to put his tunic back on. Though a childhood spent clambering over mountain slopes had developed his legs and his torso was bronzed from working in the sun, his shoulders were undeniably large. He had never thought much about his body, except to take pride in being able to work as hard and as long as his bigger foster brothers. But now he fought shame.

"Brother Gnome!" Shall I let them Name me?

Teams were forming for a new stickball game, and Stone strode onto the field. The competition drove Buck's laughter to the back of his mind, but for a moment the ball seemed to bear Buck's face, and Stone slashed down at it with a savage joy.

The game ended as Pine slammed the leather-covered ball into the goal. Stone followed the others toward the tree.

"Well, that was all very lively," said Buck, "but can't you think of anything to do besides batting a little ball around? Footraces, perhaps, since they won't let us do anything really worthwhile like riding or falconry."

"A race would be just fine!" said Pine, stretching his long legs.

"But let's run a course that's really—worthwhile—" said Stone, giving Buck a level look. "Like from here to that big rock at the top of the hill and back." He pointed to an outcropping of rock almost a quarter of a mile away.

"If you wish it, I will judge," said one of the priestesses who had been watching the game, a young woman with a thick braid of black hair down her back.

"Mistress Larissa, the honor will be ours," Buck replied. If he minded the course or the distance, he gave no sign. He was stripping off his own tunic now. Stone looked at the beautifully defined muscles of the other boy's torso, and wondered suddenly what *he* would have looked like if he had been reared in a great lord's hall. Thoughtfully he retied the thong that held his dark hair clubbed at his neck.

Eight young people lined up beside Mistress Larissa on

the grass. They stretched tight muscles and scuffed bare feet to get a better purchase on the grass. Stone hunched his shoulders nervously, then relaxed to the stillness of the hunter who waits beside the pool. He was no sprinter, but he had taken his first steps on a mountainside.

Larissa's hand came down.

Buck flashed into the lead at once, with Pine at his heels. The dark girl was saving her strength, loping easily along in third place with the others grouped into a loose knot behind her. As he had expected, Stone was last. He concentrated on binding heart and lungs and pounding feet into one smoothly running machine. When he felt the ground steepen, he smiled. Ahead, Buck and Pine and the dark girl touched the rock and turned. Stone pushed himself then. His fingers brushed the rough stone and he pivoted, thrusting strongly to get impetus for the dash downward.

The others had reached the flat now, but they could not keep up their early speed. Stone's feet touched grass. His lips drew back in a grimace of effort, and he set his teeth and ran. Buck and Pine were fighting for the lead, but the dark-skinned girl was like a swallow heading for home. She was almost level with Buck when she cried out and fell.

Neither of the leaders had paused. Had they even heard? The girl had been swinging around Buck when she fell, close to the kind of rock outcrop where rattlesnakes liked to shelter from the heat of the day. Stone's step faltered, and he dropped to his knees in the dust beside the fallen runner. He saw no fang marks, but there was a gash on her temple. The blood seemed very bright against her brown skin. Stone eased his arms beneath her body.

"Don't try to move, little Swallow—you'll be all right," he murmured as she moaned. The feel of her bare skin against his sent prickles up and down his spine.

Stone strode toward the finish line, carrying the girl. People were running toward them. Pine reached him first, his eyes clouded with concern.

"Holy Guardians, is she all right?" he stammered. "I didn't see her fall."

"I think she slipped on a loose stone and hit her head on the way down."

Pine shook his head regretfully. "She would have won!"

As the crowd parted, Stone glimpsed Buck with the victor's chaplet of sweet-smelling laurel leaves on his brown hair.

Someone had laid a cloak under the oak's spreading shade. Stone lowered the girl onto it, and one of the priests bent over her, feeling her skull. The crowd began to drift away.

"Come on," said Pine. "We're goin' down to th' river for a swim."

Stone nodded. "I'll be along." He followed slowly, trying to fight his anger at Buck's victory.

"You did well ..." Mistress Larissa was moving silently at his side. Her skin was the color of honey in the afternoon light. She seemed little older than he was, hardly old enough to have completed her training at the College of the Wise.

He shook his head. "No—" the words rushed out. "I picked the course to give myself an advantage, and I almost didn't stop when the girl fell."

"You judge yourself too harshly—you *did* stop, after all, and that is what matters in the end."

He started to kick a pebble out of his path, then halted. Why should he take out his frustrations on the innocent earth?

"When I came here, I thought that in my vision quest I might find a Calling to the Master's road as well as a Name ..." he said at last.

"Oh, dear—and so you wanted to be perfect from the very start?" Stone flushed, but her laugh was understanding. "I felt the same. But when I chose my path, I assure you it was not because I was faultless!"

"Then how *did* you choose?"

"I wanted to learn the lore of healing herbs. Such

knowledge is gathered at the College of the Wise. Once there, I grew to love the rites and ceremonies."

Stone glanced at her sidelong, wondering at her serenity. "And did you not desire to take the longer road?" he asked.

"The road to Awahna?" Larissa smiled. "The Adept's Road is for those whose strength of spirit is as great as their desire to seek the Glory that lies beyond all created things."

"I hadn't thought of it that way," said the boy. He remembered the look on the Master's face sometimes when he turned toward Awahna, eyes following the Pilgrim's Road.

Stone worked his shoulders back and forth. "But how then shall I know who I am, and what I am to do?" he cried suddenly.

"What are you good at doing?" the priestess asked him.

"I wish I knew."

Stone lay in his narrow cot, listening to the other boys' breathing. But superimposed upon the darkness he saw the figures of the dancers and the four Jewels from the pageant they had just seen. By these four talismans the kings of Westria who were descended from the priestess who made the Jewels had mediated between men and the other powers.

Earth and water, air and fire . . . on these four all life depends . . . lines from the catechism echoed in his memory.

What must it be like to possess such magic? How would a man, even a king, control it? Stone was not aware when his pondering passed into a dream in which he saw the dance once more.

Again the priestess came toward him, and he knew her for Mistress Larissa. She held out her arms, and now he was her partner, twirling closer, closer, until the world whirled around him and he entered her waiting arms.

The boy moaned and twisted in his blankets, then burrowed against the pillow and quieted once more, still feel-

ing the bliss of soft arms around him. He looked up at
dark hair framing a pale face, heard his name sung
against the singing of the wind in the pines, and breathed
in a scent of lilies.

Mother ... he murmured, and in that recognition half
awakened. *She called my name* ... he tried to remember
what that name had been. *I was dreaming about the Four
Jewels* ...

It seemed to him that he played with them like a jug-
gler: the Earthstone, the Sea Star, the Jewel of Fire, and
the Wind Crystal by whose power the priestess had created them. Faster and faster, and the Jewels began to slip
from his fingers. He cried out as the world collapsed
around him in thunder and flood and flame.

When he woke in the gray dawn, clutching vainly at images of fear and splendor, he knew that he had dreamed,
but could not remember what the dreams had been.

"Why are they stuffing us with all this history?" Stone
muttered to Pine. "Will I quarry rock any better because
I now know there've been fourteen kings of Westria since
Julian Starbairn's time?" He had awakened with a head-
ache that had persisted all day. It was clearing now, but he
still felt muzzy.

The girl he called Swallow looked up from her dinner.
"If we don' learn from what's happened before, it'll come
again. My father says things would change if we'd a king
t' hold the Jewels, but if folk don't *want* t' keep the Law,
I don' see what good a king could do ..."

A murmur ran through the group as the Initiation Master came into the firelight, followed by another man
whose purple cloak glowed like amethyst.

"A bard ... who is it?" ran the whisper. "Is it
Silverhair?" "Is it the Master of Bards?"

"Nay!" said Buck a little too loudly. "Silverhair is only
a legend, and the Master of Bards has better things to do
than serenading a pack of cubs." He peered at the man
through the glare of the firelight. "That is Aurel
Goldenthroat, who some say will lead the College of

Bards one day." He smiled, his features lit for once by honest delight. "He is Master enough—wait and see!"

He met Stone's eyes, and his face changed. Too late, Stone tried to stop scowling. Then he stopped wanting to as Buck went on—

"This will be a great treat for you, Brother Gnome—a change from the clatter of falling rocks . . ."

Stone felt Pine grip his elbow and swallowed his retort. The bard sat down by the fire and took out his dulcimer. He was still young, with mouse-fair hair and eyes of a peculiar clarity. Delicately he drew the plectrum over the dulcimer's strings, then looked around at his audience with a smile.

"I am told that you are wearied of the deeds of kings. But I must beg your indulgence, for my song tells of the first of the great lords of Westria—Julian Starbairn, who was also called the Jewel-Lord."

Stone flushed, wondering who had told the bard about his grumbling. But he could not deny the stirring of interest, for the first Master of the Jewels had been born in Awahna, and that was near Stanesvale, his home. He put down his empty bowl and crossed his legs comfortably as the bard began to sing. *"Once long ago there was no king. The land lay lorn, with warring torn—"*

The song told of the Jewel Wars, when every petty king had his sorcerer and men forgot the Covenant they had sworn with the elder powers. Aurel's voice soared, telling how Julian had come down from the mountains with the Jewels and used them to put out the fires and renew the ravaged land.

But that was not the end of the story.

> *Their own lord slain, the people chose*
> *Young Julian to lead their men.*
> *In wrath the other princes rose*
> *To crush him then.*
> *"Now use the Jewels!" the people cried,*
> *"And let the land destroy their pride!"*
> *How could such need be denied?*

Oh Jewel-Lord?

Stone leaned forward, listening.

> *If by the power of the Jewels*
> *The land could kill, at its own will*
> *It might continue without rules*
> *To deal death still.*
> *Oh rather let them lend to men*
> *The strength of earth, storm-fury when*
> *They fight, and fire's heat," said he then,*
> *The Jewel-Lord.*

And so the king battled, using the Jewels to strengthen but never for destruction, until all accepted him. The dulcimer chimed exultantly as the bard finished his song.

> *Nor shall we cease remembering*
> *The greatness of the star-born king,*
> *Whose deeds and wisdom still we sing—*
> *The Jewel-Lord.*

Stone sat still. It seemed to him that it had answered a question out of his dream, though he did not understand how. *It is just a legend,* he thought, *just a tale about an ancient king.*

The singing continued as the stars peeked through the friendly dusk. Larissa took the dulcimer and sang a ballad about a girl of the north who had lived with a wolf pack after her family was slain. The fire was warm, and she had loosened the lacing at the neck of her robe. The pale curve of her breast showed beneath it. Her voice was like honey. Stone wondered if her skin were as smooth as it looked, and whether it tasted of honey too . . .

Pine spoke into the silence that her song left behind, his voice slow and dreamy. "Tis hard to believe that when this week is past we'll go out t' seek our own visions, and come back *named , . ."*

"Well, I will be happy when it is over," said Buck.

"My brother says I may ride with his warband after the slavers when I return!"

Swallow frowned at him. "Don't ye know better than t' talk o' such things here?"

One of the other girls laughed. "I wish I had some magic Jewels—I could do anything I wanted to then!"

"No . . ." with Pine's "*named,*" still ringing in his head, Stone answered her. "That's exactly what you couldn't do. Didn't you understand the song? Julian Starbairn was a great king because he knew what he did and did not have the right to do. Wrong use of power is worse than no use at all!"

His words hung in the air like a prophecy. Stone looked around at his friends, wondering what had possessed him to speak so.

"Hah!" Buck echoed his thought abruptly. "And who do you think you are to make free with the name of a king? You'll never rule more than your own weedpatch, Brother Gnome!"

The world darkened. Without willing it, Stone reached for that mocking face, because while Buck was still speaking, Stone had realized what name it was he wanted and could never claim.

He heard Pine shout, then someone pulled him away.

"Puppies! Are you puppies to quarrel before your dinner is cold?" Larissa's icy tone congealed his anger. "Get to bed, both of you, if you cannot behave like men!"

Stone did not see the priestess on the two days that followed. He told himself that it was because she was working with the girls. Only when he was alone did he admit to himself how much it mattered what Larissa thought of him. When he and Buck could not avoid contact, they were distantly polite. Stone told himself that if there was any hope that Buck might accept an apology decently he would make one. But he had no faith in his own self-control if the other boy were to mock him again.

After the vision quest he would be able to do it. When

he had his Name, he would be immune to anything Buck might say.

During these last days Stone had begun to realize how much he was counting on that time of testing. Everyone returned from the quest with a Name. Some were given a vision of their whole life's path. Thinking about it, he became silent, and snapped at his friends. He found himself trembling unaccountably, like an overstrung bow.

On the last evening they were bathed and newly clothed in tunics of pure white. Stone and the other boys formed into a line and followed one of the priests toward the dancing ground. As they neared the clearing where they had practiced for so many hours, they heard the rapid heartbeat of knuckle drums. The posts that marked the four quarters were festooned now with ribbons and green boughs, and beyond them another line of dancers was approaching. Girls—no—women, newly robed in black, swayed in time to the drumbeat as they drew near.

Back and forth they surged, then the men began to circle sunways. But the women's line, surrounded, circled the other way. Touching hands briefly, males and females exchanged places then, and each line reversed the circle it had made before. Then they shifted again, forming a single circle around the fire.

"This is the Dance of Life!" the Initiation Master proclaimed. "Now we advance, now go back; now one is positive, but in response to another becomes passive again. You must find the point of balance between. Knowing this, let the music move you and let the dancing go on!"

The pipes let go with an exulting skirl, and the drums thudded out a rhythm that compelled the body to move. From the seekers came a shout, as, releasing all the strain and tension of the days just past, they began to dance.

Stone sat down on one of the logs laid around the edge of the dancing floor. He was tired, but not yet ready for sleeping. Many of the dancers had gone already, some in groups, some in pairs who slipped into the darkness. Couples who had found each other during Initiation often chose the great dance to complete their bond.

Stone had thought of asking a girl to go into the woods with him, but there were not many girls his age near his home, and his knowledge was still all theory. Some of the boys boasted of making conquests, but Stone did not want it to be like that. Besides, what if he had asked a girl, and she had said no? *And what if she had said yes?*

He got to his feet. The moonlight on the bare hilltops was very beautiful. He thought he would let it bathe his soul as the river had made his body clean. And the others could wonder all they pleased about where and with whom he had gone.

The path led him up the slope behind the dancing floor. The light of the full moon dimmed the stars. The hills lay open to his gaze, all shining curves and tree-furred hollows like a woman's body. Beyond them the banked ridges of the Ramparts rose, as transparent and mysterious in the moonlight as the walls of the Otherworld.

Stone started toward one of the boulders that studded the slope. It stirred; amid dark folds he saw the pale glimmer of a face. He stopped short, sight dimming to the rush of his blood. Then his vision cleared and he recognized Larissa. And still he could not move. A shift in the wind made the drums sound in his ears, or perhaps it was only the heightened pounding of his heart.

"The night is beautiful, and there is room on my cloak for two. Come and sit down . . ." she said.

With the feeling that each step had been predestined, he came to her.

Stone awoke in the light of the new day, breathing in Larissa's honey-scent upon his skin. He reached out for her and struggled for a moment against the folds of the cloak. Then he lay still, understanding that she was gone. But soon he was laughing. One way or another Larissa had given him the answer to a lot of questions before the night was done. But none of this new knowledge could explain the essential wonder that such a potentially awkward activity could result in a sense of union with all things.

He pulled his rumpled tunic over his head, bundled the cloak under his arm, and started down the hill. He was whistling by the time he reached the bathing pool.

"Well, well—look at the mockingbird!"

Stone turned, stopped, met Buck's blue gaze. Even then, it took a few moments for his happiness to fade.

"Isn't he just the picture, though?" Buck said softly. Others were turning, but no one else could hear as he went on. "Straw in his hair and dirt on his legs, and—oh—the barnyard stink of him!" He turned his head delicately aside.

Stone bit back a retort and started past.

"And so you're going to bathe—" the other boy's tone sharpened. "But don't think you can hide your rutting that way. Writhing in the muck like any beast, weren't you, but then you *are* an animal . . . What sow did you mount, beast? What bitch did you—" he leaned forward, hissing the words.

The other boy's description of the sexual act was complete and graphic. Stone heard the splendors he had just discovered made sordid and unclean. He threw up his hands to ward the words away, but he could not wipe the pictures from his mind.

"Stop!" Stone shouted at last.

"Oh, no—you've been putting on airs since the first day. I want you to understand just how wretched you are!"

All Stone's awareness focused into the desire to wipe the contempt off that aristocratic face.

"Gelding—" he struggled to control his breathing. "Are you jealous? If your male parts are as useless as the rest of you, no wonder you couldn't get anywhere with a girl!"

And he saw, in the fraction of a second before Buck's fist smashed toward him, a dumb hurt in the other boy's eyes and knew that what he had said must somehow have been true.

Stone tried to pull away and took a glancing hit that made his head ring. He dropped the cloak and swung, but the other boy danced neatly out of the way and hit him again. Buck was fast, and he had been trained well. Stone endured his blows and waited for his chance. His fist darted out and missed, but he had thrown the other boy off balance. He grabbed Buck's left wrist and bore him down.

His enemy struggled beneath him, fists drumming on Stone's back, but the heavy shoulders Buck had mocked gave Stone an advantage now. His hand rose and fell.

Desperate fingers dug into his arms. As the pounding in his head faded, Stone heard shouting. With a sob, he forced himself to stop, to let someone lift him to his feet. Buck sprawled in the dust before him, hair matted and blood trickling from his nose. His eyes were closed.

Stone ran his tongue across his lips, winced, and tasted blood there, too. In the silence that followed, Stone looked down at Buck again. He supposed that he must have won the fight. But as Pine took his arm to lead him away, he was aware only of a dreadful sense of loss.

Stone's back burned where Buck's nails had gouged him, but he remained where he was, sitting out in the full sun on the hillside, as if the pain of the body could cancel out that of the mind. Two jays were arguing in the branches of a live oak tree. Beyond it the red earth rose sharply, and three gnarled pines showed in sharp silhouette against the brilliant sky. A day and a half had been ample time for Stone to memorize every rock and leaf in his hermitage.

After the fight Stone had been terrified that he would be sent home nameless, with his shame proclaimed to all. But it might be worse to be sent on his vision quest just as if he had not broken a fundamental rule of the Initiation Encampment, with no company but the memory of his crime.

Stone felt tears pricking beneath his eyelids and did not bother to brush them away. There were only the jays to see him, and they did not care. *If they had sent me home,*

*in justice they would have had to expel Buck too. They
would not dare to treat the Lord Commander's brother
that way!* He shook his head and winced as the bruise on
his temple began to throb once more.

Abruptly he rose and began to pick his way down the
hill. There was no use in this kind of meditation! At the
bottom of the slope a little stream chuckled to itself
among the stones. He cupped his hands and drank—
carefully, for his lip was still puffy. His stomach growled,
and to quiet it he drank again.

Unless he found food here he would get nothing to eat
for another two days, but the seekers were always left
near water. In spots where there was no stream the priests
brought water bottles each day before dawn. Stone knew
that if he traveled upstream or down he would find others,
though they had all been blindfolded during the two-hour
ride.

Stone thought for a moment of what would happen if
he met a rattler . . . He progressed in imagination through
the sudden pang, the spreading numbness, the final agony.
He would not make a fire to summon help. When they
came at last, they would find him convulsed and cold.
How would they all feel then? How would Larissa look
when she heard?

"Go forth into darkness as the dead go, guided only by
faith. Go forth little knowing where you are going or
what you will find." The parting admonition of the Initiation Master had been burned into his brain. "But wake to
the Light. For this is Death, and Death is only this—to
sleep and wake renewed. When you return, you will be
different both in name and in deed."

But nearly half of the quest was over, and Stone knew
himself agonizingly the same.

Deliberately he stepped over to the driftwood pile and
stood waiting. But there was no slither of scales, no fierce
rattling. All he could hear was the laughter of the stream.
Stone laughed too, mocking himself. "If I do not return
that way, how can I return at all?"

He could run away and could call himself whatever he

wished, and no one would know. No brand upon his forehead would proclaim that his name had not been recorded
by the College of the Wise, that he had never sworn his
Oath to Westria. He could make a new life in the barbarian lands east of the mountains. Maybe he would become
one of the raiders the Westrians so feared. Or he might
lose himself in these mountains. There were songs about
men who lived alone in the wilderness, gaining kinship
among the beasts though they could not find it with men.

Stone sighed and dangled his feet in the cool water. He
had tried to think of a name. Surely not everyone had a
vision.

"But *I* had to . . ." he whispered. "I wanted to be a
Master, but I could not even ignore the words of someone
who must have been as unhappy as I was. Oh, my Master." He thought of the old man. "Why did you encourage
me to dream such dreams?" Even the sun was deserting
him. The sky held only memories of its glory, drawn in
achingly lovely shades of flame and peach and rose.

"You powers who live here, please help me!" Stone
cried to the woods and the stream. "Holy One, speak to
me now . . . touch me . . . let me see *something* . . ."

The stream hushed as the light dimmed. Stone's con-
sciousness rushed inward, straining toward that threshold
beyond which all is Light. For a moment he hovered on
the brink, then words buzzed in his mind and he was himself again, sitting on a hard rock in the dark.

The third day was like the second, and the first. Then
it was the last night. It took a long time for sleep to come,
and when his eyes closed at last, his cheeks were wet
with tears.

*He is running through the woods, trying to ward off the
branches that whip at his face. He can hear Larissa
screaming. He hears crashing in the brush behind him—
his pursuers are nearing—he turns . . .*

"Get up!"

He woke with a gasp, felt something prick his throat.

"Now—"

Stone focused on the sword blade, winced as the weapon moved down to poke his belly, and sat up quickly. Other shapes stood around him. A horse nickered softly nearby.

"Put on your boots, clod-eater, we've not much time."

Numbly he reached for his boots, struggling to tie laces with fingers that had forgotten how to bend. The world had the gray look of the hour just before dawn. These were not priests from the Initiation Encampment come to punish him. The man with the sword was dressed in riding leathers, and the speech of the others sounded strange. He began to remember stories he had heard.

As the man in leather spoke again, Stone got his feet under him. He leaped sideways and yelled as the flat of a sword slapped his ribs. Hard hands grasped him before he hit the ground. He fought for breath, certain he had been cut in two, but they flung him facedown across a saddle and bound him there.

He tried to scream as the horse jerked into motion, but the raiders only laughed. And then they were trotting up the trail, and for a time he hurt too much to think of anything at all. They stopped twice as the light grew stronger. Stone heard a scuffle and a cry and knew that the next captive had not been taken by surprise. He tugged at his bonds, but they were tight enough to make his wrists ache, and he could not reach the knots.

He wondered who else they had taken, and why. They had mentioned the outlaw city of Arena, so he knew they must be raiders from the Barren Lands. When the sun began to poke above the trees, they stopped where two trails joined. Stone was jerked off the horse, bound again with rope looped around a tree. He sat down abruptly as the circulation in his ankles began to return.

"So you were my neighbor—I wondered who was upstream from me!"

Stone looked around and saw Pine smiling at him, though his face was grimed and pale. Beyond him, lying unconscious but with his hands still bound, was Buck.

The reivers were mixing up a gruel of dried meat and

water from their canteens. As the smell reached the boys, Stone remembered how long it had been since he had tasted food.

Pine swallowed convulsively and looked at him.

"Hey, you—Eastlings! We'll be no good to you if we starve!" Stone willed his voice to steadiness as he called.

Laughter gusted from the men around the fire, but no one even looked up. One of the raiders was speaking to the others now, and Stone frowned, for the man had sounded like a Westrian. He got up, a bowl in his hand, and Stone saw that the left side of his face was marred by a purple scar.

"So, *el renegado* is soft for's old kin! *Vaya*, Mole— feed 'em—but don't giv'em my share!" shouted one of his friends.

"I told you—they've been three days fasting. They won't bring us any gold if they look starved!"

The man waited impatiently while Stone slurped mush from the bowl. When it was empty, he refilled it and fed Pine. Stone sighed as warmth spread through his limbs.

"You're raiders from the Barren Lands, aren't you?" he asked. "Where's your plunder?"

The man gave a bark of laughter and rubbed at the old scar. "Right here! Haven't you heard of the slave-marts of Arena?"

"Slave-marts!" The new voice was thin with outrage. "I'm the Lord Commander's brother! He'll pay you better than any barbarian for my return!"

Stone saw Buck sitting up, his colorless lips drawn tight. There was a short silence. Then the leader sauntered over. The silver chain around his neck winked in the morning sun.

"Oh, I don' think so—yer a pretty lad. Reckon we'll get th' worth o' our time fer you!"

"But the ransom—" sputtered Buck.

"Right enough, but who's t' go back fer it? And then what'll stop yer brother from comin' after us? Our orders was to git back t' Delasker's Hold with what we c'n carry, an' that's what we'll do. If Delasker wants t' hold

ye to ransom, that's his look-out. Don't think he will ...
I know a fat merchant or two who'd find ye just to his
taste!!"

As he realized just what the man was suggesting,
Buck's face lost all color, and the men roared with laughter. Stone could almost find it in his heart to pity the other
boy. As the mockery faded, he heard, like an echo, the
pattering of hooves on the other trail.

The raiders tensed, hands moving toward sword hilts,
and hope flamed in Buck's eyes. Then there was a soft
whistle. Four more riders clattered up, greeting the men
who had captured the boys with ribald familiarity. They
were driving half a dozen horses, most of them laden with
packs. But among them were three with human burdens—
Swallow, a girl who had been one of Buck's followers,
and Larissa.

Stone rode in agony throughout that first, interminable
day. Each step jolted his bruised ribs, and the wooden
saddle frame rubbed raw places on his inner thighs. The
only way to endure it was to force his mind to roam.

He had heard once that by the straight road over the
mountains it was two weeks from Rivered to the barbarian city of Arena. But the raiders were not taking the
straight road. The man with the Westrian accent was leading them by hidden tracks in the hills.

The others called him Mole, and Stone thought the
name fitted him well—he scanned the path with nervous
jerks of the head as if he were smelling his way. Stone
wondered if the man had been initiated, if he had ever
had a Westrian name.

The trail was growing steeper. A barked order from
ahead had men dismounting in the trail. Stone was yanked
off his horse. He bit back a whimper of agony as stiff legs
took his weight. His hands were still bound, but he got no
help other than a vicious tug on the rope when he fell. One
of the other prisoners sobbed steadily as they went on, and
Stone was in too much pain to see who it was.

If they mean to sell us, they won't let us die, went his

inner litany, and his spirit began to lighten. *I'm no worse off than if I'd run away. My foster parents may be sorry when they hear, but at least they won't be shamed. Even the Master can't blame me now!*

The first night the prisoners were tied securely to trees while the raiders loosened saddle girths and sprawled on the ground without troubling to make a fire. Stone slumped against the smooth trunk and felt curls of bark crush and flake away. The oval shapes of madrone leaves framed the stars. One of the raiders crunched through the fallen leaves. Stone gasped as a hard hand forced the neck of a waterskin between his teeth. He sucked in instinctively, thirst overcoming exhaustion and fear. Then the skin was as rudely jerked away.

"That's enough for you, cub—leave some for your denmates, now," the man growled. It was Mole, who had fed the captives that morning. How long ago that seemed! Stone peered after him as he moved toward the next tree.

It was like a Westrian to use an animal metaphor. The others called him a renegade, but Mole had known where to find the captives, and that they would be fasting. So he must have been initiated once and taken a real name. What could have turned him against his own people this way?

A muffled oath from the next tree cut short his wondering.

"Get your hands off me, filth! I've the blood of a king, and—" Buck's words abruptly ceased.

"King's blood flows like any other man's—" the renegade replied harshly. "Swallow this water while you can, and swallow your damned Westrian pride! Where you're going, a sharp tongue can spoil a pretty face."

Buck kicked convulsively and Mole cuffed him. One of the raiders called softly, and Mole grunted a reply before moving on. Stone heard stifled sobbing, but he could not tell if it was Buck or one of the others. Presently it became a background to his dreams.

It seemed to him that they were being hustled awake again before the pain in his bruised limbs had dulled. Get-

ting into the saddle brought new agony. But they pressed
on. By the time darkness fell, they were high among the
peaks, where few trees grew, and Westria was a dim blur
to the west. When they stopped at last, Stone found himself bound to the same stunted juniper as Pine.

"Are you all right?" Pine asked in a low voice.

Stone suppressed bitter laughter. "My thighs are raw,
that pack saddle is trying to pinch off my manhood, and
I'm a prisoner. Aside from that . . ."

One of the raiders walked by them and the boys fell silent. He was a big man, with dark hair showing at the
neck of his tunic and on his arms beneath rolled-up
sleeves. The others called him Martan.

"Were you hurt when they captured you?" Stone asked
when the man had gone by. Pine reddened and shook his
head. He had been asleep and had known nothing until he
felt himself being lifted and flung across the horse.

"Maybe I taught them something, then—not that it did
much good!" He paused. A little gimlety man with griz-
zled hair was walking toward them, a sack in his hand.

"'Ere—" he smirked, throwing some rounds of hard
bread at Pine's feet and dropping a skin of water beside
them. "Wouldn't want ye t' starve t' death afore we git ye
t' market! Ye c'n just thank Burkey ye've got anything at
all—say thank ye, then!" His foot shot out and caught
Stone in the thigh.

Stone gasped and mumbled a curse through set teeth.
Burkey spat and turned away. When the pain eased, he
and Pine gobbled the bread down, but his stomach was
still crying for more when they were done.

"How are the others doing?"

"About the same as us, I guess," Pine replied. "I was
tied near Buck last night, but I couldn't get him t' talk t'
me—" he stopped.

"It's all right," said Stone, forcing a smile. "Our quarrel doesn't seem very important now." *I was fighting myself, not him,* Stone thought with new clarity, and then,
Who was Buck fighting, if not me?

"Well . . ." Pine hesitated, "he seems to be takin' it hard. D'ye think th' Lord Commander'll rescue us?"

Stone shook his head and eased down against the tree. "Not if that Westrian renegade knows his job. The Commander would be at least two, three days behind us. If he can find the trail."

"Hard luck for us," Pine said tightly, "and harder for the girls."

"How could they have captured *her*—I mean the priestess?" Stone said at last. He could not speak Larissa's name aloud.

"The dark girl said Mistress Larissa was bringin' water and ran into th' raiders. She tried t' slip away, but they ran her down."

Stone sighed deeply. Rest and food had dulled his pain. Was that why it was suddenly harder to be detached? He remembered holding her; his body ached with longing to hold her again, but whether he wanted to give comfort or receive it he was not sure.

"This place where they're takin' us . . . I heard it's desert there—no trees," Pine said after awhile.

Something in his voice focused Stone's attention. Why was the other boy worrying about trees? Impulsively he turned to him. "Before we were captured, when we were alone, did something happen to you?"

"Does it matter now?" Pine's voice was full of unshed tears.

Stone leaned closer, trying to see his face in the gloom. "Yes, it does matter!" he said fiercely. "The Guardians don't give without reason . . . tell me!"

Pine took a shuddering breath. "I was lookin' at the trees," he said. "I was wishin' I could live like a tree, on soil an' sunlight, and then, there was a bit when I felt like th' sun was shinin' through my skin. An' the world went by so slowly . . ."

Stone grunted encouragement, and the other boy went on.

"When I came out of it, th' sun was settin'. I looked around, an' every leaf I saw was outlined with sparkly golden light. I thought, 'It's just the sunset, shinin' through the leaves.' But the veins in each leaf were golden too, an' I saw a glow where water was movin' up the trunks. There was the outside o' the tree, with bark and leaves an' all like I was used to, and the inside—the *real* tree, all laid out in lines o' light!" His voice was dreamy.

"So I reached out t' touch the trunk. An' I could feel a kind o' tingling. It was almost like an itch—an' it wasn't that I couldn't scratch it—more like it was in a place I never knew I had before. Then a wind came up an' rustled th' branches. The leaves were talkin'—the tree was talkin' to me, and I knew if I could stand still long enough, I'd understand." He fell silent.

"What did you do?" Stone asked after a moment or two had passed.

"Oh, when it got dark, I lay down t' sleep, an' decided t' take my grandfather's name."

Stone nodded. "Because it didn't matter what name you took, did it? You didn't mean to keep it long. When we saw you again, you'd be a friend of th' trees, and men would call you Master of the Pines!"

"How'd you know?" Pine cried.

Footsteps silenced them. "Quiet there! You that lively tomorrow, let yer own two feet carry you!" It was Madok's voice. The two boys waited until he stalked away.

Then Stone leaned closer to his friend. "*Pine* . . . that's the name I've had for you since we met!"

They lay silent in the darkness after that. After a little the sound of Pine's regular breathing told Stone that the other boy slept. But Stone listened to the snoring of the raiders and the small night noises of the land. The wind was whispering among the pines, and Stone swallowed, thinking of the boy who was being taken to a land where there were no trees.

Oh, my Master, he thought. *Here is one who'd do credit to your teaching. I wish you were here to help him now!*

The third night, they made camp in a broad basin glacier-carved into the granite of the peaks, safe from pursuit at last. The raiders laughed or swore with no attempt at silence as they unpacked their gear. Stone heard one of the girls cry out and whirled, tripping over the ropes that bound his ankles.

The fair-haired girl was still mounted, but instead of lifting her off her horse, the raider was running his hand up her leg. Until now, their captors had treated all of them as dispassionately as any other stolen goods. But clearly the general relaxation of discipline extended to more than making noise.

Burkey shouted to the man to stop fooling around so that he could get the horse settled. At that, the man burst into laughter and pulled the girl down, kissing her until she lay like a stunned rabbit in his arms.

Stone strained against his bonds. A man they called Rio had grasped Swallow by the arm. As he clamped her against him, she sank her teeth into his hairy arm. He yelled and shoved her down on the stones.

"Stop it!" Stone hobbled toward him. "We're merchandize, remember? If you damage us, who'll buy?"

Rio growled and started for him, black beard stiff with outrage. Stone stood his ground, wincing in anticipation.

"Hands off th' women, Rio! Martan—you know what virgins are worth 'n Arena! You let th' bitch go *now!*" Madok strode forward, grasping the stock of the bull whip thrust through his belt.

Martan let go of his girl, who stumbled toward Swallow and sank to her knees beside her, sobbing. He stood stroking his scanty beard, eyes narrowed, then suddenly turned to Larissa, who still sat her horse behind him.

"Well, *they* may be virgins, but here's one that's not!" He chuckled, tugged her bindings loose and pulled her down, pinioning her with one arm while with the other hand he yanked at her tunic until her breasts were bared.

There was a silence, as if all the men there had forgotten how to breathe. Larissa's eyes glittered with a desperate pride.

"We all know 'bout those Westrian temple women, *sabe?*" Martan's calloused fingers stroked Larissa's breast. "We heard what they do at those festivals," he went on. "Think I'll have a little Westrian festival right now . . ."

Mole shook his head. "Don't—not like that! It's . . . bad luck!"

Martan laughed. "Good luck, ye mean. This'll be my share o' the loot, compadres—ye can have the rest!" He began to drag Larissa aside.

"Oh, no, ye don't!" One of the others grabbed his arm. "Go first if ye must, but I'm after. Haven't poked a woman in a year!"

"Aren't any'd have ye!" There was a feverish note in the laughter.

"I'll hold'er for ye!" said the second man, shoving Larissa down. For a long moment they looked at her.

The voices came to Stone faint and tinny through the throbbing in his ears. He saw part of Larissa's breast, her shadowy hair veiling the stone, but superimposed were his own memories of her body glowing in the darkness of a summer night. This was far worse than when Buck had taunted him, for he could feel desire stirring in him, and knew himself kin to his captors even while he hated them.

He groaned and the great muscles in his shoulders bulged. He did not hear the pop as one strand of the rope that bound him snapped. It was not until much later that he noticed the rope burn on his arm.

Then all the men were rushing toward her, and Madok's bull whip cracked the silence, transforming cries of lust into yells of pain. In a moment only Martan faced him, but his knife was out and ready.

Madok laughed and struck again. The long whip curled around Martan's waist, pulled him forward as the leader whipped his sword free and in the same movement lopped off Martan's right hand. Still gripping the dagger, it dropped to the ground.

Burkey swore and snatched up a brand from the fire and thrust the wrist stump into the flame. There was an awful smell of burnt meat. Then Martan screamed.

"Bad luck . . ." whispered Mole. "I told you—" he nodded dully and turned away.

"I said, no women!" Madok spoke softly, looking around at his men. "Yer fightin' already, and Delasker's Hold is two days' ride away! The girls are for the market in Arena, an' th' Westrian witch is for Delasker."

Tension eased from the air. Already the men were beginning to look sheepish, unclenching their fists, sheathing daggers they hoped no one had seen them draw.

"So then, ye horny bastards. Go eat! Ye'll know better'n to try this again—but I don' care what ye dream!" Madok favored them with his own peculiar smile. The men laughed then, but not too loud.

Stone felt his knees suddenly weaken, and sat down.

Since there were no trees, that night the raiders bound their prisoners together. The fight had stimulated them to an unusual efficiency, and before either of them could protest, Stone and Buck found themselves tied wrist to wrist in a parody of a lover's embrace.

Stone wondered if someone had told Madok that he and Buck were enemies. Looking on the other boy's closed face, Stone found it hard to remember what they had fought about. It was very cold.

Buck lay too still, too stiff, to be asleep.

"Buck—" Stone whispered. "Buck, listen to me—we have to escape."

The other boy twitched, then shook his head. "We can't. Don't mock me!"

"I'm not. I don't hate you—how could I, now?"

The other boy's blue eyes opened. Buck stared at him. "I can't help you . . ." he said very softly. "I can't do anything useful. I never could." For a moment surprise held Stone speechless. "You knew that, didn't you? That was why you were always testing me. I had to fight you, Brother Gnome, or else they would all have known."

"Buck!" Stone remembered to lower his voice. "Buck, *what* was I supposed to have known? But it doesn't matter now. We have to get away from these people before we reach their hold!"

Buck's eyes glistened. "No. It's better this way." he answered. "I was only an extra son in case something happened to Philip. I've been fostered with one lord after another since I was four years old." Buck gulped as if he were trying to stop, but the words rushed on.

"My last 'keeper' was Diegues dos Altos. I thought I had found a real home there—but Diegues treated me like a sacred statue. It took me a long time to realize that I never got to *do* anything! I boasted that my brother would take me into the Border Patrol after Initiation." Buck went on. "If he did take me he'd have found out how little I know." Buck stopped.

"But surely you learned—"

"You can't know!" Another gulp from Buck interrupted him. "Now Philip has boys of his own. If I'm gone, he can provide for them without needing to bother about me!"

"No ... I don't know," Stone said slowly. "I was the youngest child in the house, the gift to them of a nameless woman who collapsed on their doorstep and then died. But there was work enough for us all. Your brother should be glad of a strong arm at his back. You said you studied warfare, Buck—can't you remember anything that might help us now?"

"I tried—for two whole days I've tried." Buck shook his head. "But the raiders are all strong and well armed. Even if they unbound us, what could we do? I couldn't even help that poor girl," murmured Buck, letting his head drop again.

As I couldn't help Larissa, Stone thought then. *Now there are two of us who don't care if we live or die but are responsible for others who do. There must be a way out of this—there has to be!*

The cold wind drew goose bumps down his bare arm. He heard a clicking sound and realized that Buck's teeth were chattering. Without thinking, he pulled the other boy

closer. Buck stiffened, and for a moment Stone thought he
would pull away. *Does he despise me even now?*

Then he remembered the fine future Madok had promised Buck as a catamite in Arena. He searched for some
way to help the other boy accept simple human comfort
without shame.

"Please—I'm freezing!" Stone ventured at last. "At
least you can help me keep warm . . ." After a moment's
hesitation he felt Buck relax.

Even if I weren't in love with Larissa, Stone thought
with inner laughter, *I don't think I'd want a man! But I
don't suppose Buck has ever huddled in bed between two
brothers while a blizzard drifts snow over the second-story
window sill!* He cast about for something to distract them
until their combined body heat could get them warm.

"I wonder what King Julian would have done," he said
at last.

"King Julian would never have gotten into such a fix,"
Buck replied, but his voice held a hint of humor. "Shut
your eyes, Brother Gnome. Maybe a way out will come to
you in your dreams." Buck's voice faded, and Stone
thought he had gone to sleep, but then he whispered
again, so softly Stone was not sure he heard, "Dream of
a way, brother, and I'll follow you."

Stone grew still, realizing with a shock that Buck was
now depending on *him.* The other boy's loneliness had
been added to Larissa's danger and Pine's longing, a tri-
ple weight he could not choose not to bear.

*He is standing on a hill, before a wall of fire. Smoke
stings his eyes and billows upward to hide the sky. Tree
after tree is haloed in flame as its leaves flare, then becomes a living torch. He quivers with their agony. Men
are pulling at his arm, trying to draw him away. He
shakes his head.*

*Carefully he binds around his loins a belt of woven
linen clasped by a glowing brown stone. For a moment he
stands still, rooted to the earth, feeling its strength rise
through his limbs. Then swiftly he belts the moonlight ra-*

diance of the second Jewel at his waist, hangs the great winged crystal upon his breast, sets the coronet that holds the fiery gem upon his brow. Power courses through his body from feet to fingertips. Force swirls through belly and breast, is balanced and channeled outward by his will. Light blazes from his brow.

He lifts his hands.

Soon he senses the gathering of a mighty wind. A damp gust touches his forehead, he feels upon his cheeks the tears that fortell rain. Men are cheering hoarsely. "Julian!" come the cries, "Julian."

"Julian . . ." murmured Stone. He felt the dream begin to slip away, tried to recapture that sensation of balanced power. He brought up his hands in the gesture of praise, felt pain, and opening his eyes, saw that he was bound. A horse neighed. Now Stone could hear the camp waking around him. He felt a twitch at his wrists and, turning his head, saw that Buck was trying to sit up.

"Well—so yer wakin'!" Burkey stood over them with his knife gleaming in the early sun, and Stone jerked upright. The raider grinned nastily, stooped and slashed he ropes that held him and Buck together. "Get up, slaves! Yer not in Westria anymore, and ye'd best get used t' takin' orders!" He drew back one foot as if to kick them.

They scrambled to their feet, eyeing Burkey's boot warily.

"Not in Westria?" asked Buck dully. Stone glanced upward and saw behind him the divide.

Burkey laughed. "Look—" he pointed eastward, where the mountains sheered off in a series of sculptured escarpments, then stretched away in a dust-colored sea.

"The Barren Lands," said Stone.

"The free lands!" Burkey corrected him. "No Westrian lordling tells *us* when t' squat! Free for some, anyways— not for you!" he grinned again. "Get goin' and water th' beasts so's we c'n load. 'Tis Madok's order—ye'll work yer passage now!"

It felt good to have something to do, even with no choice about doing it. But as Stone listened to the pony

slurping up the chill water, he found himself gazing eastward again.

The horse shook its head, splattering Stone. "All right,"
said the boy, slapping the pony's neck. "Come on—Madok
will pity neither of us if we make him wait!" He led the
horse back toward the others, looking for his friends.

"My dear—you must not think of me . . ." Larissa
shaded her eyes against the noonday sun. Stone let his
empty waterskin drop, not daring to touch her for fear
that one of the raiders would see. The tinkle of the little
waterfall beside which they had paused seemed very loud
in his ears.

Larissa paused, balancing her full water bottle on one
shoulder. Shadows like bruises stained the skin around
her eyes. She had fastened her torn gown together with a
wooden skewer. Did she understand what he had asked?

Stone had been able to talk to the others before they
started, but Larissa had been kept apart. Their noon stop
was in a sort of bay in the side of the mountain. Stunted
pines clung to the cliff where a trickle of water emerged
from a fissure.

"Yes, of course you must escape if you can—" Larissa
continued. "But they will never let *me* go. To have me in
their power gives them an illusion of control over their
own fears. It is all right—I will survive."

He swallowed. "Try to think of a way we can *all* escape," he said again. "Don't you understand? I love you!"
He saw her smile and stumbled onward. "If it were not
for you and Pine and Buck and the others, I wouldn't care
whether or not I got away!"

There was a shout from above. Stone retrieved the waterskin and lowered himself over the edge. When he
glanced back he saw that she was still watching him, her
brows bent in a frown.

When Stone reached the top once more, Pine took his
arm and nodded southward. Stone peered through the
haze and glimpsed a ribbon of road winding down the
mountainside.

"The Traders' Road," whispered the other boy.

"I didn't know we were so close to it!" said Stone.

"Do ye no good—" said Rio, passing them. "We don't use it. Our ways take longer, but they're secret. An' we're almost home!" He gestured across the valley. "We get down t' that valley, climb the cliffs. No good for anyone to find Delasker's Hold. He'd never find 's way out again!"

The horses had had enough water at last. The east wind was dry, aromatic with the scent of scrub pine and sage. A stray gust swirled the dust in the path. After a few moments the fair-haired girl eased down beside him. "I haven't thought of anything," she murmured. "But I'm still trying. I'll do whatever you ask."

Stone tried to smile at her. *The other side of the ridge,* he thought. Another day and it would be too late to do anything.

They camped that night on the floor of the valley. The raiders were merry and broke out some of the wine they had stolen in Westria. But Stone had begged permission for the prisoners to have their own fire. What persuaded Madok was Stone's suggestion that if the reivers were going to be drinking, it might be as well to keep the women out of the way.

They sat close together, looking into the flames. Anyone watching would have thought them overcome by despair.

Swallow shook her dark head. "I have thought and thought, but I just want to poison them all. Mistress Larissa, you told us you studied herbs. Is there anything here we could use?"

Larissa shook her head. "Not without preparation," she said. "Their cooking is so simple, they'd notice any flavoring."

"I've thought of something," said Buck. "We might die too, but at least we would be spared captivity. If one of us, going out to relieve himself, dropped a few coals in this dry scrub, within moments a wildfire would cut us off from their Hold. While the barbarians were all chasing horses we'd have a chance to get away!"

"No!" cried Pine, then covered his face and was still.

Stone realized that the others were waiting for him to say something. "It's very dangerous." He wondered if that was why Buck had thought of it. "If the wind changed, the whole valley could go." A vision of flaming trees nagged at his memory.

"The trees . . . you will kill the trees," murmured Pine.

Stone remembered his dream of King Julian. "These are not Westrian trees," he said slowly, "but they're alive. Do we have the right to sacrifice them?"

Buck bit off an oath. "The right? This is to save our lives!"

"I don't think so . . . but I *am* a Westrian. Didn't you believe what they taught us?" Stone asked. "We haven't yet sworn the Covenant, but which of us will be able to if we have to break it in order to get back to Westria?"

"But what if we don't?" asked the fair-haired girl. "You persuaded us to think about escape. Why are you trying to discourage us now?"

"I know—" Stone's voice cracked. "There are things worse than death, and if we don't get away we'll learn about them. I know that all things live by the deaths of others. But not a whole forest!" He shook his head. "I can't decide for you, but I can't vote to follow Buck's plan."

"Nor I . . ." said Larissa. Stone felt the warmth of her smile.

"If the trees burn, I'll burn too!" said Pine.

There was a short silence, then Swallow sighed. "Well, I didn't think we'd any hope anyway, and I owe ye my life already." she touched Stone's arm.

Buck glared at them. "Leave this brushpile be, if you must, but I swear that I will not go living into Delasker's Hold."

No! thought Stone. *I might be wrong. Please don't lay the burden of it all on me!* Presently they left him alone. After a while he realized wryly that at least he had made one decision with which his old master would agree. Then he wept, because whatever became of him, the Master would never know.

Stone struggled, powerless in his dreams, while Larissa was raped again and again, and Buck as well. Then gray light filtered through his eyelids and he opened them on the dim glow of the fire. He had been asleep ... those night visions had no reality. Not yet. ...

"Maker of All, forgive and help me ..." he whispered, "for I have no wisdom of my own. ..." He waited, but all he could hear was Burkey's snores.

An hour of travel took them through the last of the trees. They dismounted below a slope of broken shale, and a series of slanting cliffs whose tops were studded with rocks like dead teeth. No one would have suspected that the gap at the top began a road. They began to lead their horses cautiously across the slope. Though at times Stone found himself near his friends, no one spoke. He looked up at the cliffs and wished they would fall on him.

They stopped again while Madok, Rio, and Mole left their horses and tracked the next part of the way. Stone looked at the cliffs once more. *Maybe they* will *fall,* he thought. This certainly looked like rockslide country—he knew, he had been brought up to judge stone. After a moment he forced himself to breathe. *Powers of Earth! Is there a way? Surely it will do no harm here if the rock falls one more time* ...

Carefully he pulled his horse closer to Larissa's. "Listen—were you trained in voice projection at the College of the Wise?" She nodded and started to speak, but he motioned for silence. "When I whistle, can you scream? Aim your voice at the cliffs, there, where the crack shows just under the overhang."

"I will do it." Larissa nodded again. "Will we die?" she added softly.

"I don't know."

Rio called her to catch up then, but as she went she smiled back at Stone and pursed her lips in a kiss.

Madok and the three best scouts had been checking the trail. He must make sure they did not run back to the others when the rock began to fall. He edged toward Swallow.

"This is worse than our race course at Initiation, isn't it?" he called. She grinned. Burkey, ahead of them, turned his head and grimaced, but his horse was balking, and he had no attention to spare. In a lower voice, Stone asked, "Could you run on this stuff?"

She looked at him curiously. "Yes, but what . . ." She bent toward him as he whispered furiously, and after a moment grinned again.

Stone's heart was pounding. He breathed deeply a few times to steady himself. He was sweating too, but then they were all sweating from the heat and the strain. He pretended to be looking for a rock in his boot and waited until Pine was alongside.

"Pine—if anything happens, grab the yellow-haired girl and run back downslope. Will you do it?" he hissed. He barely waited for the other boy's muffled agreement before he pulled his boot back on and moved up the line.

Everyone stopped while Madok and Rio argued about the route. Stone fidgeted, willing them to go on. At last, Madok and his scouts moved out across the shale.

Stone let another of the raiders pass him, then led his horse beside Buck's so that it blocked the path.

"Brother!" he called softly. "I've thought of another way for us to risk our lives. Will you stand with me?"

Buck turned, his eyes gleaming, but Stone put a finger to his lips and let go his pony's reins. From now on the horses would have to take their chances with the rest of them.

Stone pursed his lips and whistled. For an eternal moment, the sound echoed thinly from cliff to cliff. His bowels cramped. He wondered whether the others, knowing less, were more or less afraid.

Swallow left her horse and began to run.

Scarcely did a rock know she had touched it before she was gone, speeding lightly across the slope a little above Madok and his men. They shouted, and Rio and Mole dashed after her.

Everyone was yelling now, but Larissa's call transcended all other sound—an intense keening that vibrated in the air, resonated in the rocks; a wordless command. Stone felt a tremor.

Swallow was nearing the gap in the cliff when the mountain began to move. A boulder bounced by her; she sped on. The cliff groaned and began to crumble. Madok was swearing, trying to fight his way upward. Rio had fallen; Mole was sliding downhill. Still the boy gazed, while the cliff sagged and exploded in a thunder of falling stone. As Martan reached them, Buck let his beast go and it leaped forward, knocking the man sprawling down the hill.

Buck turned. "Behind you!"

Stone whirled. Mole was sliding toward him, sword drawn. He picked up a rock, flung it, and knew an instant's satisfaction as he saw the sword knocked away.

Larissa screamed. Stone saw her struggling in Burkey's arms and scrambled toward them. The man saw him coming, hesitated, and Larissa tore herself away. Burkey's hand moved and Stone saw a knife flash.

The boy kept up a steady hail of stones as he moved in. Then Stone flung himself upon the raider. He felt a searing pain in his arm and remembered the knife. He groped for Burkey's wrist as they rolled down the hill, something clicked, and Burkey screamed. Stone was shocked to feel a momentary disappointment as he felt all resistance cease.

For a moment he lay still, gasping. Then Buck crashed into him. A sword flickered downward where he had been. There was a short cry. Stone glimpsed Mole's raised arm and realized the renegade had got his sword back. But the blow had struck Burkey.

The two boys rolled apart as the sword came down again. Stone struggled to his feet. Then Buck got upright, and the three formed a wavering triangle. Stepping carefully, the Westrian renegade moved forward. Stone looked around for a rock, but they had ended up in a slide of sand.

Suddenly Mole leaped toward Buck, sword sweeping outward in a stroke that would carry it through the boy's body and Stone's as well.

Buck threw himself backward as Stone dove at Mole's legs. The blade whistled past his head, he touched leather, gripped the man's knees and twisted. His enemy toppled, and together they slid down the hill; Stone grabbed for the other's throat just as Mole's fingers closed on his own.

But as he began to squeeze, they came to the end of the sand. Stone saw a boulder rushing toward them, then Mole's head struck it with a sound like a splitting melon and they ceased to move. After a moment Stone lifted his head and spat out sand.

He looked down, saw Mole's eyes on his, saw the man's lips move. *He is a Westrian!* Stone thought suddenly, *I cannot let him die this way—*

"Forgive me, brother . . ." all he could think of was the hunting prayer.

The man's eyes fixed his. "I forgive . . ." The thin sound strengthened suddenly. "In the Name of the Maker of All Things!" Then his eyes dulled like a dying deer's.

And as your death serves me, may mine serve the world . . . Silently, Stone finished his prayer. When he saw that Mole breathed no longer, he closed his eyelids gently and struggled upright.

The air was hazed with dust and resonant with small creakings and groanings as several tons of rock found a new resting place. Occasionally another shower of pebbles would clatter down.

Stone gazed around him. Buck was sitting up the slope, his brown hair white with dust. Larissa picked her way toward them. Pine and the blond girl were quieting the horses at the bottom of the hill. Someone shouted. Stone made out Swallow dancing over the waste of tumbled rock where Madok and his men had been.

The sun seemed suddenly too bright. He blinked dizzily, looked down and saw red blood welling where Burkey's knife had slashed his arm.

They met Lord Philip two days' travel into Westria along the Traders' Road. The weather had held clear and bright for them, as if trying to make up for the unkindness of their fellow men. They gazed eagerly on mountain and sky as if these things had been newly created to delight them. When Pine stopped to talk to the trees, no one complained.

Larissa had dressed Stone's wound and made a sling for his arm. Buck had strained his ankle. All of them had scrapes and bruises, but on the whole they were surprisingly well. But Stone could not keep the others from fussing over him. They told him that he deserved it, though it seemed to him that they had all had an equal part in their deliverance.

When they saw the dust cloud on the road ahead they halted, reaching for the weapons they had taken from the bodies of Madok's men. Stone's left hand closed on the hilt of Mole's sword. Anyone coming from Westria ought to be friendly, but they had been through too much to be caught unprepared. They pulled their horses into a tight group, heads outward. Though their hearts were pounding, they were a force to be reckoned with now.

It was Buck who recognized his brother's horn call. He unbent his bow, light fading from his eyes.

"By Julian's sword, Buck, you were a hero!" said Stone angrily. He nudged his horse toward the other boy. "If your brother doesn't appreciate you now, then swear brotherhood with me and we'll seek our fortunes elsewhere!"

Buck gave him a quick glance, then began to smile. "By Julian's sword?" he asked. "No—*you* are the Julian here . . ."

Stone grew very still, staring at the boy whom he had fought with, and for. "You give me that name—" he breathed. *"You?"* His throat closed.

The Lord Commander and his men were skidding to an astonished halt in the road. Buck kicked his horse forward, face set, but Stone heard a sob as Lord Philip enfolded his younger brother in his arms.

It was the name he had wanted, and would never have dared to claim.

Stone looked back and saw Larissa's triumphant smile.

The Final Challenge

Lawrence Watt Evans

The royal funerary rites were long since finished and the crowd along the high street was thinning rapidly, but the last of the auxiliary troops were still straggling past when the old soldier ducked into the tavern. He grabbed himself a tankard of ale from a passing tray, turned to face the crowded room, and hoisted it in salute.

"To the old king!" he cried. "We won't see a man like *him* again!"

Most of the tavern's patrons smiled and murmured agreement, lifting their own drinks in reply.

Not everyone did, though. "You old fool," someone called back. "The old king's dead, and now that he's properly buried, let's drink to his son, the *new* king!"

The soldier hesitated, startled. For an instant his teeth bared in an angry grimace, but then he turned it into a rather stiff smile. "Fair enough," he answered. "I'll drink the new king's health, for he's a good man, too—but I'll tell you, good as he is, he's not his father's equal." He swigged ale.

"And how is it you're so certain of that, then?" the other man called belligerently.

The soldier peered over his mug for the source of the voice, and spotted it—a strapping young man of twenty or so, wearing the livery of the crown prince's personal guard, a uniform that no longer had quite the meaning it had had three days before. He was sitting with three other young men, all three in the attire of other divisions of the royal service.

That explained the fellow's hostility. The soldier knew that this was a hard time for the prince's men, as they sought to prove themselves—the relative roles of the Prince's Guard and the King's Chosen Regiment were not yet settled. Such uncertainty could make anyone surly; there was no point in arguing with the fellow about it.

"Why, I've served with them both, boy," the soldier called back to the guardsman, "and I'll be glad to tell you all about it, if you'd like. I meant no disrespect to you, or to Prince . . . that is, King Philip."

"I don't need to hear any tall tales, old man," the guard answered.

"If by that you mean the sort of lies men usually swap in taverns," the soldier said, approaching the guard's table, "why, I don't mean to tell any—just a few memories about young King Philip, long may he reign, and old King Geoffrey, bless his memory, and every word the truth."

The guardsman hesitated; he glanced around at his companions, judging their reactions, then shrugged. "Talk if you want, old man," he said. "But I won't promise to listen."

"I'd never expected such a promise," the soldier said, sinking into an empty chair across from the guardsman and setting his tankard on the table. He gazed around, as if thinking, and asked, "Ah, where to begin?"

"You say King Philip's no match for his father," the guardsman said challengingly. "I say that's crap. His Majesty's a warrior and a match for any man."

"Oh, he knows how to wield a sword, I'll give you that," the older man agreed, "but a warrior? How's anyone to say, when he's never gone to war?"

The guard's eyes narrowed. "I've seen His Majesty fight, and to my eyes a finer swordsman never lived; certainly no bent old fossil like King Geoffrey could match him!"

"You've seen him *fence*," the soldier corrected. "And in all likelihood you've seen him wrestle and box and ride and shoot and throw the javelin. But you've never seen him fighting for his life, because he's never had to—he was born a prince, where his sire was a minor baron's second son who fought his way to the throne."

"What of it, then? All the more honorable, then, to fight for what's his by right!"

"You think so?"

"I know it!" The guardsman made as if to rise.

The soldier did not; he shrugged, lifted his mug and drank, then put the tankard down empty and wiped his mouth with the back of his hand. The guard hesitated, then settled back into his chair.

"King's son or not," the soldier said, "the old king was one hell of a man, and a warrior to the end, even when he was too old to use a blade."

The guard snorted.

"No, it's true!" the soldier insisted. "Listen, I was at Prince Philip's manhood feast—His Majesty was still the prince then, I mean no disrespect."

"Go on," the guard said. "I've heard the tale; let's hear your version. You say you were there?"

"That I was, lad, that I was. Not at the head table or anything—no, I was just one of the guards at the door, the old king had his own old regiment there as an honor, but whether for us or the boy I don't know." He looked down into his empty mug and sighed. "That was when old Geoffrey fought his last battle with the sword, that feast—you've heard the story, you said. Did you know that the king was more than sixty years of age at the time? Sixty-five, at least, I'd guess—not the typical thing for the father of a lad just coming of age, but what with the wars and the rest of it, he'd got a late start at siring sons. His hair had gone gray, and his belly sagged, but he was still a fine man, with his own teeth and his eye still bright."

"An old man," the guard said derisively. "Like you."

The soldier snorted. "If I should be half so formidable at that age, I'd thank God and sing His praises half the day!"

"Still an old man."

"Aye," the soldier admitted. "An old man—but the

king, and still a warrior. He sat at the high table with his councillors and his old cronies, the Red Duke and Tom o' the Axe and the rest, shouting and drinking and carrying on ..."

The guard muttered sarcastically, "Nothing like maintaining the royal dignity." His companions chuckled.

"The old king never worried overmuch about his dignity, true enough," the soldier agreed. "Certainly not then. He was having a fine time, he and his comrades taking turns telling stories. The boy—Prince Philip, that is—was seated at the second table, in accordance with protocol, until the stroke of midnight, when he'd be able to take his place with the men, and he had his own comrades about him. Some were men from your own company, some were courtiers and courtiers' sons, and his mother's friends, and his old playmates, all gathered about, making merry. If the truth be told, some were there because of their names and fathers, rather than because the prince actually liked them or wanted them there." He winked at the guard.

"I know the sort," the young man agreed.

"Whatever their excuses, there they all were, drinking and talking—but being young, few of them had any great tales to tell, and in large part they listened to the boasting of their elders."

"I know that sort, too," the guardsman muttered.

The soldier nodded. "Don't we all," he said. "At any rate, there was one lad there who had drunk perhaps more than was good for him, a brawny fellow of twenty-three years or thereabouts, standing six and a half feet when he was upright, and strong as an ox. Perhaps he was unused to strong drink, or perhaps the excitement overcame him, or perhaps he was just a fool, but when the festivities grew loud, he was loudest; when the boys at the second table became rowdy, he was the rowdiest; and at last, upon hearing Lord Ashleigh's account of the defense of the Crimson Gate, he stood up and announced that the tale was nonsense."

"Was it?" the guardsman asked.

The soldier shrugged. "I wasn't at the Crimson Gate,"

he said, "nor was this lad—yet he went farther, and pronounced *all* the stories being told at the high table as the
self-serving lies and senile exaggerations of useless old
men."

"Were they?"

The soldier shrugged again. "The ones I knew firsthand
were more truth than not."

"Go on."

"Well, the lords at the high table spoke out angrily and
called the lad a young idiot, among other disparagements,
but King Geoffrey called for calm, and for a moment it
appeared that reason and good will would triumph. The
lords ceased their protests, and the lad found himself
standing alone and silent, looking rather foolish.

"All might have been well, had not one of the other
boys tugged at the oaf's sleeve and urged him to sit. 'Let
the old men remember their days of glory,' the fellow
said. 'They're the king's good servants.'

"And at that, the drunkard shouted out, 'They're liars,
the lot of them, and the king's the worst of them all!' "

"Hunh," the guardsman muttered.

"Indeed," the soldier agreed. "I can still remember the
utter silence, that tension in the air—ever been in a real
battle, friend? No? Well, if you had, you'd know that moment just before the first charge is made, before the first
blow falls. It felt much like that—but in the king's own
great hall, and with no armies at the ready, only a hot-
tempered young fool making trouble.

"I watched from my post at the door as the king rose
to his feet and faced the youth. Of course, all the others
made to rise, too, as protocol demands, but the king mentioned them back in their seats.

" 'Lad,' the king said quietly, 'Think well on what
you've just said.'

"The young fool shouted back, 'I know what I said; I
called you a liar. That's what you are—a liar, and a
usurper, and a coward who'd never dare face me if he
didn't sit on a stolen throne!' "

"The boy had courage, anyway," the guardsman remarked.

"But little wit," the soldier said.

"Go on with the story."

"Well, now, you'd expect the king to rant and rage, and order the young man thrown in the deepest dungeon, but in fact he sighed, and he looked the lad in the eye, and told him, 'I know the hot temper of youth, and the courage we all find in strong drink. I suggest you take a moment to reconsider, and perhaps you'll wish to retract what you have said.' "

"Fairly spoken."

"I thought so," the soldier agreed. "I told you, the old king was one hell of a man."

The guardsman gestured for the story to continue.

"Well, as I already said, the hall was silent, so still it seemed that no one even breathed, and every soul present heard the youth pause, and draw a deep breath—and then not recant, not at all, but instead say, 'I've nothing to retract—you're a scared old man, afraid to die in an honorable combat.'

"The king answered him, 'There is nothing honorable in such a duel,' but it was clear the youth was determined to have his duel, or else, should the king fall back upon the royal prerogatives and have him imprisoned or slain, to become a martyr to the king's tyranny. I suppose the boy's family or friends had some old grudge against the king that had inspired this; I doubt it could be purely drunken folly, though that was plainly to be the excuse."

The soldier paused long enough to signal for another ale, explaining, "Talking's thirsty work." Then he continued, "The king knew the boy wanted to fight, and he made no further attempt to avoid it. Instead he called for his sword and ordered that the boy's own sword be found and brought, and then he marched down from the high table to the center of the hall, where there was room to fight.

"Everyone else just watched, the feast forgotten, as the two swords were delivered and the two men faced each other across a few yards of stone pavement.

"Whatever the lad had said, it seemed at that moment that no one could doubt the old king's courage. An old man, past sixty, against this young man in his prime.

"The sight—ah, I remember it well! What a contrast! That great hulking youth, glowing with health, took up a formal fighting stance as if he were performing for his fencing master. And the old king stood a head shorter, his face lined, the tendons standing out as he gripped the hilt, hands shaking, his gray hair partially obscuring his face. He fell from old habit into *his* preferred stance, which was a sort of wary crouch, crooked and graceless. He looked like a troll facing a god." The soldier shook his head at the memory, then swigged ale.

The young men at the table shifted restlessly, and one glanced behind, as if he feared someone might be waiting to arrest him for not objecting to such an unflattering description of the late monarch.

The soldier paid no attention; when he had wet his throat sufficiently he continued, "The youth attacked first, swinging the sword like an axe—he couldn't be troubled with fencing's fine points, not against a tired old man, not when they were both drunk. He swung with such strength that it would have gone clear through the king—had it struck him. The king stepped aside, though, and deflected the blow, sending it harmlessly aside with his sword.

" 'It's not too late to apologize,' the king said.

"The boy bellowed a wordless challenge, and attacked again, this time showing some pretty skill—in fact, now that he knew a single blow would not serve, he put on a display of the finest fencing-school flutters and flourishes that ever I saw, the blade weaving about like a snake, fast as a cat's paw striking. The king gave ground, turning each attack with his own sword, or else contriving not to be in quite the spot where the blow fell, but it appeared that only by great effort and astonishing luck did he turn the attacks.

"At last, the lad had the king backed up against a pillar.

" 'Your last chance,' the king said.

"The youth laughed, and roaring with confidence, he lunged forward in a simple thrust—and fell to the floor with a look of dumb amazement on his face, having been run through the heart once the king had his measure."

The soldier shook his head and smiled.

"Old Geoffrey knew it's not youth and strength that make a warrior, nor a king," he said. "He gave that boy his chance several times over. He never lost his temper, never did anything rash, never let his enemy know his strengths."

"You mean his weaknesses."

"No, no—I mean his *strengths*. So the boy ran right into them. The shaking hands, the seeming weakness— what better way to mislead a foe? And King Geoffrey was brave, but he was no fool; he'd not have fought had he not been certain he would win. Why risk his life when a word would have had the boy arrested and hanged? Oh, a martyrdom might be trouble, but better to face a later insurrection than to die in a stupid brawl. Dead kings do no one any good, most especially not themselves. Geoffrey knew that well." The soldier sighed. "He would never have fought if he didn't know his own strengths, and he knew them well, after all those years. Age and experience outweigh strength and bravado any day."

"So you old men would have us believe," the guardsman said.

"Oh, no," the old soldier said. "Better for us if you don't! Had that young idiot known it, he'd never have challenged the king so openly."

"Ha, a point!" one of the guard's companions shouted, and the four young men laughed.

The soldier did not join them.

"Finish your tale, old man," another said when the laughter had passed.

"Oh, that's all of it, really," the soldier said. "After the king had won, after the boy had died there on the floor, King Geoffrey called for the party to continue, apologized for the unpleasantness, and sent for servants to clean up the mess. And twenty minutes later, at midnight, young Philip came to take his seat at the high table."

"And that," said the old soldier, finishing his ale, "was twenty years ago next month."

CODA

Working Stiff

Mike Resnick
and Nicholas A. DiChario

I'm the best bus driver on the downtown line, and damned proud of it. I take the wide turn around East Elm Street—trickiest corner on my whole route—feeling the tires slide across a patch of early-morning slush and then skid to a stop right in front of the station. Twelve midnight. Right on schedule. I've always been a good schedule driver. And no one's got quicker reflexes.

There's still one passenger aboard. I open the door and the bitter cold air whisks down the aisle. Winter in upstate New York comes in hard and fast off Lake Ontario. Sometimes it hits as early as September and sticks around till May. Not exactly the kind of weather I grew up with back on the island, but I always hated tropical heat.

I turn around and this guy is still sitting on his duff. "End of the line, mister," I announce.

The guy walks up slowly from the rear, then sits in that first seat opposite me. He's a short, chunky guy. Glasses. Neatly trimmed beard. Shirt and tie under a fancy overcoat. Nice boots. Not the kind of guy you'd normally see on my line, so I've got a pretty good idea as to what's coming next. By now I can sense when one of these jokers has come looking for a story.

"Mind if we have a chat?" he says, sweet as pie. "I'm from *New York Silver Screen Magazine.*"

I shrug. "Why not?"

I crawl out of the driver's seat, and the two of us walk through the gathering snow into the bus terminal. "Wait here," I tell him. He sits on a bench in front of the tall Plexiglas windows facing South Avenue, and I go to the supervisor's station to clock off my shift, half expecting him not to be there when I get back. Some of them don't wait. Some of them, the brighter ones, can tell right off they're not going to get the story they came hunting for.

Not this guy, though; he's still waiting. He gives me a

fake smile and says, "How's about I buy you some break-fast?"

"Thanks, but no thanks," I answer. "I got some errands to run. You're welcome to tag along." I turn my back on him and head for the street. He follows.

"You know, you're not exactly what I expected," he says thoughtfully.

I sigh. "You mean I'm not as big as you expected."

He nods. "Right."

That's the first thing that strikes most of them. I'm pretty big, but they always expect bigger. *Much* bigger.

We step outdoors into the cold black morning. I start walking. I walk everywhere, or take the bus. I'm too large to fit comfortably in a car. I tried a sleek little Mazda RX7 once; three years old, 47,000 miles, drove like a dream—but I always felt like I was about to swallow my knees.

I figure the wind-chill has dropped the temperature to three or four degrees below zero. Maybe I can shake this guy yet. After all, *he* doesn't have a fur coat. Me, I live in mine.

"Why only one film?" he says.

I grimace. These journalists are so predictable. They'll ask one question, maybe two, about me, and then, inevitably, they'll ask about *her.* "Don't you miss her? What did she mean to you? What do you remember most about her? Do you still talk to her?"

So I state the obvious. "There's not a lot of opportunity for a guy like me in Hollywood. I'm not exactly your typical leading man, you know?"

We walk into this tavern on Alexander Street, brush off the snow and sleet, and take a couple of stools at the bar.

Vinnie the bartender comes right over. "What can I do for you boys?"

I pull a wad of bills out of my jacket pocket and start peeling off twenties. "What's the line on the Bengals and the Jets?"

Vinnie looks at my friend.

"He's okay," I tell him.

"What's his name?"

"I don't know. What's your name?"

The guy looks ill at ease. I can't say as I blame him. "Parker Granwell," he says, extending his hand to Vinnie. "It's a pleasure to meet you, sir."

Vinnie snickers. He's got this kind of wheezing emphysema laugh. He was shot in the ribs a few years back. The bullet left him with an air leak and a limp, as if he's got a permanent stitch in his side. "Where'd you find this nerd?"

"He found me," I answer. "What's the line?"

"Minus two," says Vinnie.

"Under-over?" I ask.

"Thirty-eight."

"What about the Dolphins and the Bills?"

"Miami plus six and a half. Forty-two."

"I'll take the Dolphs and over for a hundred, and the Bengals and under for forty ... no ... make it sixty."

Vinnie takes my money. "What about the nerd? Care to place a wager?"

"I'll pass," says Parker, fidgeting on his bar stool.

Vinnie chuckles. "Pleasure to meet you, Mr. Parker Granwell, sir"—he makes it sound like a title—and limps into the back room.

I nod toward the door. "Let's go."

We enter the storm again. Granwell seems like a decent enough guy, and I figure I might as well give him what he wants. So as we walk, I talk about the good old days, the days of Mary Pickford and Doug Fairbanks and Scott Fitzgerald, the days of Gable, Harlow, and Cagney, the glory days of Universal, Paramount, Warner Brothers, MGM, and of course RKO, the days before the Screen Actors Guild destroyed something so pure and simple as the studio contract. I even throw in some trite quotable stuff about Willis O'Brien's brilliant animation and Max Steiner's underappreciated musical score and Merian Cooper's genius. What the hell, it was all true; I just never cared.

Anyway, Granwell nods and takes some notes and

throws in a "yeah—uh-huh—okay" every now and again, and when it's all over he tucks his notebook in his coat pocket and frowns, the snow gathering in his neat beard.

"I do believe that is the longest line of bullshit I have ever heard," he says.

"I've had a lot of practice," I reply without missing a beat.

"I want the truth."

He's right, of course, about the bullshit. But he's wrong about the truth. He doesn't really want it. None of them ever do.

We stop at the Cork Screw, a liquor store about the size of a meat freezer over on Chestnut Street. Max closes at midnight but he's always in the back room till around two or three, counting receipts, punching figures into his adding machine, and drinking away his profits. I like Max. We've spent many an evening together talking football and getting drunk. He's one of the few people in the world who has never seen the movie, and has no desire to.

I rap on the back door. Max opens up and asks me in.

"Sorry, Maxy," I greet him. "I can't stay tonight. I got company I can't get rid of."

Max peeks out the door and shows the barrel end of his Remington twelve-gauge. "I'll bet *I* can get rid of your company for you."

I see Granwell go a little pale. This is more than he bargained for. He was probably looking for an easy piece of back-page fluff, not a tour of the inner city in sub-zero weather, complete with gangsters and sawed-off shotguns. "That's all right, Maxy, he's okay. You got any overstock tonight?" I peel off another twenty and, as usual, Max won't take it. He hands me a bottle of Canadian Club— not my favorite, but well worth the price—and Granwell and I make our way down Chestnut, through the windy spray of sleet and snow, to the trucking warehouse where I rent my living space.

I push through the heavy doors, click on the overhead light bulb, and invite him in. What the hell. I'm always hoping that one of these guys, one of these days, will print the truth. The *Truth*. Your king lives in a warehouse surrounded by banana crates, and sleeps on two king-size mattresses thrown on top of a concrete floor. Your king is a bus driver who gambles and drinks away his paycheck. Your king never wanted his goddamned crown, and if he regrets one thing in his life, it's that he took the role that made him king, that he died onscreen for the love of a flat-chested wig-wearing blonde, and that the world can't forget about it.

And neither can he.

Suddenly, the Canadian Club doesn't appeal to me. I need a beer. I open my fridge, crack open a Bud, and offer one to Granwell. Much to my surprise, he accepts.

"You know," he says, "rumor has it that your movie saved RKO. They were ready to file for bankruptcy when—"

"Yeah, it's true. But let's get one thing straight. It's not *my* movie."

"Without you, there *is* no movie." He sits on a banana crate and sips his Bud. "In 1975, the American Film Institute honored it as one of the favorite American films of all time. There was even a reception at the White House."

"You got guts, Parker Granwell," I say, guzzling my beer and crushing the can. "You want honesty? I like being a bus driver. I like to gamble and I like to drink. I like my friends and my life. Why not let it go at that?"

"I don't get it. Why did you leave the island if you didn't want to be king?"

I can't help but laugh at that one. How could I have known back in 1933 what I was getting myself into? I was just a big kid. So I tell him the truth, just like I tell all the others: "I *hated* that damned island. The heat, the gigantic insects, the carnivorous spiders, snakes a mile long, vultures the size of airplanes, the tyrannosaurus always hunting me. I had to fight the pterodactyls and pteranodons for every scrap of food. I was allergic to more plant life on that goddamned island than you can find on this whole fucking continent. And the natives were the worst of the lot: they'd sacrifice virgins to me one minute and chuck spears at me the next. How long do you think I could have survived in that environment?"

I take a deep breath and continue. "I needed a change, and quick—but the problem was getting off the island. I couldn't swim. (Still can't.) Anyway, I hear through the grapevine that this guy Merian Cooper is vacationing on the island and he's putting together this film in the States and it just so happens he needs an ape, so I go looking for him. Once he calms down he gives me this mock screen test and he likes what he sees. The rest is history."

"How did you get so small? I mean, you were *huge*—forty, fifty feet tall at least."

I shrug, go to the fridge, crack open another Bud. "That one's a mystery to me. But I have a theory. I think the universe has to be in a kind of balance. Over the years, as the myth grew bigger, I got smaller. It's as if there's not enough room for both of us in this world: it can accommodate either me or the myth—and the myth is a hell of a lot stronger than I am."

Granwell looks like he's mulling it over, then apparently decides to let it go. "I'd like to read you something," he says. "It's an open letter from—"

"Let me guess," I interrupt, because while I have never read his writing, I can read Granwell like a book. "It's from the one true love of my life."

"It's from the introduction to her autobiography," he answers, missing my finely wrought sarcasm. "It reads something like this: 'I wonder whether you know how strong a force you have been to me. For more than half a century, you have been the most dominant figure in my public life. To speak of me is to think of you. . . . You have accumulated so much affection over all the years that no one wants to kill you. What the whole world wants is to save you.'"

I pick up the remote, click on the television set, and flip to ESPN. Speed Week. Damn. I was hoping for a college football game.

"Don't her words mean anything to you?" asks

Granwell. "Don't you ever think of her? Don't you have anything you want to say to her?"

So at last Parker Granwell comes clean. I mute the TV and shoot him my most feral expression, curling my lips and showing my fangs, but to be perfectly honest, there isn't much in me to be afraid of anymore.

I set down my beer. "Do you think you're the only bright-eyed reporter who has ever bothered to track me down, Granwell?" I say. "Hell, it's been sixty years since I made that flick. You all come looking for the same thing. You want to find this gigantic, forlorn ape, pining after the woman of his dreams, the woman whose heart he could never capture because he's nothing but a savage beast. And none of you can bear the fact that it just isn't so." I pause long enough to stifle a growl deep in my chest. "The truth is I'm not a savage beast and never was. I never loved that screeching bitch. I never even *liked* her. In fact, I could barely tolerate her. I was *acting,* plain and simple. She used to give me migraine headaches on the set like you wouldn't believe. Cooper hired her for her piercing scream, which as far as I can tell was her only talent. And she made up for her inadequacies by burrowing into the Hollywood social scene like some pathetic maggot. Who was Cary Grant dating and was Hepburn as good an actress as everybody said and was Fitzgerald going to be at this party or at that one? Christ, she made me want to puke!" Instead I belch, which suits me and my mood just fine.

Granwell just sort of shakes his head. I can see it in his eyes: This won't do at all, he's thinking. He's already put his notebook away. He says, "Paul Johnson wrote an appreciation of you in the *New Statesman* back in the sixties. It was brilliant. He called you a creature of intelligible rage, nobility, pathos. He called you a prehistoric Lear. And he was right, you know. You're America's only king."

They all come to this realization sooner or later. Elvis won't cut it because of the drugs and some of the ugly things he did and stood for which just won't go away, and they've learned too much about Kennedy, and the world is too hard and cold and jaded now to come up with anything better. America may be a land of riches and excess and (some say) even self-made royalty, but it is not a land of monarchs. No, there's only one king. Me. The ape. "I'm sorry I don't live up to your expectations."

Granwell sighs. "So if we just leave you alone, if we let you pass your time quietly here on Earth, we can take comfort in knowing that your myth will survive."

I nod. "Don't sweat it, Parker. Most people have already forgotten about me. I'm out of the loop, man. All the golden anniversary celebrations for that stupid movie—I didn't get a single engraved invitation. Not one. De Laurentiis never called to consult with me about the remake. I didn't even get an invite to that White House thing back in '75. But *she* was there, kissing up to Jimmy and Rosalyn Carter." This time I can't hold back the growl. "She wouldn't have missed it for the world."

"Don't you think you're being a little tough on her? She was one of the most popular actresses of her day, worked with every major male lead in the business—and then, to be frank, you ruined her. After your film, the monster-movie offers came pouring in, and nobody would give her the serious roles she deserved."

Granwell's no different from the rest of them. By the time they finish talking to me, they wish they never found me, and so do I. "Look, man, I'm just a gorilla. I don't share your sense of tragedy."

Granwell sets his beer down, slides off the banana crate, and walks to the door. "Thanks for the chat."

I call after him: "If you want to make an old ape happy before he dies, print the truth."

"You will never die," he says, and walks out.

Touché.

Suddenly I could use some Canadian Club. I pour myself a tall one, drop down on my mattresses, and start flipping through the channels. I pull the covers up to my chin and listen to the fierce wind howling through the empty lot behind the warehouse. I've got a chill I can't get rid of. Regardless of the temperature, some nights are colder than others.

Fifty-seven channels and there's nothing on.

Yet on any given night, if I can keep my eyes propped open long enough to catch the late shows ... if I don't pass out from the booze or the beer or the boredom ... chances are, sooner or later, I'll come across my favorite film.

About the Authors

JOHN GREGORY BETANCOURT, a former senior editor, is now a full-time writer and book producer. His upcoming books include a science fiction cookbook co-edited with Anne McCaffrey, and a novel co-written with Greg Cox. John lives in New Jersey with his wife, their son, and an ever-growing assortment of cats and computers.

The short fiction of NICHOLAS A. DICHARIO has appeared in such diverse anthologies as *Tales from the Great Turtle, Christmas Ghosts,* and *Dinosaur Fantastic.* In his first few years as a professional writer, Nick has been a Hugo, John W. Campbell, and World Fantasy Award nominee.

STEPHEN R. DONALDSON is the author of such popular series as *Thomas Covenant the Unbeliever,* the *Mordant's Need* novels, and more recently, *The Gap.* As Reed Stevens, his mysteries include *The Man Who Killed His Brother,* and *The Man Who Tried to Get Away.* He also plays a mean game of bridge.

DEBRA DOYLE, a Ph.D. in English literature, and JAMES D. MACDONALD, a former naval officer, met in Philadelphia while she was in graduate school and he was still on active duty. They now live a big nineteenth-century house in Colebrook, New Hampshire, where they write fantasy for children, teenagers, and adults.

ALAN DEAN FOSTER's first published SF was the short story "Some Notes Concerning a Green Box" published in 1971. His first novel, *The Tar-Aiym Krang,* was published the next year, beginning his interconnected "Humans Commonwealth" sequences. His many other novels and novelizations include *Dark Star, Alien Nation,* and the *Spellsinger* series.

ESTHER M. FRIESNER is the author of such novels as *Majyk by Accident* and *Majyk by Design,* as well as the *Star Trek: Deep Space 9* novel *Warchild.* Her short fiction has appeared in many leading anthologies, and she recently edited her own satirical anthology, *Alien Pregnant by Elvis.*

RICHARD GILLIAM's editing credits include such well-regarded anthologies as *Confederacy of the Dead, Grails: Quests of the Dawn,* and *Grails: Visitations of the Night.* His novella "Caroline and Caleb" was a Bram Stoker Award nominee, and the *Grails* project was nominated for a World Fantasy Award.

The short fiction of OWL GOINGBACK has appeared in a wide variety of anthologies, including *South From Midnight, Quest to Riverworld,* and *Tales From the Great Turtle.* His nonfiction writings include a series of essays on self-defense.

By far the leading anthology editor in U.S. publishing, MARTIN H. GREENBERG has more than 600 books to his credit, including work with such best selling authors as Marion Zimmer Bradley, Dean Koontz, Robert Ludlum, Arthur C. Clarke, and Isaac Asimov.

The novels of KAREN HABER include *The Mutant Season* (written with Robert Silverberg), *The Mutant Prime,* and *Mutant Star,* as well as *Thieves Carnival,* a prequel to Leigh Brackett's *The Jewel of Bas.* Karen's short fiction has appeared in many leading anthologies and periodicals.

NANCY HOLDER has sold approximately twenty novels and sixty short stories, including appearances in such anthologies as *Confederacy of the Dead, Grails: Visitations of the Night,* and *Phobias.* She has received two Bram Stoker Awards, and has been published in over eighteen languages.

BRAD LINAWEAVER writes screenplays, fiction, and nonfiction. He has short story credits in more than two dozen anthologies, and his essays have appeared in such diverse publications as *Famous Monsters of Filmland* and *National Review.*

BILLIE SUE MOSIMAN is the Edgar–nominated author of the novel *Night Cruise.* She has published more than seventy-five stories in various magazines and anthologies, and is a columnist for *Deathrealm* magazine.

DIANA L. PAXSON is perhaps best known as the author of several successful series of fantasy novels, including the recent *Master of Earth and Water.* Her short fiction has appeared in such leading anthologies as *Grails: Quests of the Dawn* and *Excalibur.*

MIKE RESNICK is the author of thirty-six SF novels, eight short-story collections, and over one-hundred short stories not to mention editing a number of anthologies. Since 1989, he has been nominated for nine Hugo Awards, and has won two of them.

KRISTINE KATHRYN RUSCH has compiled an astounding number of awards and award nominations in the first five years of her career, including a World Fantasy Award. In addition to her novels and short stories, she is the editor of *The Magazine of Fantasy and Science Fiction.*

LAWRENCE SCHIMEL has sold stories and poetry to over forty-five anthologies, including *Grails: Visitations of the Night,* and *Tales From the Great Turtle.* He is twenty-three-years old and lives in Manhattan, where he works in a children's book store.

LARRY SEGRIFF has sold short fiction in a variety of genres, including stories in the anthology *Frankenstein: The Monster Wakes,* and in the magazine *Cemetery Dance.*

DEAN WESLEY SMITH is the author of the novel *Laying the Music to Rest,* and the editor of various projects, including *Pulphouse Magazine.* His short stories have appeared in *Grails: Quests of the Dawn* and *Quest to Riverworld.*

JUDITH TARR is the author of a number of novels including *Throne of Isis,* a novel of Cleopatra; *Pillar of Fire,* a novel of Akhenaten; and the World Fantasy award nominee, *Lord of the Two Lands.* She lives just outside of Tucson, Arizona, with two cats, a goat, a dog, and a slowly increasing herd of Lipizzan horses.

LAWRENCE WATT EVANS is the author of some two dozen novels and four score short stories in the fields of fantasy, science fiction, and horror. His most recent major work is the *Three Worlds* trilogy, whose first novel is *Out of This World.*

The short fiction of RICK WILBER has appeared in such magazines as *Analog* and *The Magazine of Fantasy & Science Fiction,* as well as such anthologies as *Grails: Quests of the Dawn,* and *Quest to Riverworld.* His story here is based on historical accounts of the first sighting of the Loch Ness monster.

* * *

JANE YOLEN is the author of over one hundred and fifty books for children and adults, which have won prizes ranging from the Caldecott Medal and the World Fantasy Award to the Mythopoeïc Society Award and the Christopher Medal. She is the editor-in-chief of Jane Yolen Books, a YA fantasy and SF imprint for Harcourt Brace & Company.